OPENING SHOTS

OPENING SHOTS

GREAT MYSTERY AND CRIME WRITERS
SHARE THEIR FIRST PUBLISHED STORIES

Edited by LAWRENCE BLOCK

CUMBERLAND HOUSE
NASHVILLE, TENNESSEE

Published by Cumberland House Publishing, Inc., 431 Harding
Industrial Drive, Nashville, Tennessee 37211

Cover design by Gore Studio, Inc.
Page design by Mike Towle

Library of Congress Cataloging-in-Publication Data
Opening shots : favorite mystery and crime writers share their first published
stories / edited by Lawrence Block.
    p. cm.
  ISBN 1-58182-125-3 (alk. paper)
    1.Detective and mystery stories, American. 2. Detective and mystery
stories, English. I. Block, Lawrence.

   PS648.D4 O64 2000
   813'.087208--dc21

                        00-058987

Printed in the United States of America
1 2 3 4 5 6 7 8 9 — 05 04 03 02 01 00

CONTENTS

An Opening Shot . . .

IN HIS WONDERFULLY READABLE memoir, *Call It Experience*, Erskine Caldwell recounts in detail the circumstances of his first sale to *Scribner's Magazine*. As he recalls (and he was, it must be acknowledged, a man given to improving a story in the recollection), he was at home in Georgia when Maxwell Perkins of *Scribner's* invited him to lunch. Caldwell got himself to New York, where Perkins took him to a good restaurant and talked about all manner of matters, literary and otherwise, before finally getting around to the pair of stories Caldwell had sent him.

"I'd like them both for the magazine," Perkins told the young writer. "Now as to payment, I could give you two-fifty for the shorter story and three-fifty for the longer piece."

Caldwell just sat there, and Perkins finally asked him if something was the matter.

"Well, I guess it's all right," Caldwell said at length, "but I have to say I thought I'd be getting more than six dollars for the pair of them."

PERKINS, OF COURSE, PROPOSED to pay $250 for the shorter story, $350 for the longer one. That doesn't sound like very much, until one considers that a dollar went a good deal further in the 1920s, when the young Caldwell first broke into print. I don't know what the equivalent would be in today's dollars—it depends which curbstone economist you listen to—but it's clear Caldwell wasn't working for subway fare. (The subway was a nickel at the time. Now it's a buck and a half. You do the math.)

Still, Perkins wasn't paying him a fortune, not in terms of the market realities of the day. At the time, the demand for short fiction of all sorts was vastly greater than it is today. Magazines flourished, and the great majority of them offered at least some fiction, and writers could make a living without ever producing a novel. On the lowest level, the pulp magazines paid a cent a word (or even less; some markets of last resort paid a half-cent, or even a quarter-cent). At the top, slick magazines like *Collier's* and the *Saturday Evening Post* paid as much as five thousand dollars for a short story by a prominent author.

The numbers shifted some and the natures of the markets changed a bit over the next couple of decades, but magazine fiction remained a rich field for readers and writers alike until shortly after the second world war. Then paperback books and television delivered a one-two punch from which the short story has never recovered. The pulps disappeared, and the all-fiction magazines that followed them, digest-sized mystery and science fiction magazines, dwindled down to a handful in each genre. General magazines reduced their fiction content or stopped publishing it entirely.

And, while inflation continued to drive up prices everywhere else, magazine fiction held the line against it, or even reversed the trend. Magazines that paid four or five cents a word in 1955 were still operating at the same word rate forty years later.

WHY THE HISTORY LESSON?

Well, it seems to me that a glance backward tells us something about short fiction today, and who writes it and why. Back when Caldwell had his lunch with Perkins, most literary wannabes started out writing short stories, and many of them did nothing else throughout lengthy careers. Magazine fiction was the way to break into print, and it was a way to make a steady and decent living.

When the pulps vanished, writers either adapted or quit. Some wrote longer fiction and published original paperback novels. Others hocked their typewriters and found something else to do.

And, increasingly, novice writers went directly to the novel. They knew that there was an eager market for book-length fiction, and almost no place to publish shorter work. And, as the years passed, the upcoming young writers had less exposure as readers to short fiction, so the novel became their frame of reference.

For experienced writers, the short story became increasingly a labor of love—and not everyone loved it enough to go on writing it. One respected crime fiction writer, a friend of mine, confided that he hadn't written a short story in years. "I can write a story and get $500 from *Ellery Queen*," he said, "or I can write an episode for a TV show. It's about the same amount of work, and I get twenty times as much for it."

That sounds clear-cut, but I wonder. Years afterward, all of those TV episodes are gone into the ether. Even the relative handful that survive on Nick at Nite are, when all is said and done, just TV. No one knows who wrote them, and no one cares.

Prose fiction has a much longer shelf life. It literally remains on shelves, where people can haul it down and read it. And it finds its way into anthology after anthology, where it becomes available to succeeding generations of readers.

WHEN I HIT ON the premise of this particular anthology, it struck me that a collection of first stories by prominent mystery writers would be not only entertaining but instructive. Besides the pleasure of the stories themselves, one would learn a little about that first successful leap into print, and could look for signs of the writer-to-be in his or her earliest effort.

And, in many of the stories that follow, that's exactly what you'll find.

Introduction

But some of the stories you'll encounter here are the work of writers who found themselves creatively and established themselves professionally before they ever wrote anything shorter than sixty thousand words. They began as novelists, and didn't write short stories until someone begged them for one for an anthology. Their aptitude for short fiction, and the delight they've taken in writing it, is unmistakably evident in the work.

WHAT SORT OF FUTURE does the short story have?

Prediction has always been a fool's errand, and never more so than now, when the rate of change has speeded up to the point that, by the time one takes a long look at anything, it has already morphed into something else. Anyone who speaks with assurance about the future of publishing is talking through his hat.

It's possible, certainly, that the Internet and e-publishing will launch a great renaissance of short fiction. And it's also every bit as possible that it won't.

Readers like to read short stories. The continuing popularity of original and reprint anthologies is proof of that. And writers like to write them. Otherwise we wouldn't bother.

But short fiction does provide the nearest thing we get to instant gratification. While it is in some ways more technically challenging than the novel, it does not demand the months and months of labor that a longer work entails. And one can experiment in short fiction, trying on the sort of characters and voices and situations and themes one wouldn't want to attempt in a novel.

I know I continue to get a kick out of writing short stories, and so, I gather, do the writers whose work you're about to enjoy. If you keep reading them, we'll go on writing them.

—*Lawrence Block*

OPENING SHOTS

Laud

DAVID BLACK

David Black's Introduction:

Every week, I sent out stories—to big slicks like the Atlantic, Harper's, and the New Yorker, literary magazines, pulps, the underground press—and every week I got rejection slips by return mail. Some had "Sorry" scrawled across the boilerplate. A few were typewritten and signed. Most were printed notes: Like errata slips in books, they seemed to be correcting mistakes in the story of my life.

Figuring my publishing career was going nowhere, I applied to the English Ph.D. program at Brown University.

It seemed my only hope of eventually making a living. But it seemed a defeat.

I'd been unsuccessfully sending stories and articles out ever since I was seven years old—when, under the influence of Moby Dick, I submitted a whaling story to Martin Levin's "Phoenix Nest" at the Saturday Review for reasons that today escape me.

Know your market! Well, at seven, I knew the Saturday Review was class. Literature. And I wanted to storm Parnassus.

So I took the train from New York City, where I was living, to Providence in time for my first seminar—a class on Poe—sat through one hour, realized graduate school was not for me. Not then, at least. And, during the break, walked down the hill to the train station and headed back to New York, convinced I had just committed economic suicide.

I was at a dead end in publishing. I was incapable of making a go of it in academia. I had no marketable skills. I believed I had only two choices: write or starve.

I got home—to my apartment on 110th Street—late. Opened the mailbox. Ready to check out any new rejections. And, along with two nine-by-twelve self-addressed, stamped manila envelopes, I found a business-size letter from the Atlantic, as odd a discovery as if I'd found a bird's egg among the mail.

Standing in the chilly hall of my apartment building, I opened the envelope and found a check for, I believe, three hundred dollars—a fortune!—and a letter accepting a short story, "Laud," which won an Atlantic "Firsts" award and later became the opening chapter of my first published novel, Like Father.

Like the initial hit of a drug, nothing beats that first acceptance. I felt not just blessed, but as if God had fallen in love with me.

To publish is human. To publish for the first time is divine.

Laud

DAVID BLACK

WHEN MY FATHER WAS fifty-eight years old, after reading Henri Troyat's biography of Tolstoy, he ran away from home. Having packed a red wool shirt, a faded pair of Levi's, a change of underwear, and three pairs of gray ski socks, he walked the mile from his house on Maplewood Terrace to Route 91 north and, sticking out his thumb, hitched a ride with a Friendly Ice Cream Shop manager to West Springfield, where after a wait of half an hour he picked up a second ride with a teenaged boy traveling from Staten Island to Warwick, Massachusetts, to visit a religious commune called the Brotherhood of the Spirit.

"They sleep during the day," my father later explained to us, his eyes squinting in the dim light of the single sixty-watt bulb that swung above our kitchen table through clouds of insects, "and farm at night. Their leader is twenty-two years old, twenty-two, twenty-three, Michael somebody, a Greek name, and he also sings in a rock band. These communities interest me . . ."

A third ride with a dairy farmer along Route 116 to Route 47 brought my father within seven miles of the farmhouse which Maxie and I had rented.

"I asked the farmer about these communes," my father said. "He seemed to like them. He kept saying over and over that his two sons couldn't wait to go to New York or San Francisco and that he admired the kids who left the cities to farm. It made me proud of you. . . ."

Before leaving Springfield, my father had written a letter which he gave to me with a warning not to read until after he'd gone. His destination was unclear. Nova Scotia perhaps, Wyoming, Mexico. The letter said:

Dear Dennis,

When you were seven under an influence we were never able to determine—Hopalong Cassidy, Tom Corbett and His Space Cadets, probably one of your television heroes—you ran away from home.

We found you around the corner, pushing along on your scooter. Since you hadn't left in anger, you evidently thought when you saw us that we'd come to give you a cheerful send-off.

You were enraged when we demanded that you turn your scooter around. We were being unreasonable in trying to abort your adventure.

I have no doubt that I will be as unsuccessful now as you were then. The terribly embarrassing thing is not being able to explain why one left in the first place.

I left your mother an inadequate note. Undoubtedly she'll also see this one, which won't explain anything either.

I didn't leave because I was unhappy. I wasn't angry. I wasn't suffocating. But I am running away. From what? Nothing.

I may not be able to tell you these things—not that any of them are particularly revealing—when I see you, but I did want to leave you with some kind of comment. At least an intimate gesture.

When we meet, both of us I'm sure will be too disturbed (or embarrassed) to make any kind of peace with each other.

FOR TWENTY-EIGHT YEARS, my father had taught English in the Springfield public school system with the passionate conviction that he was saving souls, although, because he was an atheist, he would never have phrased it that way. He had been raised in the Mount Sinai Orphanage in Boston as an Orthodox Jew and had early abandoned Yahweh to the adults in the home who beat him when he misbehaved and ignored him when he didn't.

His father, my grandfather, Aaron, deserted his children in 1921, freeing himself to scheme for various unattained fortunes. The few times he showed up at the orphanage to take my father on outings, after delicatessen lunches—whitefish with lemon, knockwurst and sauerkraut, lox, knishes, pirogi—he would give my father bootleg gin to deliver. His most horrible childhood experience, my father once told me, was when he tripped climbing onto a trolley and smashed a bottle. Terror of police and shame at having failed overwhelmed him. He watched the trolley clatter away and then, sneaking through alleys and yards, raced to the orphanage, convinced that he would be sent to the reformatory.

His second most horrible childhood experience, he said, was when he was angry with his older brother, Abraham, for beating him up in the school yard. While Abraham was showering, my father threw a canful of lye at him. Abraham, screaming, shot flat against the shower wall, his back and right side puffing like burning marshmallow. My father rushed into the orphanage kitchen, stole a half-pound slab of butter—for which he was later thrashed—and, crouching in the fetid, gray, dormitory shower, smeared the "Mississippi Mud" butter over his brother's quivering body.

Abraham goaded the orphanage kids to fight the Catholic gangs in the neighborhood. In a side street behind a kosher butcher shop, he was knifed in the chest. My father, although shorter and younger than the others, fought for and gained control of the Mount Sinai gang, to lead them in a war against those who'd killed his brother, to prove he was tougher than his brother had been.

To reinforce his leadership, my father staged a raid on the food stores in the orphanage cellar, escaping punishment by hiding in a flour barrel when he heard one of the cooks coming down the stairs. He led his cronies to the fourth-floor laundry chute, down which he jumped, sixty feet. The expected billowing pile of sheets was not waiting for him below. My father shattered his leg, driving the bone two inches into his hip. Terrified of punishment, my father hobbled on his smashed limb for the rest of the day, twisted in a white pain through the night, and fainted at the washroom sink the following morning.

While in the hospital, he did chin-ups on a bar that he had placed across his bed and, once on his feet, learned to throw his crutch; so when back on the street he was taunted by gang members who stood just out of reach, he was able to turn the crutch into a successful weapon. After cracking one tormentor's spine and permanently paralyzing him, my father was sent into a special disciplinary ward, where he learned woodwork, printing, and how to play the trumpet.

One of his teachers, a twenty-six-year-old wire manufacturer's daughter who had insisted on working with the incorrigibles, having been attracted by my father's intelligence, spent hours with him after classes, giving him books, playing him scratchy 78s of Bix Beiderbecke. On a rainy afternoon, while listening to Bing Crosby and Frank Trambauer on vocals, my father ran his hand up her skirt.

She slapped him. He slapped her back just as her boyfriend, a Harvard graduate student in mathematics, walked in the door. To escape what he assumed would be a stretch in the reformatory, my father left the orphanage that night. He was seventeen, a fair trumpet player with a love for jazz, and a determination to go to college.

HE GOT A JOB in New York at a club called the Blue Room, sitting in for the regular trumpet player, a man called D'Agostino, who was dead drunk when he wasn't gambling and gambling when he should have been performing at the club. One night in a poker game with D'Agostino and Larry Craft, a gangster with a bad stomach who drank alternately from a tumbler of rye and one of cream, my father exploited a remarkable luck and won three thousand dollars. After the game, he taxied home and, before going to bed, wrote a letter asking for an application for admission to Boston University.

He conned and wheedled his way into the B.A. program. Between the money he'd saved and the money he'd won, he had enough to pay for tuition expenses for two years. He did well, skidded from scholarship to scholarship for eleven years, during which time he collected a dozen languages, an uneasy but extensive acquaintance with English literature, a library of over two thousand books, three degrees, and a wife.

He met my mother while he was living in Gloucester, Massachusetts, with four other members of the World Socialist Party, a pure Marxist conspiracy so innocent that they were not banned from agitating on Boston Common during World War II. The five of them had rented three cabins near the beach. My father lived alone. One Saturday, he cleaned house, threw the trash into the fireplace to burn, and, having left some records stacked on the mantel, walked down the road for a swim.

Ethel Diamond, the twenty-four-year-old social worker who in two years would become my mother, was visiting her sister and her new brother-in-law. She threw (accidentally? on purpose? she claims it was a mistake) a beach ball at my father, who was stalking out of the water. He tossed it back. They introduced themselves. He wooed her with an economy of words and well-placed hands. She agreed to walk to his cabin for coffee and cake. On the path they met the postman, who said, "Do you live in the number-two cabin, up that way?"

My father said, "Yes."

"Well," said the postman, walking on and looking at the letters he was shuffling, "it's burning to the ground."

When I was a child and my father would sit in the twilight on the edge of my bed telling me the story, at this point I would bolt up with a knot in my chest as though I had swallowed a hard ball of cold water and say, "The records caught on fire, didn't they?"

He would nod and stand, making the mattress bounce, and say as he walked through the gloom to my bedroom door. "That's right. They were made of shellac and caught on fire from the trash in the fireplace."

And once, when I was older, almost too old to be told bedtime stories, I said, "That was pretty stupid, leaving them on the mantel, wasn't it?"

My father paused in the door, a dark shape against the hall dusk.

"Yes," he said, "it was stupid." And then half in anger, half in puzzlement, he added, "Don't you know most of life is made up of stupid mistakes?"

I said, "It isn't."

"Good night," said my father.

"It isn't," I repeated; and, as I felt my hold on my father weakening—he was backing into the hall, making calm-down gestures with his hands—I screamed, "It isn't! It isn't! It isn't!"

My father stopped his retreat and reentered the bedroom.

"You're in a nice rage," he said.

"No, I'm not," I said, throwing myself back on the bed.

"That's all right," he said. "It's all right to be in a rage. If I hadn't been in a rage, I never would have gone to college. And I'm glad I went." He stood, staring down at me. I twisted like the grubs I used to impale in the backyard. "But save for something worthwhile," he said at last, "because you can use it up on worthless things; and when you need it for something important, it's gone."

THE EVENING MY FATHER arrived at our farmhouse, Maxie and I were in the garden. I was squatting by the pole beans, pulling up pigweed and witchgrass. Maxie was kneeling over the carrots, thinning the row.

She straightened and, stepping over the line of feathery stalks, said, "Some old man just walked up our front porch." She turned to me. "Dennis?"

I came down the path between the furrows. My father, still carrying his suitcase, had circled back into sight around the corner of the house. He strolled, glancing up at the second-floor porch, where a Mexican hammock hung. Abandoned books, our current fancies (*Vikram and the Vampire*, Hammett's *Red Harvest*, Father Brown, Lovecraft's map of local western Massachusetts horrors, what else, some books on education, some books on garden insects, a book of popular astronomy with which Maxie and I tried to decipher the night sky), made human-looking lumps—buttocks, shoulder, elbow—in the hammock's blue web. My father put down his suitcase and called up at the shape he assumed was a resting body.

"Hello," he shouted. "Dennis? Maxie?"

The books in the hammock did not resolve themselves into some head, arms, and torso; did not sit up and peer down at my father; did not answer.

"Hey," my father called, "wake up, Dennis, greet your prodigal pop. I've suddenly become a dropout."

The sun was behind us, balanced on the horizon, large and round as a yawn. When I shouted to him, my father turned and put his hand to his forehead in a salute to shade his eyes.

Bluff and grinning—the bared teeth occasionally turning into a manic grimace—my father described his day's adventures.

"Running away was the climax," he said. "The rest will be an extended, increasingly painful denouement."

Later at dinner, his elbows propped up on the table, my father continued to sketch his running away as though it were a neatly, already completed play. His voice vibrated with the same wheedling urgency that balanced his lectures on a nice edge of curiosity. When I was a freshman in college, one vacation I sat in on his class, partly to judge him with the mean, keen eye of a nineteen-year-old son, partly to probe into the eager pride he roused in me.

He started the class by saying—I wrote it down, irked at having been nudged from my role as critical son into that of appreciative student—"By lumping certain of Shakespeare's plays together under the title of tragedies, you imaginatively annihilate the great differences among them. *Macbeth* touches our scorn as much as our pity. *Hamlet* moves us to an ecstasy of frustration. But it's impossible to read *Lear* without weeping."

That struck me as extraordinary: "It's impossible to read *Lear* without weeping."

I had just read it for a Humanities course and hadn't wept. I was sure none of my father's students had wept. My friends at college had dutifully venerated it, but as far as I knew no one had wept. I was half-sure my father hadn't wept when reading it, that his speech was merely showmanship.

But there was something in the certainty with which he said it, the absolute conviction that one could not really read the play, understand it, and believe in the old king's despair without shedding tears, which sprung some valve of respect.

At home, my father faltered from one decision to another: should he buy a new car, put up the screens, call so-and-so on the school committee to protest the exclusion of *A Connecticut Yankee in King Arthur's Court* from the list of books to be bought for the following year, wear a white or a pale blue shirt to a retirement dinner . . . At home, when I would confront him with a bristling assertion which I knew contradicted his opinion ("Wolfe wasn't a very good writer, was he, Dad?"), he would clear his throat, hesitate, temporize, shrug.

In class, there he was, speaking *ex cathedra*! And he seemed to be right.

That evening and for weeks thereafter, I tried to elicit the same sureness from him—about books, music, politics, flavors of ice cream, anything. But he would squint his eyes in pain and, my insistence prickling up against him, step back, step back again, dropping *maybe's* and *perhaps's* along the path of his retreat, as though he were both trying to escape and to leave a trail for me to follow.

I couldn't follow him, however—at least, not into his blinking, shrugging insecurity, not even into smiling, cautious—ambiguity. I wanted him to be certain, to be absolute, to slam his fist onto a tabletop and say, "Look, kid, you're wrong." But he refused to give me any further demonstration of what I assumed to be his rigid and correct self.

THE NIGHT HE ARRIVED, trying to sound casual, but giddy at the prospect of rupturing the traditional membrane of polite ignorance of each other's intimate motives or excuses which separated us, I asked him why he had always evaded my questions.

"Your questions?" my father murmured. "Your questions? Did you ever really want to know what I thought? I always felt you were throwing some kind of noose over my head, and if I had resisted the rope would slip tighter."

"Did you think that?" I asked, apparently surprised, but feeling that he was right and that I had known it all along. "Did you really think I was trying to trap *you*?"

"Weren't you?" he asked, the pained furtive glance slipping into his eyes like sizzling drops of water skittering onto a hot skillet.

We both flinched, paused at the moment when only anger or love would have carried us into each other's sealed worlds. I tapped my knees with fingers that abruptly seemed large and clumsy. My father crossed his legs and thrust his hands deep into his pockets. His chin touched his chest; and, blinking up over the tops of his glasses, he exchanged one dangerous subject for another.

"Well," he said in an innocent treble, "when am I going to be a grandfather?"

"What do you want to be a grandfather for?" I said. "Isn't being a father hard enough?"

"Hard?" he asked.

"Are you in a hurry to be one?" Maxie leaned back stiffly in her chair, the same way she tenses herself when we're in the car and I take a curve too fast.

Unsure whether Maxie was joking or provoking him, he said, "You've been married three years. I was a father nine months after the vows."

"Marvelous," said Maxie, "how did you manage that?"

"Should I explain the facts of life?" my father asked.

"I know all about them," said Maxie. "You find babies under cabbages. That's what we're growing in our garden. Dennis, why are you shaking your head at me?"

"Why are you being unpleasant?" I asked.

My father, trying to appease Maxie by defending her, accused me.

"You're always finding something wrong," he said. "She's just having a joke."

"I'm not *she*," said Maxie. "Call me by my name."

"What are you yelling at me for?" said my father. "I'm on your side."

"My side?" she said. "What are you talking about? I don't have a side."

Desperately attempting not to be misunderstood, terrified that my father would dismiss her anger as something that he, as a male, could charm away, she grabbed his hands and pulled him toward her.

The contact was not sexual, but an effort to make him know the hungry something in her which wielded her femininity like a weapon. My father became tensed attention, sensing the merely erotic.

"I want a baby," she said.

"Then why don't you have one?" my father asked.

"Because I'm not ready," I said.

The emotional acceleration stopped. There was a noticeable lag in our responses. None of us was sure what had happened. My father untangled his hands from Maxie's grasp and folded them on the table.

"Dennis has this thing about fatherhood," said Maxie, her voice flat, although her neutral tone had set up a flag: this is where I can be hurt; don't hurt me. "Dennis thinks that fathers have to choose between destroying their children or being destroyed by them."

"What about us?" my father asked me. "Do you think I destroyed you?"

Suddenly exposed by his assumption—"Do you think *I* destroyed *you*?"—he started shaking his head no, as though to cue me; and in doing so he was typically offering himself for the sacrifice. He was saving: given the choice between your destruction or my destruction, let us agree upon doing me in.

"Well," he said, "do you think you destroyed me?"

The question was rhetorical. Neither of us was prepared to admit the answer.

My father quickly said, "We were talking about babies." But it sounded as though he had said: let's talk about something less important than this male struggle of ours; let's talk about some trifling woman's complaint—"We were talking about babies . . ."

Maxie spilled her coffee over the table. My father grabbed a napkin and began mopping up the mess. When finished, he stuffed the dripping napkin into a glass.

"It's bedtime," he said. "I'm tired." At the bottom of the stairs, he half turned. "Ah, Dennis, I haven't quite settled where I'm going yet. Would it be too much of an inconvenience if I stayed here for a day or two?"

I said, "No. I'd like that."

"Good." He started to go.

"This is as good a place to run away to as any other," I said, realizing as I spoke that willfully, although unconsciously, I had maimed him as surely as if I had just laid a hot poker across his face.

He made a noise halfway between a snort and a guffaw and, having said a gloomy good night, climbed the stairs to his bedroom.

"Are you afraid your son will hate you as much as you hate him?" Maxie asked. She was testing me: if I could hate him, couldn't I also hate her?

"I don't want to have to be a model," I said.

"Do you think we could have a baby in a year?" she said, invoking one of our catechisms. We had fixed scripts for exorcising all the devils of anxiety, anger, love, lust, all the insistent affects that threatened to crowd habit and security from our lives. By varying the old questions and answers slightly every time, we walked through our roles, we safely sneaked through our roles, we safely sneaked forward toward being the people we wanted to become. When Maxie asked, "Do you think we could have a baby in a year?" she was saying, "I'm frightened. I don't recognize you. Play your role."

"Yes, in a year," I should say.

"Yes, in a year we should be settled enough . . ." I should say.

"Yes, in a year. Of course, it depends . . ." I should say.

As in a guessing game, you must try one variation after the other until you find the one that fits, the correct answer.

I said: "I don't want a baby."

"I don't believe you," said Maxie. "You're lying. Aren't you? Aren't you?" Her need had claws. I had not been lying. I had been exploring a growing panic. In bed, when she put her hands flat against my back and asked again, "Weren't you lying?" I gave her, instead of love, the devious gift of a soothing answer: "I was lying, yes."

Maxie and I slept in a large room behind the kitchen to take advantage during cold weather of the fireplace across from which we had placed our bed. Sometime before dawn, a noise woke me; and peering into the dark kitchen, I found my father, luridly lit by the blue and yellow ring of flame on the gas stove.

He wore only his tan slacks, no shirt or shoes, and was whistling Kate Smith's theme song, "When the Moon Comes Over the Mountain." As he poured steaming water from a tea kettle over the coffee in the Melita filter bag, he began singing in a low, nasal, Vaughn Monroe style. The piddling stream of dripping coffee accompanied him. After clanking the kettle back onto the stove and turning off the gas, he switched to a Bing Crosby version of "Because My Baby Don't Mean Maybe Now."

It was too dark to see him, but I heard him shuffling in an easy soft-shoe to his own music. I gauged the distance between our worlds as the difference between Crosby's chorus, nonsense sounds that slid from his mouth like water dribbling through parted lips— "Buh buh ba la, buh buh ba la, ba la"—and the music I would have babbled in the dark, a fierce spray of sound, Little Richard Penniman's "A wop bop a loo mop a lam bam boom . . ."

Not that different after all, because somehow the relaxed syllables of my father's song and the angry syllables of mine both slipped a wedge between the singer and seriousness. Neither chorus meant anything. Or rather, both choruses meant something more than words could have expressed. They were magic chants to invoke some spook of youth. Standing in the dark and letting "Tutti Frutti" bop in my mind beside the music my father was making, I for the first time felt old.

Up until that moment, I had still thought of myself as, say, nineteen. Perhaps twenty or twenty-one at the most. I was stunned. I could slide my imagination back a decade and discover myself as essentially the same person that was standing in the dark kitchen, secretly listening to my father jolt through a repertoire of early jazz and swing. I had a history! I felt like a lucky archaeologist who stumbles onto a terrain fertile with artifacts of an unknown civilization: intact temples buried under soil pocked with pottery, weapons, primitive games, uncrushed skulls, tools, coins, bracelets . . .

The screen door creaked open and banged shut, and I saw a hole in the dark move across the lawn. I followed, letting the screen door bang to alert my father to my presence.

"Maxie?" he asked. "Dennis?"

"Dennis," I said. "You're up early."

"I couldn't sleep," he said. "Sorry I disturbed you."

"I couldn't sleep either," I lied, trying to force an intimacy by admitting to a similar complaint. I couldn't say I was sorry for hurting him earlier, because by acknowledging the injury I would only enlarge it. To establish contact, I had to make myself vulnerable, but I couldn't think of anything sufficiently sensitive. Ever since we had left New York and moved to the farm, my life had been remarkably uneventful, happy. The slight annoyances of the past year were not substantial enough to offer up as a token of my defenselessness. It was like finding yourself at the altar of some bloodthirsty god with only a chipmunk to slaughter and a knife too frail for suicide.

So I lied again, sketching a general anxiety to explain my insomnia. My father rose to the bait, gave the lie flesh by making connections I had not implied.

"Are you having problems with Maxie?" he asked.

Since his question had a slight tremor of intimacy—the father probing the son's misery with the same delicacy used to tease out a splinter with a needle and the same possibility of having to dig painfully into the flesh—I assumed my father felt he'd found a sensitive spot.

"Yes," I said, "a little."

Ready to jab a nerve, he asked, "Is she unfaithful?"

We were exchanging hostages. I won't hurt you if you won't hurt me. I hoped we would make more exchanges, inching closer to each other with each revelation.

It would be painful to admit that Maxie was unfaithful (even though as far as I knew she wasn't), but I supposed my father would not make any deadly attacks. And even if I were wrong and he did, my confidence was a fraud. I wasn't ready to trust my father that entirely. So once more I lied.

"Yes," I said.

He said, "I'm sorry."

"It's nothing serious," I said.

My father laughed, I think, sympathetically.

"You don't sound convincing," he said, and after a pause added, "Well, she's a very attractive woman. Are you going to separate?"

"I don't know," I said.

"Look, Dennis," he said, "you can talk to me." Without stopping, however, to let me talk, he continued, "That would have some kind of neatness to it. Both of us leaving our wives in the same summer. We could become hoboes together." There was another pause. When he laughed again, he had changed his position. I turned quickly around, chilled, as though I feared he'd attack me if I let him get behind me.

"Do you want a drink?" I asked.

"What do you have?"

"Jack Daniel's?"

"OK," he said.

I walked back into the house to get the bottle. On my way out, I hesitated, tiptoed to my bedroom, and, feeling in the dark for Maxie's head, kissed her on the cheek. She murmured something and flung an arm up over my neck, pulling me down to kiss me on the side of the mouth. Feeling reassured—I didn't want my lies to conjure up some infidelity—I went outside into the chilly morning. The dark had become gray, and I could make out my father's face.

I offered him the bottle. He drank, wiped his lips with the back of his hand, and handed the liquor back. I drank, gave him the bottle, which he held at his side.

"That's some garden," he said. "That's some garden you've got back there."

"Yeah," I said, slowly moving in that direction beside him. "It's the thing which makes sense out of this place. We're very proud of it." My throat tightened. Here was a revelation, although I wasn't sure that my father would understand. "When we came here," I said,

"I was very unsure about giving up a lot of things. Ambition. You know, trying to be a success. Making it in New York. It was like all that was the bone in my life. All winter I'd get these flashes of desperation. I felt completely abandoned. We left this place only a dozen times between October and March—except to drive into the Piggly Wiggly for food. No one ever came out here. Too far.

"It got so I couldn't read a paper or watch TV without getting terrified and angry. Running scared. Things were happening. I thought they were important. We didn't even know about the invasion of Laos until months afterward. Funny. It was like being stuck in a dream and not being able to get out. Even though it was a fairly pleasant dream. I wanted to go back to New York. Maxie wanted to stay here."

"So that's where the trouble started," said my father.

Yes, I thought, there had been trouble between Maxie and me. Not the kind my father had assumed and I had pretended, but just as serious. Being vulnerable to others, it seemed, was also being vulnerable to yourself. And the real revelations surprise both of you.

"It wasn't true what I said before about Maxie," I said.

My father grunted. I'm not sure he believed me.

"Not in the way I meant it, at least," I added. "But there was . . ."

"Was?"

"Is . . . a little, I guess . . . is a breach. I only said that other thing because—because it seemed like you wanted to believe it and . . ."

"Like I want to believe it?" my father interrupted. "Why would I want to believe Maxie was unfaithful?"

"I don't know," I said. "Why would you?"

It had gotten much lighter. We were standing on the edge of the garden. My father tipped back the bottle and took a long drink after which he handed it to me. I drank, capped the bottle. My father said: "I envy you, Dennis. I envy you your age, the times in which you grew up, your generation, the fact that you could escape New York, ambition, whatever, I envy you this." He waved to the garden. "Yeah," he said, "this."

We were walking around the garden. I said: "In the spring, when we planted, all the terrors vanished. It was like watching things grow, having helped them grow, healed all the raw things inside."

"Yes," said my father, "and when winter comes?"

I sighed.

"That," I said, "terrifies me. It's like thinking about death."

"I think about death a lot," said my father. "I figure I've got a decade left. Ten years. Can you imagine that? Ten years." He made a noise that was the beginning of a laugh. "Next year it'll be nine years. Then eight. Then seven. Can you imagine that?"

"Yes," I said.

"No, you can't. No, you can't. What are you? Thirty. You're still invulnerable. Nothing can hurt you."

I started to say something, but he interrupted:

"Shut up. You don't know . . . You don't know . . ." He put a hand over his eyes. "Wouldn't that be remarkable? If I started to cry. God, I envy you. How were you able to do this? How?" He reached up and grabbed an overhanging branch with both hands. "Goddamn me," he said. "Goddamn me, but I want to do something outrageous."

My father went in to bed. I stayed up, made two soft-boiled eggs, which I ate while sitting in the porch rocker and listening to the birds, and an hour later left for Martin's Stables, where I worked three days a week in the barn, shoveling up manure which I spread in the fields to fertilize the grass which was cut, bailed, and carted back into the barn for the horses to eat. Once I asked Mr. Martin why he didn't let the horses graze in the fields and in the natural course of events spread the manure themselves. Tipping his red bald head to the side and opening his eyes wide, he said:

"But, my friend, that wouldn't make sense, would it?"

When I returned home at six-thirty, Maxie dropped her hoe and ran around the tomato plants toward me. She was pointing behind herself at the woods.

"I want him to leave," she said. "I want him to leave tonight." Her face was sunburned, and there was a dried spot of blood on her forehead where she'd squashed a mosquito. "He tried to make love to me today. I was swimming in the stream. He'd followed me down. I guess, since I didn't have any clothes on, he took that as some sort of invitation . . ." She waved her hands in front of her face to brush away bugs. A drop of sweat slid from her right temple down her smudged cheek and trembled on her chin. She slapped at it. "Damn flies," she said.

"Where is he?" I asked, some Oedipal nerve lighting up like a pinball machine.

She gestured. I circled around the garden and climbed the hill into the woods. The path twisted through thick pines, some hickory, birch, beech, red and silver maple . . . After peeling a curl from a black birch, I put the bark under my tongue and let the taste of wintergreen fill my mouth. That and the smell of the purple milkweed blossoms which hung on the top of the knee-high stalks in sunny patches fixed the moment for me. There was an awful joy seeping through the locks in my brain. If I'd found my father then, I would have killed him.

I walked for fifteen minutes until I came to the slope that led down to the stream. Floating in the shallow water, face up, eyes closed, his mouth warped into a miserable grin, my father looked very old. Having stopped at the edge of the bank, I said, "Put your clothes on."

My father opened his eyes.

"I've been waiting for you," he said. "I stayed down here after Maxie left. I couldn't bear to be with her after what I did."

I said, "Get out of the water and get dressed."

"At first," he said, still not moving, just floating there, "I was terrified of what would happen when you got back. It was a curious feeling, to be terrified of one's son. I had all sorts of strange thoughts. If we fought, I figured you'd have the advantage; and I even felt bad that I hadn't beat the shit out of you when you were a kid. You know? To make up for whatever you might do to me today. Then I thought, What the hell. This is what we've both been waiting for. All that talk this morning. You didn't want to get close to me because you loved me. You wanted to get close enough to . . ."

"If I'm going to beat the shit out of you," I said, "I'd rather do it when you're dressed, but if you don't get dressed I'll do it when you're naked."

"Then I thought," my father said, standing, the water running down his body, "that if we fought, maybe it wouldn't be such an uneven match after all." He picked up his shirt and wiped himself off, threw the shirt into the grass, climbed into his slacks. "You've had a pretty soft life, Dennis. You've never fought for blood. I have."

"Do you think I'm afraid of you?" I asked.

"No," he said. We were standing face to face, and I could see the muscles in his shoulders and chest tensing. "But I'm not afraid of you either."

For a long time neither of us said, did anything. A frog started croaking right by our feet. My father licked his lips. I cleared my throat and said: "You're going to leave tonight, aren't you?"

He said, "Yes."

"Are you going home?"

"Not right away." He blinked, momentarily bringing back the same vacant expression I used to hate, but then he narrowed his eyes and peered very hard at my face. "If I could figure out a way to hurt you," he said, "I would. You condescend. We're not going to be able to know each other until you realize in what way we're equal."

"Good-bye," I said.

He held out his hand. "Good-bye."

I left my father and walked back to the house. It was beginning to get dark. Maxie had set the table for two, and the absence of the third place oppressed me. I left most of my food. The meat loaf smelled stale, rancid. Maxie cleared the table, carried out the garbage, and screamed. I ran onto the porch. Maxie stood at the rocker, the garbage pail spilled on the ground beside her.

In the garden my father was dragging up pole beans, kicking over cabbages, tearing down tomato plants.

"Aren't you going to do anything?" Maxie wailed.

I leaned against the kitchen door and, ready to welcome hate or the rigid fusing of respect to love, watched my father rage.

Double Glazing

SIMON BRETT

Simon Brett's Introduction:

"Double Glazing" was first published in 1979, and that was a very important year for me. It was the year in which I gave up the day job. Up until then, from the time I left university, I'd been employed, first as a department store Santa, next as a BBC radio producer, and finally as a television producer.

But once my first mystery had been published in 1975, the fantasy I'd always nursed, of being a full-time writer, became more and more compelling. I was starting to make a bit of money from my writing; indeed I was making about as much as my salary; it was clearly the moment to halve my income.

There was one risk, so far as I could see, in becoming a full-time writer. All my hours over the calculator, all the mental sums I spent so much of my time doing, came to the same conclusion. My new lifestyle was only going to work if I produced more than I had when I was just writing in my spare time. I'd heard terrible cautionary tales of people who had given up the safe job, only to spend eight hours a day behind a desk, producing the same number of words as they previously had done in one snatched hour in the evening.

So I was determined to diversify in my writing. I'd published four of my Charles Paris mysteries by then, but I'd never tried a crime short story. Reaching this conclusion fortunately coincided with my agent mentioning a long-established anthology that was on the lookout for new stories. And so it was the "Double Glazing" came to be written.

The story was also a departure for me, in that it was my first attempt to write something that wasn't funny. Since, as a seven-year-old, I had been set the homework of writing my own epitaph and come up with:

"Here I lie, S. Brett by name,

"Killed by a lion I thought was tame,"

Almost everything I wrote had ended up with jokes in it. Certainly there was an expanding thread of humor in the Charles Paris novels.

"Double Glazing" was going to change all that.

I remember writing the story very quickly, and enjoying the process. I also remember growing delight at the prospects it opened up for me. The mystery short story was a new form to explore, and one that I felt confident would give me a lot a pleasure of the years. (I was right.)

Creating a whole book is a wonderful experience, but it's always going to be a marathon. Great to be able to vary those long hauls with a few sprints now and then. And there's something wonderfully satisfying in a piece of work that you can take from idea to completion in a matter of a few days—or every now and then, when the gods are really smiling on you, within a single day.

So I look back on "Double Glazing" with great fondness. It reminds me of that annus mirabilis, 1979, much of which I spent wandering round the house in a state of euphoria, pinching myself and saying with giddy disbelief, "I don't have to do any of that office stuff anymore. I'm a writer."

Double Glazing

SIMON BRETT

THE FIREPLACE WAS RATHER splendid, a carved marble arch housing a black metal grate. The curves of the marble supports echoed the elaborate sweep of the coving and the outward spread of petals from the central ceiling rose. The white emulsion enthusiastically splashed over the room by the Housing Trust volunteers could not disguise its fine Victorian proportions. The old flooring had been replaced by concrete when the damp course was put in, and the whole area was now snugly carpeted. This was one of the better conversions, making a compact residence for a single occupant, Jean Collinson thought as she sat before the empty grate opposite Mr. Morton. A door led off the living room to the tiny kitchen and bathroom. Quite sufficient for a retired working man.

She commented on the fireplace.

"Oh, yes, it's very attractive," Harry Morton agreed. His voice still bore traces of his Northern upbringing. "Nice workmanship in those days. Draughty, mind, if you don't have it lit."

"Yes, but there's no reason why you shouldn't use it in the winter. When they did the conversion, the builders checked that the chimney wasn't blocked. Even had it swept, I think."

"Oh, yes. Well, I'll have to see about that when the winter comes. See how far the old pension stretches."

"Of course. Do you find it hard to make ends meet?"

"Oh, no. I'm not given to extravagance. I have no vices, so far as I know." The old man chuckled. He was an amiable soul; Jean found him quite restful after most of the others. Mrs. Walker with her constant moans about how her daughter and grandchildren never came to visit, Mr. Kitson with his incontinence and unwillingness to do anything about it. Mrs. Grüber with her conviction that Jean was part of an international conspiracy of social workers devoted to the cause of separating her from a revoltingly smelly little Yorkshire terrier called Nimrod. It was a relief to meet an old person who seemed to be coping.

Mr. Morton had already made his mark on the flat although he had only moved in the week before. It was all very clean and tidy, no dust on any of the surfaces. (He had refused the Trust's offer of help with the cleaning, so he must have done it himself.) His few possessions were laid out neatly, the rack of pipes spotless on the mantelpiece, the pile of Do-It-Yourself magazines aligned on the coffee table, the bed squared off with hospital corners.

Mr. Morton had taken the same care with his own appearance. His chin was shaved smooth, without the cuts and random tufts of white hair which Jean saw on so many of the old men she dealt with. His shirt was clean, tie tight in a little knot, jacket brushed, trousers creased properly, and brown shoes buffed to a fine shine. And there didn't linger about him the sour smell which she now almost took for granted would emanate from all old people. If there was any smell in the room, it was an antiseptic hint of carbolic soap. Thank God, Jean thought, her new charge wasn't going to add too much to her already excessive workload. Just the occasional visit to check if he was all right, but, even from this first meeting, she knew he would be. Harry Morton could obviously manage. He'd lived alone all his life and had the neatness of an organized bachelor. But without that obsessive independence which so many of them developed. He didn't seem to resent her visit, nor to have complicated feelings of pride about accepting the Housing Trust's charity. He was just a working man who had done his bit for society and was now ready to accept society's thanks in the reduced circumstances of retirement. Jean was already convinced that the complaints which had led to his departure from his previous flat were just the ramblings of a paranoid neighbor.

She stifled a yawn. It was not that she was bored by Harry Morton's plans for little improvements to the flat. She had learned as a social worker to appear interested in much duller and less coherent narratives. But it was stuffy. Like a lot of old people, Harry Morton seemed unwilling to open the windows. Still, it was his flat and his right to have as much or as little ventilation as he wanted.

Anyway, Jean knew that the lack of air was not the real reason for her doziness. Guiltily, she allowed herself to think for a moment about the night before. She felt a little glow of fragile pleasure and knew she mustn't think about it too much, mustn't threaten it by inflating it in her mind beyond its proper proportions.

But, without inflation, it was still the best thing that had happened to her for some years, and something that she had thought, at thirty-two, might well never happen again. It had all been so straightforward, making nonsense of the agonizing and worry about being an emotional cripple which had seemed an inescapable part of her life ever since she'd broken up with Roger five years earlier.

It had not been a promising party. Given by a schoolfriend who had become a teacher, married a teacher, and developed a lot of friends who were also teachers. Jean had anticipated an evening of cheap Spanish plonk, sharp French bread and predictable cheese, with conversation about how little teachers were paid, how much more everyone's contemporaries were earning, how teaching wasn't really what any of them had wanted to do anyway, all spiced with staff-room gossip about personalities she didn't know, wasn't likely to meet and, after half an hour of listening, didn't want to meet.

And that's how it had been, until she had met Mick. From that point on, the evening had just made sense. Talking to him, dancing with him (for some reason, though they were all well into their thirties, the party was still conducted on the lines of a college hop), then effortlessly leaving with him and going back to his flat.

And there it had made sense, too. All the inhibitions she had carried with her so long, the knowledge that her face was strong rather than beautiful, that her hips were too broad and her breasts too small, had not seemed important. It had all been so different from the one-sided fumblings, the humorless groping and silent embarrassments which had seemed for some years all that sex had to offer. It had worked.

And Mick was coming straight round to her place after school. She was going to cook him a meal. He had to go to some Debating Society meeting and would be round about seven. Some days she couldn't guarantee to be back by then, the demands of her charges were unpredictable, but this time even that would be all right. Harry Morton was the last on her round and he clearly wasn't going to be any trouble. Covertly, with the skill born of long practice, she looked at her watch. A quarter to five. Good, start to leave in about five minutes, catch the shops on the way home, buy something special, maybe a bottle of wine. Cook a good dinner and then . . .

She felt herself blushing and guiltily pulled her mind back to listen to what Harry Morton was saying. Fantasizing never helped, she knew, it only distanced reality. Anyway, she had a job to do.

"I've got a bit of money saved," Harry was saying, "some I put aside in the Post Office book while I was still working and I've even managed to save a bit on the pension, and I reckon I'm going to buy some really good tools. I want to get a ratchet screwdriver. They're very good, save a lot of effort. Just the job for putting up shelves, that sort of thing. I thought I'd put a couple of shelves up over there, you know, for magazines and that."

"Yes, that's a very good idea." Jean compensated for her lapse into reverie by being bright and helpful. "Of course, if you need a hand with any of the heavy stuff, the Trust's got a lot of volunteers who'd be only too glad to—"

"Oh no, no, thank you. I won't need help. I'm pretty good with my hands. And, you know, if you've worked with your hands all your life, you stay pretty strong. Don't worry, I'll be up to building a few shelves. And any other little jobs around the flat."

"What did you do before you retired, Mr. Morton?"

"Now please call me Harry. I was a warehouse porter."

"Oh."

"Working up at Granger's, don't know if you know them?"

"Up on the main road?"

"Yes. We loaded the lorries. Had trolleys, you know. Had to go along the racks getting the lines to put in the lorries. Yes, I did that for nearly twenty years. They wanted me to be a checker, you know, checking off on the invoices as the goods were loaded on to the lorries, but I didn't fancy the responsibility. I was happy with my trolley."

Suddenly Jean smiled at the old man, not her professional smile of concern, but a huge, generic smile of pleasure that broke the sternness of her face into a rare beauty. Somehow she respected his simplicity, his content. It seemed to fit that the day after she met Mick, she should also meet this happy old man. She arose from her chair. "Well, if you're sure there's nothing I can do for you . . ."

"No, I'll be fine, thank you, love."

"I'll drop round again in a week or two to see how you're getting on."

"Oh, that'll be very nice. I'll be fine, though. Don't you worry about me."

"Good." Jean lingered for a moment. She felt something missing, there was something else she had meant to mention, now what on earth was it?

Oh, yes. His sister. She had meant to talk to him about his sister, sympathize about her death the previous year. Jean had had the information from a social worker in Bradford where the sister had lived. They tried to liaise between different areas as much as possible. The sister had been found dead in her flat. She had died of hypothermia, but her body had not been discovered for eleven days, because of the Christmas break.

Jean thought she should mention it. There was always the danger of being thought to intrude on his privacy, but Harry Morton seemed a sensible enough old bloke, who would recognize her sympathy for what it was. And, in a strange way, Jean felt she ought to raise the matter as a penance for letting her mind wander while Harry had been talking.

"Incidentally, I heard about your sister's death. I'm very sorry."

"Oh, thank you." Harry Morton didn't seem unduly perturbed by the reference. "I didn't see a lot of her these last few years."

"But it must have been a shock."

"A bit, maybe. Typical, though. She always was daft, never took care of herself. Died of the cold, she did. Hyper . . . hyper-something they called it."

"Hypothermia."

"That's it. Silly fool. I didn't see her when I went up for the funeral. Just saw the coffin. Closed coffin. Could have been anyone. Didn't feel nothing, really."

"Anyway, as I say, I'm sorry."

"Oh, don't think about it. I don't. And don't you worry about me going the same way. For one thing, I always had twice as much sense as she did—from a child on. And then I can look after myself."

Jean Collinson left, feeling glad she had mentioned the sister. Now there was nothing nagging at her mind, nothing she felt she should be doing. Except looking forward to the evening. She wondered what she should cook for Mick.

Harry Morton closed the door after her. It was summer, but the corridor outside felt chilly. He shivered slightly, then went to his notebook and started to make a list.

He had always made lists. At the warehouse he had soon recalled that he couldn't remember all the lines the checker gave him unless he wrote them down. The younger porters could remember up to twenty different items for their loads, but Harry recognized his limitations and always wrote everything down. It made him a little slower than the others, but at least he never got anything wrong. And the Head Checker had said, when you took off the time the others wasted taking back lines they had got wrong, Harry was quite as fast as any of them.

He headed the list "Things to do." First he wrote "Ratchet screwdriver." Then he wrote "Library."

HARRY KNEW HIS OWN pace and he never tried to go any faster. When he was younger he had occasionally tried to push himself along a bit, but that had only resulted in mistakes. Now he did everything steadily, methodically. And now there was no one to push him. The only really miserable time of his life had been when a new checker had been appointed who had tried to increase Harry's work-rate. The old man still woke up sometimes in the night in the sweat of panic and confusion that the pressure had put on him. Unwillingly he'd remember the afternoon when he'd thrown a catering-size till of diced carrots at his tormentor's head. But then he'd calm down, get up, and make himself a cup of tea. That was all over. It hadn't lasted very long. The checker had been ambitious and soon moved on to an office job.

And now he wasn't at work, Harry had all the time in the world, anyway. Time to do a good job. The only pressure on him was to get it done before the winter set in. And the winter was a long way off.

He read through all the Do-It-Yourself books he had got from the library, slowly, not skipping a word. After each one he would make a list, a little digest of the pros and cons of the methods discussed. Then he sent off for brochures from all the companies that advertised in his Do-It-Yourself magazines and subjected them to the same punctilious scrutiny. Finally, he made a tour of the local home-care shops, looked at samples and discussed the various systems with the proprietors. After six weeks he reckoned he knew everything there was to know about double glazing.

And by then he had ruled out quite a few of the systems on the market. The best method he realized was to replace the existing windows with new factory-sealed units, but, even if the Housing Trust would allow him to do this, it would be far too expensive and also too big a job for him to do on his own.

The next possible solution was the addition of secondary sashes, fixing a new pane over the existing windows, leaving the original glass undisturbed. There were a good many proprietary sub-frame systems on the market, but again these would be far too expensive for his modest savings. He did some sums in his note-book, working out how long it would take him to afford secondary sashes by saving on his pension, but he wouldn't have enough till the spring. And he had to get the double glazing installed before the winter set in. He began to regret the generous proportions on which the Victorians had designed their windows.

He didn't worry about it, though. It was still only September. There was going to be a way that he could afford and that he could do on his own. That social worker was always full of offers of help from her network of volunteers, but he wasn't reduced to that yet.

Then he had the idea of going through the back numbers of his Do-It-Yourself magazines. He knew it was a good idea as soon as he thought about it. He sat in his armchair in front of the fireplace, which was now hidden by a low screen, and, with notebook and pencil by his side, started to thumb through the magazines. He did them in strict chronological order, just as he kept them stacked on their new shelf. He had a full set for seven and a half years, all unbroken sequence from the first time he had become interested in Do-It-Yourself. That had been while he was being harassed by the new checker. He chuckled to remember that he'd bought the first magazine because it had an article in it about changing locks and he'd wanted to keep the checker out of his flat. Of course, the checker had never come to his flat.

He started on the first magazine and worked through, reading everything, articles and advertisements, in case he should miss what he was looking for. Occasionally he made a note in his notebook.

It was on the afternoon of the third day that he found it. The article was headed, "Cut the Costs of Double Glazing." His heart quickened with excitement, but he still read through the text at his regular, unvarying pace. Then he read it a second time, even more slowly, making copious notes.

The system described was a simple one, which involved sticking transparent film on the inside of the windows and thus creating the required insulation gap between the panes and the film. There were, the writer observed slyly, kits for this system available on the market, but the shrewd Do-It-Yourself practitioner would simply go to his local supermarket and buy the requisite number of rolls of kitchen clingfilm and then go to his hardware store to buy a roll of double-sided Sellotape for fixing the film, and thus save himself a lot of money. Harry Morton chuckled out loud, as this cunning plot was confided to him. Then he wrote on his list "Kitchen Clingfilm" and "Double-sided Sellotape."

As always, in everything he did, he followed the instructions to the letter. At first, it was more difficult than it sounded. The kitchen film tended to shrivel up on itself and stretch out of true when he tried to extend it over the window frames. And it caught on the stickiness of the Sellotape before it was properly aligned. He had to sacrifice nearly a whole roll of clingfilm before he got the method right. But he pressed on, working with steady care, perched on the folding ladder he had bought specially for the purpose, and soon was rewarded by the sight of two strips stretched parallel and taut over the window frame.

He was lining up the third when the doorbell rang. He was annoyed by the interruption to his schedule and opened the door grudgingly to admit Jean Collinson. Then he almost turned his back on her while he got on with the tricky task of winding the prepared film back on to its cardboard roll. He would have to start lining the next piece up again after she had gone.

Still, he did his best to be pleasant and offered the social worker a cup of tea. It seemed to take a very long time for the kettle to boil and the girl seemed to take a very long time to drink her tea. He kept looking over her shoulder to the window, estimating how many more strips it would take and whether he'd have to go back to the supermarket for another roll to make up for the one he'd ruined.

Had he taken any notice of Jean, he would have seen that she looked tired, fatigue stretching the skin of her face to show her features at their sharpest and sternest. Work was getting busy. She had ahead of her a difficult interview with Mrs. Grüber, whose Yorkshire terrier Nimrod had developed a growth between his back legs. It hung there, obscene and shiny, dangling from the silky fur. The animal needed to go to the vet, but Mrs. Grüber refused to allow this, convinced that it would have to be put down. Jean feared this suspicion was correct, but knew that the animal had to make the trip to find out one way or the other. It was obviously in pain and kept up a thin keening whine all the time while Mrs. Grüber hugged it piteously to her cardigan. And Jean knew that she was going to have to be the one who got the animal to the vet.

Which meant she'd be late again. Which would mean another scene with Mick. He'd become so childish recently, so demanding, jealous of the time she spent with her old people. He had become moody and hopeless. Instead of the support in her life which he had been at first, he was now almost another case on her books. She had discovered how much he feared his job, how he couldn't keep order in class, and, though she gave him all the sympathy she could, it never seemed to be enough.

And then there were the logistics of living in two separate establishments an awkward bus-ride apart. Life seemed to have degenerated into a sequence of late-night and early-morning rustics from one flat to the other because one of them had left something vital in the wrong place. Jean had once suggested that they should move in together, but Mick's violent reaction of fear against such a commitment had kept her from raising the matter again. So their relationship had become a pattern of rows and making up, abject self-recrimination from Mick, complaints that she didn't really care about him and late-night reconciliations of desperate, clinging sex. Always too late. She had forgotten what a good night's sleep was by the time one end had been curtailed by arguments and coupling and the other by leaving at half past six to get back to her place to pick up some case notes. Everything seemed threatened.

But it was restful in Harry's flat. He seemed to have his life organized. She found it an oasis of calm, of passionless simplicity, where she could recharge her batteries before going back to the difficulties of the rest of her life.

She was unaware of how he was itching for her to go. She saw the evidence of the double glazing and asked him about it, but he was reticent. He didn't want to discuss it until it was finished. Anyway, it wasn't for other people's benefit. It was for him.

Eventually Jean felt sufficiently steeled for her encounter with Mrs. Grüber and brought their desultory conversation to an end. She did not notice the alacrity with which Harry Morton rose to show her out, nor the speed with which he closed the door after her.

Again he felt the chill of the corridor when the door was open. And even after it was closed there seemed to be a current of air from somewhere. He went across to his notebook and wrote down "Draught Excluder."

IT WAS LATE OCTOBER when she next went round to see the old man. She was surprised that he didn't immediately open the door after she'd rung the bell. Instead she heard his voice hiss out, "Who is it?"

She was used to this sort of reception from some of her old ladies, who lived in the conviction that every caller was a rapist at the very least, but she hadn't expected it from such a sensible old boy as Harry Morton.

She identified herself and, after a certain amount of persuasion, he let her in. He held the door open as little as possible and closed it almost before she was inside. "What do you want?" he asked aggressively.

"I just called to see how you are."

"Well, I'm fine." He spoke as if that ended the conversation and edged back toward the door.

"Are you sure? You look a bit pale."

He did look pale. His skin had taken on a grayish color.

"You look as if you haven't been out much recently. Have you been ill? If you're unwell, all you have to do is—"

"I haven't been ill. I go out, do my shopping, get the things I need." He couldn't keep a note of mystery out of the last three words.

She noticed he was thinner, too. His appearance hadn't suffered; he still dressed with almost obsessive neatness; but he had definitely lost weight. She wasn't to know that he was cutting down on food so that his pension would buy the "things he needed."

The room looked different, too. She only took it in once she was inside. There was evidence of recent carpentry. No mess—all the sawdust was neatly contained on newspaper and offcuts of wood were leaned against the kitchen table which Harry had used as a sawing bench—but he had obviously been busy. The ratchet screwdriver was prominent on the tabletop. The artifact which all this effort had produced was plain to see. The fine marble fireplace had been neatly boxed in. It had been a careful job. Pencil marks on the wood showed the accuracy of measurement and all of the screws were tidily countersunk into their regularly spaced holes.

Jean commented on the workmanship.

"When I do a job, I like to do it properly," Harry Morton said defensively.

"Of course. Didn't you . . . like the fireplace?"

"Nothing wrong with it. But it was very draughty."

"Yes." She wondered for a moment if Harry Morton were about to change from being one of her easy charges to one of her problems. He was her last call that day and she'd reckoned on just a quick visit. She'd recently made various promises to Mick about spending less time with her work. He'd suddenly got very aggressively male, demanding that she should have a meal ready for him when he got home. He also kept calling her "woman," as if he were some character out of the blues songs he was always listening to. He didn't manage this new male chauvinism with complete conviction; it seemed only to accentuate his basic insecurity; but Jean was prepared to play along with it for a bit. She felt there was something in the relationship worth salvaging. Maybe when he relaxed a bit, things would be better. If only they could spend a little time on their own, just the two of them, away from outside pressures . . .

She stole a look at her watch. She could spend half an hour with Harry and still be back at what Mick would regard as a respectable hour. Anyway, there wasn't anything really wrong with the old boy. Just needed a bit of love, a feeling that someone cared. That's what most of them needed when it came down to it.

"Harry, it looks to me like you may have been overdoing it with all this heavy carpentry. You must remember, you're not as young as you were and you do have to take things a bit slower."

"I take things at the right pace," he insisted stubbornly. "There's nothing wrong with me."

But Jean wasn't going to have her solicitude swept aside so easily. "No, of course there isn't. But look, I'd like you just to sit down for a moment in front of the . . . by the fireplace, and I'll make you a cup of tea."

Grumbling, he sat down.

"And why don't you put the television on? I'm sure there's some nice relaxing program for you to see."

"There's not much I enjoy on the television."

"Nonsense, I'm sure there are lots of things to interest you." Having started in this bulldozing vein, Jean was going to continue. She switched on the television and went into the kitchen.

It was some children's quiz show, which Harry would have switched off under normal circumstances. But he didn't want to make the girl suspicious. If he just did as she said, she would go quicker. So he sat and watched without reaction.

It was only when the commercials came that he took notice. There was a commercial for double glazing. A jovial man was demonstrating the efficacy of one particular system. A wind machine was set in motion the other side of an open window. Then the double-glazed window was closed and, to show how airtight the seal was, the man dropped a feather by the joint in the panes. It fluttered straight downward, its course unaffected by any draughts.

From that moment Harry Morton was desperate for Jean to leave. He had seen the perfect way of testing his workmanship. She offered to stay and watch the program with him, she asked lots of irrelevant questions about whether he needed anything or whether there was anything her blessed volunteers could do, but eventually she was persuaded to go. In fact she was relieved to be away. Harry had seemed a lot perkier than when she had arrived and now she would be back in time to conform to Mick's desired image of her.

Harry almost slammed the door. As he turned, he felt a shiver of cold down his back. Right, feathers, feathers. It only took a moment to work out where to get them from.

He picked up his ratchet screwdriver and went over to the bed. He drew back the candlewick and stabbed the screwdriver deeply into his pillow. And again, twisting and tearing at the fabric. From the rents he made a little storm of feathers flurried.

It was cold as she walked along toward Harry's flat and the air stung the rawness of her black eye. But Jean felt good. At least they'd got something sorted out. After the terrible fight of the night before, in the sobbing reconciliation, after Mick had apologized for hitting her, he had suggested that they go away together for Christmas. He hated all the fuss that surrounded the festival and always went off to stay in a cottage in Wales, alone, until it all died down. And he had said, in his ungracious way, "You can come with me, woman."

She knew it was a risk. The relationship might not stand the proximity. She was even slightly afraid of being alone with Mick for so long, now that his behavior toward her had taken such a violent turn. But at bottom she thought it would work. Anyway, she had to try. They had to try. Ten days alone together would sort out the relationship one way or the other. And Christmas was only three weeks off.

As so often happened, her new mood of confidence was reflected in her work. She had just been to see Mrs. Grüber. Nimrod had made a complete recovery after the removal of his growth and the old lady had actually thanked Jean for insisting on the visit to the vet. That meant Mrs. Grüber could be left over the Christmas break without anxiety. And most of the others could manage. As Mick so often said, thinking you're indispensable is one of the first signs of madness. Of course they'd be all right if she went away. And, as Mick also said, then you'll be able to concentrate on me for a change, woman. Yes, it was going to work.

Again her ring at the doorbell was met by a whispered "Who is it?" from Harry Morton. It was Jean—could she come in? "No," he said.

"Why not, Harry? Remember, I do have a duplicate key. The Housing Trust insists that I have that, so that I can let myself in if—"

"No, it's not that, Jean love," his old Northern voice wheedled.

"It's just that I've got a really streaming cold. I don't want to breathe germs all over you."

"Oh, don't worry about that."

"No, no, really. I'm in bed. I'm just going to sleep it off."

Jean wavered. Now she came to think of it, she didn't fancy breathing in germs in Harry's stuffy little flat. "Have you seen the doctor?"

"No, I tell you it's just a cold. Be gone in a day or two, if I just stay in bed. No need to worry the doctor."

The more she thought about it, the less she wanted to develop a cold just before she and Mick went away together. But it was her job to help. "Are you sure there isn't anything I can do for you? Shopping or anything?"

"Oh. Well . . ." Harry paused. "Yes, I would be grateful, actually, if you wouldn't mind getting me a few things."

"Of course."

"If you just wait a moment, I'll write out a list."

Jean waited. After a couple of minutes a page from his notebook was pushed under the door. Its passage was impeded by the draught-excluding strip on the inside, but it got through.

Jean looked at the list. "Bottle of milk. Small tin of baked beans. Six packets of Polyfilla."

"Is that Polyfilla?" she asked, bewildered.

"Yes. It's a sort of powder you mix with water to fill in cracks and that."

"I know what it is. You just seem to want rather a lot of it."

"Yes, I do. Just for a little job needs doing."

"And you're quite sure you don't need any more food?"

"Sure. I've got plenty," Harry Morton lied.

"Well, I'll probably be back in about twenty minutes."

"Thank you very much. Here's the money." A few crumpled notes forced their way under the door. "If there's no reply when you get back, I'll be asleep. Just leave the stuff outside. It'll be safe."

"OK. If you're sure there's nothing else I can do."

"No, really. Thanks very much."

Harry Morton heard her footsteps recede down the passage and chuckled aloud with delight at his own cunning. Yes, she could help him. First useful thing she'd ever done for him. And she hadn't noticed the windows from the outside. Just thought the curtains were drawn. Yes, it had been a good idea to board them up over the curtains. He looked with satisfaction at the wooden covers, with their rows of screws, each one driven securely home with his ratchet screwdriver. Then he looked at the pile of new wood leaning against the door. Yes, with proper padding that would be all right. Mentally he earmarked his bedspread for the padding and made a note of the idea on the "Jobs to Do" list in his notebook.

Suddenly he felt the chill of a draught on his neck. He leapt up to find its source. He had long given up using the feather method. Apart from anything else, he had used his pillows as insulation in the fireplace. Now he used a lighted candle. Holding it firmly in front of him, he began to make a slow, methodical circuit of the room.

It was two days before Christmas, two o'clock in the afternoon. Jean and Mick were leaving at five. "Five sharp, woman," he had said. "If you ain't here then, woman, I'll know you don't give a damn about me. You'd rather spend your life with incontinent old men." Jean had smiled when he said it. Oh yes, she'd be there. Given all that time together, she knew they could work something out.

And, when it came to it, it was all going to be remarkably easy. All of her charges seemed to be sorted out over the holiday. Now Nimrod was all right, Mrs. Grüber was in a state of ecstasy, full of plans for the huge Christmas dinner she was going to cook for herself and the dog. Mrs. Walker was going to stay with her daughter, which meant that she would see the grandchildren, so she couldn't complain for once. Even smelly old Mr. Kitson had been driven off to spend the holiday with his married sister. Rather appropriately, in Bath. The rest of her cases had sorted themselves out one way or the other. And, after all, she was only going to be away for ten days. She felt she needed the break. Her Senior Social Worker had wished her luck and told her to have a good rest, and this made Jean realize how long it was since she had been away from work for any length of time.

She just had to check that Mr. Morton was all right, and then she was free.

Harry was steeping his trousers in mixed-up Polyfilla when he heard the doorbell. It was difficult, what he was doing. Really, the mixture should have been runnier, but he had not got out enough water before he boarded up the door to the kitchen and bathroom. Never mind, though, the stuff would still work and soon he'd be able to produce more urine to mix it with. He was going to use the Poly-filla-covered trousers to block the crevice along the bottom of the front door. His pajamas and pullover were already caulking the cracks on the other one.

He congratulated himself on judging the amount of Polyfilla right. He was nearly at the end of the last packet. By the time he'd blocked in the plug sockets and the ventilation grille he'd found hidden behind the television, it would all be used up. Just the right amount.

He froze when he heard the doorbell. *Lie doggo.* Pretend there's no one there. They'll go away.

The bell rang again. Still he didn't move. There was a long pause, so long he thought the challenge had gone. But then he heard an ominous sound, which at once identified his caller and also raised a new threat.

It was the sound of a key in his lock. That bloody busybody of a social worker had come round to see him.

There was nothing for it. He would have to let her in. "Just a minute. Coming," he called.

"Hurry up," the girl's voice said. She had told him to hurry up. Like the new checker, she had told him to hurry up.

He picked up his ratchet screwdriver and started to withdraw the first of the screws that held the large sheet of chipboard and its padding of bedclothes against the front door. At least, he thought, thank God I hadn't put the scaling strips along there.

Jean's voice sounded quite agitated by the time he removed the last screw. "What's going on? Can't you hurry up?"

She had said it again. He opened the door narrowly and she pushed in shouting, "Now what the hell do you think you're—"

Whether she stopped speaking because she was taken aback by the sight of the room and her half-naked host, or because the ratchet screwdriver driven into her back near her spine had punctured her heart, it's difficult to assess. Certainly it is true that the first blow killed her; the subsequent eleven were unnecessary insurance.

Harry Morton left the body on the floor and continued methodically with his tasks. He replaced the chipboard and padding over the door and sealed it round with his trousers, sports jacket, shirt and socks, all soaked in Polyfilla. Then he blocked up the plugs and ventilator grille.

He looked round with satisfaction. Now that was real insulation. No one could die of cold in a place like that. Always had been daft, his sister. But he didn't relax. One more final check-round with the candle, then he could put his feet up.

He went slowly round the room, very slowly so that the candle wouldn't flicker from his movement, only from genuine draughts.

Damn. It had moved. He retraced a couple of steps. Yes, it fluttered again. There was a draught.

By the fireplace. That fireplace had always been more trouble than it was worth.

It needed more insulating padding. And more Polyfilla to fill it.

But he'd used everything in the room and there was no water left to mix the Pollyfilla with. He felt too dehydrated to urinate. Never mind, there was a solution to everything. He sat down with his notebook and pencil to work it out.

Well, there was his underwear, for a start. That was more insulation. He took it off.

Then he looked down at Jean Collinson's body and saw the solution. To both his problems. Her body could be crammed into the chimney to block out the draughts and her blood (of which there was quite a lot) could mix with the Polyfilla.

He worked at his own pace, unscrewing the boxwork he had put around the marble fireplace with his ratchet screwdriver. Then he pulled out the inadequate insulation of pillows and Do-It-Your-self magazines and started to stuff the body up the chimney.

It was hard work. He pushed the corpse up head first and the broad hips stuck well in the flue, forming a good seal. But he had to break the legs to fit them behind his boxwork when he replaced it. He crammed the crevices with the pillows and magazines and sealed round the edges with brownish Polyfilla.

Only then did he feel that he could sit back with the satisfaction of a job well done.

THEY FOUND HIS NAKED body when they broke into the flat after the Christmas break.

He would have died from starvation in time, but in fact, so good was his insulation, he was asphyxiated first.

Public Servant

MAX ALLAN COLLINS

Max Allan Collins's Introduction:

"Public Servant" was written in 1967 for a community college creative writing class, where it stirred controversy to say the least. It's a Jim Thompson pastiche, and the most significant thing about the pastiche is that I was imitating Thompson before anybody had ever heard of him (except other writers and R. V. Cassill and Anthony Boucher, that is). It was published in the first issue of the fanzine Hardboiled *in 1985.*

The most distressing thing about the story is how much it still reads like my work . . .

Public Servant

MAX ALLAN COLLINS

I FELT GREAT, MY heart was pounding, but I should have slugged her harder. Or killed her, one of the two. I was hardly out the window and onto the lawn when she woke up and started in screaming her head off.

"Shut up, you bitch . . ." My voice hissed through my teeth like air from a punctured tire. "I'll hit you again, Goddamnit, shut the fuck up."

But it was too late.

Too late to climb back in and shut her up and too late to get away. I moved past the bushes along the side of the house and went back to my car in the alley. I could hear voices only a block or so away, so I had to work fast. I pulled the tactic I'd thought about a few times but never used. I reached in the back seat and grabbed my holstered gun, blue shirt with badge, and cap. Put them on faster than hell. Then I reached around into the front seat and flipped on the radio and grabbed off the mike and spoke into it.

"Ralph, hello Ralph, this is Harry."

His voice came back tinny over the cheap squawkbox speakers. "What's the trouble, officer?"

The mayor must have been in the station or Ralph wouldn't have called me "officer." Ralph was the chief but we didn't have many formalities, not in a town of a few thousand.

"Look, Ralph, I think the raper's hit again. There's a woman screaming and I'm heading over to look into it. Okay, Ralph?"

He forgot the newfound formality fast. "Jesus H. Christ, another rape! Damn it, damn. Any sign of the bastard?"

"Ralph, I'll shoot the damn bull with you some other time, okay? I'm going over and see what the hell's going on, you don't mind."

"I better send somebody over to help you."

"Good idea."

"Frank's hanging around the building somewhere. He's off duty, but he's the only one here so I'll send him."

"We're going to get this guy, Ralph."

"Damn right we will, Harry."

I clicked the mike off and put it back on the radio and headed for the house. Things'd been happening fast. Almost forgot to zip my fly.

SHE WAS STILL SCREAMING, so I didn't go in. Besides, there was a crowd of people in bathrobes and dressing gowns and such milling around, and I had to keep them cleared away as best I could till Frank got there to lend a hand.

When Frank finally did show, I told him to go in and do the questioning. An ambulance, Frank said, was on the way. I stood outside and worked at moving the funseekers away.

After a while the ambulance pulled up and I went inside and helped Frank and some guy from the hospital ease the bitch onto a stretcher and out the door and into the back of the ambulance. She looked right at me once and didn't bat an eye. The ambulance tore away and Frank stood there looking after it, shaking his head.

"Damn that bastard anyway, Harry, that damn bastard's going to get his, I swear."

"Same guy, suppose?"

"Sure as hell is. Same as always. Woman at home alone, her husband on the night shift or off on a National Guard stint or something of the like. The son of a bitch jimmies open a window and attacks her in her sleep, then knocks hell out of her."

"Have a cigarette, Frank."

Frank was in civvies, a T-shirt and white jeans as a matter of fact, and he stood there looking toward where the ambulance'd been, rubbing his hand over the place on his sandy crewcut where it was thinning. He said "Thanks" when I handed him the cigarette and lit it off his own lighter.

"You ain't letting this thing get you, are you, Frank?"

"Guess maybe I am. Jesus, let me tell you, it's enough to scare hell out of a married man. Christ, I mean you, you aren't married, you can't understand just how bad it is. But me, hell. A young wife. A kid in a crib. Me gone nights a lot. Scares the crap right out of me, a nut like this loose."

"Sure, Frank," I said. "I can see what you mean. I mean, I ain't married or anything, but I can see what you mean."

Frank rubbed his eyes with the heels of his hands. "Hell, Harry, how do you figure him? A psycho, sure, but how do you figure him?"

I smiled. "How *do* you figure a psycho?"

"I don't know. I honest to God don't know. But he gets his jollies making people hurt, I can see that plain enough. He always slugs hell out of the women, after he's had 'em. Didn't beat this as bad as the others, though, did you notice? Must be getting careless or something. Getting used to getting away with it. I mean, shit, we make it easy enough for him with our Mickey Mouse force."

"We're doing our best, Frank, ain't we?"

"Yeah. Our best. Dedicated public servants. Yeah."

He arched the hardly smoked cigarette out into the street.

"He'll probably be more careful next time, you know," I said.

"No next time about it," he said, "not if I can help it."

"Know what you mean, Frank, mean wouldn't you just like to get this bastard down and kick the hell out of him?"

Seemed like Frank's eyes were almost glowing. "That would be sweet. That sure as Christ would be sweet."

I patted his shoulder. "Well, we'll get him, Frank, don't you worry. I mean, after all, you figure him a nut, how long can a nut last?"

"Oh, but a damn smart nut, remember. There's never a fingerprint or clue of any kind around."

I checked my watch. "I wonder what's keeping Ollie with that damn boy scout crime lab of his? He ought to be here by now."

Frank shrugged. "Probably so used to this he's finishing the *Late Show* or something before he comes over. Besides, what's the use? That nut's a thinker, he never leaves anything to trace him. Anyway, nothing a small-scale set-up like we got could ever pick up on."

I lit myself a smoke. "But like you said, he's getting more careless. Had so much fun raping this one he didn't slug her as hard as he should've. Maybe this time he slipped up."

"Maybe you're right, Harry. Maybe old Ollie'll find something this time around."

"Here, Frank, have another smoke." I shook one out of the pack and fired him up off my lighter. "Stay out here and relax, I'll go back in and make sure none of the neighbors messed anything up before we got here."

Frank nodded. I went back in and looked around. Wiped off the windowsill with my handkerchief, a few other things, too. Had to make sure I wasn't getting *too* damn careless.

WHEN I WAS ON night duty I'd go to bed around nine o'clock in the morning and sleep till six or seven. Then I'd go over to the Seaside Motel to see Molly, and sometimes sponge a meal off her. Molly was sort of my girl. She thought she was, at least. She ran the Seaside, which is right by the lake. Her old man, who built the place (both him and the old lady kicked off in an auto wreck five, six years back), would've called it the Lakeside instead of the Seaside, only somebody else on the other side of town thought of it first. And the other motel wasn't even *on* the damn lake, ain't *that* the shits.

The "No Vacancy" sign wasn't on because the Seaside's whole neon system'd blown a few months before. But a wooden sign hung in the window of the office saying no dice to any travelers. Not that many stopped, only the regular round of salesmen who filled the

Seaside's seven dumpy little cabins during the week and the teenagers and college kids who used 'em on weekends.

The door was locked but I had a key. I went on in to Molly's living quarters beyond the office. She wasn't around. Probably down the hill by the lake.

The night air was chilly, though it was summer, high summer. Of course it's always cool on the lake, nights. I don't like the lake much. It's pretty, like a picture in a travel book, with the neon reflected on the rippling water and all that sort of shit. I'm not much for pretty things, except for pretty things like Molly. Or most any woman.

Down the gravel hill path and onto the beach I went, keeping my hand over the holstered rod at all times. Never could tell when somebody would catch up with me and then all my fun and games'd be over. So I kept my hand over the rod constant, so I could take the pleasure of blowing out some guy's guts before they took me. Sure they said I was a nut, a psycho (don't you believe it!) but I was having a hell of a good time being one.

Molly was standing on the beach in a blouse and loose skirt that was blowing up over her thighs in the gentle lake breeze. She was looking out onto the picture-book lake, watching the easy movement of the waves.

She'd heard me coming, knew I was there without looking around.

"Hi, Harry. Nice night."

"Hi."

"How about some supper? I could go back up and fix us some."

I didn't answer her right away, so she turned and looked at me. She was pretty, pretty near, her nice hazel-blue eyes the best part about her. Her hair was all right, too, for being all bleached out.

"Well, Harry, what do you say? Is it going to be supper? It's a really nice night, maybe you just want to go for a row or something?"

I grabbed her at the waist, pulled her in close to me.

"A row, Harry? How's that sound? The boat's tied down at the dock. Come on, Harry, what do you want to do?"

I squeezed. Tight. "Trouble with you, Molly, is that you don't know when to shut up. You shouldn't talk so damn much."

"Harry . . ." She laughed. I was squeezing her so hard it must have hurt like hell, but she only laughed. "Jesus, you're mean, Harry, you're one mean son of a bitch."

I squeezed even harder. "And that's what you like about me, ain't it, baby?"

She threw back her head and laughed some more. "You're god-damn right, Harry, you're goddamn right."

I latched onto her blouse and ripped it half off in one yank.

"Hey, you bastard! Take it easy on the clothes."

"What's wrong, honey? Thought you liked your Harry to be mean."

She stood there and the cold got at her, turning her blue and goose-pimply. She clutched her arms over her breasts and her teeth chattered as she said, "Be . . . be-being mean's one thing, Har . . . Harry . . . But wasting my damn m . . . money like that's an . . . another."

I wasn't worried, even if I'd cost her some in torn clothes and the like. What the hell. I reached for her skirt to rip that off her, too, but she jumped out of reach.

"Damn you, Harry! Damn you!" But she wasn't as mad as she was acting. "I'll unhook it, damn it, don't rip it off!"

She got out of the skirt before I could get my hands on it. She walked up to me and I slugged her right in the teeth and she went down like soft rope. I gripped her shoulders and pulled her up and bit into her mouth.

"Oh . . . Oh, Jesus, Harry, I love you . . ."

I laughed and bit into her bloody lips again. I liked the taste.

AFTER I LEFT MOLLY'S I stopped at the diner along Fourth Street for a bite to eat. Usually I ate at Molly's, but she had this thing about if I came to supper, fine, I can have supper and what else I wanted after, but if I took what else first, I could go out and buy my own damn chow after.

The counterman's name was Lou and he said, "Evening, Harry, what's it to be?"

"Gimme number two on the breakfasts, Lou."

I sat down on a stool at the counter and brushed the crumbs away from in front of me. A guy sat next to me sipping at his coffee. He turned and smiled and started in to talking like people do to cops sometimes, like they're trying to get in good with them or something. He sounded like a salesman, they're always getting friendly with cops. That's how a lot of them find a woman for the night in towns. But you'd think a guy could tell just looking at me I'm no goddamn pimp. Anyway, he starts in to talking:

"You always have breakfast here, officer, at eight o'clock in the evening like this?"

"Sure I do, mister, if I don't eat at my girl's place."

"Why breakfast? Any special reason, or you just like it?"

"I'm on night duty this week, pal, just got up. So I'm having breakfast."

"Oh." Back to his coffee for a minute, then: "Hear you've been having some trouble around here lately."

"Yeah," I said, trying not to get pissed at the guy; I hate pests, but I had to grin and bear it with guys like this so's folks wouldn't find out about the "beast" in me. "Yeah, trouble."

"I don't envy you guys on night duty when there's a lunatic running loose. You work in pairs, surely?"

"Nope. Can't afford to. Ain't enough men to go around."

"One man to a car? You have a small force, huh?"

"Yeah, the wages for a cop ain't worth crap."

"Pay is low, huh? That's the trouble everywhere. It's a wonder they find decent guys like you to take the job, fella."

"Thanks, pal."

"When a town pays low wages to cops, lots of times it attracts scum. You know, some nut who wants to wear a uniform and a badge. And carry a gun and a club."

I turned around on my stool and looked the guy over. A short guy in a brown suit, with small blue eyes in an oval face and receding gray-brown hair. Little punk.

I said, "I don't mean to be nasty, mister, but don't put cops down, okay? They get paid nothing while they work their tails off for the public. Jesus, the b.s. people hand out to cops! How would you like to be a cop where there's a psycho loose? You got some nerve, buddy, some nerve, you and all the others who don't appreciate what cops do for you. Police brutality, police brutality, that's all we get from Mister Public. Why, it wouldn't be safe to walk the streets at night without us suckers in blue to do the dirty work for John Q. Citizen."

The guy was sort of shaking now, spilled a little of his coffee. "Look . . . look . . . I didn't mean anything . . . I just think you guys should get paid better, that's all. That's all."

I smiled at him, both rows of whites. "Want sugar'n cream in your coffee, pal?"

He nodded nervously. I passed them to him and he poured a touch of each into his cup, then started in stirring, still nervous-like.

"I always take sugar'n cream in mine," I said. "Can't stand coffee black. Too damn bitter."

My breakfast came and I started in on it, three pancakes, two sausages, some scrambled eggs, milk, and coffee. The guy next to me went through a hamburger and fries. Or tried to anyway. He was so damn nervous he could hardly swallow a bite. I convinced him to stay on with me for another cup of coffee. After a bit we started in walking out of the diner together, having gotten more palsy with each other.

Out in the cold night air he put a hand on my shoulder and said, "You seem like a decent guy to me, officer. I didn't mean for you to take offense back there or anything. I just meant for you to see how I felt about cops getting paid bad. I mean, they should pay you guys more and keep out the riffraff, is what I mean. Those guys that just want to be a cop so they can hurt people and get away with it, you know, wear a blue suit and badge and carry a gun. No offense, right?"

I said sure. Did he want a lift?

"Well . . . my hotel's just a couple blocks, officer."

"Come on, I'll take ya there."

"Well . . . oh hell, okay."

He climbed into the front seat of the car. He fiddled around with the call box under the middle part of the dashboard like a kid in a toy shop. I began to think he'd had a little to drink or something, the way he fooled with things and the way his mouth was slack. But I couldn't tell for sure. Anyway, I got in and started the car.

"I'm staying at the Carleton, officer."

"My name's Harry. Wish you'd call me Harry."

"Sure, Harry. Mine's Joe, Joe Comstock. Salesman. Never been here before."

"We got a nice little town here. Friendly."

"Say, uh, Harry, I'm at the Carleton."

"Yeah, Joe, I know that."

"Well, uh, that's the other way . . . down the street that way . . ."

"I thought maybe we'd go riding for a while, Joe. I sure could use a little spot of company. Nothing wrong with a little ride is there, Joe?"

"Oh . . . no. Okay. Sure. Hell, I got nothing else to do."

He lit a cigarette and we drove in silence for a while. Then he came up with the best yet:

"You know, Harry, I been thinking. About this low pay for cops bit? Why, hell, Harry, what with the low pay luring the kooks and sadist-types, these eight rapes you've had here over the past few months? Guy in a bar told me about them this afternoon, you know. Those eight rapes?"

I kept my eyes on the road. "Yeah?"

"What with the low salaries and all, the rapist, don't you think he . . . well, hell, he could even be a cop."

I didn't say anything.

"I don't mean anything against cops, mind you, Harry, you know that, I explained that . . . But don't you think that could be possible?"

I braked the car.

"What are you stopping for?"

"Get out of the car, Joe."

He opened the door and climbed out; I got out and walked around the car and motioned him over toward the bushes. He started looking around but he didn't see nothing but trees and bushes and empty highway and night. I went over and clutched him by the arm.

"Now, Joe," I said, nice and friendly like, walking him along, "let me tell you the real reason I brung you out here. You look like a fella I saw on a wanted circular at the station the other day. Now since you seem like a right guy, I brung you out here where you ain't likely to be embarrassed. So now talk to me like a brother and tell me who you really are."

His mouth dropped open. "Hell, Harry, I'm just a salesman."

"The truth . . ."

"Harry . . . hell, Harry . . ."

"Put your hands in the air."

He shrugged and put them up. I swung a hard right to his groin. He rolled up into a little ball and made crying sounds. Then I got him by the scruff of the neck and dragged him behind the clump of bushes, where we wouldn't be seen if a car happened by on the highway. He kept on crying as I'd hit him pretty hard and I proceeded in to kicking him a few times while I fished out my big revolver. I spent a good five minutes whipping him with the gun butt. He made some sounds but didn't say anything, except "Jesus," once, just before he died.

The rest of the night was quiet.

THAT WAS MY LAST shift of night duty before the weekend, which I got free. I'd be back to days starting Monday, always got a free weekend after working seven nights straight.

I stopped in at the station to see the chief. It's not much as stations go, really, just one room in the city hall basement. It's a white-walled room with lots of dirt rubbed in; only part that doesn't show the dirty white walls is the part covered by the big bulletin board with the wanted posters and the like plastered to it. The chief sits in one corner behind a desk piled high with papers and a file on each end like two big bookends holding him in. That's about it for our station, except for our traffic officer who's got a real small office all to himself and the tons of unpaid tickets. Also there are a few cells adjoining the one main room. Otherwise, there's only Jim Oliver, a guy who is a technician of some kind out at the hospital and tries to help with our "scientific methods" since our force ain't exactly crime lab size. Mostly Ollie has been a joke with us.

Anyway, I stopped in to see the chief.

"Hiya, Ralph," I said, both rows of white on parade.

"Hi, Harry." Ralph didn't look up from the paper he was reading. He was in his TV cop mood today, I could tell right off. Chewing on a cigar and not smiling. Rubbing a hand over his bald spot and tweaking his bulbous nose once in a while. Maybe he pictured himself *like* a TV cop, since he had an actual case on his hands for the first time. The rapes, I mean.

"Got anything on the raper yet?" I asked him.

"Nope. Not a damn thing. Ollie tried looking around that place the other night but, hell, he doesn't do any good. I wish some of the state cops'd help out."

"Ain't their affair. 'Sides, Ralph, they wouldn't do much better than old Ollie."

"Sure they would. The bastard'd get his if there was some kind of responsible-type investigation made. But there's not much chance of that in this town."

I shook my head in concern. "It's an outright shame a nut like that runs loose. A damn shame. Too bad the feds ain't in on it."

Ralph smiled around the cigar. "Damn right. They'd crack this thing in a hurry, wouldn't they? But how the hell would the FBI get in on a local deal like this? Rape's no federal offense."

I shrugged, said, "No chance of the feds coming in, I guess. But this lad'd get caught real soon if somebody who knew what they was doing was after him, 'stead of us."

Ralph shook his head. "Sometimes I wish I would have stayed over at the cigar store, but I thought this job'd prove easier."

With a grin, I lit up a cigarette and said, "It would have if this sex nut hadn't've turned up."

"He's not so nuts, Harry."

"Oh, no, he's not nuts, he just rapes and kills."

"Kills?"

"Well, damn near kills. You know what I mean."

"Yeah. Well, I don't think he's a nut all the way, you know. After all, he picked a town where he'll like as not get away with all of it."

"Maybe, Ralph. How about pouring me some of that coffee?"

There was a pitcher of hot coffee on his desk, from which he kindly poured me a cup.

"You know, Ralph," I said, taking the cup from him, "there's a joke been going around town lately."

"That a fact?"

"Uh-huh. It's about this girl who was married three times and was still a virgin. Know how she managed that? First she married a midget, see, and he was too small. Next she married a preacher, and he was too religious. Then she married a small-town cop, and he couldn't find it."

Ralph laughed and said, "There's more truth than poetry in that one, Harry."

"Got sugar?" I asked. "And cream? I always take sugar'n cream. Coffee's way too bitter without 'em."

IT WAS A PITY what happened with Molly.

It was a couple weeks later, I was back on the night shift and the night before I'd pulled off number nine, a plump blonde bitch whose hubby was off at reserve camp. It had been awful quiet on the day shift, no one had found the salesman's body. They were all too busy worrying about rape number eight. Now that rape number nine'd come along, I figured that would give everybody something else to worry about for a while.

But I was wrong.

Because that night when we were sitting together down on the beach, Molly dropped a bombshell and told me she figured me for the raper.

"You're wrong, Molly, dead wrong. I didn't ever lay a hand an any woman but you."

"You're lying to me, Harry, I know you are." Her eyes looked green in the light of the quarter moon. I smoothed a hand over her arm as gentle as I could, but she jerked away and looked out toward the water. The lake was smooth, with only a few easy waves.

"Nice night, ain't it?" I said. "Be a nice night for a row."

"I don't . . . I don't feel like a row tonight, Harry. I don't . . . don't know anymore."

I grabbed a handful of her hair and pulled her head back—real gentle-like, of course—and said, "Molly, honey, would I ever think of touching another woman? You think I'd need to *force* a woman to get love off her?"

She pulled away again and started drawing in the sand with her finger.

"You ain't listening to me, Molly."

She kept on drawing in the sand. She seemed like maybe she was crying, but her voice was steady. "You're a funny man, Harry. You like your love to hurt. You're all take and not a damn bit of give."

I gripped her arm, hard, and she yelped a little. "You're dead wrong, Molly," I said again. "Let me prove it to you. Go out for a row with me. Come on. I love you, Molly, you'll see. Come on out for a row."

She stood up, circling her bare feet in the sand. Her face looked almost beautiful streaked with tears the way it was. "You're all I've got, Harry . . . I guess, if I'm right in what I say about you, then I don't want to live anymore. And if I'm wrong about you, well, then things'd be okay again. But even then, even if you didn't rape those women, it'll be bad, though, won't it? You and me just aren't right, Harry, so I guess things couldn't ever be fine, or good. Cause just like you like to hurt me, I like getting hurt by you, Harry . . . and that's not right. But if you . . . if you haven't been the one doing all those bad things around town, then a little boat ride wouldn't hurt, would it?"

"Why, course not."

"But if you *were* the one raping and all, then I probably wouldn't be coming back from that little boat ride, would I?"

"That's right, Molly. *If* I was."

"But if not . . ."

"Then it wouldn't hurt nothing at all, Molly, nothing at all. Come on, it's a nice night. Come on."

She turned and headed for the dock down the beach where the rowboat was tied. Her hair looked nice in the moonlight. She had nice legs when she walked, too.

We untied the boat, then I kicked off my shoes and together we waded into the water and pushed the boat out a ways. We climbed in and I started rowing. She didn't look at me, just stared out at the reflection of the quarter moon on the glassy surface of the lake.

About halfway out I threw her over, held her head down till she drowned. She didn't fight it at all. The place where she went under rippled out for a while, like a target, then got smooth again.

LATER ON I STOPPED at the diner on Fourth Street. I ordered a breakfast from the counterman, Lou, and started reading the evening paper.

Lou brought me my coffee and said, "Those guys ever find you, Harry?"

"What guys?"

A voice from behind me said, "Hiya, Harry."

"Well, Frank, how the hell're you? Going on duty soon?"

"Yeah, in a few minutes. You just finishing up your shift, huh?"

"That's right. How've ya been?" I hadn't seen much of Frank lately, since that night a while back when I had to stick around and play cop after that one deal. Should have hit that bitch harder.

"Been rough, Harry, what with my regular tours of duty and trying to look into this rapist thing in my spare time."

"Any luck?"

"Not a bit."

Frank was a small guy, but even a heel like me couldn't help but take a shine to the son of a bitch. He was everything a cop ought to be, honest and family-loving and all like that. Only his clean living was taking wear, putting deep lines in his face, around his clear blue eyes, and it seemed like his sandy crewcut was starting back farther on his head every time I saw him.

"Say, Harry," Frank said, "did you hear about the guy on the highway?"

I put down the paper. "What guy?"

"State cops found a dead guy out here along the highway a couple weeks ago, hushed it all up, not even the chief knew about it."

"Oh, really? Ain't that something." Lou was there with my breakfast, but all of a sudden I wasn't hungry.

"That's what I was trying to tell you about, Harry," Lou said, putting the food down in front of me.

"What?"

"Those two FBI men was in asking about that little guy you was talking to in here a couple weeks ago. That little guy, remember? He was the one got killed, I guess."

"FBI?" I said.

"Yeah," Frank chimed in, "seems this guy was important or something. Joker was a government courier of some kind."

"Govern . . . government courier?" I took a sip of my coffee as casually as I could.

"These FBI guys are putting on a full-scale investigation," Frank said. "I talked to them this afternoon, before they started going 'round town to ask questions. Too bad we can't get them to work on this rapist deal while they're at it."

"Yeah, too bad."

"What's this about you seeing that guy the night he was killed? And right here in the diner?"

"Oh, uh, I was just . . ."

Lou said, "Haven't you talked to those guys yet, Harry? I sent 'em out to your girl's place, figured you'd be out there at the Seaside with Molly. You must've just missed 'em."

I took another swallow of the coffee and tried to think.

"What's wrong, Harry?" Frank said.

"Hell," Lou laughed, slapping the counter, "he's drinking his coffee black. What's with you, Harry? You know you can't stomach it without cream and sugar."

Spring Fever

DOROTHY SALISBURY DAVIS

Dorothy Salisbury Davis's Introduction:

I think I was lacking confidence in myself at a couple of levels. I was well up into my thirties, a few pounds overweight, and if I'd kept plucking out the gray hairs as they showed up I'd have been bald at forty. As a writer I had some pretty good books behind me, but running scared of the next, I turned to the short story. Ha! I've always been susceptible to the influence of a good stylist and shameless in emulating their craft. At the time Joyce Cary had me in thrall. I'd have stolen outright chunks of The Horse's Mouth *if I thought I could get away with it. What I got away with was my version of an old rogue with enormous derring-do. I called him Joyce. I even stole the horse, for God's sake. But if it wasn't for the provocative editing of Fred Dannay (Ellery Queen) the story might not have worked as a mystery. Like a horse at the scent of something foul, I shied away from murder. That is a terrible affliction for a crime writer. Fred cured me. I won a second prize in that year's EQMM contest, and my friendship with Fred Dannay lasted his lifetime.*

Something I learned on the publication of "Spring Fever": Be not afraid. I don't mean only in snatching at the style of one's betters. I'd sent a copy of my forthcoming novel, A Town of Masks, *to a friend who I feared would see herself in its hapless heroine. Not at all. I breathed easy until she responded to "Spring Fever": "Well, you certainly took me apart in that one!" I'd never have made it in true crime.*

I'm very glad to have, all these years later, another "Spring Fever."

Spring Fever

DOROTHY SALISBURY DAVIS

SARAH SHEPHERD WATCHED HER husband come down the stairs. He set his suitcase at the front door, checked his watch with the hall clock, and examined beneath his chin in the mirror. There was one spot he sometimes missed in shaving. He stepped back and examined himself full length, frowning a little. He was getting paunchy and not liking it. That critical of himself, how much more critical of her he might be. But he said nothing either in criticism or compliment, and she remembered, uncomfortably, doing all sorts of stunts to attract his eye: coy things—more becoming a girl than a woman of fifty-five. She did not feel her twelve years over Gerald . . . most of the time. Scarcely aware of the movement, she traced the shape of her stomach with her fingertips.

Gerald brought his sample spice kit into the living room and opened it. The aroma would linger for some time after he was gone. "There's enough wood, dear, if it gets cold tonight," he said. "And I wish you wouldn't haul things from the village. That's what delivery trucks are for . . ." He numbered his solicitudes as he did the bottles in the sample case, and with the same noncommittal attention.

As he took the case from the table, she got up and went to the door with him. On the porch he hesitated a moment, flexing his shoulders and breathing deeply. "On a morning like this I almost wish I drove a car."

"You could learn, Gerald. You could reach your accounts in half the time, and . . ."

"No, dear. I'm quite content with my paper in the bus, and in a town a car's a nuisance." He stooped and brushed her cheek with his lips. "Hello there!" he called out as he straightened up.

Her eyes followed the direction in which he had called. Their only close neighbor, a vegetable and flower grower, was following a plow behind his horse, his head as high as the horse's was low, the morning wind catching his thatch of gray hair and pointing it like a shock of wheat.

"That old boy has the life," Gerald said. "When I'm his age that's for me."

"He's not so old," she said.

"No. I guess he's not at that," he said. "Well, dear, I must be off. Till tomorrow night, take care of yourself."

His step down the road was almost jaunty. It was strange that he could not abide an automobile. But not having one was rather in the pattern. A car would be a tangible link between his life away and theirs at home. Climbing into it of an evening, she would have a feeling of his travels. The dust would rub off on her. As it was, the most she had of him away was the lingering pungency of a sample spice kit.

When he was out of sight she began her household chores—the breakfast dishes, beds, dusting. She had brought altogether too many things from the city. Her mother had left seventy years' accumulation in the old house, and now it was impossible to lay a book on the table without first moving a figurine, a vase, a piece of delft. Really the place was a clutter of bric-a-brac. Small wonder Gerald had changed toward her. It was not marriage that had changed him—it was this house, and herself settling in it like an old Buddha with a bowl of incense in his lap.

A queer thing that this should occur to her only now, she thought. But it was not the first time. She was only now finding a word for it. Nor had Gerald always been this remote. Separating a memory of a particular moment in their early days, she caught his eyes searching hers—not numbering her years, as she might think were he to do it now, but measuring his own worth in her esteem.

She lined up several ornaments that might be put away, or better, sold to a junkman. But from the lineup she drew out pieces of which she had grown especially fond. They had become like children to her, as Gerald made children of the books with which he spent his evenings home. Making a basket of her apron she swept the whole tableful of trinkets into it.

Without a downward glance, she hurried them to the ashbox in the backyard. Shed of them, she felt a good deal lighter, and with the May wind in her face and the sun gentle, like an arm across her shoulders, she felt very nearly capersome. Across the fence the jonquils were in bloom and the tulips, nodding like fat little boys. Mr. Joyce had unhitched the horse. He saw her then.

"Fine day this morning," he called. He gave the horse a slap on the rump that sent him into the pasture, and came to the fence.

"I'm admiring the flowers," she said.

"Lazy year for them. Two weeks late they are."

"Is that a fact?" Of course it's a fact, she thought. A silly remark, and another after it: "I've never seen them lovelier, though. What comes out next?"

"Snaps, I guess this year. Late roses, too. The iris don't sell much, so I'm letting 'em come or stay as they like."

"That should bring them out."

"Now isn't that the truth? You can coax and tickle all year and not get a bloom for thanks. Turn your back on 'em and they run you down."

Like love, she thought, and caught her tongue. But a splash of color took to her checks.

"Say, you're looking nice, Mrs. Shepherd, if you don't mind my saying it."

"Thank you. A touch of spring, I suppose."

"Don't it just send your blood racing? How would you like an armful of these?"

"I'd be very pleased, Mr. Joyce. But I'd like to pay you for them."

"Indeed not. I won't sell half of them—they come in a heap."

She watched his expert hand nip the blooms. He was already tanned, and he stooped and rose with a fine grace. In all the years he had lived next to them he had never been in the house, nor they in his except the day of his wife's funeral. He hadn't grieved much, she commented to Gerald at the time. And little wonder. The woman was pinched and whining, and there wasn't a sunny day she didn't expect a drizzle before nightfall. Now that Sarah thought of it, Joyce looked younger than he did when Mrs. Joyce was still alive.

"There. For goodness' sakes, Mr. Joyce. That's plenty."

"I'd give you the field of them this morning," he said, piling her arms with the flowers.

"I've got half of it now."

"And what a picture you are with them."

"Well, I must hurry them into water," she said. "Thank you."

She hastened toward the house, flying like a young flirt from her first conquest, and aware of the pleased eye following her. The whole morning glowed in the company she kept with the flowers. She snapped off the radio: no tears for Miss Julia today. At noon she heard Mr. Joyce's wagon roll out of the yard as he started to his highway stand. She watched at the window. He looked up and lifted his hat.

At odd moments during the day, she thought of him. He had given her a fine sense of herself and she was grateful. She began to wish that Gerald was returning that night. Take your time, Sarah, she told herself. You don't put away old habits and the years like bric-a-brac. She had softened up, no doubt of it. Not a fat woman, maybe, but plump. Plump. She repeated the word aloud. It had the sound of a potato falling into a tub of water.

But the afternoon sun was warm and the old laziness came over her. Only when Mr. Joyce came home, his voice in a song ahead of him, did she pull herself up. She hurried a chicken out of the refrigerator and then called to him from the porch.

"Mr. Joyce, would you like to have supper with me? Gerald won't be home, and I do hate cooking for just myself."

"Oh, that'd be grand. I've nothing in the house but a shank of ham that a dog wouldn't bark for. What can I bring?"

"Just come along when you're ready."

Sarah, she told herself, setting the table, you're an old bat trying your wings in daylight. A half-hour later she glanced out of the window in time to see Mr. Joyce skipping over the fence like a stiff-legged colt. He was dressed in his Sunday suit and brandishing a bottle as he cleared the barbed wire. Sarah choked down a lump of apprehension. For all that she planned a little fun for herself, she was not up to galloping through the house with an old Don Juan on her heels. Mr. Joyce, however, was a well-mannered guest. The bottle was May wine. He drank sparingly and was lavish in his praise of the dinner.

"You've no idea the way I envy you folks, Mrs. Shepherd. Your husband especially. How can he bear the times he spends away?"

He bears it all too well, she thought. "It's his work. He's a salesman. He sells spices."

Mr. Joyce showed a fine set of teeth in his smile—his own teeth, she marveled, tracing her bridgework with the tip of her tongue while he spoke. "Then he's got sugar and spice and everything nice, as they say."

What a one he must have been with the girls, she thought, and to marry a quince as he had. It was done in a hurry no doubt, and maybe at the end of a big stick.

"It must be very lonesome for you since Mrs. Joyce passed away," she said more lugubriously than she intended. After all, the woman was gone three years.

"No more than when she was with me." His voice matched hers in seriousness. "It's a hard thing to say of the dead, but if she hasn't improved her disposition since, we're all in for a damp eternity." He stuffed the bowl of his pipe. "Do you mind?"

"No, I like the smell of tobacco around the house."

"Does your husband smoke?"

"Yes," she said in some surprise at the question.

"He didn't look the kind to follow a pipe," he said, pulling noisily at his. "No, dear lady," he added when the smoke was shooting from it, "you're blessed in not knowing the plague of a silent house."

It occurred to her then that he was exploring the situation. She would give him small satisfaction. "Yes, I count that among my blessings."

There was a kind of amusement in his eyes. You're as lonesome as me, old girl, they seemed to say, and their frankness bade her to add: "But I do wish Gerald was home more of the time."

"Ah, well, he's at the age when most men look to a last trot around the paddock," he said, squinting at her through the smoke.

"Gerald is only forty-three," she said, losing the words before she knew it.

"There's some take it at forty, and others among us leaping after it from the rocking chair."

The conversation had taken a turn she certainly had not intended, and she found herself threshing around in it. Beating a fire with a feather duster. "There's the moon," she said, charging to the window as though to wave to an old friend.

"Aye," he said, "there's the moon. Are you up to a trot in it?"

"What did you say, Mr. Joyce?"

"I'd better say what I was thinking first. If I hitch Micky to the old rig, would you take a turn with me on the Mill Pond Road?"

She saw his reflection in the window, a smug, daring little grin on his face. In sixteen years of settling she had forgotten her way with men. But it was something you never really forgot. Like riding a bicycle, you picked it up again after a few turns. "I would," she said.

The horse ahead of the rig was a different animal from the one on the plow that morning. Mr. Joyce had no more than thrown the reins over his rump than he took a turn that almost tumbled Sarah into the sun frames. But Mr. Joyce leaped to the seat and pulled Micky up on his hind legs with one hand and Sarah down to her cushion with the other, and they were off in the wake of the moon . . .

THE SUN WAS FULL in her face when Sarah awoke the next morning. As usual, she looked to see if Gerald were in his bed by way of acclimating herself to the day and its routine. With the first turn of her body she decided that a gallop in a rusty-springed rig was not the way to assert a stay of youth. She lay a few moments thinking about it and then got up to an aching sense of folly. It remained with her through the day, giving way at times to a nostalgia for her bric-a-brac. She had never realized how much of her life was spent in the care of it.

By the time Gerald came home she was almost the person he had left the day before. She had held out against the ornaments, however. Only the flowers decorated the living room.

It was not until supper was over and Gerald had settled with his book that he commented.

"Sarah, what happened to the old Chinese philosopher?"

"I put him away. Didn't you notice? I took all the clutter out of here."

He looked about him vacantly as though trying to recall some of it. "So you did. I'll miss that old boy. He gave me something to think about."

"What?"

"Oh, I don't know. Confucius says . . . that sort of thing."

"He wasn't a philosopher at all," she said, having no notion what he was. "He was a farmer."

"Was he? Well, there's small difference." He opened the book.

"Aren't the flowers nice, Gerald?"

"Beautiful."

"Mr. Joyce gave them to me, fresh out of his garden."

"That's nice."

"Must you read every night, Gerald? I'm here all day with no one to talk to, and when you get home you stick your nose into a book . . ." When the words were half out she regretted them. "I didn't tell you, Gerald. I had Mr. Joyce to dinner last night."

"That was very decent of you, dear. The old gentleman must find it lonesome."

"I don't think so. It was a relief to him when his wife died."

Gerald looked up. "Did he say that?"

"Not in so many words, but practically."

"He must be a strange sort. What did she die of?"

"I don't remember. A heart condition, I think."

"Interesting." He returned to his book.

"After dinner he took me for a ride in the horse and buggy. All the way to Cos Corner and back."

"Ha!" was his only comment.

"Gerald, you're getting fat."

He looked up. "I don't think so. I'm about my usual weight. A couple of pounds maybe."

"Then you're carrying it in your stomach. I noticed you've cut the elastic out of your shorts."

"These new fabrics," he said testily.

"They're preshrunken," she said. "It's your stomach. And haven't you noticed how you pull at your collar all the time?"

"I meant to mention that, Sarah. You put too much starch in them."

"I ran out of starch last week and forgot to order it. You can take a size fifteen-and-a-half now."

"Good Lord, Sarah, you're going to tell me next I should wear a horse collar." He let the book slide closed between his thighs. "I get home only three or four nights a week. I'm tired. I wish you wouldn't aggravate me, dear."

She went to his chair and sat on the arm of it. "Did you know that I was beginning to wonder if you'd respond to the poke of a hat pin?"

He looked directly up at her for the first time in what had seemed like years. His eyes fell away. "I've been working very hard, dear."

"I don't care what you've been doing, Gerald. I'm just glad to find out that you're still human."

He slid his arm around her and tightened it.

"Aren't spring flowers lovely?" she said.

"Yes," he said, "and so is spring."

She leaned across him and took a flower from the vase. She lingered there a moment. He touched his hand to her. "And you're lovely, too."

This is simple, she thought, getting upright again. If the rabbit had sat on a thistle, he'd have won the race.

"The three most beautiful things in the world," Gerald said thoughtfully, "a white bird flying, a field of wheat, and a woman's body."

"Is that your own, Gerald?"

"I don't know. I think it is."

"It's been a long time since you wrote any poetry. You did nice things once."

"That's how I got you," he said quietly.

"And I got you with an old house. I remember the day my mother's will was probated. The truth, Gerald—wasn't it then you made up your mind?"

He didn't speak for a moment, and then it was a continuance of some thought of his own, a subtle twist of association. "Do you remember the piece I wrote on the house?"

"I read it the other day. I often read them again."

"Do you, Sarah? And never a mention of it."

It was almost all the reading she did these days. His devotion to books had turned her from them. "Remember how you used to let me read them to you, Gerald? You thought that I was the only one besides yourself who could do them justice."

"I remember."

"Or was that flatter?"

He smiled. "It was courtship, I'm afraid. No one ever thinks anybody else can do his poetry justice. But Sarah, do you know—I'd listen tonight if you'd read some of them. Just for old time's sake."

For old time's sake, she thought, getting the folder from the cabinet and settling opposite him. He was slouched in his chair, pulling at his pipe, his eyes half-closed. Long ago this same contemplativeness in him had softened the first shock of the difference in their ages.

"I've always liked this one best—*The Morning of My Days*."

"Well you might," he murmured. "It was written for you."

She read one piece after another, wondering now and then what pictures he was conjuring up of the moment he had written them. He would suck on his pipe at times. The sound was like a baby pulling at an empty bottle. She was reading them well, she thought, giving them a mellow vibrancy, an old love's tenderness. Surely there was a moment coming when he would rise from the chair and come to her. Still he sat, his eyes almost closed, the pipe now in hand on the chair's arm. A huskiness crept into her voice, so rarely used to this length any more, and she thought of the nightingale's singing, the thorn against its breast. A slit of pain in her own throat pressed her to greater effort, for the poems were almost done.

She stopped abruptly, a phrase unfinished, at a noise in the room. The pipe had clattered to the floor, Gerald's hand still cupped its shape, but his chin now on his breast. Laying the folder aside, she went over and picked up the pipe with a rather empty regret, as she would pick up a bird that had fallen dead at her feet.

GERALD'S DEPARTURE IN THE morning was in the tradition of all their days, even to the kiss upon her cheek and the words, "Till tomorrow evening, dear, take care."

Take care, she thought, going indoors. Take care of what?

For what? Heat a boiler of water to cook an egg? She hurried her chores and dressed. When she saw Mr. Joyce hitch the wagon of flowers, she locked the door and waited boldly at the road for him.

"May I have a lift to the highway?" she called out, as he reined up beside her.

"You may have a lift to the world's end, Mrs. Shepherd. Give me your hand." He gave the horse its rein when she was beside him. "I see your old fella's taken off again. I daresay it gave him a laugh, our ride in the moonlight."

"It was giddy business," she said.

"Did you enjoy yourself?"

"I did. But I paid for it afterward." Her hand went to her back.

"I let out a squeal now and then bending over, myself. But I counted it cheap for the pleasure we had. I'll take you into the village. I've to buy a length of hose anyway. Or do you think you'll be taken for a fool riding in on a wagon?"

"It won't be the first time," she said. "My life is full of foolishness."

"It's a wise fool who laughs at his own folly. We've that in common, you and me. Where'll we take our supper tonight?"

He was sharp as mustard.

"You're welcome to come over," she said.

He nodded. "I'll fetch us a steak, and we'll give Micky his heels again after."

Sarah got off at the post office and stayed in the building until Joyce was out of sight—Joyce and the gapers who had stopped to see her get out of the wagon. Getting in was one thing, getting out another. A bumblebee after a violet. It was time for this trip. She walked to the doctor's office and waited her turn among the villagers.

"I thought I'd come in for a check-up, Dr. Philips," she said at his desk. "And maybe you'd give me a diet?"

"A diet?" He took off his glasses and measured her with the naked eye.

"I'm getting a little fat," she said. "They say it's a strain on the heart at my age."

"Your heart could do for a woman of twenty," he said, "but we'll have a listen."

"I'm not worried about my heart, Doctor, you understand, I just feel that I'd like to lose a few pounds."

"Uh-huh," he said. "Open your dress." He got his stethoscope.

Diet, apparently, was the rarest of his prescriptions. Given as a last resort. She should have gone into town for this, not to a country physician who measured a woman by the children she bore. "The woman next door to us died of a heart condition," she said, as though that should explain her visit.

"Who's that?" he asked, putting away the instrument.

"Mrs. Joyce. Some years ago."

"She had a heart to worry about. Living for years on stimulants. Yours is as sound as a bullet. Let's have your arm."

She pushed up her sleeve as he prepared the apparatus for measuring her blood pressure. That, she felt, was rising out of all proportion. She was ashamed of herself before this man, and angry at herself for it, and at him for no reason more than that he was being patient with her. "We're planning insurance," she lied. "I wanted our own doctor's opinion first."

"You'll have no trouble getting it, Mrs. Shepherd. And no need of a diet." He grinned and removed the apparatus. "Go easy on potatoes and bread, and on the sweets. You'll outlive your husband by twenty years. How is he, by the way?"

"Fine. Just fine, Doctor, thank you."

What a nice show you're making of yourself these days, Sarah, she thought, outdoors again. Well, come in or go out, old girl, and slam the door behind you . . .

MICKY TOOK TO HIS heels that night. He had had a day of ease, and new shoes were stinging his hooves by nightfall. The skipping of Joyce with each snap of the harness teased him, the giggling from the rig adding a prickle. After the wagon, the rig was no more than a fly on his tail, He took the full reins when they slapped on his flanks and charged out from the laughter behind him. It rose to a shriek the faster he galloped and tickled his ears like something alive that slithered from them down his neck and his belly and into his loins. Faster and faster he plunged, the sparks from his shoes like ocean spray. He fought a jerk of the reins, the saw of the bit in his mouth a fierce pleasure. He took turns at his own fancy and only in sight of his own yard again did he yield in the fight, choking on the spume that lathered his tongue.

"By the holy, the night a horse beats me, I'll lie down in my grave," Joyce cried. "Get up now, you buzzard. You're not turning in till you go to the highway and back. Are you all right, Sarah?"

Am I all right, she thought. When in years had she known a wild ecstasy like this? From the first leap of the horse she had burst the girdle of fear and shame. If the wheels had spun out from beneath them, she would have rolled into the ditch contented.

"I've never been better," she said.

He leaned close to her to see her, for the moon had just risen. The wind had stung the tears to her eyes, but they were laughing. "By the Horn Spoon," he said, "you liked it!" He let the horse have his own way into the drive after all. He jumped down from the rig and held his hand up to her. "What a beautiful thing to be hanging in the back of the closet all these years."

"If that's a compliment," she said, "it's got a nasty bite."

"Aye. But it's my way of saying you're a beautiful woman."

"Will you come over for a cup of coffee?"

"I will. I'll put up the horse and be over."

The kettle had just come to the boil when he arrived.

"Maybe you'd rather have tea, Mr. Joyce?"

"Coffee or tea, so long as it's not water. And I'd like you to call me Frank. They christened me Francis, but I got free of it early."

"And you know mine, I noticed," she said.

"It slipped out in the excitement. There isn't a woman I know who wouldn't of collapsed in a ride like that."

"It was wonderful." She poured the water into the coffee pot.

"There's nothing like getting behind a horse," he said, "unless it's getting astride him. I wouldn't trade Micky for a Mack truck."

"I used to ride when I was younger," she said.

"How did you pick up the man you got, if you don't mind my asking?"

And you the old woman, she thought; where did you get her? "I worked for a publishing house and he brought in some poetry."

"Ah, that's it." He nodded. "And he thought with a place like this he could pour it out like water from a spout."

"Gerald and I were in love," she said, irked that he should define so bluntly her own thoughts on the matter.

"Don't I remember it? In them days you didn't pull the blinds. It used to put me in a fine state."

"Do you take cream in your coffee? I've forgotten."

"Aye, thank you, and plenty of sugar."

"You haven't missed much," she said.

"There's things you see through a window you'd miss sitting down in the living room. I'll wager you've wondered about the old lady and me?"

"A little. She wasn't so old, was she, Mr. Joyce?" Frank, she thought. Too frank.

"That one was old in her crib. But she came with a greenhouse. I worked for her father."

Sarah poured the coffee. "You're a cold-blooded old rogue," she said.

He grinned. "No. Cool-headed I am, and warm-blooded. When I was young, I made out it was the likes of poetry. She sang like a bird on a convent wall. But when I caged her she turned into an old crow."

"That's a terrible thing to say, Mr. Joyce."

The humor left his face for an instant. "It's a terrible thing to live with. It'd put a man off his nut. You don't have a bit of cake in the house, Sarah, to go with this?"

"How about muffins and jam?"

"That'll go fine." He smiled again. "Where does your old fella spend the night in his travels?"

"In the hotel in whatever town he happens to be in."

"That's a lonesome sort of life for a married man," he said.

She pulled a chair to the cupboard and climbed up to get a jar of preserves. He made no move to help her although she still could not reach the jar. She looked down at him. "You could give me a hand."

"Try it again. You almost had it that time." He grinned, almost gleeful at her discomfort.

She bounced down in one step. "Get it yourself if you want it. I'm satisfied with a cup of coffee."

He pounded his fist on the table, getting up. "You're right, Sarah. Never fetch a man anything he can fetch himself. Which bottle is it?"

"The strawberry."

He hopped up and down, nimble as a goat. "But then maybe he doesn't travel alone?"

"What?"

"I was suggesting your man might have an outside interest. Salesmen have the great temptation, you know."

"That's rather impertinent, Mr. Joyce."

"You're right, Sarah, it is. My tongue's been home so long it doesn't know how to behave in company. This is a fine cup of coffee."

She sipped hers without speaking. It was time she faced that question, she thought. She had been hedging around it for a long time, and last night with Gerald should have forced it upon her. "And if he does have an outside interest," she said, lifting her chin, "what of it?"

"Ah, Sarah, you're a wise woman, and worth waiting the acquaintance of. You like me a little now, don't you?"

"A little."

"Well," he said, getting up, "I'll take that to keep me warm for the night."

And what have I got to keep me warm, she thought. "Thank you for the ride, Frank. It was thrilling."

"Was it?" he said, coming near her. He lifted her chin with his forefinger. "We've many a night like this ahead, Sarah, if you say the word." And then when she left her chin on his finger, he bent down and kissed her, taking himself to the door after it with a skip and a jump. He paused there and looked back at her. "Will I stay or go?"

"You'd better go," she choked out, wanting to be angry but finding no anger in herself at all.

ALL THE NEXT DAY Sarah tried to anchor herself from her peculiar flights of fancy. She had no feeling for the man, she told herself. It was a fine state a woman reached when a kiss from a stranger could do that to her. It was the ride made you giddy, she said aloud. You were thinking of Gerald. You were thinking of . . . the Lord knows what. She worked upstairs until she heard the wagon go by. She would get some perspective when Gerald came home. It seemed as though he'd been gone a long time.

The day was close and damp, and the flies clung to the screens. There was a dull stillness in the atmosphere. By late afternoon the clouds rolled heavier, mulling about one another like dough in a pan. While she was peeling potatoes for supper, Frank drove in. He unhitched the horse but left him in the harness, and set about immediately building frames along the rows of flowers. He was expecting a storm. She looked at the clock. It was almost time for Gerald.

She went out on the front porch and watched for the bus. There was a haze in the sweep of land between her and the highway, and the traffic through it seemed to float thickly, slowly. The bus glided toward the intersection and past it, without stopping. She felt a sudden anger. Her whole day had been strung up to this peak. Since he had not called, it meant merely he had missed the bus. The next one was in two hours. She crossed the yard to the fence. You're starting up again, Sarah, she warned herself, and took no heed of the warning.

Frank looked up from his work. "You'd better fasten the house," he said. "There's a fine blow coming."

"Frank, if you're in a hurry, I'll give you something to eat."

"That'd be a great kindness. I may have to go back to the stand at a gallop."

He was at the kitchen table, shoveling in the food without a word, when the heavy sky lightened. He went to the window. "By the glory, it may blow over." He looked around at her, "Your old boy missed the bus, did he?"

"He must have."

Frank looked out again. "I do like a good blow. Even if it impoverished me, there's nothing in the world like a storm."

An automobile horn sounded on the road. It occurred to Sarah that on a couple of occasions Gerald had received a ride from the city. The car passed, but watching its dust she was left with a feeling of suspended urgency. Joyce was chatting now. He had tilted back in the chair and for the first time since she had known him, he was rambling on about weather, vegetables, and the price of eggs. She found it more disconcerting than his bursts of intimate comment, and she hung from one sentence to the next waiting for the end of it. Finally she passed in back of his chair and touched her fingers briefly to his neck.

"You need a haircut, Frank."

He sat bolt upright. "I never notice it till I have to scratch. Could I have a drop more coffee?"

She filled his cup, aware of his eyes on her. "Last night was something I'll never forget—that ride," she said.

"And something else last night, do you remember that?"

"Yes."

"Would you give me another now to match it if I was to ask?"

"No."

"What if I took it without asking?"

"I don't think I'd like it, Frank."

He pushed away from the table, slopping the coffee into the saucer. "Then what are you tempting me for?"

"You've a funny notion of temptations," she flared up, knowing the anger was against herself.

Joyce spread his dirt-grimed fingers on the table. "Sarah, do you know what you want?"

The tears were gathering. She fought them back. "Yes, I know what I want!" she cried.

Joyce shook his head. "He's got you by the heart, hasn't he, Sarah?"

"My heart's my own!" She flung her head up.

Joyce slapped his hand on the table. "Ho! Look at the spark of the woman! That'd scorch a man if there was a stick in him for kindling." He moistened his lips and in spite of herself Sarah took a step backward. "I'll not chase you, Sarah. Never fear that. My chasing days are over. I'll neither chase nor run, but I'll stand my ground for what's coming to me." He jerked his head toward the window. "That was only a lull in the wind. There's a big blow coming now for certain."

She watched the first drops of rain splash on the glass. "Gerald's going to get drenched in it."

"Maybe it'll drown him," Joyce said, grinning from the door. "Thanks for the supper."

Let it come on hail, thunder, and lightning. Blow the roof from the house and tumble the chimney. I'd go out from it then and never turn back. When an old man can laugh at your trying to cuckold a husband, and the husband asking it, begging it, shame on you. She went through the house clamping the locks on the windows. More pleasure putting the broom through them.

An early darkness folded into the storm, and the walls of rain bleared the highway lights. There was an ugly yellow tinge to the water from the dust swirled into it. The wind sluiced down the chimney, spitting bits of soot on the living room floor. She spread newspapers to catch it. A sudden glow, it would soon be spent. She went to the hall clock. The bus was due in ten minutes. What matter? A quick slipper, a good book, and a long sleep. The wily old imp was right. A prophet needing a haircut.

The lights flickered off for a moment, then on again. Let them go out, Sarah. What's left for you, you can see by candlelight. She went to the basement and brought up the kerosene lamp and then got a flashlight from the pantry. As she returned to the living room, a fresh gust of wind sent the newspapers out of the grate like scud. The lights flickered again. A sound drew her to the hall. She thought the wind might be muffling the ring of the telephone. When she got there, the clock was striking. The bus was now twenty minutes late. There was something about the look of the phone that convinced her the line was dead. It was unnerving to find it in order. Imagination, she murmured. Everything was going perverse to her expectations. And then, annoyed with herself, she grew angry with Gerald again. This was insult. Insult on top of indifference.

She followed a thumping noise upstairs. It was on the outside of the house. She turned off the light and pressed her face against the window. A giant maple tree was rocking and churning, one branch thudding against the house. There was not even a blur of light from the highway now. Blacked out. While she watched, a pinpoint of light shaped before her. It grew larger, weaving a little. A flashlight, she thought, and wondered if Gerald had one. Then she recognized the motion: a lantern on a wagon. Frank was returning.

When she touched the light switch there was no response. Groping her way to the hall she saw that all the lights were out now. Step by step she made her way downstairs. A dankness had washed in through the chimney, stale and sickening. She lit the lamp and carried it to the kitchen. From the window there, she saw Frank's lantern bobbing as he led the horse into the barn. She could not see man or horse, only the fading of the light until it disappeared inside. When it reappeared she lifted her kerosene lamp, a greeting to him. This time he came around the fence. She held the door against the wind.

"I've no time now, Sarah. I've work to do," he shouted. "He didn't come, did he?"

"No!"

"Is the phone working?"

She nodded that it was and waved him close to her. "Did the bus come through?"

"It's come and gone. Close the door or you'll have the house in a shambles." He waved his lantern and was gone.

She put the pot roast she had prepared for Gerald in the refrigerator and set the perishables close to the freezing unit. She wound the clock and put away the dishes. Anything to keep busy. She washed the kitchen floor that had been washed only the day before. The lantern across the way swung on a hook at the barn, sometimes moving toward the ground and back as Joyce examined the frames he was reinforcing.

Finally she returned to the living room. She sat for a long time in Gerald's chair, watching the pattern of smoke in the lamp-chimney. Not even a dog or cat to keep her company. Not even a laughing piece of delft to look out at her from the mantelpiece; only the cold-eyed forebears, whom she could not remember, staring down at her from the gilt frames, their eyes fixed upon her, the last and the least of them who would leave after her—nothing.

It was not to be endured. She lunged out of the chair. In the hall she climbed to the first landing where she could see Joyce's yard. He was through work now, the lantern hanging from the porch although the house was darkened. It was the only light anywhere, and swayed in the wind like a will-o'-the-wisp.

She bounded down the stairs and caught up her raincoat. Taking the flashlight she went out into the storm. She made her way around the fence, sometimes pushing into the wind, sometimes resting against it. Joyce met her in his driveway. He had been waiting, she thought, testing his nerves against her own, expecting her. Without a word, he caught her hand and led her to his back steps and into the house. "I've an oil lamp," he said then. "Hold your light there till I fix it."

She watched his wet face in the half-light. His mouth was lined with malicious humor, and his eyes, as he squinted at the first flame of the wick, were fierce, as fierce as the storm, and as strange to her. When the light flared up, she followed its reaches over the dirty wall, the faded calendar, the gaping cupboards, the electric cord hanging from a naked bulb over the sink to the back door. There were dishes stacked on the table where they no doubt stood from one meal to the next. The curtains were stiff with dirt, three years of it. Only then did she take a full glimpse of the folly that had brought her here.

"I just ran over for a minute, Frank . . ."

"A minute or the night, sit there, Sarah, and let me get out of these clothes."

She took the chair he motioned her into, and watched him fling his coat into the corner. Nor could she take her eyes from him as he sat down and removed his boots and socks. Each motion fascinated her separately, fascinated and revolted her. He wiped between his toes with the socks. He went barefoot toward the front of the house. In the doorway he paused, becoming a giant in the weird light.

"Put us up a pot of coffee, dear woman. The makings are there on the stove."

"I must go home. Gerald . . ."

"To hell with Gerald," he interrupted. "He's snug for the night, wherever he is. Maybe he won't come back to you at all. It's happened before, you know, men vanishing from women they don't know the worth of."

Alone, she sat stiff and erect at the table. He was just talking, poisoning her mind against Gerald. How should she get out of here? Run like a frightened doe and never face him again? No, Sarah. Stay for the bitter coffee. Scald the giddiness out of you once and for all. But on top of the resolve came the wish that Gerald might somehow appear at the door and take her home. Dear, gentle Gerald.

She got up and went to the sink to draw the water for coffee. A row of medicine bottles stood on the windowsill, crusted with dust. Household remedies. She leaned close and examined a faded label: "Mrs. Joyce—take immediately upon need."

She turned from the window. A rocker stood in the corner of the room. In the old days the sick woman had sat in it, on the back porch, rocking, and speaking to no one. The stale sickness of her was still about the house, Sarah thought. What did she know of people like this?

He was threshing around upstairs like a penned bull. His muddy boots lay where he had taken them off, a pool of water gathering about them. Again she looked at the windowsill. No May wine there. Suddenly she remembered Dr. Philips's words: "Lived on stimulants for years." She could almost see the sour woman, even to her gasping for breath . . . "Take immediately."

Fix the coffee, Sarah. What kind of teasing is this? Teasing the dead from her grave before you. Teasing. Something in the thought disturbed her further . . . an association: Joyce watching her reach for the preserves last night, grinning at her. "Try it again, Sarah. You almost had it that time." And she could still hear him asking, "Which bottle?" Not which jar, but which bottle.

She grabbed the kettle and filled it. Stop it, Sarah. It's the storm, the waiting, too much waiting . . . your time of life. She drew herself up against his coming, hearing his quick step on the stairs.

"Will you give us a bit of iodine there from the window, Sarah? I've scratched myself on those blamed frames."

She selected the bottle carefully with her eyes, so that her trembling hand might not betray her.

"Dab it on here," he said, holding a white cuff away from his wrist.

The palm of his hand was moist as she bent over it and she could smell the earth and the horse from it. Familiar, too familiar. Everything about him had become familiar, too familiar. She felt his breath on her neck, and the hissing sound of it was the only sound in the room. She smeared the iodine on the cut and pulled away. His lips tightened across his teeth in a grin.

"A kiss would make a tickle of the pain," he said.

Sarah thrust the iodine bottle from her and grabbed the flashlight. "I'm going home."

His jaw sagged as he stared at her. "Then what did you come for?"

"Because I was lonesome. I was foolish . . ." Fear clicked off her voice. A little trickle of saliva dribbled from the corner of his mouth.

"No! You came to torture me!"

She forced one foot toward the door and the other after it. His voice rose in laughter as she lumbered away from him. "Good Lord, Sarah. Where's the magnificent woman who rode to the winds with me last night?"

She lunged into the electric cord in her retreat, searing her cheek on it. Joyce caught it and wrenched it from the wall, its splayed end springing along the floor like a whip. "And me thinking the greatest kindness would be if he never came home!"

The doorknob slipped in her sweaty hand. She dried it frantically. He's crazy, she thought. Mad-crazy.

"You're a lump, Sarah," he shouted, "And Mr. Joyce is a joker. A joker and a dunce. He always was and he will be till the day they hang him!"

The door yielded and she plunged down the steps and into the yard. In her wild haste she hurled herself against the rig and spun away from it as though it were something alive. She sucked in her breath to keep from screaming. She tore her coat on the fence hurtling past it, leaving a swatch of it on the wire. Take a deep breath, she told herself as she stumbled up the steps. Don't faint. Don't fall. The door swung from her grasp, the wind clamoring through the house. She forced it closed, the glass plate tingling, and bolted it. She thrust the flashlight on the table and caught up the phone. She clicked it wildly.

Finally it was the operator who broke through. "I have a call for you from Mr. Gerald Shepherd. Will you hold on, please?"

Sarah could hear only her own sobbing breath in the hollow of the mouthpiece. She tried to settle her mind by pinning her eyes on the stairway. But the spokes of the stairway seemed to be shivering dizzily in the circle of light, like the plucked strings of a harp. Even the sound of them was vibrant in her head, whirring over the rasp of her breath. Then came the pounding footfalls and Joyce's fists on the door. Vainly she signaled the operator. And somewhere in the tumult of her mind she grasped at the thought that if she unlocked the door, Joyce would come in and sit down. They might even light the fire. There was plenty of wood in the basement. But she could not speak. And it was too late.

Joyce's fist crashed through the glass and drew the bolt. With the door's opening the wind whipped her coat over her head; with its closing, her coat fell limp, its little pressure about her knees seeming to buckle them.

"I'm sorry," came the operator's voice, "the call was canceled ten minutes ago."

She let the phone clatter onto the table and waited, her back still to the door. Ten minutes was not very long ago, she reasoned in sudden desolate calmness. She measured each of Joyce's footfalls toward her, knowing they marked all of time that was left to her. And somehow, she felt, she wanted very little more of it.

For only an instant she saw the loop he had made of the electric cord, and the white cuffs over the strong, gnarled hands. She closed her eyes and lifted her head high, expecting that in that way the end would come more quickly . . .

The Tree on Execution Hill

LOREN D. ESTLEMAN

Loren D. Estleman's Introduction:

I suppose it's fitting, given my split-personality career, that my first pub-lished fiction should have blended elements of the contemporary suspense story and historical fiction.

It was even more complicated in its first incarnation. While attend-ing college, I wrote ten pages of an allegorical short story that attempted to employ this same theme, and many of the characters who appear here in pursuit of some cosmic comment on flawed humanity; but since no one, and certainly no publisher, understands just what an allegory is or why it exists, I shelved those pages and only discovered them years later while scouting up an idea for a mystery. I jettisoned the murky symbolism and the more top-lofty narrative comments, introduced a clear destination, and incidentally wound up with a better demonstration of human frailty than anything I learned from reading Thomas Mann.

The Tree on Execution Hill

LOREN D. ESTLEMAN

IT SEEMED AS IF everybody in Good Advice had turned out for the meeting that night in the town hall. Every seat was taken, and the dark oaken rafters hewn and fit in place by the ancestors of a good share of those present resounded with a steady hum of conversation while the broad pine planks that made up the floor creaked beneath the tread of many feet.

Up in front, his plaid jacket thrown back to expose a generous paunch, Carl Lathrop, the town's leading storekeeper and senior member of the council, stood talking with Birdie Flatt from the switchboard. His glasses flashed a Morse code in the bright overhead lights as he settled and resettled them on his fleshy nose. I recognized the gesture from the numerous interviews I had conducted with him as a sign that he was feeling very satisfied with himself, and so I knew what was coming long before most of my neighbors suspected it.

I was something of a freak in the eyes of the citizenry of Good Advice, New Mexico. This was partly because I had been the first person to settle in the area since before 1951, when the aircraft plant had moved on to greener pastures, and partly because, at forty-two, I was at least ten years younger than anyone else in town. Most people supposed I stayed on out of despair after my wife Sylvia left me to return to civilization, but that wasn't strictly true. We'd originally planned to lay over for a week or two while I collected information for my book and then move on. But then the owner of the town newspaper had died and the paper was put up for sale, and I bought it with the money we'd saved up for the trip. It had been an act of impulse, perhaps a foolish one—certainly it had seemed so to my wife, who had no intention of living so far away from her beloved beauty parlors—but my chief fear in life had always been that I'd miss the big opportunity when it came along. So now I had a newspaper but no Sylvia, which, all things considered, seemed like a pretty fair trade.

The buzz of voices died out as Lathrop took his place behind the lectern. I flipped open my notebook and sat with pencil poised to capture any pearls of wisdom he might have been about to drop.

"We all know why we're here, so we'll dispense with the long-winded introductions." A murmur of approval rippled through the audience. "You've all heard the rumor that the state may build a superhighway near Good Advice," he went on. "Well, it's my pleasant duty to announce that it's no longer a rumor."

Cheers and applause greeted this statement, and it was some minutes before the room grew quiet enough for Lathrop to continue.

"Getting information out of these government fellows is like pulling teeth," he said. "But after about a dozen phone calls to the capital, I finally got hold of the head of the contracting firm that's going to do the job. He told me they plan to start building sometime next fall." He waited until the fresh applause faded, then went on. "Now, this doesn't mean that Good Advice is going to become another Tombstone overnight. When those tourists come streaming in here, we're going to have to be ready for them. That means rezoning for tourist facilities, fixing up our historic landmarks, and so on. The reason we called this meeting is to decide on ways to make this town appealing to visitors. The floor is open to suggestions."

I spent the next twenty minutes jotting down some of the ideas that came from the enthusiastic citizens. Birdie Flatt was first, with a suggestion that the telephone service be updated, but others disagreed, maintaining that the old upright phones and wall installations found in many of the downtown shops added to the charm of the town. "Uncle Ned" Scoffield, at ninety-seven Good Advice's oldest resident, offered to clean out and fix up the old trading post at the end of Main Street in return for permission to sell his wood carvings and his collection of handwoven Navajo rugs. Carl Lathrop pledged to turn the old jail, which he had been using as a storeroom, into a tourist attraction. The fact that outlaw Ford Harper had spent his last days there before his hanging, he said, could only add to its popularity. Then, amidst a chorus of groans from scattered parts of the room, Avery Sharecross stood up.

Sharecross was a spindly scarecrow of a man, with an unkempt mane of lusterless black hair spilling over the collar of his frayed sweater and a permanent stoop that made him appear much older than he was. Nobody in town could say how he made his living. Certainly not from the bookstore he had been operating on the corner of Main and Maple for thirty years; there were never any more than two customers in the store at a time, and the prices he charged were so ridiculously low that it was difficult to believe that he managed to break even, let alone show a profit. Everyone was aware of the monthly pension he received from an address in Santa Fe, but no one knew how much it was or why he got it. His bowed shoulders and shuffling gait, the myopia that forced him to squint through the thick tinted lenses of his eyeglasses, the hollows in his pale cheeks were as much a part of the permanent scenery in Good Advice as the burned-out shell of the old flour mill north of town. I closed my notebook and put away my pencil, knowing what he was going to talk about before he opened his mouth. It was all he ever talked about.

Lathrop sighed. "What is it, Avery? As if I didn't know." He rested his chin on one pudgy hand, bracing himself for the ordeal.

"Mr. Chairman, I have a petition." The old bookseller rustled the well-thumbed sheaf of papers he held in one talonlike hand. "I have twenty-six signatures demanding that the citizens of Good Advice vote on whether the tree on Execution Hill be removed."

There was an excited buzz among the spectators. I sat bolt upright in my chair, flipping my notebook back open. How had the old geezer got twenty-five people to agree with him?

For 125 years the tree in question had dominated the high-domed hill two miles outside of town, its skeletal limbs stretching naked against the sky. Of the eighteen trials that had been held in the town hall during the last century, eleven of those tried had ended swinging from the tree's stoutest limb. It was a favorite spot of mine, an excellent place to sit and meditate. Avery Sharecross, for reasons known only to himself, had been trying to get the council to destroy it for five years. This was the first time he had not stood alone.

Lathrop cleared his throat loudly, probably to cover up his own astonishment. "Now, Avery, you know as well as I do that it takes fifty-five signatures on a petition to raise a vote. You've read the charter."

Sharecross was unperturbed. "When that charter was drafted, Mr. Chairman, this town boasted a population of over fourteen hundred. In the light of our present count, I believe that provision can be waived." He struck the pages with his fingertips. "These signatures represent nearly one-tenth of the local voting public. They have a right to be heard."

"How come you're so fired up to see that tree reduced to kindling, anyway? What's the difference to you?"

"That tree"—Sharecross flung a scrawny arm in the direction of the nearest window—"represents a time in this town's history when lynch law reigned and pompous hypocrites sentenced their peers to death regardless of their innocence or guilt." His cheeks were flushed now, his eyes ablaze behind the bottle-glass spectacles. "That snarl of dead limbs has been a blemish on the smooth face of this community for over a hundred years, and it's about time we got rid of it."

It was an impressive performance, and he sounded sincere, but I wasn't buying it. Good Advice, after all, had not been my first exposure to journalism. After you've been in this business awhile, you get a feeling for when someone is telling the truth, and Sharecross wasn't.

Whatever reasons he had for wishing to destroy the town's oldest landmark, they had nothing to do with any sense of injustice. Of that I was certain.

Lathrop sighed. "All right, Avery, let's see your petition. If the signatures check out, we'll vote." Once the papers were in his hands, Lathrop called the other members of the town council around him to look them over. Finally he motioned them back to their seats and turned back toward the lectern. For the next half hour he read off the names on the petition—many of which surprised me, for they included some of the town's leading citizens—to make sure the signatures were genuine. Every one of those mentioned spoke up to assure him that they were. At length the storekeeper laid the pages down.

"Before we vote," he said, "the floor is open to dissenting opinions—Mr. Macklin?"

My hand had gone up before he finished speaking. I got to my feet, conscious of all the eyes upon me.

"No one is arguing what Mr. Sharecross said about the injustices done in the past," I began haltingly. "But tearing down something that's a large part of our history won't change anything." I paused, searching for words. I was a lot more eloquent behind a typewriter. "Mr. Sharecross says the tree reminds us of the sordid past. I think that's as it should be. A nagging reminder of a time when we weren't so noble is a healthy thing to have in our midst. I wouldn't want to live in a society that kicked its mistakes under the rug."

The words were coming easier now. "There's been a lot of talk here tonight about promoting tourist trade. Well, destroying a spot where eleven infamous badmen met their rewards is one sure way of aborting any claims we might have had upon shutter-happy visitors." I shook my head emphatically, a gesture left over from my college debating club days. "History is too precious for us to turn our backs on it, for whatever reason. Sharecross and his sympathizers would do well to realize that our true course calls for us to turn our gaze forward and forget about rewriting the past."

There was some applause as I sat down, but it died out when Sharecross seized the floor again. "I'm not a Philistine, Mr. Chairman," he said calmly. "Subject to the will of the council, I hereby pledge the sum of five thousand dollars for the erection of a statue of Enoch Howard, Good Advice's founder, atop Execution Hill once the tree has been removed. I, too, have some feeling for history." His eyes slid in my direction.

That was dirty pool, I thought as he took his seat amid thunderous cheering from those present. In one way or another, Enoch Howard's blood flowed in the veins of over a third of the population of Good Advice. Now I knew how he had obtained those signatures. But why? What did he hope to gain?

"What about expense?" someone said.

"No problem," countered Sharecross, on his feet again. "Floyd Kramer there has offered to bulldoze down the tree and cart it away at cost."

"That's true, Floyd?" Lathrop asked.

A heavy-jowled man in a blue work shirt buttoned to the neck gave him the high sign from his standing position near the door.

I shot out of my chair again, but this time my eyes were directed upon my skeletal opponent and not the crowd. "I've fought you in print and on the floor of the town hall over this issue," I told him, "and if necessary I'll keep on fighting you right to the top of Execution Hill. I don't care how many statues you pull out of your hat; you won't get away with whatever it is you're trying to do."

The old bookseller made no reply. His eyes were blank behind his spectacles. I sat back down.

I could see that Lathrop's attitude had changed, for he had again taken to raising and lowering his eyeglasses confidently upon the bridge of his nose. Enoch Howard was his great-grandfather on his mother's side. "Now we'll vote," he said. "All those in favor of removing the tree on Execution Hill to make room for a statue of Enoch Howard signify by saying aye."

RAIN WAS HISSING ON the grass when I parked my battered pickup truck at the bottom of the hill and got out to fetch the shovel out of the back. It was a long climb to the top and I was out of shape, but I didn't want to risk leaving telltale ruts behind by driving up the slope. Halfway up my feet began to feel like lead and the blood was pounding in my ears like a pneumatic hammer; by the time I found myself at the base of the deformed tree I had barely enough energy left to find the spot I wanted and begin digging. It was dark, and the soil was soaked just enough so that each time I took out a shovelful the hole filled up again, with the result that it was ten minutes before I made any progress at all. After half an hour I stopped to rest. That's when all the lights came on and turned night into day.

The headlights of half a dozen automobiles were trained full upon me. For a fraction of a second I stood unmoving, frozen with shock. Then I hurled the shovel like a javelin at the nearest light and started to run. The first step I took landed in the hole. I fell headlong to the ground, emptying my lungs and twisting my ankle painfully. When I looked up, I was surrounded by people.

"I've waited five years for this." The voice belonged to Avery Sharecross.

"How did you know?" I said when I found my breath.

"I never did. Not for sure." Sharecross was standing over me now, an avenging angel wearing a threadbare coat and scarf. "I once heard that you spent all the money you had on the newspaper. If that was true, I wondered what your wife used for bus fare back to Santa Fe when she left you. Everyone knew you argued with her bitterly over your decision to stay. That you lost control and murdered her seemed obvious to me.

"I decided you buried her at the foot of the hanging tree, which was the reason you spent more time here than anyone else. The odds weren't in favor of my obtaining permission to dig up the hill because of a mere supposition, so it became necessary to catch you in the act of unearthing her yourself. That's when I got the idea to propose removing the tree and force you to find someplace else to dispose of the body."

He turned to a tall man whose Stetson glistened wetly in the unnatural illumination of the headlights at his back. "Sheriff, if your men will resume digging where Mr. Macklin left off, it's my guess you'll find the corpse of Sylvia Macklin before morning. I retired from the Santa Fe Police Department long before they felt the need to teach us anything about reading rights to those we arrested, so perhaps you'll oblige."

Now's the Time

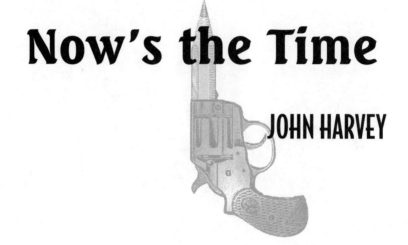

JOHN HARVEY

John Harvey's Introduction

In the more or less twenty years of writing prior to the publication of "Now's the Time," I'd tried my hand at pretty much everything in the professional's armory. Westerns; spy fiction and political thrillers; novelizations of everything from Herbie Rides Again *to the television sitcom* Duty Free; *a couple of "classic" serials for BBC television; scripts for* Spender *and* Hard Cases; *radio adaptations and originals; teenage fiction, ranging from romance on the beaches of Mablethorpe to suicidal angst in Stevenage New Town; a quartet of sub(very)-Chandler private eye novels; pulp novels by the score and then some (the pulpiest cowritten with the late Laurence James over six days; he did the violence and I did the rest—and this before the age of word processing and computers. Our tools were two electric typewriters, scissors, and paste). A few pieces of lightly disguised and heartfelt autobiographical fiction aside, the one thing I hadn't turned my hand to was the short story.*

The reasons were twofold: first, in the UK, there's only a very small commercial market for short fiction, and second, I'd always thought writing a short story would be fiendishly difficult and demanding an amount of time disproportionate to the results. After all, if in six days . . . but you get my point.

All this, however, reckoned without the redoubtable Maxim Jakobowski, bookseller, anthologizer, and writer. And Maxim, as those who have met him will know, is quite a determined man. So when he told me he wanted a Resnick story for a collection he was putting together— London Noir, *featuring the hippest crime writers around, the noirest of the noir, and the newest of the new—who was I to say no? Admittedly, none of the Resnick novels were set in London, and I didn't really consider what I was doing as particularly noir, never mind hip, but those were only incidentals to be swept aside.*

What gave me the go-ahead for the actual story was a small, easy-to-miss entry in the Death Notices of the Guardian newspaper, announcing the death of a Scottish jazz trumpeter named Al Fairweather, a musician whose playing I'd enjoyed listening to since I was a club-visiting schoolboy. Just a few lines, that's all there were—not much for a life. And then I got to thinking about the character of Ed Silver, a fictitious alcoholic ex-sax player who features in the third Resnick novel, Cutting Edge—if and when he died, is that what one might see, half a dozen lines near the foot of page 21 and nothing more. So I was off, filling in, as I have done in other stories since, the dots that surround the lives of those who people the books but are not sufficiently central to be more fully drawn. Charlie Resnick comes down to London for the funeral and takes the opportunity to catch a little jazz at Ronnie Scott's. What could be more natural? All right, I accept that as a story it's slight, with just a touch of plot involving a teenage run-away thrown in to keep it afloat, but, as I've said, it was my first and I think—and hope—I've got better. Read the stories in Now's The Time: The Complete Resnick Short Stories (Slow Dancer Press) to find out.

A final footnote: Spike Robinson, whom Resnick goes to hear at the Scott Club, is an actual musician, an Anglicized American who plays tenor sax like Lester Young with wings. I showed Spike the story, which I think he quite liked, save for the lines describing him as "stooped and fragile look-ing," which he considered worthy of improvement. He did come and play, though, at the London launch of my own Slow Dancer Press's short-lived fiction list—and I got to climb up on the stage of the 100 Club and say into the mike: "Spike Robinson, ladies and gentlemen, Spike Robinson."

Now's the Time

JOHN HARVEY

"THEY'RE ALL DYING, CHARLIE."

They had been in the kitchen, burnished tones of Clifford Brown's trumpet, soft like smoke from down the hall. Dark rye bread sliced and ready, coffee bubbling, Resnick had tilted the omelette pan and let the whisked eggs swirl around before forking the green beans and chopped red pepper into their midst. The smell of garlic and butter permeated the room.

Ed Silver stood watching, trying to ignore the cats that nudged, variously, around his feet. Through wisps of gray hair, a fresh scab showed clearly among the latticework of scars. The hand which held his glass was swollen at the knuckles and it shook.

"S'pose you think I owe you one, Charlie? That it?"

Earlier that evening, Resnick had talked Silver out of swinging a butcher's cleaver through his own bare foot. "What I thought, Charlie, start at the bottom and work your way up, eh?" Resnick had bundled him into a cab and brought him home, stuck a beer in his hand and set to making them both something to eat. He hadn't seen Ed Silver in ten years or more, a drinking club in Carlton whose owner liked his jazz; Silver had set out his stall early, two choruses of "I've Got Rhythm" solo, breakneck tempo, bass and drums both dropping out and the pianist grinning, open-mouthed. The speed of thought; those fingers then.

Resnick divided the omelette on to two plates. "You want to bring that bread?" he said. "We'll eat in the other room."

The boldest of the cats, Dizzy, followed them hopefully through. The *Clifford Brown Memorial* album was still playing "Theme of No Repeat."

"They're all dying, Charlie."

"Who?"

"Every bugger!"

AND NOW IT WAS true.

> SILVER Edward Victor. Suddenly at home, on February 16, 1993. Acclaimed jazz musician of the be-bop era. Funeral service and memorial meeting, Friday, February 19, at Golders Green Crematorium at 11:45 A.M. Inquiries to Mason Funeral and Monumental Services, High Lanes, Finchley.

Resnick was not a *Guardian* reader; not much of a reader at all, truth to tell. *Police Review*, the local paper, Home Office circulars and misspelled incident reports, *Jazz Journal*—that was about it. But Frank Delaney had called him Tuesday morning; Frank, who had continued booking Ed Silver into his pub long after most others had turned their backs, left Ed's calls unanswered on their answer-phones. "Seen the *Guardian* today, Charlie?" Resnick had taken it for a joke.

Now he was on the train as it approached Saint Pancras, that copy of the newspaper folded on the seat beside him, the debris of his journey—plastic cups, assorted wrappings from his egg mayonnaise sandwich, bacon and tomato roll, lemon iced gingerbread—pushed to one side of the table. There was the Regent's Canal; and as they passed the gas holders at King's Cross, Resnick got to his feet, lifted his coat down from the rack, and shrugged his way inside it. He would have to walk the short distance from one terminal to another and catch the underground.

EVEN AT THAT HOUR, King's Cross seemed jaded, sour, down at heel, broad corners and black cabs, bare-legged girls whose pallid skin was already beginning to sweat; men who leaned against walls and railings and glanced up at you as you passed, ready to sell you anything that wasn't theirs. Ageless and sexless, serious alcoholics sat or squatted, clutching brown bottles of cider, cans of Special Brew. High above the entrances, inside the wide concourse, security cameras turned slowly with remote-control eyes.

The automatic doors slid back at Resnick's approach and beyond the lights of the computerized arrivals board, the Leeds train spilled several hundred soccer fans across the shiny floor. Enlivened by the possibility of business, two girls who had been sharing a breakfast of chips outside Casey Jones, began to move toward the edges of the throng. One of them was tall, with badly hennaed hair that hung low over the fake fur collar of her coat; the other, younger, smudging a splash of red sauce like crazy lipstick across her cheek, called for her to wait. "Fuck's sake, Brenda." Brenda bent low to pull up the strap of her shoe, lit a cigarette.

"We are the champions!" chanted a dozen or more youths, trailing blue and white scarves from their belts.

In your dreams, Resnick thought.

A couple of hapless West Ham fans, on their way to catch an away special north, found themselves shunted up against the glass front of W. H. Smith. Half a dozen British rail staff busied themselves looking the other way.

"Come on, love," the tall girl said to one of the men, an ex-squaddis with regimental colors and a death's head tattooed along his arms, "me and my mate here. We've got a place."

"Fuck off!" the man said. "Just fucking fuck off!"

"Fuck you, too!" Turning away from the tide of abuse, she saw Resnick watching. "And you. What the hell d'you think you're staring at, eh? Wanker!"

Loud jeers and Resnick moved away between the supporters but now that her attention had been drawn to him, Brenda had him in her sights. Middle-aged man, visitor, not local, not exactly smart but bound to be carrying a quid or two.

"Don't go."

"What?"

The hand that spread itself against him was a young girl's hand. "Don't go."

"How old are you?" Resnick said. The eyes that looked back at him from between badly applied makeup had not so long since been a child's eyes.

"Whatever age you want," Brenda said.

A harassed woman with one kiddie in a pushchair and another clinging to one hand banged her suitcase inadvertently against the back of Brenda's legs and, even as she swore at her, Brenda took the opportunity to lose her balance and stumble forward. "Oops, sorry," she giggled, pressing herself against Resnick's chest.

"That's all right," Resnick said, taking hold of her arms and moving her, not roughly, away. Beneath the thin wool there was precious little flesh on her bones.

"Don't want the goods," her friend said tartly, "don't mess them about."

"Lorraine," Brenda said, "mind your own fucking business, right?"

Lorraine pouted a B-movie pout and turned away.

"Well?" Brenda asked, head cocked.

Resnick shook his head. "I'm a police officer," he said.

"Right," said Brenda, "and I'm fucking Julia Roberts!" And she wandered off to join her friend.

THE UNDERTAKER LED RESNICK into a side room and unlocked a drawer; from the drawer he took a medium-size manila envelope and from this he slid onto the plain table Ed Silver's possessions. A watch with a cracked face that had stopped at seven minutes past eleven; an address book with more than half the names crossed through; a passport four years out of date, dog-eared at the edges; a packet of saxophone reeds; one pound, thirteen pence in change. In a second envelope there were two photographs. One, in color, shows Silver in front of a poster for the North Sea Jazz festival, his name, partly obscured, behind him in small print. He is wearing dark glasses but, even so, it is clear from the shape of his face he is squinting up his eyes against the sun. His gray hair is cut in a once-fashionable crew cut and the sports coat he is wearing is bright dogtooth check and overlarge. His alto sax is cradled across his arms. If that picture were ten, fifteen years old, the other is far older—black and white faded almost to sepia, Ed Silver on the deck of the *Queen Mary*, the New York skyline rising behind him. Docking or departing, Resnick couldn't tell. Like many a would-be bopper, he had been part of Geraldo's navy, happy to play foxtrots and waltzes in exchange for a fervid forty-eight hours in the clubs on 52nd Street, listening to Monk and Bird. Silver had bumped into Charlie Parker once, almost literally, on a midtown street and been too dumb-struck to speak.

Resnick slid the photographs back from sight. "Is that all?" he asked.

Almost as an afterthought, the undertaker asked him to wait while he fetched the saxophone case, with its scuffed leather coating and tarnished clasps; stuck to the lid was a slogan: *Keep Music Live!* Of course, the case was empty, sax long gone to buy more scotch when Ed Silver had needed it most. Resnick hoped it had tasted good.

In the small chapel there were dried flowers and the wreath that Frank Delaney had sent. The coffin sat, cheap, before gray curtains and Resnick stood in the second row, glancing round through the vicar's perfunctory sermon to see if anyone else was going to come in. Nobody did. "He was a man, who in his life, brought pleasure to many," the vicar said. Amen, thought Resnick, to that. Then the curtains slowly parted and the coffin slid forward, rocking just a little, just enough, toward the flames.

Ashes to ashes, dust to dust,
If the women don't get you, the whisky must.

While the taped organ music wobbled through "Abide with Me," inside his head Resnick was hearing Ed Silver in that small club off Carlton Hill, stilling the drinking and the chatter with an elegiac "Parker's Mood."

"No family, then?" the vicar said outside, anxious to find time for a cigarette and a pee before the next service.

"Not as far as I know."

The vicar nodded sagely. "If you've nothing else in mind for them, we'll see to it the ashes are scattered here, on the rose garden. Blooms are a picture, let me tell you, later in the year. We have one or two visitors, find time to lend a hand keeping it in order, but of course there's no funding as such. We're dependent on donations."

Resnick reached into his pocket for his wallet and realized it was gone.

THE "MEAT RACK" STRETCHED back either side of the station, roads lined by lock-up garages and hole-in-the-wall businesses offering third-hand office furniture and auto parts. Resnick walked the gauntlet, hands in pockets, head down, the best part of three blocks and neither girl in sight. Finally, he stopped by a woman in a red coat, sitting on an upturned dustbin and using a discarded plastic fork to scrape dog shit from the sole of her shoe. There were bruises on her neck, yellow and violet, fading under the soiled white blouse which was all she was wearing above the waist.

"Ought to be locked up," the woman said, scarcely glancing up, "letting their animals do either business anywhere. Fall arse over tit and get your hand in this, God knows what kind of disease you could pick up." And then, flicking the contents of the fork out toward the street, "Twenty-five, short time."

"No," Resnick said, "I don't . . ."

She shook her head and swore as the fork snapped in two. "Fifteen, then, standing up."

"I'm looking for someone," Resnick said.

"Oh, are you? Right, well," she stood straight and barely came level with his elbows, "as long as it's not Jesus."

He assured her it was not.

"You'd be amazed, the number we get round here, looking to find Jesus. Mind you, they're not above copping a good feel while they're about it. Took me, one of them, dog collar an' all, round that bit of waste ground there. Mary, he says, get down on your knees and pray. Father, I says, I doubt you'll find the Lord up there, one hand on his rosary beads, the other way up my skirt. Mind you, it's my mother I blame, causing me to be christened Mary. On account of that Mary Magdalene, you know, in the Bible. Right horny twat, and no mistake." Resnick had the impression that even if he walked away she would carry on talking just the same. "This person you're looking for," she said, "does she have a name or what?"

THE HOTEL WAS IN a row of similar hotels, cream paint flaking from its walls and a sign that advertised all modern conveniences in every room. And then a few, Resnick thought. The manager was in Cyprus and the youth behind the desk was an archaeology student from King's, working his way, none too laboriously, through college. "Brenda?" he said, slipping an unwrapped condom into the pages of his book to keep his place. "Is that the one from Glasgow or the one from Kirkby-in-Ashfield?"

"Where?"

"Kirkby. It's near . . ."

"I know where it's near."

"Yes? Don't sound as though you're from round there."

"Neither do you."

"Langwith," the student said. "It's the posh side of Mansfield."

Resnick had heard it called some things in his time, but never that. "That Brenda," he said. "Is she here?"

"Look, you're not her father, are you?"

Resnick shook his head.

"Just old enough to be." When Resnick failed to crack a smile, he apologized. "She's busy." He took a quick look at his watch. "Not for so very much longer."

Resnick sighed and stepped away. The lobby was airless and smelled of . . . he didn't like to think what it smelled of. Whoever had blue-tacked the print of Van Gogh's sunflowers to the wall had managed to get it upside down. Perhaps it was the student, Resnick thought, perhaps it was a statement. A—what was it called?—a metaphor.

If Brenda was as young as she looked and from Kirkby, chances were she'd done a runner from home. As soon as this was over, he'd place a call, have her checked out. He was still thinking that when he heard the door slam and then the scream.

RESNICK'S SHOULDER SPUN THE door wide, shredding wood from around its hinges. At first the man's back was all he could see, arm raised high and set to come thrashing down, a woman's heeled shoe reversed in his hand. Hidden behind him, Brenda shrieked in anticipation. Resnick seized the man's arm as he turned and stepped inside his swing. The shoe flew high and landed on top of the plywood wardrobe in the corner of the room. Resnick released his grip and the man hit the doorjamb with a smack and fell to his knees. His round face flushed around startled eyes and a swathe of hair hung sideways from his head. His pale blue shirt was hanging out over dark striped trousers and at one side his braces were undone. Resnick didn't need to see the briefcase in the corner to know it was there.

From just beyond the doorway the student stood thinking, there, I was right, he is her father.

"She was asking . . ." the man began.

"Shut it!' said Resnick. "I don't want to hear."

Brenda was crying, short sobs that shook her body. Blood was meandering from a cut below one eye. "Bastard wanted to do it without a rubber. Bastard! I wouldn't let him. Not unless he give me another twenty pounds."

Resnick leaned over and lifted her carefully to her feet, held her there. "I don't suppose," he said over this shoulder, "you've got anything like first aid."

The man snatched up his briefcase and ran, careening between the banister and the wall. "I think there's plasters or something," the student said.

RESNICK HAD GONE TO the hospital with her and waited while they put seven stitches in her cheek. His wallet had been in her bag. Warrant card, return ticket and, astonishingly, the credit card he almost never used were still there; the cash, of course, was gone. He used the card to withdraw money from the change kiosk in the station. Now they were sitting in the Burger King opposite Saint Pancras and Resnick was tucking into a double cheeseburger with bacon, while Brenda picked at chicken pieces and chain-smoked Rothmans King Size.

Without her makeup, she looked absurdly young.

"I'm eighteen," she'd said, when Resnick had informed her he was contacting her family. "I can go wherever I like."

She was eleven weeks past her fifteenth birthday; she hadn't been to school since September, had been in London a little over a month. She had palled up with Lorraine the second or third night she was down. Half of her takings went to Lorraine's pimp boyfriend, who spent it on crack; almost half the rest went on renting out the room.

"You can't make me go back," she said.

Resnick asked if she wanted tea or coffee and she opted for a milk shake instead. The female police officer waiting patiently outside would escort her home on the last train.

"You know you're wasting your fucking time, don't you?" she called at Resnick across the pavement. "I'll only run off again. I'll be back down here inside a fucking week!"

The officer raised an eyebrow toward Resnick, who nodded, and the last he saw was the two of them crossing against the traffic, Brenda keeping one clear step ahead.

THE MAITRE'D AT RONNIE Scott's had trouble seating Resnick because he was stubbornly on his own; finally he slipped him in to one of the raised tables at the side, next to a woman who was drinking copious amounts of mineral water and doing her knitting. Spike Robinson was on the stand, stooped and somewhat fragile-looking, Ed Silver's contemporary, more or less. A little bit of Stan Getz, a lot of Lester Young, Robinson had been one of Resnick's favorite tenor players for quite a while. There was an album of Gershwin tunes that found its way onto this record player an awful lot.

Now Resnick ate spaghetti and measured out his beer and listened as Robinson took the tune of "I Should Care" between his teeth and worried at it like a terrier with a favorite ball. At the end of the number, he stepped back to the microphone. 'I'd like to dedicate this final tune of the set to the memory of Ed Silver, a very fine jazz musician who this week passed away. Charlie Parker's "Now's the Time."

And when it was over and the musicians had departed backstage and Ronnie Scott himself was standing there encouraging the applause—"Spike Robinson, ladies and gentlemen, Spike Robinson"—Resnick blew his nose and raised his glass and continued to sit there with the tears drying on his face. Seven minutes past eleven, near as made no difference.

Death of a
Romance Writer

JOAN HESS

Joan Hess's Introduction:

For the unenlightened few who have not heard this dirty little secret of mine, I'm now going to immortalize it in print. Those of you who already have heard it, please fast-forward.

I had never attempted to write fiction (or anything else not due on Monday) until a friend swept into town in the early 1980s and convinced me that we could make gazillions writing romance novels. Because of the aforementioned and because I'd never read a romance novel, I had reservations. However, the market was hot and the advances were hefty, even by today's standards. I convinced my white-haired mother to check out a few romances at the library, read a couple of them, and decided to try. On the first page of what would eventually be the first of ten unpublishable literary gems, I discovered that I loved writing fiction: Dawn and Derek on the beach as the sun set in a blaze of color; Tiffany and Brett, gazing longingly into each other's emerald green/slate gray eyes, the wild gallop across the pasture on a dewy morning, the steamy passion beside the waterfall, etc.

The letters of rejection were eerily uniform: good characters and dialogue, intriguing premise, and then the inevitable "too much plot; not enough romance." Rather than sit down and actually read some popular romance novels to find out what the editors wanted, I merely went back into the manuscript and stuck in more sex.

I was on my fourth agent when I finally acknowledged that it might be time to have a bonfire in the backyard, toast a marshmallow or two, and go back to grad school. Agent No. 4 convinced me to write a mystery. I delayed the screwy grad-school scheme and wrote the first Claire Malloy novel, which aptly might have been subtitled "Death of a Romance Writer."

I realized I'd found my genre and my voice. The characters in Strangled Prose seemed richer, wittier, and more textured. They certainly were having more fun than Dawn, Derek, and the rest of the gang. Rather than repressing their emotions, they could act on them. What's more, they tended to take charge and say and do things that I, their decreasingly omnipotent creator, hadn't anticipated (this is not quite as schizophrenic as it sounds; many writers admit as much).

And thus I began to feel sorry for my romance novel cast, forever gnawing their knuckles in frustration. Then I considered the plight of the poor heroine of historical romance fiction, doomed to be banished from the family estate and forced to survive as an ill-treated nanny, scullery maid, or governess until the hero—aka the guy with the mysterious scar—swept her into his arms and made her the lady of the manor.

In "Death of a Romance Writer," my very first attempt at a short story, I decided to take a dollop of revenge for all the abused heroines of romantic fiction and let one of them, at least, have some fun for a change. The story's peculiar; you'll either get a kick out of it, or react in the same manner as the above-mentioned white-haired lady, who read it and, with a deeply perplexed look, said, "I don't get it."

Death of a Romance Writer

JOAN HESS

THE YOUNG WOMAN HESITATED at the top of the great curving stair-case, grumbling rather rudely to herself as she gazed at the scene below. "Hell's bells!" she muttered under her breath. "Doesn't she like anything besides waltzes? A little New Wave rock, or at least jazz?"

In the grand ballroom ladies dressed in pastel gowns swept across the floor under the benevolent eyes of elegant gentlemen in black waistcoats and ruffled shirts. A stringed orchestra labored its way through the familiar melodies with grim concentration. Servants moved inconspicuously along the walls of the vast room, their expressions studiously blank. The same old thing, down to the canapes and sweet sherry.

Gathering up her skirt with pale, delicately tapered fingers, the woman forced herself to move down the stairs. Her heart-shaped mouth was curled slightly, and her deep jade eyes flittered across the crowd without curiosity. He would make an appearance in a few minutes, she reminded herself glumly, but perhaps she could have a bit of fun in the meantime. The fun would certainly end when he appeared—whoever he was.

"Lady Althea!" gushed a shrill, nasal voice from the shadows behind her. "I was so hoping to see you this evening. The ball is absolutely delightful."

Lady Althea, the woman repeated to herself. A silly name, as usual, invoking images of moonlit gardens and scented breezes. Why not a simple "Kate" or "Jane"? Oh, no. It was always "Desiree" or "Bianca," as if her bland personality must be disguised by alluring nomenclature.

The dowager tottered out of the shadows on tiny feet. In her seventies (hundreds, Althea sniffed to herself), the woman's face was a mesh of tiny lines, and her faded blue eyes glittered with malevolence. Her thin white hair was decorated with a handful of dusty plumes, one of which threatened to sweep across her hawkish nose with every twitch of the woman's head.

"Who're you?" Althea demanded bluntly.

The dowager raised a painted eyebrow. "I am your mother-in-law's dearest friend, Lady Althea. You had tea only yesterday at my summer home. Your first introduction to society, I believe. I'm amazed that it has slipped your mind."

"Yeah, sorry." Althea moved away from the woman's rancid breath and fluttery hands. Surely these people could be induced to brush their teeth, she thought testily. They didn't, of course. As far as she could tell, they had no bodily functions whatsoever. A few bouts of the vapors, a shoulder slashed by a dueling sword, a mysterious scar across the check. But nothing mundane to interrupt the flow of their lives.

Ignoring the woman's frown, Althea stood on her toes to peer around the room. He wasn't here yet. Good. Now, if she could only liven up the music and get these nameless people to loosen up a little bit, the evening might provide some amusement. A ball could be a ball, but it seldom was.

The dowager was not ready to allow Althea to escape. "Your dear mother-in-law has told me of your tragic history, and I must tell you how much I admire your courage," she hissed. Little drops of spittle landed on Althea's check, like a fine mist of acid rain.

"Sure, thanks," Althea said. "I'm a plucky sort, I understand. Personally, I'd rather watch television or read a confession magazine, but I never get the chance."

"Television? What might that be, my dear girl?"

Althea shook her head. "Never mind. Hey, which one of these ladies" (dames, broads) "is my mother-in-law? The one with the chicken beak or that fat slug in the corner?"

"Lady Althea! I must tell you that I am somewhat shocked by your manner," the dowager gasped. Her hand fluttered to her mouth. "I was led to believe you had been raised most properly in a convent; that you were of gentle birth and delicate nature."

"Is that so? I guess I'd better behave," Althea said dryly. She tucked a stray curl of her raven black hair into place, and checked the row of tiny seed pearl buttons on her elbow-length gloves. Now that, she told herself sternly, was the accepted and expected behavior. She glanced at the dowager.

"So which one is my mother-in-law?"

"Your mother-in-law is there," the dowager said, gesturing with a molting fan toward a grim-visaged woman sitting on a straight-backed chair. "But where is your dear husband, Lady Althea? I had such hopes of speaking to him."

"Beats me," Althea said. So she was already married, she thought with a sigh. These rapid shifts were disconcerting. Dear husband, huh! Gawd, he was probably a bodice ripper like the rest of them. And she had decided to wear her new gown—genuine silk and just the right color for her eyes. Perhaps there was enough time to change into something more expendable.

Frowning, Althea glanced across the coifed heads of the guests to study her mother-in-law. A real loser, with a profile that ought to be illegal. Translucent blue complexion, hooded eyes, mouth tighter than a miser's purse. But the woman did have a smidgen of charm— all found in the garish diamond broach on her chest. From across the room, Althea could see the brilliance of the stone, and even the dull glow of the gold setting. Now *that* was charming.

Leaving the dowager puffing resentfully at the bottom of the staircase, Althea began to thread her way between the dancers. Despite her intention of finding the punch bowl, she found herself curtsying in front of her mother-in-law. Damn.

"Althea, dear child," the woman said frostily. She extended a limp white hand, as though she expected Althea to clasp it to her bosom—or kiss it, for God's sake!

Althea eyed it warily. At last she touched it timidly, then snatched her hand away and hid it behind her back. "Good evening," she said, swallowing a sour taste in the back of her throat. The diamond broach. It would keep her in penthouses and champagne for the rest of her life, if only . . .

"Excrutia, this child is charming!" the dowager said, shoving Althea aside. "But where is your son? Dear Jared must be eager to present his charming bride to his friends . . ."

Jared, huh. Althea brushed a black curl off her eyebrow as she checked the crowd. She was destined to be stuck with an elegant moniker, and so was he. Once, she remembered with a faint sigh, she had particularly liked a chap named Sam—but of course he had become a Derek. Sam had had bulging biceps and a busted nose, but it hadn't kept him from stirring up a bit of inventiveness between the covers. Derek, on the other hand, had spent hours gazing into her eyes and murmuring (bleating) endearments that were supposed to sweep her off her feet. Sam's approach was brisker—and a hell of a lot more interesting.

The mother-in-law was sniveling down her nose. "Where is my son, Althea? Have you already managed to . . . distract him from his duties as host?"

Althea thought of several snappy remarks but again found herself in an awkward curtsy. "No, ma'am. I haven't seen him since—"

Since what? It was impossible to keep track of the convoluted framework. Since he rescued her? Married her? Raped her? Jared would never do such a thing, she amended sourly. No doubt he had kept her from being raped by one of the marauding highwaymen that accosted virgins. Considering Jared, it might have been more fun to be accosted . . .

"Well, Althea," the mother-in-law snorted in a well-bred voice, "you must feel most fortunate to have snared my son. He is, after all, the owner of this charming manor and of all the land from here to the cliffs. And you, a penniless orphan, destined to become a scullery maid—had not heaven intervened on your behalf."

Sam's mother was a cheery drunkard who was still producing babies on an annual basis. This one had probably produced Jared by virgin birth. Forget that; birth was messy. Jared had no doubt simply appeared one day, lisping French and nibbling cucumber sandwiches under his nanny's approving smile.

Althea swallowed in angry response. Fluttering her thick lashes, she murmured, "Yes, ma'am, I was most fortunate to have met your son. When my father died, leaving me a penniless orphan at the mercies of my unscrupulous uncle, I feared for my life." Melodrama, pure and nauseating. Why couldn't she have been a barmaid? A bit of slap and giggle in the shadows behind the stables, a feather bed to keep warm for a guy like Sam. But instead she had to hang around with the aristocracy. Snivellers and snorters, bah!

But there was no point in worrying about this Jared fellow. Maybe he was a Sam in disguise. Maybe chickens had lips, and the moon was made of green cheese. Maybe it was time to start expecting the Easter bunny to show up with a bunch of purple eggs.

The mother-in-law person stood up imperiously and held a lace handkerchief to her nose. "I am going into the garden for a bit of fresh air," she announced. "Send Jared to me when he appears, Althea. I must speak to him; it is of the greatest importance."

Hummm? Had the old bat noticed her repeated glances at the diamond broach? If she were to tattle to this Jared person, Althea might find herself scrubbing pots after all. It seemed prudent to assume the dutiful role.

"Please don't take a chill, Lady Excrutia," Althea said in a solicitous whine. "Shall I fetch a shawl for you from your dressing room? Allow me to bring it to you in the garden."

The dowager with the plumes beamed approvingly at Althea's meek posture. "Charming child, just charming. But look, here's Jared!"

Oh, hell. Althea tried to forget about the promised encounter in the garden—for a few minutes anyway. Forcing herself into a semblance of pleased surprise, she lifted her eyes to meet those of the unknown Jared.

Oh, my God, she thought with a scowl. Another arrogant one. There went another bodice, ripped into shreds. Endless lovemaking, with nothing but simmering frustration as the result. And those granite gray eyes boring into her, for God's sake! It was more than anyone would have to bear . . . it really was.

"DAMNEDEST THING I'VE EVER seen!" The lieutenant leaned against the kitchen counter, watching the body being wheeled out of the tiny office. For the first time in his career even the paramedics were subdued.

The two men waited for the medical examiner to finish wiping the inky smudges off his hands, then crowded into the room. The desk was cluttered with notebooks, chewed pencil stubs, and an overflowing ashtray. A lipstick-stained coffee cup lay on the floor in a dried brown puddle. A typewriter hummed softly, and with a snort the second of the plainclothes detectives leaned over to switch it off.

"How'd you discover the body?" the medical examiner asked. Like Lady Macbeth, he seemed obsessed with the invisible marks on his hands, rubbing them against each other nervously.

"The woman in the next apartment called the super. It seems the woman who lived here was a writer, and the neighbor was used to the sound of the typewriter clattering all day long. She told the super the last couple of days there was no sound, and it was driving her crazy," the first detective said.

The second snorted again. "If I lived next door to one of these writers, and had to listen to that noise all day, I might have strangled the broad myself. As it is, I have to listen to my wife screaming at the kids every night and—"

"Damnedest thing," the first repeated, shaking his head. "In twenty-nine years on the force, I've seen a lot of weird things—but I've never seen anyone strangled with a typewriter ribbon."

The medical examiner laughed. "As good as a wire or a rope, but a hell of a lot messier. All you have to do now is find someone with ink-stained hands."

The second detective was reading the titles of the paperback books on a shelf above the desk. "Look at this, Carl. Do you know what the victim wrote? Romance novels, by damn! You know the things: *Sweet Moonlight, The Towering Passion of Lady Bianca*, etc., etc."

"My wife reads that stuff," the first admitted. He shook his head. "I dunno why, though. Gimme a good ball game on television and a six-pack to keep me cool. That's my idea of romance—me, Budweiser, and the Yankees."

The medical examiner raised his hand in a farewell gesture. "I'll get back to you in a day or two, Carl. Don't waste your time reading the victim's books—unless you think the intellectuals of the world conspired to do her in!" Chuckling to himself, he left the two detectives exchanging glances.

"Naw, Carl," the second said, "don't get your hopes up. It was a prowler or something. Let's go talk to the doorman and the elevator operator."

The first sighed, thinking of the tedious interviews that would prove necessary, the trivial gossip that the neighbors would feel obliged to share, the dinner he would not have a chance to eat that night.

"Too bad it wasn't a suicide," he grumbled. "My wife always makes meatballs on Mondays and then goes bowling with a bunch of the girls. Good game on tonight."

"Then we'd have our note," the second added, pointing at a piece of paper sticking out of the typewriter. "But nobody, not even dippy romance writers, can strangle themselves. My money's on the neighbor; she's probably half-deaf from the noise. She just couldn't stand the sound of the typewriter any longer and went berserk. I would've."

"She's eighty-three," the first one said. He leaned over to read the manuscript page, then straightened up. "My wife will get a kick out of this, you know. Yours will, too. All women think this stuff is great—all the damned moonlight and wine and deep soulful stares! It spoils them for the real world, Marv."

"Yeah, my wife wanted me to take her out to dinner for her birthday. Hell, the baby sitter drives a damn Mercedes! I can't see spending half a week's salary on fancy food."

"So what'd you do?" Carl asked as they went out the door of the office and started for the living room.

The one named Marv shrugged his shoulders. "I brought home a real nice pizza."

LADY ALTHEA WRAPPED HER arms around Sam's stocky waist and snuggled against him, ignoring the black smudges on his back from her previous caresses. For a long time, the horse's rhythmic clops were the only sound on the road. The moon illuminated the trees on either side of them with a silver haze, and the light breeze had an earthy redolence. At last the horse and its two riders were gone into the darkness, although a faint giggle seemed to linger in the air.

Back at the cold and lifeless manor house, the ball was over. The nameless gentility had disappeared, the orchestra vanished, the vast room as quiet as a tomb. In the center of the room lay a body. Two arrogant eyes stared at the darkened chandelier, unblinking and glazed with faint surprise. Blood had long since coagulated on the gash across his neck.

There was more blood in the garden. The figure there had the same surprised expression, and a similar slash across the neck. The bosom no longer heaved, although it had the appearance of a mountain range arising from the manicured lawn. The surface of this alpine region was smooth, except for a tiny rip in its surface where a broach had been removed hastily and without regard for the crinoline fabric.

His majesty's guards remained puzzled by the scene for a few weeks, then dismissed it from their minds. One or two of the younger ones sometimes mentioned it over pints of ale in the new roadhouse, but the older officers usually ignored them. The barmaid, always full of throaty laughter and ready for a frolic, kept them more amused on the feather beds upstairs.

Compliments
of a Friend

SUSAN ISAACS

Susan Isaacs's Introduction:

Not counting one ghastly love poem ("Ode to David") I wrote when I was sixteen that, even now, causes my face to turn aubergine and my kishkas to seize up into a knot, my writing career had consisted of eight novels, a couple of movies, book reviews, magazine articles, political speeches, op-ed pieces—with a little cultural criticism on the side. But never a short story. Why? I don't know. To me, less was never more: More was more. Once I managed to devise an opening sentence, I'd keep plugging away until I got a nice round number, like a hundred fifty thousand words.

When I joined the Adams Round Table, I didn't know the group published anthologies of the members' stories. (If I were as worldly wise as I like to think I am, I would have understood no company of writers—particularly mystery writers—could sit around a table month after month, year after year, and forego the chance to strut their stuff and/or make a buck.) However, one Tuesday night, there was an "Oh, by the way . . . and talk of the latest collection, Murder Among Friends, got under way.

I must have whimpered, or at least shuddered, because suddenly I heard my colleagues' voices murmuring reassurances like "You don't have to" and "Don't feel compelled." I explained that the short story wasn't my form. I smiled at them. They smiled back. And that was that. But as we were leaving, Mary Clark enthused: "You know, you can do it!" as if she hadn't a doubt. And Larry Block backed her up with a low-key: "Give it a shot. You'll have fun."

Fun? But my compadres' optimism was contagious enough that by the time I got back to Long Island I knew whom I was going to kill off. But who would be my detective? I didn't have to give that a lot of thought: By the time I was turning out the downstairs lights, the protagonist was knocking on the door of my consciousness; when I opened it, I saw she was an old pal, Judith Singer, the heroine of my first novel (and first attempt at fiction), Compromising Positions.

If Judith were the investigator who would track down the killer, I could relax, or at least not hyperventilate. She and I went back more than twenty years. Her voice was familiar and dear to me. And this would give me the chance to find out what she'd been doing all this time, how life had turned out for her. (Listen, there was never really any question that she would remain the same age as she was in 1978, when she first appeared. If I had to go through menopause, she would, too.)

So as it turned out, the short story, that scary form, turned out to be one of the happiest writing experiences I'd ever had. Judith Singer came back into my life. It truly was murder among friends.

Compliments of a Friend

SUSAN ISAACS

ON A CHILL AND sodden Tuesday in March at one in the afternoon, the awesomely slender Deirdre Giddings, founder and CEO of Panache, the largest employment agency on Long Island, slipped into a chair in the designer shoe department in Bloomingdale's in Garden City cradling a black snakeskin Manolo Blahnik sling-back in her hands. She closed her eyes. A few minutes later, when Oliver, her usual salesman, gently tapped her shoulder and murmured, "Ms. Giddings? Seven-and-a-half, right? *Ms. Giddings?*" he got no response. That was because she was comatose.

She passed from the world before the gray dawn of the following morning. The Nassau County Medical Examiner ruled her exit self-inflicted—an overdose of barbiturates. The Nassau County Police Department's spokesman (elbowing aside the M.E. so he could stand squarely in front of the microphone) announced that a suicide note had been found among her personal papers. When I came home from work that Wednesday evening and heard the first of four messages about her death on my answering machine—"Judith, did you hear . . . ?"—I wasn't just surprised. I was shaken.

Deirdre, of all people! So alive. Now, when I say "alive," I'm not talking about in that congenitally chirpy no-Prozac sense. I mean alive as in seemingly invulnerable. Dressed for success in a Prada suit and Gucci shoes, though I admit my grasp of fashion is a little iffy and it could have been the other way around. Anyway, her shoes were those clunky things that make me look clubfooted. However,

145

on women like Deirdre, they look not merely stylish; they also make already slender legs appear even trimmer. Deirdre's hair? Blonde, the expensive kind that gave off glints of platinum and gold. Her lips—outlined in burgundy, lipsticked in Chianti, glossed with a daring touch of strawberry—showed she was so much the captain of her fate that, while recognizing her own mortality, she could go for her mammogram without her guts in a knot.

Whenever I saw her at the semiannual meetings of the Board of Trustees of the Long Island Heritage Council, a group dedicated to preserving the region's historical sites, she was all business, never wasting even a microsecond. She'd stroll around the Peconic-Deutschebank's conference room exchanging power handshakes and networking with her fellow and sister hotshots—whereas I hung out with the other academic, an anthropologist from Southampton College, and watched while he wrapped the titanic bagels and raisin-glutted muffins on the hospitality table in napkins and stuffed them into his backpack.

But it would be inaccurate to think of Deirdre as a stereotypical career crone, hard-eyed and tight-lipped. Her face was peaches-and-cream pretty, with all-American apple cheeks. Her eyes were true blue. She had a pink rose petal of a voice. Further, she was unfailingly polite. Still, it was easy to understand how people could call her aloof. She seemed to hold back not from shyness, but as if getting to know you too well would inevitably be disappointing, and she truly preferred to think well of you. Not at all the brash gladhander you'd expect from an employment-agency type. That reticence not only made her stand out, but made people assume that the housemaids from Panache Home, the bookkeepers from Panache Office, and the pharmacists from Panache Professional were somehow endowed with Deirdre's cool professionalism.

At her funeral, the minister had called her "caring" because not even the most charitable Christian soul could go so far as "warm." However, for some reason, Deirdre was always cordial to me—so if not actually warm, at least tepid in the nicest possible way. She'd walk toward me with both hands outstretched. "Judith Singer." Then she'd grip my shoulders and stick out her head to bestow a kiss on the cheek. All right, so not an actual kiss: As her satiny, alphahydroxied cheek grazed mine she merely made a chirping sound. But then she would draw back and regard me with something like satisfaction and inquire: "And how is my friend Judith doing?"

I hadn't the foggiest notion of how come I rated her friendship. Outside of council meetings, we never saw each other except in casual situations—coming out of Shorehaven Hardware on Main Street, or at the harbor band-shell at the Sunday night concerts each summer. Perhaps it was because we both lived in Shorehaven, a Long Island suburb which, despite being twenty-six miles from mid-Manhattan and filled with a fair number of urbane business types and cutting-edge professionals, had the aggressive neighborliness of an Andy Hardy movie.

To be honest, Deirdre's special treatment might have been pity: I was—am—a widow. For the past two years, since my husband Bob died half a day after finishing the New York Marathon in four hours and twelve minutes, I'd noticed that the same people who would treat a middle-aged divorcée with the same *tendresse* as they would a rabid dog could be surprisingly compassionate toward a woman who had lost her husband—as opposed to one who somehow sloppily allowed her man to slip through her fingers.

Or perhaps Deirdre was merely grateful to me. I am a historian who works two jobs. Half the time I'm adjunct professor of history at the formerly all-female, formerly nun-run, formerly first-rate Saint Elizabeth's College across the county border in the borough of Queens; the other half I head my town's oral history project at the Shorehaven Public Library. A few years earlier, Deirdre had come to me for help: A potential client, the president of Kluckers, a kosher chicken distributor, wasn't sure if Long Island had the right "vibes" for his new corporate headquarters. I'd worked with her to compose a lively *précis* of the history of poultry farming on Long Island. Apparently, our effort wowed the guy. Naturally, I wouldn't take the money she offered for my work. So she'd sent the library a generous contribution and, to me, a gorgeously bound copy of *Leaves of Grass*, somehow having learned I'm a fool for Walt Whitman. Now she was dead.

"This Deirdre business has really gotten to me," I declared to my true friend Nancy Miller two nights later. "Not that I actually was her friend, even if that's what she called me but . . ." Nancy was eagle-eyeing the waiter as he opened a bottle of Rosso di Montalcino so I demanded: "Are you listening to me?"

"How can I avoid it?" We were in a new restaurant, La Luna Toscana. For some reason I cannot explain, whenever a new culinary trend gets underway in Manhattan, such as Tuscan cuisine, it gets out to Kansas City—with a side trip to Emporia—before it can manage to schlep the twenty-six miles east to Shorehaven.

"About Deirdre . . ." I went on. "I'm upset . . . But not really touched . . . Shit, I wish I could find the right words to express what I feel."

"How about 'shocked and saddened'?" Nancy suggested. "Tell me, when Bob died, did you get one single note that didn't say: 'I was shocked and saddened to hear of your loss'? I mean—" Her "I mean" came out "Ah main." Although Nancy hasn't been back to her native Georgia in thirty years, she has clung to its syrupy accent, convinced, correctly, that it adds to her charm. "I mean, did anyone even have the originality to say 'saddened and shocked'?"

"Of course not. But someone like Deirdre committing suicide? It is genuinely shocking. Look, I know no one can get through life without pain, but she seemed so impervious to the usual slings and arrows."

"Please. Stan Giddings dumped her for a younger woman." Nancy lifted her wineglass, held it to the light, and looked perturbed. Once she took a sip, she shook her head with weariness and regret, but waved the waiter away. "Didn't he dump his first missus too, for Deirdre?"

"Yes," I replied. "Her name is Barbara. It was all in your paper. Don't you read it, for God's sake?"

"Not the stories that pander to salivating semi-literates, though I sense that's most of our readership." Several years earlier, Nancy had given up freelance writing to become an associate editor of *Newsday's* op-ed page. "When I want my trash, I go right to the *New York Post*. They do it right. None of this genteel suburban shit like 'The Medical

Examiner refused to speculate why Ms. Giddings chose to end her life in a department store after taking an overdose of the prescription drug Nembutal, a common sleep-inducing barbiturate.'" She finished off the wine in her glass and immediately poured herself another.

"Why not stick a straw into the wine bottle and just glug away?" I suggested. "Save all that tedious pouring."

"Why don't you put a cork in it about my drinking?"

With a sigh that I hoped was sufficiently passive-aggressive to induce guilt, I went back to the subject at hand. "A woman like Deirdre doesn't kill herself over a man."

"If she were crazy enough to actually marry that slick, do-nothing piece of work, you don't think she might decide to pack it in when he took a walk?"

"First of all," I said patiently, "he's not slick."

In fact, the couple times I'd seen Stan Giddings—at the Long Island Heritage Council's annual dinner-dance, on line at Let There Be Bagels, I'd found him pleasingly unslick. Tall, broad-shouldered, square-jawed, given to rumpled denim work shirts and tweedy jackets, he looked like an East Coast version of the Marlboro Man. His gray-flecked brown hair was longish, chopped more than cut, and his smile was wide, yet somehow sensual. It let you know he was aware you were woman and he was man—and that he was excited by the difference. A for-real smile, not that lips-together smirk of the Long Island Lothario. A smile from a guy like Stan and you find yourself grinning back, so imbued with your own lusty wench-hood that you momentarily forget you're old enough to be his mother— had you experienced an early menarche. You'd remember that smile, too—for days, or weeks, even though you knew that as soon as he smiled it you were already erased from his consciousness.

"He's not slick," I declared, "just smooth."

"I don't mean slick in the Michael-Douglas-slime-on-his-hair sense. Slick in that his charm has nothing to do with his feelings, assuming he has any." She set down her glass, picked up a bread stick and snapped it in two. "Inherited money," Nancy observed.

Over the years I've become so used to her non sequiturs that such statements, coming from her, acquire their own logic. "Inherited

money has something to do with being emotionally deficient," I artic-
ulated for her.

"Obviously."

"Not quite."

"Stan's money comes from socks, for crissakes!"

"For the U.S. armed forces. From Iwo Jima to the Persian Gulf
and that's a lot of socks, enough to make his family incredibly rich
for—what?—three generations. What do socks or being rich have to
do with Stan's personality?"

Nancy shook the half bread stick at me the way a teacher would
shake a pointer at a deliberately dense student. "He never had to
earn a living. He never had to *do* anything. He just had to *be*, and
people would vacuum his floors and groom his horse and admit him
to Princeton and treat him in every respect as if he had done something important."

I tried to come up with a piercingly clever rejoinder to counter
her argument, but I finally said, "You're right."

"Supposedly he runs the company. Except he spends two
months in Vail skiing. And two months up in Maine sailing. And two
months someplace warm golfing, plus everyone knows that if he
actually did run the company the only place he'd run it is into the
ground. He was born to play, not to think. On the other hand," she
added, "he's hung like King Kong."

"How do you know that?"

"How do you think I know?" In Nancy's mind, Mount Sinai was
the place God had given Moses the Nine Commandments. In her
thirty-one years of marriage, at least four score lovers had come—
and gone.

"You slept with Stan?" Her head moved slightly: an acknowl-
edgment. "I can't believe you! How come you left out this one?" I'd
sometimes felt as if Nancy was relying on me to be her official score-
keeper.

"It must have been when you were writing your doctoral dissertation," Nancy muttered. "You were already overstimulated. How
could I burden you? Anyhow, everyone in town knows about his
equipment."

"I don't."

"You! You can name every member of Roosevelt's Cabinets from whenever—"

"From 1933 to 1945."

"—but anything truly interesting always comes as a surprise. 'Golly! You mean Stan Giddings has a foot-long hot dog? No kidding!' By the way, he knows what to do with it, too."

All I could say was "Golly!"

"Of course, there's always the 'but,'" Nancy added.

"What's his?"

"He's an idiot ultra-conservative and he can't stop babbling about it. It's like fucking Oliver North, except Stan has decent teeth."

"So if he's that much of a *dummkopf*, his leaving wouldn't have sent Deirdre over the edge."

"I heard something about other reasons," Nancy muttered to her wine.

"Like what?" I probably sounded a tad overeager because she responded with an elegant flaring of her nostrils. I leaned forward, rested my hands on the annoying, chic sheet of butcher paper the restaurant was using instead of a cloth, and demanded: "*What* other reasons?"

"Serious business reverses."

"Where did you hear that?"

She took a slow sip of wine. "I suppose as I wafted past the city room."

"How serious is 'serious'?" Nancy peered into her glass once again. She seemed surprised to find it empty, as though someone had sneaked over and drained it while she was talking. Shrugging, she poured herself another glass. I took my third sip of the night and, for the umpteenth time in the thirty-three years since we'd been in college together, worried about her liver. "Nancy, how bad were Deirdre's business reverses?"

"Why are you so interested?"

"Something's fishy."

"Nothing's fishy."

"I don't buy this suicide story."

She gripped the stem of her glass. "You're not thinking of doing a little detecting, are you, Judith?"

"Please!" I tried to act amused, but the derisive chuckle came out as if I were having some unpleasantness with phlegm. "I only did that once. Twenty years ago. A blip on the radar screen of life. It's just . . ."

"Just what?"

"Hear me out. Suicide makes no sense. Say you want to kill yourself. But your whole persona is being one cool cookie. So you wouldn't do it violently, like leaping off an overpass into rush-hour traffic on the Northern State, would you? And if you're as meticulous as Deirdre, would you risk breaking a nail hooking up a hose to the exhaust of your car? No. You'd probably do the girl thing, take sleeping pills. Right?"

"Probably," she conceded, although reluctantly.

"And what would happen then? You might just go to sleep forever. But you could also upchuck and choke on your own vomit."

"Must you be so vivid before the first course?"

"And why in God's name would you choose to die in Bloomingdale's?" I continued. "Why would you be looking at shoes in the final moments of your life? Think, Nancy: If you were depressed enough to actively contemplate suicide, would you be worrying about what to wear with your new spring suit?"

"No. Accessorizing is definitely life-affirming."

"Also, if you're one of these controlled types like Deirdre," I went on, "are you going to risk dropping down dead over a display of Ferragamos and losing control of your bowels while you still have your pantyhose on?" With that I waved the waiter over and inquired how much garlic there was in the ribollita.

But after dinner, back home alone, I was still asking questions. So I hauled in the tied-up newspapers I'd put in the garage for recycling and sat in the kitchen. Intermittently, I was distracted by the noise of sleet against the window, like thousands of long-nailed fingers tapping impatiently against a glass tabletop. I read and reread Deirdre's obituary and everything about her death. There wasn't much. She'd been born Deirdre Graubart in Rockville Centre, a town on Long Island. She'd gone to Hofstra College, also on the Island, and after a brief stint (although I never heard of a stint that wasn't brief) working at a gigantic employment agency in the city, she'd founded Panache while still in her twenties. Her clients ranged from Kluckers to a computer software giant, from socialites to professional athletes. By the time she was in her early thirties, she had not only married Stan, but had also gotten him to build her a fifteen-room house on a bluff overlooking Long Island Sound, a place so abounding in Doric columns it was clear she had seen *Gone With the Wind* too many times during preadolescence.

One of the articles had a picture of Deirdre in a coatdress perched on the edge of her Louis the Somethingth desk. She was flanked on the left by a woman in a maid's uniform and a man holding a pipe wrench, and on the right by a man in a three-piece banker's suit and another in a one-piece mechanic's coverall. "Her former husband, Stanley Giddings," the *Shorehaven Sentinel* reported, "could not be reached for comment, although a spokesman released a statement that said Mr. Giddings was 'shocked and saddened to learn of Deirdre's suicide.'" The shocked and saddened Stan, the paper noted, had, three months earlier, married an artist who went by the name of Ryn and had moved out of Shorehaven.

The next time I glanced up it was long past eleven o'clock. I'd made a nifty pile of clippings about Deirdre's death, arranged in chronological order, interspersed with older features about her career I found on the Internet. Why had I spent the night doing this when I had twenty-two first drafts of term papers on New Deal agencies to evaluate? Well, Deirdre had called me her friend. On the slim chance she hadn't been full of it, that she was truly so friendless that she considered a near-stranger a friend, maybe I owed her something. Or it could have been a gut reaction—suicide is bullshit—and I've learned over the years my gut is right more often than wrong. Who knows? Maybe it was that after dinner with Nancy, on yet one more bleak night alone, a mystery was just what I needed to put a little life in my life.

My husband was gone. True, Bob and I hadn't had a fairy-tale marriage. Still, even when all that's left is polite conversation and predictable marital sex, you have to remember (I had told myself all those years) that once upon a time it had to have been a love story. So I always half-expected the plot would get moving again: Some incident would touch off a great conflict and, lo and behold, not only would the air finally become clear, but there'd be romance in it! The two of us would walk hand in hand into a sunset, happily ever after—or until one of us went gently into the night in our eighth or ninth decade.

Imagine my surprise when he died before my eyes in the emergency room of North Shore Hospital. One minute he squeezed my hand, a reassuring pressure, but I could see the fear in his eyes. As I squeezed back, he slipped away. Just like that. Gone, before I could say, "Don't worry, honey, you'll be fine." Or, "I love you, Bob."

Not only no husband. No prospect of another one. Not one more blind date, that was for sure, not after the two Nancy referred to as Old and Older. Periodically I went to the movies or the theater with Geoff, a post-modernist from the English Department. I rarely understood what he was talking about, and his clothes smelled as if he patronized a discount dry cleaner. No one else was knocking at my door. My son and daughter were grown, gone from the house. So who knows? Maybe I was entertaining thoughts about murder because it was one of those dark and stormy nights, both without and within, when the notion of suicide—anybody's—was so terrifying it had to be denied.

I should have felt better the next day. A smiley yellow sun rose into an azure sky. In the cold air, I sniffed the first sweetness of impending spring. Actually, I did feel better. But that was probably because I was sitting across from Dr. Jennifer Spiros, the number-two pathologist in the Nassau County Medical Examiner's office. "I'm not authorized to give you a copy of the autopsy report," she said, taking her time with each word. Her long, shiny *Alice in Wonderland* hair was tied with a dainty blue ribbon with rickrack edges. That was the good news. The bad was she had a rectangle of a face—along with such a thick neck she looked as if she was the result of her mother's quickie with a Lipizzaner stallion.

"I understand that you can't hand over the actual report," I replied. "But this is for Shorehaven Library's *oral*-history project."

We both glanced at the red light on the tape recorder I'd set on her desk between us. Dr. Spiros moistened her lips with her tongue. "It's not a matter of documentation," I explained. "What I'm trying to capture here is the reality of a single death, a view from all perspectives of the passing of one citizen of Shorehaven. From Deirdre Gidding's friends and colleagues to her minister who gave the eulogy to . . . well, to the officials charged with investigating that death." Naturally, I didn't add that if news of this little caper got back to Shorehaven Library's administrator, Snively Sam, I'd be out of a job. I pressed on. "I understand she left a note?"

Dr. Spiros pressed her hands together, prayer-like, and held them demurely under her chin. "I'm not authorized . . ." Her nails, disturbingly long for a pathologist's, were a hideous purplish orangey-pink, about the color of a plastic flamingo at twilight.

I reached out and switched off the recorder. "On background," I said boldly, crossing my legs, more Rosalind Russell–*His Girl Friday* than historian. Except two seconds later my heart started to race. It demanded what my brain hadn't permitted itself to ask: What the hell was I doing here? Each heartbeat was more powerful than the one before until my entire chest was filled with what felt like a life-threatening hammering. "I want to get the big picture," I was telling her. Was I nuts? Any minute she'd come to her senses and toss me out on my ear.

"The suicide note said something like 'I can't take it anymore,'" she was saying. "'It's got to end.' That's about it."

"Was it signed?"

"Yes. Signed 'Deirdre.' On her personal stationery."

"Was it handwritten?" She nodded. "Was she carrying it with her?" I got a blank look. "In her handbag or her coat pocket. When she was at Bloomingdale's."

"No. It was . . ." She glanced at me, a little too suspiciously but, unable to figure out my angle, she continued. "In a manila folder right in her top desk drawer. The drawer was open slightly. The file was marked 'Personal Papers.' Her marriage certificate was in there. Her divorce decree. In a sense, she'd assembled her whole relationship with Stanley Giddings in that file."

I turned on the recorder again. "I'd like to go over what's been released publicly." She nodded, then lifted her hair and let it fall back onto her shoulders. Clearly, and not without reason, she considered it her best feature. "How many pills did she take?" I inquired.

"Our estimate is about thirty."

"Do you actually see them when you do the autopsy?"

"The pills? No. They were dissolved. But we can ascertain from the blood chemistry . . ."

"How do you know someone didn't just grind up thirty Nembutal and sprinkle them over her Raisin Bran?"

Her patronizing smile was barely more than a puff of air blown past compressed lips. "That's where the police investigation comes in," she explained, too patiently. "They tell us there was a suicide note on her own paper, in her own handwriting—believe me, that was checked out—signed by her. They tell us her friends reported she was depressed over the breakup of her marriage. They find out she was having serious business reverses. And she had a new boyfriend, except she'd broken a series of dates with him."

"What does that mean?"

"It's often a sign of depression," Dr. Spiros said.

"Maybe it's a sign he was a dork and she wanted to lose his number," I replied. She inched forward in her chair. I sensed she was about to lose my number. "If you wanted to end it all," I asked quickly, "would you do it in a public place?"

Empathy did not seem to be Dr. Spiros's strong suit. Instead of looking contemplative, her horse face grew even longer with concern: Had she made an egregious bureaucratic boo-boo by agreeing to talk with me? "Lots of people kill themselves in public places," she asserted. "They jump from buildings and bridges, they—"

"In a shoe department, holding a sling-back?"

"The effects of the barbiturate aren't immediate. She might have decided to distract herself rather than lying down and just, you know, waiting for it to happen."

"Who from Homicide is in charge . . ." Suddenly, I had such a lump in my throat I could not complete the sentence.

"Detective-Sergeant Andrew Kim," she replied, and gave her hair a definitive flip. Interview over.

I suppose an explanation of my emotional reaction at the mention of the Nassau County Police Department's Homicide Bureau is in order. All right, it's like this. Twenty years earlier, shortly before I passed over to the dark side of thirty-five, at a time when my now-lawyer daughter and film-critic son were little more than toddlers, a local periodontist named M. Bruce Fleckstein was murdered. I recall hearing about it on the radio and thinking: Who could have done such a thing? The next thing I knew I was investigating. Before too long I actually was instrumental in determining just who the killer was. But in the course of my detective work, I came into contact with a real detective, Lieutenant Nelson Sharpe of the Nassau County Police Department.

To make a long story short, I had an affair with him. That was it. Six months of faithlessness in a twenty-eight-year marriage. Even for a historian like me, aware of the significance of the past, it should have been ancient history—except I fell in love with Nelson. And he with me. For a time we even discussed leaving our spouses, getting married. We simply couldn't bear being without each other. Not just for the erotic joy, but for the sheer fun we had together. But even more than my secret belief that a marriage that rises from the ashes of other marriages is doomed from the start was our mutual, acknowledged awareness of what our leaving would do to our children. At the time, my daughter Kate was six, my son Joey four. Nelson had three kids of his own. And so he stayed with his wife June and I remained with Bob Singer. Nelson and I never saw or spoke to each other. Twenty years.

"If you want my opinion," Nancy Miller began later that evening.

"No," I said. I definitely do not."

"Hush," she commanded southernly. Her telephone voice was splendid, pure magnolia blossom, the sort that in her reporting days evoked in an interviewee an overwhelming desire to be indiscreet. "My opinion is that your going to the Medical Examiner's offices to interview Dr. Horse-face was just an excuse."

"Right," I said. "A ploy to get closer to Nassau County law enforcement so I could somehow contrive to see Nelson Sharpe and rekindle a twenty-year-old flame that still burns brightly despite the pathetic depletion of the estrogen that fueled it?" My usual six-thirty, end-of-the-workday Hour of Fatigue was upon me. Bad enough when you have a husband for whom you have to prepare the eight thousandth dinner of your marriage. Worse when you don't and you lack the energy to even dump the egg drop soup from its single-serving cardboard container into a bowl before you microwave it. "Give me a break, Nancy."

"You don't deserve a break on this. Except I'll give you one. I spoke to the reporter on the Deirdre suicide. He heard something about her business reverses."

"Doesn't it bother you that the authorities are so quick to label a high-powered woman's death as a suicide?"

"Might I remind you your friend Deirdre left a note? Might I remind you as well that her beloved Stan, he of the power pecker, had only recently deserted her for a younger woman? Might I also add I have information about her business problems that could prove to be the final nail in her coffin as far as your murder theory is concerned? Might you be interested?"

"Go ahead." I held my excitement in check. Pretty calmly, I thought, I stuck the soup in the microwave and cradled the phone against my shoulder while I worked to get the wire handle off the carton of sautéed tofu and broccoli so I could zap that too.

"Deirdre lost Sveltburgers."

"What in God's name are you talking about?"

"Sveltburgers. *Sveltburgers!*" Nancy repeated. "They're famous."

"Not in my universe."

"They're veggie burgers, you ignoramus. Made around here. In Commack or Center Moriches, Cutchogue or one of those C places I've never been to. Instead of being those flat things that look like a hockey puck, they're thick, so they look like a real hamburger. You never heard of Sveltburgers?" I hate when the person I'm talking to acts stunned by my ignorance, like when my son, Joey, a movie critic for the *très chic*, near-insolvent 'zine called *night* gasped and demanded: "You call yourself a movie-lover and you never heard of H. Peter Putzel?"

"I don't know," I muttered. "Sveltburgers? Maybe I have."

"I thought you were a historian. Sveltburgers are a Long Island legend."

"I'm obviously not as good a historian as I think I am."

"This woman, Polly Terranova—How's that for a mixed metaphor?—built Sveltburgers into a multimillion-dollar company from something she started in her kitchen in Levittown." Nancy waited for me to say, Oh, yeah, right. I've heard of her. I didn't, so she continued. "She signed on with Panache for some kind of package deal—office help, factory workers. Anyway, her story is the accountant Deirdre got for her was a complete incompetent and now she's in trouble with the IRS. Also, she's claiming the factory workers were drop-outs from some drug rehab program and kept nodding off when operating the machinery. The FDA health inspectors found pieces of fingers in the Sveltburgers."

"Then they're not vegetarian." The bell dinged and I took the container of soup from the microwave.

"Right. Anyway, Pissed-off Polly told our reporter Deirdre was completely unresponsive to her complaints because she was too busy obsessing over the failure of her marriage."

"If Deirdre was obsessed with the failure of her marriage, then losing the Sveltburger account wouldn't make her OD on Nembutal. And while we're at it, if Power Pecker's leaving her was so devastating, how come she had herself a new boyfriend?"

"I'm only reporting what the reporter told me," Nancy snapped. "According to him, Polly told the cops that when she pulled her business out of Panache, Deirdre was *shattered*."

Shattered? Fine, shattered. For the next few days, having other fish to fry, I gave the cops the benefit of the doubt and let Deirdre rest in whatever peace suicides are permitted. I taught my three classes at Saint Elizabeth's, then put on my other hat and recorded an interview with a retired gardener, an eighty-five-year-old man who had come to Shorehaven from Umbria to work in the greenhouses of one of the grand old estates in nearby Manhasset.

But by Saturday night of that week, sometime after watching *Radio Days* for the hundredth time and discovering (and devouring) seven miniature Mounds bars left over from Halloween and reading an article in a history journal on the formation of the Women's Trade Union League in 1903, I decided Deirdre Giddings's demise still needed looking into.

So on Sunday I went into the city, to Soho and the Acadia-Fensterheim Gallery. "Group show" a banner hanging outside proclaimed. The group in question included two finger paintings by Ryn, the newest Mrs. Giddings—a tidbit I'd come up with after going through a half-dozen issues of *ArtNews* at the library.

I hate when people contemplate a work of art, say an abstract-expressionist painting, and then make nincompoop remarks like "My three-year-old kid could do the same thing." Nevertheless, I spent five minutes in the high-ceilinged, white-walled gallery studying Ryn's "Purple Opinion" and saw nothing in the swirl of four fingers and one thumb that Kate or Joey could not have brought home from Temple Beth Israel Nursery School.

"Like it?" a man's voice inquired. He was in his twenties, with the requisite Soho shaved head and unshaven face, so I concluded his question was not a pick-up line. He was either an Acadia-Fensterheim employee or an admirer of Ryn's *oeuvre*. I nodded with what I hoped was a combination of enthusiasm and reverence. "Are you familiar with Ryn's work?" he asked.

"No. Is the name some reference to Rembrandt van Rijn?"

He glanced around: It was only us. "The truth? Her name's *Karyn* with a *Y*. Her last name is—was—Bleiberman."

"And now?"

"Now it's—" He lifted his head and pursed his lips to signify snootiness, although he did it in an appropriately ironic Gen-X manner. "—Giddings."

I gave him an I-get-it nod and inquired: "How much is the painting?" Apparently it wasn't *de rigueur* to actually speak of price, but he was kind enough to hand me a list. "Purple Opinion" was going for sixteen thousand. I said: "I hope this doesn't sound incorrigibly crass, but—"

"Isn't that somewhat high for a painting made with fingers? She's not Chuck Close, right?" He looked to see if I'd gotten his reference, so I nodded my appreciation. "It's not high at all, to tell you the truth," he went on. "Ryn spends an incredible amount of time prepping the canvas to give it the *appearance* of paper."

I offered some vague sound of comprehension, like "Aaah." We both gazed respectfully at the purple whorls. "Is she from around here?" I asked.

"Well, she has a studio in Williamsburgh, but these days . . ." He smiled and shook his head with a clearly unresolved mix of condescension and awe. "She's living out on Long Island. She's married to a rich older guy . . ." He hesitated for an instant, perhaps unsure whether it was chivalrous to say "older" to someone as old as I. "They have a mansion," he confided.

"A mansion?" I repeated, appropriately wowed.

"It has a stable!" he declared. "*And* he gave her a five-carat diamond ring. Like, is that a statement or what? Not that any of those things would make a dent in Ryn's consciousness. You know? I mean, when I spoke to her after she first saw the place, you know the only thing she mentioned? The quality of the light."

"So she works out there?"

"Well, right now she's not working."

"Taking a rest after this?" I inquired, waving my hand toward "Purple Opinion" and "Green Certainty."

"Getting ready to have a baby. She's due any second. I mean, when we had the opening two weeks ago, we were all praying she wouldn't . . ." He shuddered as if seeing a puddle of amniotic fluid on the gallery's polyurethaned oak floor. I thanked him and, price list neatly folded in my handbag, hurried off to catch the 4:18 back to Shorehaven.

It wasn't until eleven that night, defeated by the lower left-hand corner of the Sunday *Times* crossword puzzle, that it occurred to me that when Stan Giddings married Ryn, she had been close to six months pregnant. A pregnant piece of information, but what did it mean? Having spent twenty-eight years married and only two widowed, I still wasn't used to having some late-night question pop into my head and not being able to ask, *What do you make of this?* Even if the reaction was a mumbled *I dunno* or even an antagonistic *What business is it of yours, Judith?*, it was enough of a response for me to begin either to start speculating silently or to think *Beats the hell out of me* and drift off to sleep.

Plainly, Bob would not have taken well to my inquiring into the death of Deirdre Giddings. Like the last time around, twenty years earlier, when I got involved in investigating the Fleckstein murder: At his best he'd been exceedingly aggravated with me. At his worst, enraged. For him, my business was to be his wife. A historian? Why not? He lived in an era in which powerful men's wives did not churn butter. They held jobs, the more prestigious the better, though not so prestigious as to outshine their husbands.

But even if I couldn't have asked *Do you think Ryn's six-months-pregnant marriage means anything?* without getting a harsh rejoinder, I still couldn't bear the loss of him. Late Sunday nights hurt the most. I yearned to be a wife, to hear Bob's sleepy voice murmuring *G'night* as he turned over, to sense the warmth of his body across a few inches of bed, to smell the fabric softener on his pajamas. Of course, if I'd have left him and married Nelson, he and I would be riveted, sitting up discussing—*Stop!*

Over the years I'd become my own tough cop, policing myself from crossing the line from the occasional loving or lustful memory of Nelson to hurtful fantasy: What is he doing now? Still married? Is he happy? Would it be so terrible to call him and offhandedly say, "You just popped into my head the other day and I was wondering . . ." *Stop!*

The next morning, on my way to Saint Elizabeth's, I dropped by the house of my semi-friend Mary Alice Mahoney Hunziger Schlesinger Goldfarb—the woman who talked more than any other in Greater New York and said the least. Annoying? Truly. Vacuous? Definitely. Stupid? Indubitably. However, somehow her pea-brain was optimally structured for the absorption and retention of every item of Shorehaven gossip that wafted through the air, no matter how vague. So I asked her: "How come Stan Giddings waited until Ryn was six months pregnant to marry her?"

"It's a looong story," Mary Alice began. Awaiting the arrival of her personal trainer, she was decked out in cornflower blue Spandex shorts and tank top with a matching cornflower blue terry headband. Clearly, irrationally, she was proud of her body. Her arms had the approximate diameter of the cardboard tube inside a roll of toilet tissue. Her hip bones protruded farther than her breasts. "A *very* long story."

"I have to get going in ten minutes, Mary Alice. I have a class."

"My trainer is due then. Tucker? You know him?" She rolled her eyes to let me know how out of it I was. "I mean, he's only *the* most well-known trainer on the North Shore. God, you're an intellectual in an ivory tower! Deirdre used him, you know." She sighed. Not a mere exhalation of air, but the drawn-out vocalization a bad actress would make if she'd read a bracketed *sighing* in a script. "What can I tell you? Deirdre knew Ryn was—" Mary Alice gazed ceilingward, searching for the right words. "—*avec* child, like the French say, and she wanted to put the pressure on Stan."

"To get a good settlement?"

"Well, *of course*," she responded, a bit impatiently. Ours was not a natural friendship. Like cell mates, Mary Alice and I had come together while doing time—in our case, as class mothers years earlier. "Naturally," she went on, "Deirdre signed a prenup." Mary Alice, on her fourth marriage, this one to Lance Goldfarb, urologist to Long Island's best and brightest, obviously knew prenuptial agreements. She took the blue sweater that had been draped over a chair and arranged it artfully around her skeletal shoulders. "I mean, someone with Stan's resources isn't going to go into a marriage without protection, is he?"

"He obviously went into Ryn without protection."

"Can you *believe* that? Well, I can, as a matter of fact. He'd had two kids with his first wife but they weren't working out. Neurotic or dyslexic or something. And Deirdre couldn't have any. Or wouldn't. Whatever. Anyhow, Stan was absolutely dying for a family."

"Isn't that a little risky? I mean, getting your girlfriend pregnant while you're still married to someone else."

Mary Alice blew out an impatient gust of air. "Grow up, Judith."

"What am I pathetically naive about?"

"About that sooner or later he'd get out of the marriage without fatal damage because he had an air-tight prenup. And that if Ryn had the baby before they were married, big damn deal. She's an *artist*. Do you think artists care about having a child being a bastard or a non-bastard?"

"You've got a point," I conceded. "But Stan's not an artist, so he would want the baby to be legitimate. Ergo, Deirdre knew time was on her side."

Mary Alice gave a weary nod which said: *Finally* she's getting it. It's so annoying to be condescended to by a birdbrain. "Right," she said. "She didn't need her lawyer to tell her it was time to put the squeeze on Stan. Trust me. Deirdre got the picture. And she wound up with the house *and* the pied-à-terre on Central Park West *and* enough cash to choke a horse, except she needed it because she was going to redecorate plus get the works: face-lift, tummy tuck, tush tightening, and lipo, lipo, and more lipo. Maybe implants. I can't remember if I heard she wanted them."

"Did she get all that done?" I asked. The last time I'd seen Deirdre, a couple of months before she died, she hadn't looked as if she needed anything tightened or implanted, though for all I know I might have been looking at the results.

"No, no, no. She met someone."

"Who?"

"Do you want some ginger tea?"

"No thanks. Whom did she meet?"

"His name is Tony. Like in Tony Bennett." Mary Alice's white-blonde hair was pulled up into a pretty topknot, and she twisted it around her index finger, a gesture that led me to believe Tony was not unattractive.

"What's Tony's last name?"

"Tony Marx."

"As in Karl?"

"What?"

"Never mind. Did you ever meet him?"

"No. I mean, yes. See, she also got the country club member-ship as part of the settlement, which I hear just about *killed* Stan because his grandfather had been a founder. Very, very rare for the wife to get the membership, which shows you how much Stan was willing to give to get out of that marriage. He and Ryn are living in the grandfather's house now. Way out in Lloyd's Neck. Practically a chateau I hear. It's called Giddings House, but it needs *major* fixing up. It'll take *years*. That's why Deirdre didn't want any part of it. Anyhow, I know someone like you with a Ph.D. doesn't take country clubs seriously, Judith, but they mean a lot to people. Anyhow, Lance and I were there as the Shays' guests—" She gave her wedding band, a knuckle-to-knuckle diamond dazzler, a twist. "They don't accept Jews as members." She paused, waiting for a response. I offered none so she explained: "Lance is Jewish."

"I guessed it, Mary Alice. The 'Goldfarb' was a clue."

"That's why we were there as *guests*."

"So you just happened to see this Tony there with Deirdre?"

"Right. Well, we chatted for a few minutes. He was wearing a sports jacket in the teeniest houndstooth. I mean, when you first looked at it, you'd think charcoal gray, not black and white. Cashmere. Stunning detail. You could tell—"

"What does Tony do?"

"He owns a car dealership."

"What kind?"

"Volvo. He kidded around and called it Vulva. Well, I guess not to his customers."

"Is it here on the Island?" She nodded. "How serious was Deirdre about him?"

"How serious?" Mary Alice chewed her thin but well-glossed lower lip, then smoothed over the chewed area with her pinky. "It's serious in that he's very, *very* attractive. But not so serious because he only owns one dealership." I must have looked confused because she exhaled impatiently: "Forget that he's not in Stan Giddings's league moneywise. He wasn't even in *Deirdre's* league. So how serious could she be about a man who couldn't earn as much as she could? No, she'd let the relationship play out, which might take her through the summer. That way, she'd have someone for mixed doubles, then in September she'd just get busy with her business or whatever, then go away after Christmas and come back and get her plastic surgery over with so that by the next summer she could really be a contender. You very well know what I mean, Judith, so don't look like 'Duh?'. Contender: be eligible for a really important guy."

"So then why did she kill herself?" I asked.

Mary Alice shrugged. "Maybe what everyone's saying is right. Losing Stan and Sveltburgers just took too much out of her. When all you want is to die of a broken heart and you don't, what do you do?"

"What?"

"Suicide!" she said brightly.

Just as I opened the door to leave, Tucker the trainer ambled in. He was an exceedingly muscular but very short man, not much longer than his gym bag. Yes, he said slowly when I asked him, he had seen Deirdre the morning of her death. Not only had she not been in the zone, she'd actually cut their session short when she glanced out the window of her workout room and spotted a silver Volvo, an S80, pulling into the driveway. When I asked if he'd seen who was driving the car, Tucker gazed up at me suspiciously. Fortunately, Mary Alice gave him a she's-okay pat on the deltoid, so he conceded: The boyfriend. Tony? I asked. Yeah, Tony.

That afternoon I got stuck in a particularly noxious history department meeting which ended with Medieval European shaking his fist at Modern Asian. The day after that I had a three-week pile of oral-history transcriptions at the library to contend with, so I didn't get to Volvo Village until the following morning. I felt I was losing not only time, but ground. If there was anything fishy about Deirdre's death, the person or persons responsible had had more than enough time to execute an exquisite cover-up.

I suppose dealing with the American public in the highly emotional arena of car-buying can make someone inured to surprise, so Tony Marx did not think it at all odd that I wanted to trade in my 1998 Jeep for a 1999 Volvo or that I wanted to talk about Deirdre. "I don't know if Deirdre ever mentioned me—" I said.

"Of course she did," he said courteously, clearly never having heard my name.

"I'm so upset," I told him. "I still can't believe it."

"I know." Except for a bit of a paunch, he was a sleek man in his early forties, with the sort of lifelong, worked-at tan that turns skin to leather. In Tony's case, it was a butter-soft pecan-colored leather. "You're looking to unload the Jeep for a V70 AWD, Judy?" he asked.

"Pardon me?"

"All-wheel drive."

"Right." His dress was conservative—gray suit, white shirt, maroon rep tie—the get-up someone selling safety and solidity would put on. He himself, though, tall, slender, graceful, and sloe-eyed, was keeping his inborn flash under control. He should have been selling Maseratis. "Deirdre told me you were the man to see about a car." He nodded. "She seemed to think the world of you," I went on. I expected him to nod again and move on to the turbo charger, whatever that was, but instead he swallowed hard. "Was she . . ." I began. "I apologize. I shouldn't ask."

"It's okay," he responded. "Depressed? Yeah. But not like, you know, depressed-depressed."

"Not suicidal?" I asked softly.

"No! I mean, when they told me, I thought it was some sick joke. Except I knew it was real because it was a couple of cops who came here and told me. Asked me questions. They had to. Because she died at Bloomie's, not, like, in a hospital."

"Was she depressed about the Sveltburger business?"

His head moved from side to side. "Depressed, angry. Why shouldn't she be angry?" The showroom lights that brought out the gleam of his Volvos made his dark brown hair shine. His eyes appeared moist, too, but I couldn't tell if it was the lighting or tears. "It was so unfair. Like what was Deirdre supposed to do? Run Polly Terranova's business for her?" He answered his own question. "No. Deirdre did her job—got the employees. Polly or whoever Polly picked was supposed to supervise them."

"That was unfair," I agreed. Then, lowering my voice, I said: "Was Deirdre still *that* upset about her divorce?"

"No! At least, not to me she wasn't."

"When was the last time you saw her?" I inquired.

"The night before." Tony touched his paunch gently as if to help him recollect. "We went out to dinner. She'd just put me on a diet. High protein." His eyes grew damper. A tear formed in the corner of his left eye and meandered down his cheek. "She told me I was . . ." He stopped and took a deep breath to compose himself ". . . insulin-resistant. That's how come so much protein."

"The explanation about the suicide," I said as gently as possible. "It doesn't feel right to me. Could she have been upset about something else? Some other business thing? Could someone she knew have been giving her a hard time?"

"No," he said firmly. "She would've said something to me. We had a completely—" He blinked back another potential tear. "We talked all the time."

On the way back to Shorehaven, having vowed to think about the all-wheel drive's viscous coupling, I bought myself a cup of coffee and sat in my Jeep in the parking lot of a Starbucks. Snow began to fall, just enough to frost the windshield, so I gazed ahead into its soothing whiteness. Tony's deal wasn't good enough to tempt me. Neither was Tony. However, I was touched by the tear that trickled down his cheek—although my sentiment was tempered by the fact that he'd lied to me about when he'd last seen Deirdre. On the last morning of Deirdre's life, she had told Tucker the trainer to leave because she'd seen Tony driving up. Tucker himself had seen Tony. Yet Tony had told me the last time he'd seen her was at dinner the night before, when she put him on a diet. Unless Tucker was the one who wasn't telling the truth.

I warmed my hands on the cup and sipped the coffee. Tony seemed genuinely upset by Deirdre's death. Still, I remembered Nelson telling me that if he had a buck for every tear shed by killers he'd be the richest guy on Long Island. But why would Tony want to kill Deirdre? Actually, why would anyone? For once I stopped being my own bad cop and let myself think about Nelson. I asked him. Okay, what was to be gained by her death? He counseled: Approach it by thinking about each person she had a relationship with. I probably did something humiliating, like nodding and smiling at him—

good idea!—because I recall how relieved I felt that the window was snowed over.

All right, what about Tony? If he hated Deirdre, he could simply stop going out with her . . . unless, of course, she knew some dark secret about this business or his sexuality and was blackmailing him. If Nelson were really beside me he'd be shaking his head: Far-fetched. Keep it on your list, but make it last. Move on.

Polly Terranova? From the bit of research I'd done, it seemed that nothing—not even the doofus accountant and the doped-up assembly line workers sent out by Panache—could stop the inex-orable march of Sveltburgers into America's freezers. Polly might be angry, but she could better get even by taking away her business than by offering Deirdre a Nembutalburger.

Stan Giddings? He might have wanted to get rid of Deirdre in order to marry Ryn, but that had been months earlier. It had proba-bly cost him above and beyond what his prenuptial contract speci-fied. But she hadn't bankrupted him, not by a long shot: He was still loaded enough to give Ryn a five-carat ring and to be refurbishing Giddings House.

Ryn? Again, she might have wished to get rid of the second Mrs. Giddings so she could become the third sooner rather than later. But for once, I thought, Mary Alice was right. It wouldn't matter to someone like Ryn whether a child was born in or out of wedlock. Admittedly, if Deirdre had dug in her heels and tried to sue Stan over the prenup claiming whatever about-to-be exes usually claim, the baby could be born and Stan might have second thoughts. Sure, he'd support the kid, but support didn't mean a five-carat rock and a house with a name for its mother. So it was in Ryn's interest to marry Stan as quickly as she could. Since she had done that, there was no reason to risk killing Deirdre Giddings.

I turned on the windshield wipers. The snow was fluffy and dry, a benevolent end-of-winter snow sent to remind the impatient yearning for spring how ravishing winter can be. I felt one of those by now-familiar waves of sadness crash over me, being alone, with no one to share the beauty. Sure, at the end of the day, I could call one of my children, or Nancy, and describe the fat, silent snowflakes descending on Starbucks, but the "Oh, nice!" that I'd get would be syllables of charity. Well, to tell the truth, Bob would not have been seized by ecstasy either. I put the Jeep into reverse and backed out to go home.

Until I thought of the first Mrs. Giddings. Barbara. Who, according to Bell-Atlantic Information—which probably had only cost me thirty dollars on my cell phone—lived at 37 Bridle Path West in Shorehaven Acres. Shorehaven Half-Acres would be more exact. And as for the so-called bridle path, it was, like Cotillion Way and Andover Road that crossed it, an allusion to a way of life that the residents themselves had probably never experienced. Still, it was a pleasant development of neo-colonials and putative Tudors. The pathetic little saplings planted in the sixties had grown into fine oaks and august gingkos. It all looked perfectly nice—except for Barbara Giddings's house.

Even the camouflage of snow couldn't hide the neglect. The driveway had deep gouges; chunks of asphalt lay around these holes as if the driveway had been strafed. The house itself was even more forlorn, its white-painted clapboard peeling. Once it must have been a dark red because carmine patches blotched the white facade like some dreadful skin condition.

Barbara Giddings wasn't in such good shape either. At two in the afternoon, her frizz of bleached hair was flattened on one side. Her eyes had the blinky look of someone wanting not to be caught napping. Nevertheless, she hadn't had the energy to pull back her slumping shoulders. Her blue eyes and small, pouty lips indicated she had probably once been pretty, although her face was now so puffy it was impossible to tell if it had been in a Sandra Dee or Kim Novak way. I felt if I went into my now-familiar vaudeville routine—library, oral history, important contribution—it would wipe her out. So I just whipped out a pad and muttered something about just having only a few questions about Deirdre Giddings.

"I don't think . . . I should call my lawyer," she said. Surprise. I had expected a voice of the living dead, but she had the rich, cultivated tones of an announcer on a classical music station. So I performed my vaudeville act. And she invited me inside.

After ten years of wear and a couple of kids, the house was less neglected than simply rundown. We sat on her living room couch covered with one of those beige slipcovers you see in catalogues that are supposed to look fashionably shabby, as if your great-grandparents had old money, but which, sadly, look as though you have a battered couch you can't afford to replace.

"Would you mind if I record . . ." She shook her head so vehemently, I quickly said, "Just for background then," and sat forward, hands in my lap. "Were you surprised by Deirdre's death?"

"No."

"How come?"

Her lips compressed in disapproval until they looked like a pale prune. "She was always a pill-popper."

"Deirdre?"

A quick, dismissive, almost cruel laugh—heh—meant to tell me how uninformed I was. "Yes. Deirdre. You know those long, Monday to Sunday pill cases?" she asked. I nodded. "She carried *two* of them in her purse. And that was in the days, let me tell you, that she should have been flying high on her own accord. That was when she was carrying on with Stan—lunch, dinner, no wonder she never had a weight problem. She never ate, just banged her brains out." Barbara's words may have been coarse, but her voice sounded so cultivated. You expected to hear *Haydn's Symphony Number 96 in D major*, so what she did say was doubly jarring. But she made me feel so sad, too. With her defeated posture and straw hair, Barbara Giddings had the despondent air of a welfare mother who no longer has the energy to hope. All her aspects didn't add up. It was like a game show and I couldn't figure out which contestant was the real Barbara.

"Do you know what kind of pills?" I asked. "Did she have some illness?"

"Illness?" she laughed. "Diet pills. Amphetamines, I suppose. And downers. And who knows what else. But two pill cases. A blue and a yellow."

"Do you believe it really was suicide?" I tried to sound offhand.

"Do I believe it was suicide?" she demanded, irritably. Her pasty cheeks suddenly bloomed scarlet. "Do you think I give a good goddamn?"

"I'm sorry."

"No, no, *I'm* sorry," she quickly apologized, trying to comb her hair behind her ears with her fingers. "What can I tell you? It's one thing to take someone's husband away. Fair and square in the game of love and all that." She managed a small smile, but her combing grew more intense, so she was almost raking her scalp. "I mean, Stan had it all: looks, charm, intelligence. And money." I made myself keep looking at her and not at the graying rug under our feet that had once been some cheerier color. "Money," Barbara Giddings said. "There's a reason they call it the root of all evil."

"That's for sure," I mumbled, just to have something to say.

"She wasn't going to settle for Stan and his—his wealth and social position. No, Deirdre had to have everything."

"Everything?"

"Everything."

"How did she go about it?" I inquired. I was a little nervous that all of a sudden she'd come to her senses and think: Why in God's name am I talking like this to a stranger? Instead, she seemed relieved I was there, to sit on her couch and be a witness to the outrage that had been perpetrated against her.

"How? She manipulated Stan—trust me, he was a babe in the woods and she knew just how to take him over. She got him to con me into signing a divorce agreement that gave me next to nothing. You couldn't bring up two hamsters, much less kids—one who just happens to have ADD—on what I'm getting. Stan gave me a song and dance about how he wanted to give me the money off the books, you know, like under the table. For tax purposes. What did I know? I was just the ex-maid."

"You'd been working as a—"

"No!" she barked, suddenly showing so much spirit it seemed as though some passionate doppelgänger had supplanted her on the couch. "I was going to Stony Brook! Studying botany. I got a summer job after sophomore year helping out their gardener. Not in a lab, but what the hell, at least it paid. But the story got out that Stan had eloped with the *maid*. I could never shake it."

"How come your lawyer allowed you to go along with the money-under-the-table business?"

"Please. Stan got me my lawyer. A kid from one of the law firms that Atlantic Hosiery used. Atlantic is Stan's family's company. Need I say more?"

I shook my head, but that didn't stop Barbara Giddings's rant. For the next three-quarters of an hour, I heard how Stan's visits to his children dwindled from twice a week to once every month or two—because of pressure from Deirdre. How Deirdre got Stan to hire an architect from Los Angeles to design a new house in Shore-haven Estates. How Deirdre had Stan employ a chauffeur and how the chauffeur would drive in her personal shopper from Manhattan with trunks full of clothes. Prada. Comme des Garcons. Zoran for at-home. Size six. Alligator handbags with gold clasps. A wall of shoes, size seven-and-a-half. How Deirdre was much too much for Stan. How she'd made him over, from the tips of his once-machine-made shoes to the top of his beginning-to-bald head. Italian handmade loafers. Hair plugs. Private wine-tasting lessons. How she'd taken an ordinary rich Joe whose greatest joy had been his fifty-yard-line box at Giants' games and yearly golf weekend at Pebble Beach and trans-formed him into croquet-playing Social Man who either dined out every night with friends who weren't really friends or who hosted dinner parties in his new waterfront mansion for corporate types who were . . . Here Barbara stopped to take a breath to propel the words out . . . Deirdre's clients!

At last I drove off, relieved to be out of a house that smelled like dirty laundry, grateful to get away from Barbara's fixation. Not on her ex-husband, the man she'd presumably loved, the man who'd bam-boozled her. But on the Other Woman. It was one thing to be aware of a rival's key asset, a law degree from Harvard or a hand-span waist. Quite another to know she had fourteen size-six suits in her closet.

Two hours later I demanded: "Could Barbara Giddings be gullible enough to believe that a man who's cheated on you with another woman, who's leaving you for her, who's sticking you and your children in a house that probably costs about the same as the Hepplewhite breakfront in your former dining room . . . could she honestly believe he would honor an agreement to pay up under the table?" I was sitting beside Nancy's desk at *Newsday* watching her perform microsurgery on somebody's op-ed essay on government subsidies for the arts. I'd never been to see her at work before and was both dazzled and comforted that the newsroom I'd walked through actually looked like all the newsrooms in movies.

"You know what the answer is," Nancy replied, but gently. She understood I had not dropped by to shoot the breeze. With three clicks of her mouse, she highlighted a paragraph on her computer screen and, with one dismissive tap of a key, deleted it. "Yes. Barbara Giddings could be that gullible," she replied. "If all you're offered is a lie and you're desperate for hope, when you're fucked up the ass you tell yourself you're queen of the May and the thing up your ass is a maypole."

"I know," I conceded. "But is she telling the truth? Could she actually have been given a generous settlement and blown it at the racetrack or on some gigolo or a bad investment? And as far as Deirdre goes . . . Barbara has a dull, lost look, like 'What do I do now that Deirdre's dead? Whom can I hate?' What I want to know is if what I saw was an act or the real thing."

"You mean Barbara's really a conniving, murdering bitch?"

"I mean, was she telling me the truth? *Was* Deirdre so into drugs? Could you just ask the reporter who's—"

"Shit on a stick, Judith!" But after glaring at me she picked up the phone. Two minutes later—and some whispered prompting by me—she hung up and declared: "The only drug they found in her system was the Nembutal that killed her. Yes, she did have two pill cases in her handbag. Mostly those big mothers, megavitamins. And a couple of Xanax. The only prescriptions in her name were for the Nembutal, Xanax, and Halcion, you know, the sleeping pill."

"Did they find the Nembutal bottle?" I demanded.

"I didn't ask. I am not going to call him again and have him think Lord knows what—that I'm after his job, or him."

"Then call the cops," I said softly. Nancy shook her head. "I swear to you, Nan, I'm not using this as a devious way to get to Nelson."

"Like hell."

"The police must have a PR person. Just find out if they found the bottle. Also, get the prescription dates and anything else about her drugs."

It's often eye-opening to watch a friend doing what she does for a living: Her authority is so startling, you forget the complex and often vulnerable woman and see only the champ. For someone calling cold, Nancy was amazingly adroit. Hi! Nancy Miller from *Newsday* Viewpoints. We're thinking of running a piece on suicide with a mention of the Deirdre Giddings case. Direct, businesslike, but still, she was laying on the Georgia peach jam so thick I could tell she was talking to a man. When she hung up she reported: "No Nembutal bottle. They surmise she must have thrown it out on her way to Bloomingdale's."

"That's one hell of a surmise."

"The Nembutal prescription was from March '98. The Halcion is from this January."

"Call him back."

"No."

"Please. Find out where Stan and Tony Marx and Barbara Giddings and Ryn were the day she died."

"In a pig's eye."

Call-Me-Mike, Nancy's new conquest in the Nassau County Police Department's PR office, phoned her back a half-hour later, during which time I watched her eviscerate the essay on her screen and call the writer to inform her of having made a couple of minor edits. Call-Me-Mike told her—off the record—that Ryn had gone to her obstetrician in the morning, then had Stan's chauffeur drive her into the city, to the Acadia-Fensterheim Gallery in Soho where, presumably, she admired her own work. Tony Marx went from his condo to his Volvo dealership, a fact which did not square with what Tucker the Trainer had told me about seeing Tony's car drive up to the house. Stan was on a plane coming back from Palm Beach where he had spent the previous day looking at real estate. As for Barbara, well, she had not been interviewed.

"Would you stop it now?" Nancy snapped. Well, not quite snapped, but I could sense she was less than delighted with me. "Deirdre killed herself. Period. *She was not your friend.* You owe her nothing! She was a woman who was losing her husband, losing her big client, probably losing her looks if you got up close enough. Would you want to spend the rest of your life finding jobs for steam-fitters and sleeping with a guy who calls his car a Vulva? No, you'd OD and be done with it."

"I would not," I said as I stood. "And even if I were going to, would I take thirty Nembutal in the morning and then go shopping?" I put on my coat. "Or would I take them at a time a person would logically take a sleeping pill—the night before—and just fall asleep and never wake up?"

"Where are you going?" Nancy grilled me, in the manner of a parent sensing her child is about to do something reckless.

I gave her head a comforting pat. "Relax. I'm going to Mineola to look up some records."

"What kind of records?"

"Martha and the Vandellas. Public records, to see what information there is about Stan's divorces. I want to find out if the house Barbara is in now is the one she got stuck with ten years ago when Stan left . . . or if she had something better and lost it. Then I'll go back to the library to run a more thorough search on Ryn and Tony."

"Why?"

"Why? Because they seem like the sort of people who could possibly have checkered pasts. And because the alternative is my book group and they're doing *The Golden Notebook* which I've successfully avoided my entire life."

I drove west on the Long Island Expressway listening to a National Public Radio interview with an expert on lichens. He explained how lichens are formed by a fungus and an alga living together "intimately." The intimacy must have gotten to me because instead of driving to the County Clerk's office, I found myself heading for police headquarters. This is nuts, I told myself. What if

Nelson sees you? He'll think you've been stalking him for twenty years. Get out. Except I had an idea.

I gripped the wheel. Cool it, I ordered myself as I pulled into the parking lot. It's just a glimmering. Now what was the name of the guy from the police conducting the investigation? I'd only heard it from Dr. Horse Face and come across it a hundred times in the newspaper accounts, but naturally at the moment I wanted it, the particular neuron that had this cop's name on it refused to fire. Well, I could walk right in and ask and they'd say, Oh, it's Detective-Sergeant Whatever and I'd go to his office and just say, Hi, I'm a neighbor of Deirdre Giddings's and what do you think about this? I know it's just a theory but . . . Kim! That was his name! On one hand, maybe Detective-Sergeant Kim had enormous intellectual curiosity and would reopen the case. On the other hand, maybe he'd think I was demented. Or I'd go inside headquarters and my heart would be in my throat at the thought that I could possibly see Nelson and so I'd stand before Detective-Sergeant Kim and make hideous gurgling noises.

Naturally I was an utter wreck, wanting, not wanting, so I won't even describe my walking in there and finding Detective-Sergeant Kim's office, which took maybe four minutes but which felt like four years. It normally would have taken half that time, except I kept my head down just in case Nelson walked by, and I had to wait until I sensed the halls clear before I could look up and see the numbers on the doors.

"It's an interesting theory," Detective-Sergeant Kim remarked fifteen minutes later. He was a large man in his late thirties who looked as if he'd gained twenty pounds since the time he'd bought his suit. "And I appreciate your sharing it with me, Ms. Singer. Except for one thing."

"No one had any reason to want to kill her," I replied. He smiled, a gracious, be-nice-to-upper-middle-class-citizens smile. "At least no one had any reason at the time she died. On that score you're absolutely right. But what about four or five months before that?"

"What do you mean?" He looked less impatient than perplexed, which I took as a hopeful omen.

"If she wanted to kill herself, why would she take pills from an old prescription? She had a prescription for Halcion, so if she wanted to go to sleep permanently, why not take those?" He waited. He crossed his arms over his chest and tried to lean back, except his chair didn't want to. He gave up and rested his elbows on his desk. "Look," I went on, "say you want to kill Deirdre Giddings. Make it look like a suicide. What do you do? Well, you could slip a compromising letter on her note paper into a file marked personal papers, 'I can't take it anymore. It's got to end.' With her signature."

"Doesn't that sound like a suicide note to you?" he asked, still patient. I couldn't tell if he was a naturally easygoing man or a canny cop who used pleasantness as an investigatory technique.

"It could mean *anything* has got to end. It could have been a note to her housekeeper, that she's ironing on too high a heat and burning blouses right and left and it's got to end. To her secretary, that she's calling in sick too often. To her boyfriend, that it's over. Or to her husband, that his philandering or his lying or his late nights have got to end." Kim took a deep breath that looked as if it were meant to propel a sentence, so I talked faster. "To her husband's lover, to end the affair. To her husband's ex-wife—who seemed more than a little preoccupied with Deirdre—to stop snooping around town about what she's doing."

"So you're saying someone got her note and—if it wasn't the maid with the iron—they sneaked in and stuck it into her folder?" Kim had a sweet face with a pudgy chin and bright, dark eyes, but he raised one eyebrow in the cool, skeptical manner of a film noir antihero.

"No. I'm saying whoever did it did it months ago, when he or she had easier access to Deirdre's things, like her file of personal papers." Kim waited. The smile vanished. On the other hand, it wasn't replaced with a snarl. "It was done before the prescription for Halcion was written, before Deirdre's marriage was over. Was the note on top of the papers in the folder?"

"No," he said cautiously.

"So in the ensuing months, she just stuck other papers in there—like her divorce decree—and never saw the note."

"Okay, then what?" he asked slowly, trying to see where I was going. But there was not enough light for him to make it out.

"Look, if someone dies a suspicious death what happens? Guys like you look into it. You'll find out what people close to the victim were doing around the time of the death. So if you want to make a murder look like a suicide, the best thing to do is to distance yourself from the place and time of death as much as possible."

"What do you think happened?" Kim asked. It was less a request than a demand to put up or shut up.

"I'm not sure." This did not put the smile back on Kim's face. "Tony Marx lied to me and probably to you about not seeing Deirdre on the day she died." Before he could interject another question I explained: "Deirdre's personal trainer, a guy named Tucker, saw Tony driving up to her house that morning." His mouth opened slightly, that how—do—you—know—that gape. I kept going. "My guess is Tony had some trouble in the past and got frightened about being part of any investigation. That's why he lied about when he last saw her." I waited.

Kim finally said: "It's a matter of public record. An arrest for insurance fraud, second degree. Suspended sentence."

"Tony seems to have genuinely loved her." No reaction. "Now Barbara Giddings didn't love Deirdre, although she's obsessed with her. Knows the precise number of suits in her closet."

"So you're saying she had access?"

"I don't know. Deirdre and Stan lived in a huge, expensive house that must have a sophisticated alarm system. It would be hard to break in, although I concede Barbara might have been able to con a housekeeper or someone to let her in. But have you met Barbara Giddings?" Kim didn't respond, so I kept going. "She seems too dispirited to be able to pull off a maneuver that would take that kind of guts and inventiveness. My guess is she's got highly sensitive antennae that picks up any snippet of information that was around town about the second Mrs. Giddings."

"And the third Mrs. Giddings, the artist?" Kim inquired. He was listening, that was for sure. Sitting motionless: no paper clip bending, no pen chewing.

"Well, for Ryn, a clock was ticking. She was having a baby. Not that she'd be worried about it being born out of wedlock. It wasn't social stigma that concerned her. It was getting Stan to marry her. Once the baby was born, it would be a fact of life. Clearly, Stan would support it. But would he be willing to go through another divorce? Another marriage? There's no way Deirdre would have let him off cheap the way Barbara did. Ryn was running the risk that if a divorce dragged on for too long, Stan would lose interest. She'd wind up with a kid and child support. Sure, that would keep her in finger paints, but it wouldn't buy her a five-carat ring, a family manse, and a husband with the wherewithal to make her career happen."

"Any other suspects?" Kim tried to query lightly, as if amused, but he was too absorbed to pull off.

I sat forward in the stiff-backed chair and rested my arm on his desk as if we were two colleagues shooting the breeze. "I don't know the other people in Deirdre's life," I told him. "Did anyone strike you as having a motive? Anyone who might have wanted to get Deirdre out of the way?"

Kim caught himself before he answered, but not before he swiveled his head to the right, a prelude to a shake that would have told me, "No, no one." He was so annoyed at his lapse of control that he glanced at his watch, did a Damn-I'm-late-for-a-meeting push back from his desk. "I really have to go. Listen, Ms. Singer, what you told me: Interesting." He stood and inhaled to close his jacket. "Creative. Believe it or not, there's a lot of creativity in police work. But you have no evidence for your theory that it was a homicide. On the other hand, we have evidence—the note, people saying how depressed she was, the fact that the drug that killed her was one prescribed for her. All our evidence adds up to one thing—"

"The pills in those two cases she carried were mostly vitamins," I cut him off. "Megavitamins. Big capsules, a lot of them. Gelatin, or whatever for the outside, that dissolves in the stomach. Some of them, you can pull the two gelatin halves apart. It wouldn't take a pharmacological genius to grind up thirty Nembutal, stick the grindings into a capsule and slip it back into her pill case. Then go out of town, or do something to give you a good alibi just in case there was an investigation. But this is the thing. Deirdre didn't take that pill. How come? Maybe she read about some new study that too much Vitamin X leads to liver disease, or dry skin. Or maybe she was beside herself because she knew her husband was cheating on her, or maybe he'd actually asked for a divorce, and she stopped taking care of herself. Meanwhile, the killer is waiting for the kill. Except it doesn't happen. So what does he or she conclude?"

"What?" Kim asked, walking me to the door, but slowly.

"That she took it. That she probably had one of the longest naps on record, but it didn't kill her."

"So how come she finally did take the pill?" The question was tossed off casually enough, but he wasn't going anywhere. In fact, he lounged against the door frame.

"Maybe she read another study that said the earlier study was based on false methodology. Or maybe she was feeling better and getting back to her old, health-conscious routine. The point is, the killer wasn't going to try again because he or she got what he or she wanted."

"Which was?"

"Deirdre let Stan go." He smiled, a how-amusing smile, like a sophisticate in a Coward comedy. "Tell me, Sergeant Kim, who's your money on?"

"What?" The smile disappeared and he stood straight. Seeing he was about to step out into the hall, I stood in the doorway, blocking his way.

"Is it on Barbara Giddings?" I asked. "She was obsessed with Deirdre. She knew about the two pill cases. But she didn't know there were vitamins in them; she thought they were full of uppers and downers. And then there's the problem of access. Could Barbara really have gotten into Deirdre's handbag not once, but twice—to get the capsule, then to return it to the pill case?"

Kim decided to revert to amusement. "The new wife," he suggested. He waited, an appreciative expression on his face, as if he were waiting for a standup comic to take center stage.

"Same problem of access. How could she have done it without Stan's complicity?"

"Then you're saying . . ." He waited.

The problem wasn't whether Kim was interested. I could see he was, if only to the extent that, if he were the diligent type, he'd review the case the minute I left. The problem was that if he were a shrewd department politician without a conscience, he wouldn't now holler murder when he'd already gone public and said suicide.

"Listen," I told him. "I teach history on the college level. Plus I work in a public library that serves a population of thirty thousand."

"What?"

"I know from bureaucracy. It might seem to you that saying it's a homicide now is like announcing 'I goofed.' But it doesn't have to be viewed as *your* mistake. More than likely, it could be sloppy work by the Medical Examiner's office, or by the first cops on the scene, or something. And you could be the hero because you had doubts and the courage of your convictions and went after the truth."

"And what is the truth?" Kim asked.

Before I could answer, a voice from behind me, in the hall, called out to Kim: "How's it going, Andy?" Oh, God. I knew whose voice that was. I could not bring myself to turn around and look.

"Not bad. How're you doing?"

"Not bad either," the voice said. The footsteps continued down the hall for another second or two. Maybe it wasn't extrasensory perception that made Nelson stop, but a cop's sensitivity to some infinitesimal motion. For all I know it could have been my telltale heart.

Nelson looked lousy. He looked wonderful. His salt-and-pepper hair had turned white. His skin had turned the chalky color of a lifelong civil servant. Although I didn't dare give him the once-over, his body still looked fine. His eyes were still beautiful, large and velvety brown. For that instant, they did not leave my face. Naturally, I immediately thought there was some hideous flaw he'd spotted, one of those imperfections of middle age I couldn't see because my eyesight has gone to hell—a giant hair growing out of my nose, an entire cheek covered by a liver spot. I held my hands tight to my sides so I wouldn't reach up and feel for what was wrong and swallowed hard. And nothing more happened. Nelson gave me a barely perceptible nod and walked on.

Now all I wanted was to get out of police headquarters. But I forced myself to talk to Detective-Sergeant Kim: "You and I both know who had access to Deirdre's things a few months back."

"You're talking about Stan Giddings?"

"We know Deirdre was too much for him. Pushing him farther than he wanted to go socially. Making him over, from his shoes to hair plugs for a bald spot. He couldn't take that. He was a man used to unquestioning acceptance, a man used to people moving earth and sky for *him*. He wanted someone more than Barbara, but he didn't want a wife who would not just outshine him, but drive him. A man like Stan wants someone with a cute career, not an important one. And he wanted someone who could have a baby, so he could have a do-over the way so many men do when they hit middle age. He wanted to live in Giddings House, be lord of his manor. He wanted to do rich man's things, like winter in Palm Beach. What was he doing the day Deirdre died? Coming home from Florida after looking at real estate. But what was the only thing that kept him from doing what he wanted to do? Deirdre."

"Why couldn't he just wait till the divorce was over? Why push it?"

"Because he is spoiled worse than rotten. He wanted what he wanted when he wanted it. He wanted out of the marriage and he wanted a baby, so he got Ryn pregnant. But Deirdre wouldn't cooperate with him. Somehow she got wind that the baby was coming. Maybe he even told her. But she started holding him up for more than what the prenuptial agreement stipulated. That kind of chutzpah wasn't in his calculations, and he became enraged. He wanted out, and fast, and if Deirdre was going to make it difficult for him, she'd have to go. Why don't you check? I bet there's a period of time when he was out of town. That would be the days or weeks when he expected her 'suicide' to happen. Except it didn't."

Kim stuck his hands in his pockets. Finally he asked: "And how am I supposed to prove this?"

Kim called me that night. The Medical Examiner's report stated that the stomach contents had included a trace amount of gelatin, enough for a large dissolved capsule.

I waited. In a whodunit, I would have been Kim's partner, leading him (carrying a search warrant) to a dusting of Vitamin X and Nembutal mixture in the pocket of Stan Giddings's cashmere sports jacket. Or I'd be luring Stan into an Edward Hopper diner for a coffee and then snatch the cup and discover—Aha!—the dribblings on the so-called suicide note turned out to be saliva that matched Stan Giddings's DNA from the saliva on the cup. But in life the scales of justice hardly ever achieve the exquisite balance that they do in a whodunit.

To give Detective-Sergeant Kim credit, he did his homework, albeit a little late. Two artist friends told him how Ryn had given Stan an ultimatum: a month to finalize his divorce. If he couldn't, she would get an abortion. As to having a child out of wedlock, they laughed. Ryn? No, Ryn knew what she wanted and having a baby was a means of getting it. No "it," no kid.

And yes, Stan had gone to his house in Maine for a month in October with Ryn, around the time he left Deirdre, around the time he was waiting for her to kill herself so he and Ryn could come back and get married. But nothing happened and so Stan's freedom, according to Detective-Sergeant Kim, cost him an extra three and a half million dollars.

Finally, the cops did find Stan Giddings's fingerprints on a brown amber bottle of Sunrise Anti-Ox Detox in a bathroom adjacent to Deirdre Giddings's workout room. What does that prove? Stan's lawyer screamed to the District Attorney of Nassau County. And the DA conceded meekly: It means maybe he took a vitamin. Thus, Stan's long-standing policy of giving campaign contributions to the local candidates of all parties except blatant Commies was vindicated. And, sad to report, Stan Giddings himself was vindicated.

It was too late for true justice, although *Newsday* somehow got wind that Deirdre Giddings's suicide was once again under investigation, as was her former husband, Stanley Giddings. Suicide . . . or murder? A dandy photograph of Stan and Ryn ran on the front page, along with insets of Giddings House and Deirdre's Tara. "Good enough for your friend Deirdre?" my friend Nancy Miller demanded that morning. I held the phone away from my ear as she made one of those hideous Southern ya-hoo sounds, half yell, half screech. "None of that 'respected businessman' shit. 'Heir to a footwear fortune' was the best I could do. The powers that be rejected 'playboy' out of hand."

"Nancy, thank you! God bless you!" I held the paper at arm's length and smiled at the photograph of an unhappy Ryn and an outraged Stan leaving church the previous Sunday. They held their baby, wrapped in a pink blanket, awkwardly between them, as if it were a football hand-off neither would accept.

"Are you okay on the Nelson front, kiddo?" Nancy quizzed me.

"Fine."

"Being so close to him and not having him even say hello really got to you."

"Yes."

"You're not going to do anything moronic, like call him."

"No," I assured her.

"Or fax him Bob's obit."

"Stop it, Nancy!"

"Hey, aren't I a good friend?" she asked.

"There's none better," I told her.

"No. There's none better than you, Judith. To me and even to that boring clothes-horse Deirdre, poor thing. I just don't want you getting hurt, is all and—"

"Call waiting. Hold on."

I never got back to her that day. It was Nelson Sharpe. He said "Judith," and then—

But that's another story.

The Bathroom

PETER LOVESEY

Peter Lovesey's Introduction:

Where are you reading this? If, like me, you enjoy relaxing in a steaming bathtub with a short story, then you could be in the perfect place to get the most out of it.

I wasn't aware when I wrote "The Bathroom" that it contained themes I would revisit many times in short stories and novels: characters in warm, secure places with no inkling of the terrors lurking nearby; a blend of real and fictional crime; and the past affecting the present.

Where did the idea come from? It was a visit to the Black Museum at Scotland Yard. In 1973, when it was written, I was a new and junior member of the Crime Writers' Association. I'd heard of the Black Museum, but in those days it wasn't open to the public, so when a CWA tour was arranged, I was pleased to go along. I think about twenty of us were on the trip, including that charming and inventive writer, Christianna Brand, the author of Green for Danger.

Christianna noticed I knew hardly anyone among the crime writers, and soon introduced herself and got talking. She was such entertaining company that I don't recall very much about the Black Museum except that it badly needed rearranging and labeling. In those days, it was basically a storeroom cluttered with exhibits from over a century of famous crimes. Our guide showed us death masks, and a Jack the Ripper poster and torture implements, while Christianna, well-versed in criminology, made a few sharp asides that lightened up the occasion. She was propped on the edge of an old tin bath to take some of the weight off her feet. Suddenly our guide pointed and said, "And that's one of the baths used by George Joseph Smith in the Brides in the Baths murders." Christianna said, "Holy Moses!" and shot up like a champagne cork.

Later, I read the trial of Smith, dubbed "the most atrocious English criminal since Palmer." He was callous and cruel beyond belief, but like Sweeney Todd he devised a method of murder that has a horrid fascination even now. I can understand Christianna's reaction. Thanks to her, I wrote this first short story, and I'll always be grateful for that.

The Bathroom

PETER LOVESEY

"SORRY, DARLING. I MEAN to have my bath and that's the end of it!" With a giggle and a swift movement of her right hand, Melanie Lloyd closed the sliding door of her bathroom. The catch fastened automatically with a reassuring click. Her husband William, frustrated on the other side, had installed the gadget himself. "None of your old-fashioned bolts or keys for us," he had announced, demonstrating it a week before the wedding. "The door secures itself when you slide it across from the inside. You can move it with one finger, you see, but once closed, it's as safe as your money in the bank."

She felt between her shoulders for the tab of her zip. William could wait for her. Sit in bed and wait whilst she had a leisurely bath. What was the purpose of a luxurious modern bathroom if not to enjoy a bath at one's leisure? William, after all, had spent weeks before the wedding modernizing it. "Everything but asses' milk," he had joked. "Mixer taps, spray attachment, separate shower, bidet, heated towel-rails and built-in cupboards. You shall bathe like a queen, my love. Like a queen."

Queenly she had felt when she first stepped through the sliding door and saw what he had prepared for her. It was all there exactly as he had promised, in white and gold. All that he had promised, and more. Ceramic mosaic tiles. Concealed lighting. Steam-proof mirrors. And the floor—wantonly impractical!—carpeted in white, with a white fur rug beside the bath. There was also a chair, an elegant antique chair, over which he had draped a full-length lace negligee.

"Shameless Victoriana," he had whispered. "Quite out of keeping with contemporary design, but I'm incurably sentimental." Then he had kissed her.

In that meeting of lips she had shed her last doubts about William, those small nagging uncertainties that would probably never have troubled her if Daddy had not kept on so. "I'm old-fashioned, I know, Melanie, but it seems to me an extraordinarily short engagement. *You* feel that you know him, I've no doubt, but he's met your mother and me only once—and that was by accident. The fellow seemed downright evasive when I questioned him about his background. It's an awkward thing to do, asking a man things like that when he's damned near as old as you are, but, dang it, it's a father's right to know the circumstances of the man who proposes marrying his daughter, even if he is past fifty. Oh, I've nothing against his age; there are plenty of successful marriages on record between young women and older men. Nothing we could do to stop you, or would. You're over twenty-one and old enough to decide such things for yourself. The point is that he knew why I was making my inquiries. I wasn't probing his affairs from idle curiosity. I had your interests at heart, damn it. If the fellow hasn't much behind him, I'd be obliged if he'd say so, so that I can make a decent contribution. Set you both up properly. I would, you know. I've never kept you short, have I? Wouldn't see you come upon hard times for anything in the world. If only the fellow would make an honest statement . . ."

One didn't argue with Daddy. It was no use trying to talk to him about self-respect. Every argument was always swept aside by that familiar outpouring of middle-class propriety. God, if anything drove her into William Lloyd's arms, Daddy did!

She stepped out of the dress and hung it on one of the hooks provided on the wall of the shower compartment. Before removing her slip, she closed the Venetian blind; not that she was excessively modest, nor, for that matter, that she imagined her new neighbors in Bismarck Road were the sort who looked up at bathroom windows. The plain fact was that she was used to frosted glass. When she and William had first looked over the house—it seemed years ago, but it could only have been last April—the windows, more than anything else, had given her that feeling of unease. There were several in the house—they had been common enough in Victorian times when the place was built—small oblong frames of glass with frostwork designs and narrow stained-glass borders in deep red and blue. They would have to come out, she decided at once, if William insisted on living there. They seemed so out of keeping, vaguely ecclesiastical, splendid in a chapel or an undertaker's office, but not in *her* new home. William agreed at once to take them out—he seemed so determined to buy that one house. "You won't recognize the place when I've done it up. I'll put a picture window in the bathroom. The old frames need to come out anyway. The wood's half-rotten outside." So the old windows went and the picture window, a large single sheet of glass, replaced them. "Don't worry about ventilation," William assured her. "There's an extractor fan built in above the cabinet there." He had thought of everything.

Except frosted glass. She *would* have felt more comfortable behind frosted glass. But it wasn't *contemporary*, she supposed. William hadn't consulted her, anyway. He seemed to know about these things. And there *were* the Venetian blinds, pretty plastic things, so much more attractive than the old brown pelmet they replaced.

She fitted the plug and ran the water. Hot and cold came together from a lion's-head tap; You blended the water by operating a lever. Once you were in the bath you could control the intake of water with your foot, using a push-button mechanism. What would the first occupants of 9 Bismarck Road, eighty years ago, have thought of that?

Melanie reviewed the array of ornamental bottles on the shelf above the taps. Salts, oils, crystals, and foam baths were prodigally provided. She selected an expensive bath oil and upended the bottle, watching the green liquid dispersed by the cascading water. Its musky fragrance was borne up on spirals of steam. How odd that William should provide all this and seem unwilling for her to use it! Each evening since Monday, when they had returned from the honeymoon, she had suggested she might take a bath and he had found some pretext for discouraging her. It didn't matter *that* much to her, of course. At the hotel in Herne Bay she had taken a daily bath, so she didn't feel desperately in need of one immediately after they got back. It was altogether too trivial to make an issue of, she was quite sure. If William and she *had* to have words some time, it wasn't going to be about bath nights, at any rate. So she had played the part of the complaisant wife and fallen in with whatever distractions he provided.

Tonight, though, she had deliberately taken him by surprise. She had hidden nightie and book in the towel chest earlier in the day, so when she hesitated at the head of the stairs as they came to bed he was quite unprepared. You don't go for a late-night bath empty-handed, even when your bathroom has every convenience known to the modern home designer. She was sliding the bathroom door across before he realized what had happened. "Sorry, darling! I mean to have my bath and that's the end of it!"

The door slid gently across on its runners and clicked, the whole movement perfectly timed, without a suspicion of haste, as neatly executed as a pass in the bull ring. That was the way to handle an obstructive husband. Never mind persuasion and plead- ing; intelligent action was much more dignified, and infinitely more satisfying. Besides, she *had* waited till Friday.

She tested the water with her hand, removed her slip, took her book and plastic shower-cap from the towel chest, shook her mass of flaxen hair, and then imprisoned it in the cap. She turned, saw herself unexpectedly in a mirror, and pulled a comical face. If she had remembered, she would have brought in a face pack—the one thing William had overlooked when he stocked the cosmetic shelf. She wasn't going into the bedroom to collect one now, anyway. She took off the last of her underclothes and stepped into the bath.

It was longer than the bath at home or the one in the hotel. Silly really: neither William nor she was tall, but they had installed a six-foot, six-inch bath—"Two meters, you see," the salesman had pointed out, as though that had some bearing on their requirements. Over the years it would probably use gallons more hot water, but it was a beautiful shape, made for luxuriating in, with the back at the angle of a deck chair on the lowest notch, quite unlike the utility five-footer at home, with its chipped sides and overhanging geyser that allowed you enough hot water to cover your knees and no more. William had even insisted on a sunken bath. "It will sink to four inches below floor level, but that's the limit, I'm afraid, or we'll see the bottom of it through the kitchen ceiling."

Accustomed to the temperature now, she pressed the button with her toe for more hot water. There was no hurry to rise from this bath. It wouldn't do Mr. William Lloyd any harm to wait. Not simply from pique, of course; she felt no malice toward him at all. No, there was just a certain deliciousness—a man wouldn't understand it even if you tried to explain—in taking one's time. Besides, it was a change, a relief if she was honest, to enjoy an hour of solitude, a break from the new experience of being someone's partner, accountable for every action in the day from cooking a dinner to clipping one's toenails.

She reached for the book—one she had found on William's bookshelf with an intriguing title, *Murder is Methodical*. Where better to read a thriller than in a warm bath behind locked doors? There hadn't been much opportunity for reading in the last three weeks. Or before, for that matter, with curtains to make and bridesmaids to dress.

She turned to the first page. Disappointing. It was not detective fiction at all, just a dreary old manual on criminology. "William Palmer: The Rugeley Poisoner" was the first chapter. She thumbed the pages absently. "Dr. Crippen: A Crime in Camden Town." How was it that these monsters continued to exert such a fascination on people, years after their trials and executions? The pages fell open at a more whimsical title—from her present position, anyway— "George Joseph Smith: The Brides in the Bath." Melanie smiled. That chapter ought to have a certain piquancy, particularly as one of the first placenames to catch her eye was Herne Bay. Strange how very often one comes across a reference to a place soon after visiting there. With some slight stirring of interest, she propped the book in the chromium soap holder that bridged the sides of the bath, dipped her arms under the water, leaned back, and began to read.

George Joseph Smith had stayed in Herne Bay, but not at the New Excelsior. Wise man! If the food in 1912 was anything like the apologies for cuisine they dished up these days, he and his wife were far better off at the house they took in the High Street. But it wasn't really a honeymoon the Smiths—or the Williamses, as they called themselves—spent at Herne Bay, because they had been married two years before and he had deserted her soon after, only to meet her again in 1912 on the prom at Weston-super-Mare. In May they had come to Herne Bay and on July 8 they made mutual wills. On July 9, Smith purchased a new five-foot bath. Bessie, it seemed, decided to take a bath on the twelfth, a Friday. At 8 A.M. the next morning a local doctor received a note: *Can you come at once? I am afraid my wife is dead.* On July 16, she was buried in a common grave, and Smith returned the bath to the supplier, saying he did not require it after all. He inherited twenty-five hundred pounds.

Twenty-five hundred pounds. That must have been worth a lot in 1912. More, almost certainly, than the five-thousand-pound policy William had taken out on her life. Really, when she considered it, the value of money declined so steadily that she doubted whether five thousand pounds would seem very much when they got it in 1995, or whenever it was. They might do better to spend the premiums now in decorating some of the rooms downstairs. *Super* to have a luxury bathroom, but they would have to spend a lot to bring the other rooms up to standard. "Insurance policies are security," William had said. "You never know when we might need it." Well, security seemed important to him, and she could understand why. When you'd spent your childhood in an orphanage, with not a member of your family in the least interested in you, security was not such a remarkable thing to strive for. So he should have his insurance—it was rather flattering, anyway, to be worth five thousand pounds—and the rest of the house would get decorated in due course.

There was another reason for insurance which she did not much like to think about. For all his energy and good looks William was fifty-six. When the policy matured he would be over eighty, she fifty-two. No good trying to insure him; the premiums would be exorbitant.

For distraction she returned to the book, and read of the death of Alice Burnham in Blackpool in 1913. Miss Burnham's personal fortune had amounted to 140 pounds, but the resourceful George Smith had insured her life for a further five hundred pounds. She had drowned in her bath a month after her wedding, on a Friday night in December. Strange, that Friday night again! Really, it was exquisitely spine chilling to be sitting in one's bath on a Friday night reading such things, even if they had happened half a century ago. The Friday bath night, in fact, she learned as she read on, was an important part of Smith's infamous system. Inquest and funeral were arranged before there was time to contact the relatives, even when he wrote to them on the Saturday. Alice Burnham, like Bessie Mundy, was buried in a common grave early the following week. "When they're dead, they're dead," Smith had explained to his landlord.

Melanie shuddered slightly and looked up from the book. The appalling callousness of the murderer was conveyed with extraordinary vividness in that remark of his. For nearly twenty years he had exploited impressionable girls for profit, using a variety of names, marrying them, if necessary, as unconcernedly as he seduced them, and disappearing with their savings. In the early encounters, those who escaped being burdened with a child could consider themselves fortunate; his later brides were lucky if they escaped with their lives.

It was reassuring for a moment to set her eyes on her modern bathroom, its white carpet and ceramic tiles. Modern, luxurious, and *civilized*. Smith and his pathetic brides inhabited a different world. What kind of bathroom had those poor creatures met their fates in? She had a vision of a cheap tin bath set on cold linoleum and filled from water jugs, illuminated by windows with colored-glass panels. Not so different, she mused, from the shabby room William had converted—transformed rather—for her into this dream of a modern bathroom. Lying back in the water, she caught sight of the cornice William had repainted, highlighting the molding with gold paint. So like him to preserve what he admired from the past and reconcile it with the strictly contemporary.

Friday night! She cupped some water in her hands and wetted her face. George Joseph Smith and his crimes had already receded enough for her to amuse herself with the thought that his system would probably work just as well today as it did in 1914. The postal service hadn't improved much in all those years. If, like Daddy, you insisted on living without a telephone, you couldn't get a letter in Bristol before Monday to say that your daughter had drowned in London on Friday evening.

How dreadfully morbid! More hot water with the right toe and back to the murders, quite remote now. When had Smith been tried and executed? 1915—well, her own William had been alive then, if only a baby. Perhaps it wasn't so long. Poor William, patiently waiting for her to come to bed. It wouldn't be fair to delay much longer. How many pages to go?

She turned to the end to see, and her eye was drawn at once to a paragraph describing the medical evidence at Smith's trial. *The great pathologist, Sir Bernard Spilsbury, stated unequivocally that a person who fainted whilst taking a bath sitting in the ordinary position would fall against the sloping back of the bath. If water were then taken in through the mouth or nose it would have a marked stimulating effect and probably recover the person. There was no position, he contended, in which a person could easily become submerged in fainting. A person standing or kneeling might fall forward on the face and then might easily be drowned. Then, however, the body would be lying face downward in the water. The jury already knew that all three women had been found lying on their backs, for Smith's claim that Miss Lofty was lying on her side was nonsense in view of the bath in Bismarck Road.*

Bismarck Road. Melanie jerked up in the water and read the words again. Extraordinary. God, how horrible! It couldn't possibly be. She snatched up the book and turned back the pages, careless of her wet hands. There it was again! *Margaret made her will and bequeathed everything, nineteen pounds (but he had insured her life for seven hundred pounds) to her husband. Back at Bismarck Road, Highgate, a bath was installed that Friday night. Soon after 7:30 the landlady, who was ironing in her kitchen, heard splashes from upstairs and a sound which might have been wet hands being drawn down the side of the bath. Then there was a sigh. Shortly after, she was jolted by the sound of her own harmonium in the sitting room. Mr. John Lloyd, alias George Joseph Smith, was playing "Nearer, my God to Thee."*

Mr. John Lloyd. Mr. John *Lloyd*. That name. Was it possible? William said he knew nothing of his parents. He had grown up in the orphanage. A foundling, he said, with nothing but a scrap of paper bearing his name; abandoned, apparently, by his mother in the summer of 1915. The summer, she now realized, of the trial of George Joseph Smith alias John Lloyd, the deceiver and murderer of women. It was too fantastic to contemplate. Too awful . . . An unhappy coincidence. She refused to believe it.

But William—what if he believed it? Rightly or wrongly believed himself the son of a murderer. Might that belief have affected his mind, become a fixation, a dreadful, morbid urge to relive George Joseph Smith's crimes? It would explain all those coincidences: the honeymoon in Herne Bay; the insurance policy; the house in Bismarck Road; the new bath. Yet he had tried to keep her from having a bath, barred the way, as if unable to face the last stage of the ritual. And tonight she had tricked him and she was there, a bride in the bath. And it was Friday.

Melanie's book fell in the water and she sank against the back of the bath and fainted. An hour later, her husband, having repeatedly called her name from outside the bathroom, broke through the sliding door and found her. That, at any rate, was the account William Lloyd gave of it at the inquest. She had fainted. Accidental death. A pity Sir Bernard Spilsbury could not have been in court to demonstrate that it was impossible. Even in a two-meter bath.

The Death of Me

MARGARET MARON

Margaret Maron's Introduction:

In the fall of 1966, I tried to stop smoking.

Again.

I had been quit for about three hours, had gone through two packs of gum, and was ready to kill for a cigarette. Which made me wonder, "Would someone really kill for a cigarette? Why?"

I walked up to the corner drugstore, and as I walked back home with a carton of cigarettes tucked under my arm, I finished plotting out this story. It was eventually rejected by Ellery Queen's Mystery Magazine, but the printed rejection slip carried a handwritten note of encouragement, the first I'd ever received. I was over the moon. In the spring of 1967, Ernest M. Hutter, the editor at Alfred Hitchcock's Mystery Magazine, bought it for the magnificent sum of $63.75. Your family may love everything you write, your friends may say you're another Jane Austen, but nothing validates you like a check from an editor you've never met.

Here's the story exactly as it was first printed in January 1968 under my maiden name.

The Death of Me

MARGARET MARON

YOU KNOW, FATHER, THE most irritating thing about all tired, worn-out, cliché-ridden platitudes and moralistic aphorisms is that they're so infuriatingly, smugly true: haste does make waste; a stitch in time will save nine; and Myrtle, a walking cliché . . . well, Myrtle was right, too.

"Cigarettes will be the death of you," she nagged whenever she had exhausted my other faults. "Not to mention me. Always smelling up the house with those filthy things, leaving ashtrays to be washed and ashes all over the furniture and rugs."

She left magazines in conspicuous places, opened to articles ringed in red which expounded on nicotine-linked diseases or the dangers of smoking in bed; and she took great relish in reading aloud obituaries in which lung cancer was the cause of death.

"You could stop if you tried. It's just simple mind over matter," she'd harangue.

When I had the temerity once to point out that *her* mind wasn't so hot at controlling her own corpulent matter, she flared indignantly, "You know I'm a glandular case. I can't help it if a slight heaviness runs in my family. And don't try to change the subject. It's been proved that smoking takes years off a person's life. Do you think I want to spend my last years a widow?" The thought so depressed her that she consoled herself with another handful of chocolates.

I often wondered why Myrtle was so concerned about my life span. It wasn't as if she loved me; that was over before our first year of marriage, eighteen years ago. My insurance would more than keep her clothed, sheltered, and sated with chocolates, so perhaps she thought worrying about my longevity (or lack of it) was the proper wifely thing to do, or that she would genuinely miss my being around to nag.

Why did I stay with her? Habit, I guess. Too, she kept the house immaculate, cooked delicious meals, and was so fat that I didn't have to worry about unfaithfulness.

If she hadn't been such an obese harpy, I suppose we could have jogged along as happily as any other married couple, but she just wouldn't understand that I haven't the least desire to stop smoking. It's my one real enjoyment. We had no children, my job is boring, I don't make friends easily, and I have no hobbies except reading.

Do you smoke, Father? No? Then you don't know the pleasure of sipping a second cup of hot, black coffee after a good breakfast, the newspaper opened to an interesting editorial, as you strike a match to light your first cigarette of the day. That first whiff of sulfur as the match flares and catches the end of the cigarette—what perfume to a smoker's nose! A few tentative puffs to get it going, then you inhale deeply and your whole body relaxes. At work, it eases the pressures, helps you concentrate; at night, it's soothing to sit in an easy chair with a book in your lap watching the transparent ribbon of smoke curl and undulate upward in thin blue swirls. With a cigarette in my hand I could even shut out Myrtle's droning complaints, as she was well aware.

I must have ignored her once too often because last winter she really became determined to make me quit. Until then, she'd only sniped at me; now it became serious guerrilla warfare. She began to keep the ashtrays in the kitchen on the pretext that she'd just washed them and hadn't gotten around to putting them back in the living room, forcing me to go hunting for one. She kept "forgetting" where she'd put the matches, and disavowed any knowledge of the disappearance of the last two or three packs in each carton.

"Am I to blame if you're smoking so much you can't keep track of how many packs you have?" she would ask with an injured expression.

So I began secreting them around the house, and as quickly as Myrtle would find one hiding place, I'd discover a different one. It became almost a game. My best cache was in the box of dietetic cookies she once bought in the vague hope of reducing. She never did find that particular place.

I don't know how long we'd have kept up that cat-and-mouse farce if I hadn't broken my leg while standing on a rickety step stool to reach a pack of cigarettes hidden on the top shelf of the linen closet behind some blankets.

The crash brought Myrtle waddling upstairs and, as the pain closed in on me, I heard her half-satisfied wail, "I told you cigarettes were going to be the death of you!"

When I came to, I was lying in bed and Dr. Mason was putting the final touches on a very heavy plaster cast. "A few weeks in bed, a month or two on crutches and you'll be good as new," he told me cheerfully. "It's just a simple fracture and you're lucky it was your leg and not your neck. I'll check in on you in a few days."

Then he was gone—my last link with the outside world. Still dazed and groggy, I didn't realize what it meant until Myrtle brought me my breakfast tray the next morning.

"It was delicious," I told her truthfully, reaching for a new book by one of my favorite authors which she had picked up from the library for me. I actually felt a wave of affection for her, Father.

"You're really a very good wife in many ways, my dear," I said appreciatively, indicating the breakfast tray, the steaming coffee, the book, my fresh pajama shirt. "I know it's going to be a lot of extra work for you."

Myrtle stood by the door, smiling, silent, while I opened the book and fumbled for cigarettes on the night table. Realizing they were missing, I met Myrtle's exultant eyes.

"This is no time for fun and games," I told her quietly. "Bring me my cigarettes."

"No!" she cried triumphantly. "Haven't you learned anything from that fall? What caused it? Cigarettes!"

"I fell because you made me resort to hiding them," I yelled back. "I should have slapped you down the first time you took them!"

"You would hit me, would you?" She leaned over the foot of the bed and shook a thick finger at me, her face mottled with rage. "You listen to me! I'll cook for you, I'll fetch and carry, I'll try to make you comfortable, but I will not give you cigarettes!" Smoothing her dress down over her nonexistent waist, she added, "I just can't be a party to your getting lung cancer and now is a perfect time to quit."

She collected the dishes, lumbered out of the room, and that was that. Neither pleading nor cursing moved her. She was as firm as the Rock of Gibraltar which she so much resembled; and on the issue of cigarettes, she would not be budged. After that first day, pride kept me from trying. If only I had broken something less handicapping than a leg!

True to her word, Myrtle did make me as comfortable as possible. She lugged the portable television up from the den, kept me supplied with books and magazines, and served new delicacies, but the sheer physical craving for cigarettes gnawed at my nerve ends, and everything reminded me of them.

I'd never realized before how much television time is devoted to cigarette commercials. I would be helpless and immobile, watching an actor demonstrate how enjoyable his brand was, and break out in envious sweat.

Every magazine carried at least a dozen ads for different forms of tobacco, and every chapter in every book described a character puffing a cigarette "nervously," "disdainfully," "confidently," or "lazily," while I longed to puff one "avidly."

The next two days dragged though Myrtle kept refilling the dish of lemon drops with which she had replaced my ashtray. I munched and nibbled constantly but grew more and more irritable from the sudden withdrawal.

"You'll get over it and someday you'll thank me," said Myrtle complacently.

"Thank you! If I hold onto my sanity, I'll divorce you as soon as I'm on my feet again!"

Before, I'd felt nothing for her but indifference. Now she became the embodiment of all my frustrations.

On the fourth day, my pride shattered and I groveled before her. "Just one!" I pleaded. "How will one cigarette hurt me?"

"It'll get you right back where you were before," she panted, stooping heavily to pick up the papers I'd scattered on the floor beside my bed. "You don't realize it, but you're over the worst part now."

She was so smugly self-righteous that I couldn't bear her any longer. Without thinking, I swung my broken leg, and sixteen pounds of plaster cast smashed down on her bent head. Howling with pain and pent-up frustration, I hit her again and again even after she lay still. Finally, my leg throbbed so unbearably that I fainted.

The insistent peal of the doorbell brought me to, and then I heard Dr. Mason calling from the hallway, "Anybody home?"

MY LAWYER PLEADED TEMPORARY insanity under mitigating circumstances; and although one is entitled to be judged by his peers, you'll never convince me that there were any smokers on my jury. Well, they do let you have a few last cigarettes on Death Row.

The most discouraging thing, though, Father, is how right Myrtle was. At least she's not around to say, "I told you so!"

Just a minute more, Guard; I haven't finished my cigarette yet.

Freedom

SUSAN MOODY

Susan Moody's Introduction:

It was the worst of times; it was the best of times. Revolution was stirring in middle Europe; candles were blowing in the wind while snowflakes fell, walls were tumbling, freedom was finally becoming a reality to people who for years had been locked in a despotic grip of iron.

I was in wintry Czechoslovakia, attending, for the first time, an international conference of crime writers. We were staying in a fairy-tale castle some kilometers outside Prague, which belonged to the writers of the country. The castle was painted pink and stood above a lake which, at that time, was deeply frozen, covered not only in feet of ice, but in a heavy fall of snow. I was reminded of the chapter in Virginia Woolf's pretty conceit, Orlando, where she describes the great frost in London, when the Thames froze over, shoals of eels lying motionless within the ice, and the old Burnboat woman sat frozen fathoms deep, with her lap full of frozen apples.

To the conference table came the news that in Iran, the Ayatollah Khomeini had issued a fatwah against Salman Rushdie, author of The Satanic Verses. *We were already aware that only days earlier, dissident Czech playwright Vaclav Havel had been flung into jail for inciting unrest. These were stirring times, unsettling times. Collectively, we shivered. Surely we writers were, by our very trade, granted immunity, granted freedom of speech. Surely we could write what we pleased, say what we liked, state our opinions, and not expect to be punished for them. And yet here were two of our colleagues, one in England, one in Czechoslovakia, nearby places, civilized places, who had not been accorded such freedom.*

It was in this fervent atmosphere that I walked through the early dusk in Prague, between high houses where lights blinked on behind shutters and doors were firmly closed to the elements. Snow was falling, the few people on the streets hurried past me with their heads bent against the wind. Every now and then I passed a café where small windows showed dim yellow lights. In the public buildings, offices were still brightly lit, although the working day was over.

I was startled by fresh blood on the snow. High above me, hanging from a balcony, was a dead hare with blood dripping from its mouth. Emerging from the streets, I walked slowly across the Charles Bridge. Terror suddenly seized me. The water below was black, white-flecked, very cold. There was almost nobody about. As crime writers are prone to do, I thought: What if . . . ? What if someone approached me, what if a stranger with murder on his mind walked along the bridge toward me, and, for no reason, threw me over into the black river below? Who would know? Who, in this frozen city with freedom on its mind, would care?

Back home in England, I discovered that the trails of fear were still there. This, my first crime story, was one I needed to write, if only to exorcise the fear that I felt at that moment.

Freedom

SUSAN MOODY

DEATH HAD BANISHED HIM from the city.

Only another death could have brought him back. Only this particular death.

He watched without emotion as his mother's coffin was lowered into the solid red earth, shivering when the brutal wind bit at the soft edges of his face. There were flowers in his hand, a few stiff carnations, half a dozen forced roses, all he could find at this dead time of year. He wondered if he would have dared to come back to the city if she had died in the summer. Without the excuse of cold, he would have been unable to hide himself behind the folds of his woolen scarf.

The handful of other mourners were all strangers to him. How could they be otherwise, after so many years away? He loosened the layers of wool and watched his breath plume in the icy air. Although it was mid-afternoon, the raw sides of the grave were still sealed with a sheen of frost which sparkled where the thick red sun caught it. Beyond the little chapel, pine forests marched endlessly away toward an oyster-gray sky. Behind him straggled a dozen or so of the little wooden houses which made up this village on the outskirts of the city. Their painted facades were faded, the green curlicues and once-bright flowers now almost invisible against the cracked plaster. Otherwise the place had changed little in the ten years since he was last here. He and his mother had taken a bus out from the city. It had been summer then: there had been grass to sit on. They had followed the river for a while before they ate the sausage and bread they had brought with them, and drank the strong pilsen beer for which their country was famous. The river had been full of movement, its surface rippled by the force of its flow from the cold mountains to the sea; now it lay locked under a thick crust of ice.

In memory, that distant summer day glowed with the translucence of polished glass. As well as the sunshine and the brilliant water, there was the unaccustomed feeling of freedom. In the drab routines laid down by the State, a day off was a rarity. His mother had taken off her shoes and tucked up her skirts; he had looked at her strong brown thighs as though they belonged to a pretty girl he might have passed in the street, and realized, as he did so, that he had not before seen her as an individual, female and separate, but only as a parent, only as an adjunct to himself. Standing knee-deep in the clear water, head thrown back to the sun so that her breasts showed round against the whiteness of her blouse, she had seemed carefree, happy. For the first time he was aware that she had been young once, that she was still an attractive woman, that the same desires probably shook her body as shook his own.

Glancing over her shoulder at him, she had said: "This is a nice place. I think I should like to be buried here," and the two of them had laughed at the remoteness of death.

Only a few months later, death had changed his life forever.

ABOVE THE OPEN GRAVE, the priest lifted an arm: His embroidered cape, cream and gold, hung solidly from his shoulders; the cold wind tugged at its hem. As the sign of the cross hallowed the air, Erben found himself remembering . . . nighttime. Shadows, solid as shut doors, and between them, occasional pools of yellow light. The empty bridge. The sound of rain hissing against the cobbles, pierced by the faint night-cry of a seagull drawn upriver by the hope of city pickings. The statues stood black against the blacker sky, twelve of them, six on either side, their plinths set into the parapet. He stopped by the largest of them. His feelings of humiliation and pain had reached such a pitch that he felt as though he was spinning like a top, faster and faster, out of control. Should he throw himself over? It would be one way to calm his agitation. He stared down at the river. Even in darkness, long lines of foam showed white where it tumbled over the shallow weirs.

He was conscious of the action of his heart; he saw it glowing red inside his chest, like a small furnace, pumping love and anger and despair through the bloodways of his body. Its beat filled his ears; he could hear nothing else. Afterward, he had no idea how long he had been looking down at the water before he heard the footsteps coming.

He could hear them still, would always hear them advancing toward him out of the wet night, would always remember the way they sounded like the blow of an ax or the thud of a spade and then the sudden shocking silence is the man responsible for them was thrown from the bridge, without word or threat or explanation, to plunge, arms flailing, toward his death in the black water.

Ever since, Erben had wondered at the emotions involved in the murderous deed. Was it only a random moment of impulse snatched out of the rain-filled air? Was it a need to impose some kind of singularity—however perverted—in a society which insisted on conformity, which subsumed the rights of the one within the greater good of the many? Or was it simply an act of revenge, the extracting of an eye for an eye by punishing another for the punishment one had received oneself?

And what would have happened afterward if there had not been a witness to the shocking deed? Would there have been other similar deaths, other victims after that first one, if a third person had not walked out of the pooled shadows into the light, his face staring, his mouth a hole of astonishment and fear?

In the years since his flight from the city, he had endlessly reviewed the what-ifs and the if-onlys, seeking explanations for what happened that night. He could find none. That particular concatenation of events, that precise sequence of action and result *had* taken place; thinking about it could change nothing. Would anything have been otherwise, if Nadja had been kinder, had chosen terms less damaging to his pride with which to inform him that she no longer wished to see him? Or if he had sat for ten minutes longer in the warm fug of the café, had drunk just one more beer as he tried to forget the contemptuous twist of her mouth and the words she had tossed at him. Or even if the weather had been different, if it had not rained that night and kept people indoors; what then? Would the victim have passed safely on his way? Would murder have been defeated by the proximity of others?

How many times the footage had unrolled itself against the screen of his mind: the rain, the darkness, the looming statues on the empty bridge above the black river. And the three of them, locked forever in uneasy brotherhood: victim, murderer, and witness.

Afterward, he had scarcely known how he found his way home. Shock made his feet unsteady. He had stumbled into his room, past his mother already asleep on the pull-out sofa in the tiny living room, and slumped against the stale pillows on his bed. His entire body quivered. His eyes felt as though they were on fire. He held his hand up to the light and watched the whole fine structure of bone and skin and blood shake like a wind-tugged kite. A man was dead, deliberately thrust into oblivion between one moment and the next. And what should have been a secret single act had become a steel-strong rope that bound murderer and witness closer than twins. For each of them, meeting suddenly in the rain after the deed was done, had seen the other, had come unmistakably face to face.

By the next morning he had already made up his mind to leave. The city was too small for him to brazen it out, the chances of them meeting again so likely that he knew he had no alternative but to run. It was the only way he could be free.

His mother had cried, not understanding. He wanted to explain but the words simply would not come. He should have gone to the police headquarters in the old part of the city, should have explained what had happened, taken the consequences. Cringingly, he knew he did not possess the moral strength for that. Instead, he had packed a bag and traveled south to the only other city big enough to hide in. At first, he thought of leaving the country, heading for England or Russia, or even America, but there would have been visas and passports to apply for, which would have meant delays and queues. Both increased the chances for disaster. The only way he would survive was by ensuring that as far as possible, murderer and witness would not again come face to face, then or . . . now he could hear another grave being prepared, somewhere behind the little baroque chapel. The steady *chunk chunk* of spades hitting the frost-bound earth sounded like the raucous call of a crow. He wanted to weep for his mother, but could not. Coming back had been unnecessary, irrelevant, really: it made no difference to her whether he came or not. Yet he could not let her go into the earth unwitnessed.

He threw his flowers onto the lowered coffin. His mother had loved fresh flowers. As he turned away from the grave and the unknown priest and the faces of strangers, the first flakes of winter began to fall.

The most sensible option was to get into his ugly State-manufactured car and drive back to the place he now called home. Nonetheless, he hesitated, his mind fingering the stuff of other options, wider choices. Now that he was back in the city of his youth, there were places he wanted to see once more. After all, he might never again return.

HE HAD KNOWN HE would not be able to stay away from the center of the city. The little area of cobbled streets and impossibly peaked roofs, of alleyways and statues and goldtipped wrought iron called to him. He had been a student here; fallen in love with Nadja, drunk endless beers in the cafés, listened to the great clock on the Town Hall strike the hour and watched with other pausing citizens as the figure of Death wagged its bony jaw and shook its hourglass. He had left once before; it would be harder to leave a second time. In the dusk, the old castle lay on its hill like a sleeping lion, spotlit behind the flakes of snow which fell from a brooding sky. Already the ground underfoot was thick with it; people passed in fur hats and thick coats, shoulders hunched against the cold. He felt safe, unrecognizable. Ten years had changed him from the young man he had once been. Anyone throwing more than a glance at him would see only a face marked with long-borne stress, hair already graying at the temples, eyes that were wary behind rimless glasses.

He walked between yellow painted walls where the snow had begun to drift, past the Jewish cemetery with its crowded black headstones, past the doorways of gothic churches, and into the big main square. Here in the past, his countrymen had stood against invading tanks, had defied oppressors. Now, again, there were massed crowds, placards raised, voices demanding freedom and democracy. He stood on the edge of the crowd, watching.

"Free-dom! Free-dom!" The lion-roar drifted through the snowflakes. Some of the people held flowers in their hands; they seemed unaware of the cold. On the cobbles, a few torn and soggy pamphlets called for strikes and demonstrations. The shop windows were unlit; everywhere dirt and decay reflected how, until now, the spirit of the people had been crushed.

"Free-dom! Free-dom!"

It all seemed remote, unrelated to himself. He moved away, into the side streets where black shadows creased the snow. The air was pure and piercingly cold. Voices retreated from him under archways as he shivered inside his coat. Behind the tall buildings he was always conscious of the river.

In the dark, the swelling cry of the demonstrators ebbed and flowed, covering the snowy roofs with a thin strong web of hope. As it grew later, the streets seemed emptier, as though the whole life of the city had been sucked into the square. Did that lessen or increase the possibility that the next face he saw might belong to the person he most dreaded meeting, his fellow conspirator in ten years of silence? His mind could not grasp the concept firmly enough to work it out. For too long he had worried about it, always terrified that the necessary demands of his work might throw him suddenly into the company of a stranger whose face he knew. Now, back in his own city, he almost welcomed the possible encounter. He wondered if his adversary had spent the past ten years in the same state of nervous isolation. Had he also suffered for the random chance that had led him to the bridge on that cold evening? Did he long for freedom too?

It was even possible that he was dead. In that case, Erben's nightmare could cease. But how would he know? He had nothing to go on, no means of identification, no means of checking. His only real choice was to continue living as he had been, never absolutely at peace.

Or was it? Ten years is a long time, a large percentage of one's life to sacrifice to fear. Perhaps it was time to confront his destiny head on. Perhaps he had been aware all along that his insistence on attending his mother's funeral masked the need to change the way things had been. He could no longer go on as he had been doing. Recently, he had met a woman. It was not the way it had been with Nadja: although some of the same passion was there, it was diminished, like embroidered flowers on silk that have faded in the sun. She liked him, he knew; she was ready to care for him, if he would let her. But until he had resolved his problems, he did not feel he could allow himself the luxury of affection. Coming back here was the only way.

"Free-dom!" The cry billowed down the shivering streets and he straightened his shoulders, bracing himself for conflict. He was not going to leave the city until he had tracked down the face that haunted him. Although it was impossible to conduct any kind of systematic search, in a city as small as this, the two of them were bound to come across each other sooner or later.

And when they did, what then?

It was quiet on the streets now. Erben had been walking for hours and in spite of his thick fur-lined boots and sheepskin coat, was beginning to feel chilled. Occasional windows threw a buttery glow into the dark. In a narrow alley running between all houses, he saw blood on the snow, almost black where it caught the faint light from the gas lamps attached to the wall. The blood had melted a little crater in the snow; lighter splashes lay round the edge. For a moment the *thunk thunk* of his heart drowned out all sound. Blood meant death. Had the man who fell from the bridge bled before he drowned? He stared about, then, as another drop splashed near his boot, looked up. Something was hanging head downward from the ornate balcony of the fifth floor. In this light it was difficult to be sure; an illegal pheasant, was it, or possibly a hare? He almost smiled.

He was near the State Offices now. Many of the rooms were still lit, full of bureaucrats refining the endless details without which the State would cease to function, or considering the consequences of the new spirit of unrest which was abroad in the city. He was about to pass by when one of the big double doors of polished wood opened and three people came out. For a moment they stood together at the top of the shallow flight of steps, talking quietly, pulling gloves on, tucking scarves around their necks, before setting off in opposite directions. One man went alone, the other couple, man and woman, turned toward the center of the city. As they passed, Erben saw, almost without surprise, that what he dreaded had occurred.

The man's face was as familiar as his own.

He noticed with resentment that he did not appear to have suffered, as Erben himself had. He was warmly dressed, his coat was thick and his scarf fine. Yet he, too, had aged. Somehow Erben had not expected that. In his imagination, he saw him always as he was then, white-faced, open-mouthed, eyes black with fear and surprise.

"Free-dom! Free-dom!" The sound was fainter now, but no less strong.

He followed the couple, keeping close to the wall, head down. Against his face the wind drove a freezing mixture of something that was more than rain, yet less than snow. The man held the woman's arm. At a side street, she broke away from him, waving briefly before hurrying off into the darkness. Erben continued to follow. Once, the man in front of him looked back over his shoulder. Perhaps he was as fearful as Erben himself had always been. Perhaps he too had waited for the chance encounter, dreaded the turn in the street, the opening of a door, in case it brought him face to face with his unknown yet all too familiar adversary.

They were heading for the river. No one else was about except the occasional passerby hurrying toward the warmth of home, footsteps muffled by the settling snow. They reached the deserted bridge where, implacable as a lury, the statues lined the parapet. For a moment Erben paused. Should he call? Should he run swiftly after the other man, tap his shoulder, swing him round so they faced each other again as so briefly they had done ten years before? Should he try to explain or excuse himself?

He thought of the woman who waited in the city farther south. Remembered Nadja's scornful face and his own stewing emotions as he looked down into the river in those fateful seconds before circumstance had precipitated him into murder. He knew he had a choice. He told himself that he had surely paid for that moment ten years earlier, paid in fear, isolation, exile. Now at last was his chance to change things for himself.

He ran after the hurrying figure, his boots slipping on the sleet-slippery pavement. The snow had turned to rain; he could see the parallel lines of it against the lamps. To the left was the castle; below, the river moved grayly past concrete apartment blocks and leafless trees.

Halfway over, the other man paused beneath the largest of the statues and looked up at the blindfold figure of justice which dominated the center of the bridge. What was he thinking? Light haloed his black hat, his sturdy neck and body. In their woolen gloves, his hands looked huge.

Erben remembered with bitterness how, all those years before, he had not dared go to the police. Only the week before he and his fellow-students had been involved in demonstrations against some new State injustice. With others of his friends he had been rounded up by the security forces, flung into the back of the police vans, and taken to headquarters. For two days he had been brutalized and degraded. He had finally been released with the warning that next time he was in trouble, the police would remember him. It was his reaction to this, his obvious terror, which had caused Nadja's contemptuous dismissal.

It was why he had felt unable to go to the police with the story of what had happened on the bridge.

"Free-dom!" The sound of the crowd rolled down the bridge toward him. He caught up with that man in front. Without thinking, he grabbed him round the neck with one arm and lifted him by the skirts of his thick gray coat. He twisted him up and onto the granite edge of the parapet and flung him out into the darkness. The man's long seagull-mew of terror floated for a moment and then was abruptly cut off. After that, there was only silence.

Panting a little, Erben looked up and down the wet length of the bridge. Would history repeat itself? Would another witness step from the shadows as he had once done, face white and accusing, mouth open with shock? But nothing stirred on the bridge except the whirling snow.

He felt at peace for the first time in years. The links of circumstance had snapped at last. Witness, murderer, and victim had been chained together in that unholy moment: now only he was left.

He had reached the shadows on the far side of the bridge before he began to wonder exactly which of the three he was.

The Dripping

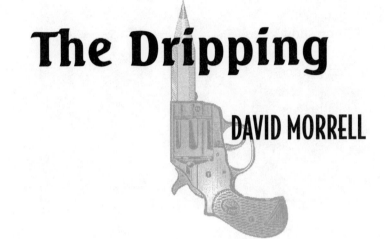

DAVID MORRELL

David Morrell's Introduction:

When I was seventeen, I realized that, more than anything, I wanted to be a writer. How can I be so specific about the time? Because my inspiration came from Stirling Silliphant's scripts for the classic TV series Route 66 *(two young men in a Corvette in search of America and themselves), which premiered in the fall of 1960, my seventeenth year. If I was going to be a writer, I decided, it wouldn't hurt to learn something about putting words together. I finished high school and went to college (a goal that had been in doubt).*

Eventually, though, I came to understand that the odds against earning a living as a writer were considerable and that a day job would be a good idea. Why not get a graduate degree in American literature? I thought. Become a professor. Write fiction when I wasn't teaching. So I went to Penn State University, and there I met Philip Klass (William Tenn), the first honest-to-God writer I'd ever talked to face-to-face. Klass reinspired me to want to be a writer. He generously put me through a crash course in technique. And with a sense of him looking encouragingly over my shoulder, in 1968 I began a novel about a disaffected Vietnam veteran named Rambo in a novel called First Blood.

That novel was begun eight years after the premiere of Route 66. *I was now twenty-five. But I still wasn't confident about my writing abilities. After numerous drafts that I struggled through when I wasn't studying for classes, I decided that I'd set myself an impossible goal.*

I put the frustrating manuscript in a drawer and began what seemed a much more sensible project: my dissertation on the contemporary American writer, John Barth. I remember a snowy night in Buffalo when Barth and I, having interrupted one of our interviews, were driving to a State University of New York function that he needed to attend. Somehow he'd heard (probably from my dissertation director) that I was working on a novel. He asked me how it was going, and I replied that I'd abandoned it, that I'd finally admitted to myself that I didn't have what it took to be a published fiction writer.

That was in 1969, nine years after the premiere of Route 66. The following year, I finished the dissertation, and with time on my hands before I moved to the University of Iowa to start teaching, I happened across the interrupted novel. To my surprise, it somehow didn't read so badly. The next thing I knew, I was cutting and rearranging, then moving the story forward. In June 1971, I finally finished it and sent it to an agent, Henry Morrison, to whom Philip Klass had introduced me, although I was still so uncertain that I also sent a typescript of my dissertation.

Which brings me to "The Dripping." That June of 1971, I had a dream so vivid and disturbing that I set to work the next morning to put it on paper. The first draft of its thirty-three hundred words was completed in one day. The second and final draft took the next day. I had no idea where to submit so troubling a tale, so I went to a store that sold magazines, scanned the racks, and decided that my subject matter was compatible with Ellery Queen's Mystery Magazine. I mailed the story, began teaching summer school, finished teaching summer school, and had pretty much given up on ever selling anything when my wife phoned my office at the university and told me that I'd just received a letter from Ellery Queen's Mystery Magazine.

I couldn't believe it. They'd bought the story. For three cents a word. A hundred dollars. That certainly wasn't going to make me rich, but then neither was being a professor—my second-year salary was $13,500. The point was, I'd been validated. I could finally call myself a professional writer. A few weeks later, Henry Morrison called to say that he'd sold my book. Assuming that he was talking about my dissertation, I needed a minute to realize that he meant First Blood, for which I was going to receive the lofty advance of thirty-five hundred dollars. That wasn't going to make me rich, either, especially since Henry reminded me that I was going to have to pay 40 percent of that in various taxes, and of course an agent's fee would have to be deducted. But the amount I earned didn't matter as much as the fact of the sale. Again I'd been validated, although the adrenaline kick (as great as *it was) didn't equal what I'd felt when I'd received that letter from* Ellery Queen's Mystery Magazine.

As things turned out, First Blood *was published in May 1972. "The Dripping" came out in August. I wish that the schedule had been the other way around, that my first sale had also been my first publication. The magazine got it right, however. "The Dripping" appeared in its Department of First Stories. Each time it's been reprinted (this is the eleventh occasion), I remember fondly and vividly that summer of 1971 (my twenty-eighth year) when I wrote something that somebody else thought was good enough to pay for, and the dream of a seventeen-year-old was fulfilled.*

The Dripping

DAVID MORRELL

THAT AUTUMN, WE LIVE in a house in the country, my mother's house, the house I was raised in. I have been to the village, struck even more by how nothing in it has changed, yet everything has, because I am older now, seeing it differently. I feel as though I am both here now and back then, at once with the mind of a boy and a man. It is so strange a doubling, so intense, so unsettling, that I am moved to work again, to try to paint it, studying the hardware store, the grain barrels in front, the twin square pillars holding up the drooping balcony onto which seared, wax-faced men and women from the old people's hotel above come to sit and rock and watch. They look like the same aging people I saw as a boy, the wood of the pillars and balcony as splintered.

Forgetful of the hours while I work, I do not begin the long walk home until late, at dusk. The day has been warm, but now in my shirt I am cold, and a half mile along I am caught in a sudden shower, forced to leave the gravel road for the shelter of a tree, its leaves already brown and yellow. The rain becomes a storm, streaking at me sideways, drenching me. I cinch the neck of my canvas bag to protect my painting and equipment and decide to run. My socks are spongy in my shoes, repulsive, when at last I reach the lane down to the house and barn.

The house and barn. They and my mother alone have changed, as if as one, warping, weathering, their joints twisted and strained,

228

their gray so unlike the brightness I recall as a boy. The place is weakening her. She is in tune with it. She matches its decay. That is why we have come here to live. To revive. Once I thought I could convince her to move away. But of her sixty-five years, she has spent forty here, and she insists that she will spend the rest, what is left to her.

The rain falls stronger as I hurry past the side of the house, the light on in the kitchen, suppertime and I am late. The house is connected to the barn the way the small base of an *L* is connected to its stem. The entrance I have always used is directly at the joining, and when I enter, out of breath, my clothes cling to me cold and wet. The door to the barn is to my left, the door to the kitchen straight ahead. I hear the dripping in the basement, down the stairs to my right.

"Meg. Sorry I'm late," I call to my wife, setting down my water-beaded canvas sack, opening the kitchen door. There is no one. No settings on the table. Nothing on the stove. Only the yellow light from the sixty-watt bulb in the ceiling, the kind my mother prefers to the brightness of a one-hundred-watt. It reminds her of candlelight, she says.

"Meg," I call again, and still no one answers. They're asleep, I think. With dusk coming on, the dark clouds of the storm have lulled them, and they have lain down for a nap, expecting to wake before I return.

Still the dripping. Although the house is very old, the barn long disused, the roofs crumbling, I have not thought it all so ill-maintained, the storm so strong that water can be seeping past the cellar windows, trickling, pattering on the old stone floor. I switch on the light to the basement, descend the wooden stairs to the right, worn and squeaking, reach where the stairs turn to the left the rest of the way down to the floor, and see not water dripping, but milk. Milk everywhere. On the rafters, on the walls, dripping on the film of milk on the stones, gathering, speckled with dirt, in the channels between them. From side to side and everywhere.

Sarah, my child, has done this, I think. She has been fascinated by the big wooden dollhouse that my father made for me when I was young, its blue paint chipped and peeling now. She has pulled it from the far corner to the middle of the basement. There are games and toy soldiers and blocks that have been taken from the wicker storage chest and played with on the floor, all covered with milk, the dollhouse, the chest, the scattered toys, milk dripping on them from the rafters, milk trickling on them.

Why has she done this? I think. Where can she have gotten so much milk? What was in her mind to do this thing?

"Sarah," I call. "Meg." Angry now, I mount the stairs to the quiet kitchen. "Sarah," I shout. She will clean the mess and stay indoors the remainder of the week.

I cross the kitchen, turn through the sitting room, past the padded flower-patterned chairs and sofa that have faded since I knew them as a boy, past several of my paintings that my mother has hung on the wall, brightly colored old ones of pastures and woods from when I was in grade school, brown-shaded new ones of the town, tinted as if old photographs. Two stairs at a time up to the bedrooms, my wet shoes on the soft, worn carpet on the stairs, my hand streaking on the smooth, polished maple banister.

At the top, I swing down the hall. The door to Sarah's room is open. It is dark in there. I switch on the light. She is not on the bed, nor has she been. The satin spread is unrumpled, the rain pelting in through the open window, the wind fresh and cool. I have a bad feeling then and go uneasily into our bedroom. It is dark as well, empty. My stomach has become hollow. Where are they? All in my mother's room?

No. As I stand at the open door to my mother's room, I see from the yellow light that I turned on in the hall that only she is in there, her small torso stretched across the bed.

"Mother," I say, intending to add, "Where are Meg and Sarah?" But I stop before I do. One of my mother's shoes is off, the other askew on her foot. There is mud on the shoes. There is blood on her cotton dress. It is torn, her brittle hair disrupted, blood on her face. Her bruised lips are swollen.

For several moments, I am silent with shock. "My God, Mother," I finally manage to say, and as if the words are a spring releasing me to action, I touch her to wake her. But I see that her eyes are open, staring toward the ceiling, unseeing although alive, and each breath is a sudden full gasp, then a slow exhalation.

"Mother, what has happened? Who did this to you? Where are Meg and Sarah?"

But she does not look at me, only toward the ceiling.

"For God sake, Mother, answer me! Look at me! What has happened?"

Nothing. Her eyes are sightless. Between gasps, she is like a statue.

WHAT I THINK IS hysterical. Disjointed, contradictory. I must find Meg and Sarah. They must be somewhere, beaten like my mother. Or worse. Find them. Where? But I cannot leave my mother. When she becomes alert again, she, too, will be hysterical, frightened, in great pain. How did she end up on the bed?

In her room, there is no sign of the struggle she must have put up against her attacker. It must have happened somewhere else. She crawled from there to here. Then I see the blood on the floor, the swath of blood down the hall from the stairs. Who did this? Where is he? Who would beat a gray, wrinkled, arthritic old woman? Why in God's name would he do it? I imagine the pain of the arthritis as she struggled with him.

Perhaps he is still in the house, waiting for me.

To the hollow sickness in my stomach now comes fear, hot, pulsing, and I am frantic before I realize what I am doing, grabbing the spare cane that my mother always keeps by her bed, flicking on the light in her room, throwing open the closet door and striking in with the cane. Viciously, sounds coming from my throat, I flail the cane among faded dresses.

No one. Under the bed. No one. Behind the door. No one.

I search all the upstairs rooms that way, terrified, constantly checking behind me, clutching the cane and whacking into closets, under beds, behind doors with a force that would certainly crack a skull. No one.

"Meg! Sarah!"

No answer, not even an echo in this sound-absorbing house.

There is no attic, just an overhead entry to a crawl space under the eaves, and that has long been sealed. No sign of tampering. No one has gone up.

I rush down the stairs, seeing the trail of blood my mother has left on the carpet, imagining her pain as she crawled. I search the rooms downstairs with the same desperate thoroughness. In the front closet. Behind the sofa and chairs. Behind the drapes.

No one.

I lock the front door, lest he be outside in the storm, waiting to come in behind me. I remember to draw every blind, close every drape, lest he be out there peering at me. The rain pelts insistently against the windows.

I cry out again and again for Meg and Sarah. The police. My mother. A doctor. I grab for the old phone on the wall by the front stairs, fearful to listen to it, afraid he has cut the line outside. But it is droning. Droning. I ring for the police, working the handle at the side around and around and around.

THEY ARE COMING, THEY say. A doctor with them. Stay where I am, they say. But I cannot. Meg and Sarah. I must find them. I know they are not in the basement, where the milk is dripping—all the basement is open to view. Except for my childhood things, we cleared out all the boxes and barrels and shelves of jars the Saturday before.

But under the stairs. I have forgotten about under the stairs, and now I race down and stand, dreading, in the milk, but there are only cobwebs there, already re-formed from Saturday, when we cleared them. I look up at the side door I first came through, and as if I am seeing through a telescope, I focus on the handle. It seems to fidget. I have a panicked vision of the intruder bursting through, and I charge up to lock it, and the door to the barn.

And then I think, If Meg and Sarah are not in the house, they are likely in the barn. But I cannot bring myself to unlock the barn door and go through. *He* must be there, as well. Not in the rain outside, but in the shelter of the barn, and there are no lights to turn on there.

And why the milk? Did he do it, and where did he get it? And why? Or did Sarah do it before? No, the milk is too fresh. It has been thrown there too recently. By him. But why? And who is he? A tramp? An escapee from some prison? Or asylum? No, the nearest institution is far away, at least a hundred miles. From the town then. Or a nearby farm.

I know my questions are a delaying tactic, to keep me from entering the barn. But I must. I take the flashlight from the kitchen drawer and unlock the door to the barn, forcing myself to go in quickly, cane ready, flashing my light. The stalls are still there, listing—and some of the equipment—churners, separators—dull and rusted, cobwebbed and dirty. The must of decaying wood and crumbled hay, the fresh wet smell of the rain gusting through cracks in the walls.

Flicking my light toward the corners, edging toward the stalls, hearing boards creak, I try to control my fright. I remember when I was a boy how the cattle waited in the stalls for my father to milk them, how the barn was once board-tight and solid, warm to be in, how there was no connecting door from the barn to the house because my father did not want my mother to smell the animals when she was cooking.

I scan my light along the walls, sweep it in arcs through the darkness before me as I draw nearer to the stalls, and in spite of myself, I recall that other autumn when the snow came early, deep drifts by morning and still storming thickly, how my father went out to the barn to do the milking and never returned for lunch, or supper. The phone lines were down, no way to get help, and my mother and I waited all night, unable to make our way through the storm, listening to the slowly dying wind. The next morning was clear and bright and blinding as we waded out, finding the cows in agony in their stalls from not having been milked and my father dead, frozen rock-solid in the snow in the middle of the next field, where he must have wandered when he lost his bearings in the storm.

There was a fox nosing at him under the snow, and my father's face was so mutilated that he had to be sealed in his coffin before he could lie in state. Days after, the snow was melted, gone, the barnyard a sea of mud, and it was autumn again and my mother had the connecting door put in. My father should have tied a rope from the house to his waist to guide him back in case he lost his way. Certainly he knew enough. But then he was like that, always in a rush. When I was ten.

Thus I think as I aim my flashlight toward the shadowy stalls, terrified of what I may find in any one of them, Meg and Sarah, or him, thinking of how my mother and I searched for my father and how I now search for my wife and child, trying to think of how it was once warm and pleasant in here, chatting with my father, helping him to milk, the sweet smell of new hay and grain, the different sweet smell of fresh droppings, something I always liked, although neither my father nor my mother could understand why. I know that if I do not think of these good times, I will surely go insane, dreading what I might find. I pray to God that they have not been killed.

What can he have done to them? To rape a five-year-old girl. Split her. The hemorrhaging alone can have killed her.

Then, even in the barn, I hear my mother cry out for me. The relief I feel to leave and go to her unnerves me. I do want to find Meg and Sarah, to try to save them. Yet I am eager to go. I think my mother will tell me what has happened, tell me where to find them. That is how I justify my leaving as I wave the light in circles around me, guarding my back, retreating through the door and locking it.

UPSTAIRS, MY MOTHER SITS stiffly on her bed. I want to make her answer my questions, to shake her, to force her to help, but I know that will only frighten her more, push her mind down to where I can never reach it.

"Mother," I say to her softly, touching her gently. "What has happened?" My impatience can barely be contained. "Who did this? Where are Meg and Sarah?"

She smiles at me, reassured by the safety of my presence. Still she cannot answer.

"Mother. Please," I say. "I know how bad it must have been. But you must try to help. I must know where they are so I can find them."

She says, "Dolls."

It chills me. "What dolls, Mother? Did a man come here with dolls? What did he want? You mean he looked like a doll? Wearing a mask like one?"

Too many questions. All she can do is blink.

"Please, Mother. You must try your best to tell me. Where are Meg and Sarah?"

"Dolls," she says.

As I first had the foreboding of disaster at the sight of Sarah's unrumpled satin bedspread, now I begin to understand, rejecting it, fighting it.

"Yes, Mother, the dolls," I say, refusing to admit what I suspect. "Please, Mother. Where are Meg and Sarah?"

"You are a grown boy now. You must stop playing as a child. Your father. Without him, you will have to be the man in the house. You must be brave."

"No, Mother." My chest aches.

"There will be a great deal of work now, more than any child should know. But we have no choice. You must accept that God has chosen to take him from us, that you are all the man I have to help me."

"No, Mother."

"Now you are a man and you must put away the things of a child."

Eyes streaming, I am barely able to straighten, leaning wearily against the doorjamb, tears rippling from my face down to my shirt, wetting it cold where it had just begun to dry. I wipe my eyes and see my mother reaching for me, smiling, and I recoil along the hall, then stumble down the stairs, down through the sitting room, the kitchen, down, down to the milk, splashing through it to the doll-house, and in there, crammed and doubled, Sarah. And in the wicker chest, Meg. The toys not on the floor for Sarah to play with, but taken out so Meg could be put in. And both of them, their stomachs slashed open, stuffed with sawdust, their eyes rolled up like dolls' eyes.

The police are knocking at the side door, pounding, calling out who they are, but I am powerless to let them in. They crash through the door, their rubber raincoats dripping as they stare down at me.

"The milk," I say.

They do not understand. I wait, standing in the milk listening to the rain pelting on the windows while they come to see what is in the dollhouse and in the wicker chest, while they go upstairs to my mother and then return so I can tell them again, "The milk." But they still do not understand.

"She killed them, of course," one man says. "But I don't see why the milk."

Only when they speak to the neighbors down the road and learn how she came to them, needing the cans of milk, insisting that she carry them herself to the car, the agony she was in as she carried them, only when they find the empty cans and the knife in a stall in the barn, can I say, "The milk. The blood. There was so much blood, you know. She needed to deny it, so she washed it away with milk, purified it, started the dairy again. You see, there was so much blood."

That autumn we live in a house in the country, my mother's house, the house I was raised in. I have been to the village, struck even more by how nothing in it has changed, yet everything has, because I am older now, seeing it differently. I feel as though I am both here now and back then, at once with the mind of a boy and a man.

A Taste of Life

SARA PARETSKY

Sara Paretsky's Introduction:

My very first crime story, written when I was fourteen, will I think be better published posthumously. So my first adult story, called "A Taste of Life," is the one I offer you. I wrote it in 1978; it was turned down by many mystery magazines and ultimately published in 1989 by the women's press as part of an anthology called Reader, I Murdered Him.

A Taste of Life

SARA PARETSKY

DAPHNE RAYDOR WORKED IN the bookkeeping department at Rapelec, Inc. Her capacity for work—her appetite for it—was insatiable. In January, when accountants go mad closing previous years' books, Daphne flourished. She worked best in the night's dark hours, comparing ledgers and totting up columns with greedy delight.

Everyone at Rapelec loved Daphne in January. Helen Ellis, the petite, arrogant assistant controller, stopped to flatter Daphne on her plant arrangements or her perfume. Carlos Francetta, the budget director, lavished Latin compliments on her. Flowers appeared on her desk, and chocolates.

In February, these blandishments disappeared and Daphne lived alone behind her barricade of ferns for another eleven months. She was smart, she was willing, she was capable. But she was also very fat. She was so fat that she had to make all her own clothes: no store carried garments in her size. Her walk was slow. She gasped for breath after climbing a short flight of stairs. Daphne lived on the first floor of a three-story walk-up. By the time she carried her groceries up one staircase and into her kitchen, she had to collapse for forty-five minutes to recover her breath.

Daphne was an excellent cook. She could make elaborate French dinners, including elegantly decorated pastries. Food and wine were both so outstanding that Helen, Carlos, and other staff members would accept her dinner invitations. They would exclaim at their hostess, who barely touched her food: how could she be so fat, when she scarcely ate? After they left, Daphne would pull another four portions from the oven and devour them.

Daphne ate constantly. Elegant French dinners she reserved for company. She shopped almost daily, at five different supermarkets so that no one would see the volume of food she purchased. She had chocolate cookies tucked into a corner of the couch, bags of potato chips at her bedside and in the bathroom. The freezer and refrigerator were always overloaded. Some food rotted and had to be thrown out, but Daphne consumed a lot more. She brought home packages of frozen hors d'oeuvres and ate them while they thawed. She kept frozen pizzas under her bed and ate them raw. She slipped chocolates into drawers and closets. She was never more than three steps from some nourishing little snack.

Daphne's present condition was especially sad to those who knew her as an elfin child. What had happened to her? Family friends blamed Sylvia Raydor.

Twenty years ago, Sylvia's face appeared regularly on the covers of *Harper's Bazaar* and *Vogue*. She was one of the top ten models in the country and could pick her jobs. When Daphne was born, Sylvia delighted in the photographs—hovering sentimentally over a white-clad infant, blowing a sad kiss to baby and nurse from the railing of the *QE2*—that only enhanced her popularity.

But as Daphne moved from infant seats to kindergarten, she became an encumbrance to Sylvia. If the child was growing up, the mother must be aging. And worse, friends—former friends—commented often on Daphne's angelic beauty. Photographers tried to bring her into the child-model business. Others prophesied a beauty that would far outshine Sylvia's, for it had a sweetness to it lacking in the mother.

Sylvia began force-feeding her daughter ("Mummy won't love you if you don't eat all of this." "But Mummy, I'm not hungry!" "Then Mummy will have to shut you in your room and leave you by yourself. She can't be with you if you hurt her feelings") until Daphne weighed close to three hundred pounds.

As for Sylvia, she hardened into a still beautiful, if somewhat lacquered, jet-setter. She did a good business in television commercials (the housewife in the wildly successful Greazout detergent campaign) but was considered too brittle for magazines. She jetted to Minorca for the winter, spent spring in Paris, summered in the temperate zones off La Jolla, and generally alighted on Daphne's Chicago doorstep for a fleeting display of maternity in mid-October. ("Daphne, my pet! Darling, how *do* you manage to stay so fat? I eat and eat and can't put on an *ounce!*") Usually she had a young escort in tow, flattered by Sylvia's beauty and sophistication, yet contriving to make her appear a trifle old.

Daphne longed for love. She tried to satisfy her dreams with novels, beauty magazines (carefully cutting out Sylvia's face the few times it still appeared), and daydreams of an impossibly romantic character. And while she read, or dreamed of herself slim and desirable, she ate: a pound of pork chops with French fries, a chocolate layer cake, and a quart of ice cream. And later a few pretzels and potato chips with beer. And so to bed.

ONE WINTER, A YOUNG man joined Rapelec's accounting department. He had a type of serious youthful beauty and was very shy. Daphne's fat, and her vulnerability, struck a responsive chord in Jerry. After thinking the matter over for several weeks, he waited until they were both alone at the end of the day and asked her to go to a movie with him. Daphne, whose dreams had been filled with Jerry's fine-etched features, at first thought he was making fun of her. But he persisted, and she finally agreed to go.

The first terrifying date took place in March. By May, Jerry and Daphne were lovers and Daphne had lost thirty-seven pounds. In September, she bought her first shop-made garment in eight years. A size twenty, to be sure, but a delirious occasion for her. In October, she and Jerry signed a lease together on Chicago's north side. That was where Sylvia found them some ten days later.

"Daphne, darling! Why didn't you let me know you were moving? I've searched everywhere for you, and finally your genius of a secretary dug up your address for me!"

Daphne muttered something which a charitable listener could interpret as delight at seeing her mother. Sylvia eyed Jerry in a way which made him blush uncomfortably. "Introduce me to your friend, darling," she cried reproachfully. Daphne did so, reluctantly, and then muttered that they were going to paint cabinets, and didn't paint always make Sylvia sick?

"You don't want to paint the first night your mother is in town," Sylvia said archly, inviting Jerry to compare mother with daughter, indeed pausing for the expected remark ("You can't be her mother— if anything, she looks older than you!"). Jerry said nothing, but blushed more than ever.

"Why, you two babies," Sylvia finally said. "Anyone would think I'd found you out in some guilty secret. Instead, here you are setting up house in the most delightful way. Let's go over to Perroquet to celebrate!"

"Thanks, Sylvia, but I—I guess I'm not hungry and these cabinets do need painting."

Sylvia cried out some more, drew the embarrassed Jerry into the conversation—"You must be making this goose of a daughter perfectly *miserable*, Jerry: she's never lost her appetite in all the years I've known her"—and finally dragged them off to Perroquet where she ordered for all of them and pouted when Daphne refused several courses. "If you were a model, darling, one could understand. But you can eat whatever you feel like."

Back home, Daphne burst into tears. How could Jerry love her, as fat as she was, and why didn't Sylvia drop dead? Jerry consoled her, but uneasily. And Sylvia, back in her suite, Sylvia could not rest. Daphne happy and in love? Impossible. Daphne thin? Never!

Sylvia's courtship of Jerry was long and difficult. She postponed her winter plans and stayed in Chicago, hosting parties, making a splash at all the society events, getting Jerry to escort her when Prince Philip hosted a dress ball at the British consulate.

Daphne watched wretchedly, hopeless and unable to act. She began eating again, not at her previous levels, but enough to put ten pounds back on by Thanksgiving.

Jerry, too, was miserable and unable to cope with Sylvia. He dreaded her summonses, yet could not refuse them. The night finally came when he did not return to the apartment.

Desolate, Daphne sat up in bed waiting for him. By three, it was clear that he wasn't coming home. She began to eat, consuming the roast she had prepared for their dinner and what little other food they had—for her sake they didn't stock much.

As soon as the stores were open, Daphne went to the nearest grocery and bought as much as she could carry. Returning home, she dropped two heavy sacks in the middle of the living room and sat down to eat. She did not take off her coat, nor bother to call her office. She ate a dozen sweet rolls, a cherry pie, and two pizzas. She was working her way through a box of chips with dip when Sylvia appeared.

Sylvia stopped in the middle of the room. "What on earth are you doing here? I was sure you would be at work!"

Daphne got clumsily to her feet. She looked at Sylvia, furiously angry, yet feeling passive and remote. She wanted to cry, to eat a pound of chocolates, to throw Sylvia out the window, yet she only stood. Finally she spoke. Her voice sounded so far away that she wondered if she'd said the words aloud and repeated herself. "What are you doing here, Sylvia? Get out."

Sylvia laughed. "Oh, I came to get Jerry's clothes—he didn't want to come himself—felt awkward, poor thing."

Daphne followed her into the bedroom. "You can't have Jerry's clothes," she whispered. "I want them myself."

"Oh, do be reasonable, Daphne: Jerry won't be coming back. Why he ever wanted a fat lump like you I don't know, but at least it gave me a chance to meet him, so I suppose it was all to the good." As she spoke, Sylvia began pulling drawers open, impatiently pawing through jeans and T-shirts.

"You can't take his clothes," Daphne whispered hoarsely, pulling at Sylvia's arm.

"Buzz off now, Daphne, and finish your cookies," Sylvia snapped, slapping her across the face.

Daphne screamed in rage. Scarcely knowing what she was doing, she picked up the dressing-table lamp and began pounding Sylvia's head with it. Sylvia fell against the dressing table and at last lay crumpled on the floor, dead long before Daphne stopped screaming and hitting her.

Finally Daphne's rage subsided. She collapsed on the floor by Sylvia's body and began to cry. Jerry would never come back to her. No one would ever love her again. She wanted to die herself, to eat and eat until she was engulfed by food. Mechanically, methodically, still weeping, she lifted Sylvia's left arm to her mouth.

Fan Mail

PETER ROBINSON

Peter Robinson's Introduction:

"Fan Mail" first appeared in Cold Blood II, *published in 1989 by Mosaic Press and edited by Peter Sellers. Since then, it has been anthologized many times and has even been issued on audiocassette, read by Jerry Orbach.*

I see from my old notebook that I started writing the story (originally titled "Fan Letter") on December 23, 1987, after "the idea woke me at 4:00 A.M. and persisted in dreams." Judging by the notes I made at the time, the plot seems remarkably complete right from the start. The next notebook reference occurs on January 19, 1988, where I name the characters and flesh out the bare bones of the plot with specific details. Believe it or not, the main character was originally called Denzil Quigley!

At that time, I was working on Caedmon's Song, *my first non-series novel. Penguin had already published the first Inspector Banks novel,* Gallows View, *while the second,* A Dedicated Man, *was due out at any moment, and I had finished numbers three and four. As I was a member of the Crime Writers of Canada, I was invited to submit a short story to the organization's ongoing series of anthologies.*

This request caused me a great deal of anxiety. I had never written a short story before. I had written poetry, but that was no help to me now. I had also written prose pieces of about ten or twenty pages in length, but not by any stretch of the imagination could these youthful experiments be called stories, let alone crime stories. I was just getting used to the novel form, with all its room to develop character and create suspense, and here I was, faced with the challenge of doing all that in a few pages. It weighed heavily on my mind.

When I mention that the idea for "Fan Mail" came to me in a dream, then, I know that dream was a result of all the conscious and unconscious anxiety that Peter Sellers's request caused me. I also know that while I had been given the idea, I still had to sweat over the details and general coherence of it all. I also had to research poisons, which I discovered was incredibly easy to do.

Since "Fan Mail," I have written many other stories and the process has never got any easier for me. It would be a great help if all the ideas came in dreams, but unfortunately that hasn't happened again.

Fan Mail

PETER ROBINSON

THE LETTER ARRIVED ONE sunny Thursday morning in August, along with a Visa bill and a royalty statement. Dennis Quilley carried the mail out to the deck of his Beaches home, stopping by the kitchen on the way to pour himself a gin and tonic. He had already been writing for three hours straight, and he felt he deserved a drink.

First he looked at the amount of the royalty check, then he put aside the Visa bill and picked up the letter carefully, as if he were a forensic expert investigating it for prints. Postmarked Toronto, and dated four days earlier, it was addressed in a small, precise hand and looked as if it had been written with a fine-nibbed calligraphic pen. But the postal code was different; that had been hurriedly scrawled in with a ballpoint. Whoever it was, Quilley thought, had probably got his name from the telephone directory and had then looked up the code in the post office just before mailing.

Pleased with his deductions, Quilley opened the letter. Written in the same neat and mannered hand as the address, it said:

Dear Mr. Quilley,

Please forgive me for writing to you at home like this. I know you must be very busy, and it is inexcusable of me to intrude on your valuable time. Believe me, I would not do so if I could think of any other way.

I have been a great fan of your work for many years now. As a collector of mysteries, too, I also have first editions of all

251

your books. From what I have read, I know you are a clever man, and, I hope, just the man to help me with my problem.

For the past twenty years, my wife has been making my life a misery. I put up with her for the sake of the children, but now they have all gone to live their own lives. I have asked her for a divorce, but she just laughed in my face. I have decided, finally, that the only way out is to kill her, and that is why I am seeking your advice.

You may think this is insane of me, especially saying it in a letter, but it is just a measure of my desperation. I would quite understand it if you went straight to the police, and I am sure they would find me and punish me. Believe me, I've thought about it. Even that would be preferable to the misery I must suffer day after day.

If you can find it in your heart to help a devoted fan in his hour of need, please meet me on the roof lounge of the Park Plaza Hotel on Wednesday, August 19, at 2:00 P.M. I have taken the afternoon off work and will wait longer if for any reason you are delayed. Don't worry, I will recognize you easily from your photo on the dust-jacket of your books.

Yours, in hope,

A Fan

The letter slipped from Quilley's hand. He couldn't believe what he'd just read. He was a mystery writer—he specialized in devising ingenious murders—but for someone to assume that he did the same in real life was absurd. Could it be a practical joke?

He picked up the letter and read through it again. The man's whining tone and clichéd style seemed sincere enough, and the more Quilley thought about it, the more certain he became that none of his friends was sick enough to play such a joke. Assuming that it was real, then, what should he do? His impulse was to crumple up the letter and throw it away. But should he go to the police? No. That would be a waste of time. The real police were a terribly dull and literal-minded lot. They would probably think he was seeking publicity.

He found that he had screwed up the sheet of paper in his fist, and he was just about to toss it aside when he changed his mind.

Wasn't there another option? Go. Go and meet the man. Find out more about him. Find out if he was genuine. Surely there would be no obligation in that? All he had to do was turn up at the Park Plaza at the appointed time and see what happened.

Quilley's life was fine—no troublesome woman to torment him, plenty of money (mostly from American sales), a beautiful lakeside cottage near Huntsville, a modicum of fame, the esteem of his peers—but it had been rather boring of late. Here was an opportunity for adventure of a kind. Besides, he might get a story idea out of the meeting. Why not go and see?

He finished his drink and smoothed the letter on his knee. He had to smile at that last bit. No doubt the man would recognize him from his book-jacket photo, but it was an old one and had been retouched in the first place. His cheeks had filled out a bit since then, and his thinning hair had acquired a sprinkling of gray. Still, he thought, he was a handsome man for fifty: handsome, clever, and successful.

Smiling, he picked up both letter and envelope and went back to the kitchen in search of matches. There must be no evidence.

OVER THE NEXT FEW days, Quilley hardly gave a thought to the mysterious letter. As usual in summer, he divided his time between writing in Toronto, where he found the city worked as a stimulus, and weekends at the cottage. There, he walked in the woods, chatted to locals in the lodge, swam in the clear lake, and idled around getting a tan. Evenings, he would open a bottle of Chardonnay, reread P. G. Wodehouse, and listen to Bach. It was an ideal life: quiet, solitary, independent.

When Wednesday came, though, he drove downtown, parked in the multi-story at Cumberland and Avenue Road, then walked to the Park Plaza. It was another hot day. The tourists were out in force across Bloor Street by the Royal Ontario Museum, many of them Americans from Buffalo, Rochester, or Detroit: the men in loud checked shirts photographing everything in sight, their wives in tight shorts looking tired and thirsty.

Quilley took the elevator up to the nineteenth floor and wandered through the bar, an olde-worlde place with deep armchairs and framed reproductions of old Colonial scenes on the walls. It was busier than usual, and even though the windows were open, the smoke bothered him. He walked out onto the roof lounge and scanned the faces. Within moments he noticed someone looking his way. The man paused for just a split second, perhaps to translate the dust-jacket photo into reality, then beckoned Quilley over with raised eyebrows and a twitch of the head.

The man rose to shake hands, then sat down again, glancing around to make sure nobody had paid the two of them undue attention. He was short and thin, with sandy hair and a pale gray complexion, as if he had just come out of hospital. He wore wire-rimmed glasses and had a habit of rolling his tongue around in his mouth when he wasn't talking.

"First of all, Mr. Quilley," the man said, raising his glass, "may I say how honored I am to meet you." He spoke with a pronounced English accent.

Quilley inclined his head. "I'm flattered, Mr. . . . er . . ."

"Peplow, Frank Peplow."

"Yes . . . Mr. Peplow. But I must admit I'm puzzled by your letter."

A waiter in a burgundy jacket came over to take Quilley's order. He asked for an Amstel.

Peplow paused until the waiter was out of earshot: "Puzzled?"

"What I mean is," Quilley went on, struggling for the right words, "whether you were serious or not, whether you really do want to—"

Peplow leaned forward. Behind the lenses, his pale blue eyes looked sane enough. "I assure you, Mr. Quilley, that I was, that I *am* entirely serious. That woman is ruining my life and I can't allow it to go on any longer."

Speaking about her brought little spots of red to his cheeks. Quilley held his hand up. "All right, I believe you. I suppose you realize I should have gone to the police?"

"But you didn't."

"I could have. They might be here, watching us."

Peplow shook his head. "Mr. Quilley, if you won't help, I'd even welcome prison. Don't think I haven't realized that I might get caught, that no murder is perfect. All I want is a chance. It's worth the risk."

The waiter returned with Quilley's drink, and they both sat in silence until he had gone. Quilley was intrigued by this drab man sitting opposite him, a man who obviously didn't even have the imagination to dream up his own murder plot. "What do you want from me?" he asked.

"I have no right to ask anything of you, I understand that," Peplow said. "I have absolutely nothing to offer in return. I'm not rich. I have no savings. I suppose all I want really is advice, encouragement."

"If I were to help," Quilley said. "*If* I were to help, then I'd do nothing more than offer advice. Is that clear?"

Peplow nodded. "Does that mean you will?"

"If I can."

And so Dennis Quilley found himself helping to plot the murder of a woman he'd never met with a man he didn't even particularly like. Later, when he analyzed his reasons for playing along, he realized that that was exactly what he had been doing—playing. It had been a game, a cerebral puzzle, just like thinking up a plot for a book, and he never, at first, gave a thought to real murder, real blood, real death.

Peplow took a handkerchief from his top pocket and wiped the thin film of sweat from his brow. "You don't know how happy this makes me, Mr. Quilley. At last, I have a chance. My life hasn't amounted to much, and I don't suppose it ever will. But at least I might find some peace and quiet in my final years. I'm not a well man." He placed one hand solemnly over his chest. "Ticker. Not fair, is it? I've never smoked, I hardly drink, and I'm only fifty-three. But the doctor has promised me a few years yet if I live right. All I want is to be left alone with my books and my garden."

"Tell me about your wife," Quilley prompted.

Peplow's expression darkened. "She's a cruel and selfish woman," he said. "And she's messy, she never does anything around the place. Too busy watching those damn soap operas on television day and night. She cares about nothing but her own comfort, and she never overlooks an opportunity to nag me or taunt me. If I try to escape to my collection, she mocks me and calls me dull and boring. I'm not even safe from her in my garden. I realize I have no imagination, Mr. Quilley, and perhaps even less courage, but even a man like me deserves some peace in his life, don't you think?"

Quilley had to admit that the woman really did sound awful—worse than any he had known, and he had met some shrews in his time. He had never had much use for women, except for occasional sex in his younger days. Even that had become sordid, and now he stayed away from them as much as possible. He found, as he listened, that he could summon up remarkable sympathy for Peplow's position.

"What do you have in mind?" he asked.

"I don't really know. That's why I wrote to you. I was hoping you might be able to help with some ideas. Your books . . . you seem to know so much."

"In my books," Quilley said, "the murderer always gets caught."

"Well, yes," said Peplow, "of course. But that's because the genre demands it, isn't it? I mean, your Inspector Baldry is much smarter than any real policeman. I'm sure if you'd made him a criminal, he would always get away."

There was no arguing with that, Quilley thought. "How do you want to do it?" he asked. "A domestic accident? Electric shock, say? Gadget in the bathtub? She must have a hair curler or a dryer?"

Peplow shook his head, eyes tightly closed. "Oh no," he whispered, "I couldn't. I couldn't do anything like that. No more than I could bear the sight of her blood."

"How's her health?"

"Unfortunately," said Peplow, "she seems obscenely robust."

"How old is she?"

"Forty-nine."

"Any bad habits?"

"Mr. Quilley, my wife has nothing *but* bad habits. The only thing she won't tolerate is drink, for some reason, and I don't think she has other men—though that's probably because nobody will have her."

"Does she smoke?"

"Like a chimney."

Quilley shuddered. "How long?"

"Ever since she was a teenager, I think. Before I met her."

"Does she exercise?"

"Never."

"What about her weight, her diet?"

"Well, you might not call her fat, but you'd be generous in saying she was full-figured. She eats too much junk food. I've always said that. And eggs. She loves bacon and eggs for breakfast. And she's always stuffing herself with cream-cakes and tarts."

"Hmmm," said Quilley, taking a sip of Amstel. "She sounds like a prime candidate for a heart attack."

"But it's me who—" Peplow stopped as comprehension dawned. "I see. Yes, I see. You mean one could be *induced*?"

"Quite. Do you think you could manage that?"

"Well, I could if I didn't have to be there to watch. But I don't know how."

"Poison."

"I don't know anything about poison."

"Never mind. Give me a few days to look into it. I'll give you advice, remember, but that's as far as it goes."

"Understood."

Quilley smiled. "Good. Another beer?"

"No, I'd better not. She'll be able to smell this one on my breath and I'll be in for it already. I'd better go."

Quilley looked at his watch. Two-thirty. He could have done with another Amstel, but he didn't want to stay there by himself. Besides, at three it would be time to meet his agent at the Four Seasons, and there he would have the opportunity to drink as much as he wanted. To pass the time, he could browse in Book City. "Fine," he said, "I'll go down with you."

Outside on the hot, busy street, they shook hands and agreed to meet in a week's time on the back patio of the Madison Avenue Pub. It wouldn't do to be seen together twice in the same place.

Quilley stood on the corner of Bloor and Avenue Road among the camera-clicking tourists and watched Peplow walk off toward the Saint George subway station. Now that their meeting was over and the spell was broken, he wondered again what the hell he was doing helping this pathetic little man. It certainly wasn't altruism. Perhaps the challenge appealed to him; after all, people climb mountains just because they're there.

And then there was Peplow's mystery collection. There was just a chance that it might contain an item of great interest to Quilley, and that Peplow might be grateful enough to part with it.

Wondering how to approach the subject at their next meeting, Quilley wiped the sweat from his brow with the back of his hand and walked toward the bookshop.

ATROPINE, HYOSCYAMINE, BELLADONNA . . . QUILLEY flipped through Dreisbach's *Handbook of Poisoning* one evening at the cottage. Poison seemed to have gone out of fashion these days, and he had only used it in one of his novels, about six years ago. That had been the old standby, cyanide, with its familiar smell of bitter almonds that he had so often read about but never experienced. The small black handbook had sat on his shelf gathering dust ever since.

Writing a book, of course, one could generally skip over the problems of acquiring the stuff—give the killer a job as a pharmacist or in a hospital dispensary, for example. In real life, getting one's hands on poison might prove more difficult.

So far, he had read through the sections on agricultural poisons, household hazards, and medicinal poisons. The problem was that whatever Peplow used had to be easily available. Prescription drugs were out. Even if Peplow could persuade a doctor to give him barbiturates, for example, the prescription would be on record and any death in the household would be regarded as suspicious. Barbiturates wouldn't do, anyway, and nor would such common products as paint thinner, insecticides, and weed killers—they didn't reproduce the symptoms of a heart attack.

Near the back of the book was a list of poisonous plants that shocked Quilley by its sheer length. He hadn't known just how much deadliness there was lurking in fields, gardens, and woods. Rhubarb leaves contained oxalic acid, for example, and caused nausea, vomiting, and diarrhea. The bark, wood, leaves, or seeds of the yew had a similar effect. Boxwood leaves and twigs caused convulsions; celandine could bring about a coma; hydrangeas contained cyanide; and laburnums brought on irregular pulse, delirium, twitching, and unconsciousness. And so the list went on—lupins, mistletoe, sweet peas, rhododendron—a poisoner's delight. Even the beautiful poinsettia, which brightened up so many Toronto homes each Christmas, could cause gastroenteritis. Most of these plants were easy to get hold of, and in many cases the active ingredients could be extracted simply by soaking or boiling in water.

It wasn't long before Quilley found what he was looking for. Beside "Oleander," the note read, "See *digitalis*, 374." And there it was, set out in detail. Digitalis occurred in all parts of the common foxglove, which grew on waste ground and woodland slopes, and flowered from June to September. Acute poisoning would bring about death from ventricular fibrillation. No doctor would consider an autopsy if Peplow's wife appeared to die of a heart attack, given her habits, especially if Peplow fed her a few smaller doses first to establish the symptoms.

Quilley set aside the book. It was already dark outside, and the downpour that the humid, cloudy day had been promising had just begun. Rain slapped against the asphalt roof-tiles, gurgled down the drainpipe, and pattered on the leaves of the overhanging trees. In the background, it hissed as it fell on the lake. Distant flashes of lightning and deep rumblings of thunder warned of the coming storm.

Happy with his solitude and his cleverness, Quilley linked his hands behind his head and leaned back in the chair. Out back, he heard the rustling of a small animal making its way through the undergrowth—a raccoon, perhaps, or even a skunk. When he closed his eyes, he pictured all the trees, shrubs, and wild flowers around the cottage and marveled at what deadly potential so many of them contained.

THE SUN BLAZED DOWN on the back patio of the Madison, a small garden protected from the wind by high fences. Quilley wore his sunglasses and nursed a pint of Conner's Ale. The place was packed. Skilled and pretty waitresses came and went, trays laden with baskets of chicken wings and golden pints of lager.

The two of them sat out of the way at a white table in a corner by the metal fire escape. A striped parasol offered some protection, but the sun was still too hot and too bright. Peplow's wife must have given him hell about drinking the last time, because today he had ordered only a Coke.

"It was easy," Quilley said. "You could have done it yourself. The only setback was that foxgloves don't grow wild here like they do in England. But you're a gardener; you grow them."

Peplow shook his head and smiled. "It's the gift of clever people like yourself to make difficult things seem easy. I'm not particularly resourceful, Mr. Quilley. Believe me, I wouldn't have known where to start. I had no idea that such a book existed, but you did, because of your art. Even if I had known, I'd hardly have dared buy it or take it out of the library for fear that someone would remember. But you've had your copy for years. A simple tool of the trade. No, Mr. Quilley, please don't underestimate your contribution. I was a desperate man. Now you've given me a chance at freedom. If there's anything at all I can do for you, please don't hesitate to say. I'd consider it an honor."

"This collection of yours," Quilley said. "What does it consist of?"

"British and Canadian crime fiction, mostly. I don't like to boast, but it's a very good collection. Try me. Go on, just mention a name."

"E. C. R. Lorac."

"About twenty of the Inspector MacDonalds. First editions, mint condition."

"Anne Hocking?"

"Everything but *Night's Candles*."

"Trotton?"

Peplow raised his eyebrows. "Good Lord, that's an obscure one. Do you know, you're the first person I've come across who's ever mentioned that."

"Do you have it?"

"Oh, yes." Peplow smiled smugly. "X. J. Trotton, *Signed in Blood*, published 1942. It turned up in a pile of junk I bought at an auction some years ago. It's rare but not very valuable. Came out in Britain during the war and probably died an immediate death. It was his only book, as far as I can make out, and there is no biographical information. Perhaps it was a pseudonym for someone famous?"

Quilley shook his head. "I'm afraid I don't know. Have you read it?"

"Good Lord, no! I don't read them. It could damage the spines. Many of them are fragile. Anything I want to read—like your books—I also buy in paperback."

"Mr. Peplow," Quilley said slowly, "you asked if there was anything you could do for me. As a matter of fact, there is something you can give me for my services."

"Yes?"

"The Trotton."

Peplow frowned and pursed his thin lips. "Why on earth . . . ?"

"For my own collection, of course. I'm especially interested in the war period."

Peplow smiled. "Ah! So that's how you knew so much about them? I'd no idea you were a collector, too."

Quilley shrugged modestly. He could see Peplow struggling, visualizing the gap in his collection. But finally the poor man decided that the murder of his wife was more important to him than an obscure mystery novel. "Very well," he said gravely. "I'll mail it to you."

"How can I be sure . . . ?"

Peplow looked offended. "I'm a man of my word, Mr. Quilley. A bargain is a bargain." He held out his hand. "Gentleman's agreement."

"All right." Quilley believed him. "You'll be in touch, when it's done?"

"Yes. Perhaps a brief note in with the Trotton, if you can wait that long. Say two or three weeks?"

"Fine. I'm in no hurry."

Quilley hadn't examined his motives since the first meeting, but he had realized, as he passed on the information and instructions, that it was the challenge he responded to more than anything else. For years he had been writing crime novels, and in providing Peplow with the means to kill his slatternly, overbearing wife, Quilley had derived some vicarious pleasure from the knowledge that he—Inspector Baldry's creator—could bring off in real life what he had always been praised for doing in fiction.

Quilley also knew that there were no real detectives who possessed Baldry's curious mixture of intellect and instinct. Most of them were thick plodders, and they would never realize that dull Mr. Peplow had murdered his wife with a bunch of foxgloves, of all things. Nor would they ever know that the brains behind the whole affair had been none other than his, Dennis Quilley's.

The two men drained their glasses and left together. The corner of Bloor and Spadina was busy with tourists and students lining up for charcoal-grilled hot dogs from the street vendor. Peplow turned toward the subway and Quilley wandered among the artsy crowd and the Rollerbladers on Bloor Street West for a while, then he settled at an open air cafe over a daiquiri and a slice of kiwi-fruit cheesecake to read the *Globe and Mail*.

Now, he thought as he sipped his drink and turned to the arts section, all he had to do was wait. One day soon, a small package would arrive for him. Peplow would be free of his wife, and Quilley would be the proud owner of one of the few remaining copies of X. J. Trotton's one and only mystery novel, *Signed in Blood*.

THREE WEEKS PASSED, AND no package arrived. Occasionally, Quilley thought of Mr. Peplow and wondered what had become of him. Perhaps he had lost his nerve after all. That wouldn't be surprising. Quilley knew that he would have no way of finding out what had happened if Peplow chose not to contact him again. He didn't know where the man lived or where he worked. He didn't even know if Peplow was his real name. Still, he thought, it was best that way. No contact. Even the Trotton wasn't worth being involved in a botched murder for.

Then, at ten o'clock one warm Tuesday morning in September, the doorbell chimed. Quilley looked at his watch and frowned. Too early for the postman. Sighing, he pressed the save command on his PC and walked down to answer the door. A stranger stood there, an overweight woman in a yellow polka-dot dress with short sleeves and a low neck. She had piggy eyes set in a round face, and dyed red hair that looked limp and lifeless after a cheap perm. She carried an imitation crocodile-skin handbag.

Quilley must have stood there looking puzzled for too long. The woman's eyes narrowed and her rosebud mouth tightened so much that white furrows radiated from the red circle of her lips.

"May I come in?" she asked.

Stunned, Quilley stood back and let her enter. She walked straight over to a wicker armchair and sat down. The basket-work creaked under her. From there, she surveyed the room, with its waxed parquet floor, stone fireplace, and antique Ontario furniture.

"Nice," she said, clutching her purse on her lap. Quilley sat down opposite her. Her dress was a size too small and the material strained over her red, fleshy upper arms, and pinkish bosom. The hem rode up as she crossed her legs, exposing a wedge of fat, mottled thigh. Primly, she pulled it down again over her dimpled knees.

"I'm sorry to appear rude," said Quilley, regaining his composure, "but who the hell are you?"

"My name is Peplow," the woman said. "Mrs. Gloria Peplow. I'm a widow."

Quilley felt a tingling sensation along his spine, the way he always did when fear began to take hold of him.

He frowned and said, "I'm afraid I don't know you, do I?"

"We've never met," the woman replied, "but I think you knew my husband."

"I don't recall any Peplow. Perhaps you're mistaken?"

Gloria Peplow shook her head and fixed him with her piggy eyes. He noticed they were black, or as near as. "I'm not mistaken, Mr. Quilley. You didn't only know my husband, you also plotted with him to murder me."

Quilley flushed and jumped to his feet. "That's absurd! Look, if you've come here to make insane accusations like that, you'd better go." He stood like an ancient statue, one hand pointing dramatically toward the door.

Mrs. Peplow smirked. "Oh, sit down. You took very foolish standing there like that."

Quilley continued to stand. "This is my home, Mrs. Peplow, and I insist that you leave. Now!"

Mrs. Peplow sighed and opened the gilded plastic clasp on her purse.

She took out a Shoppers Drug Mart envelope, picked out two color photographs, and dropped them next to the Wedgwood dish on the antique wine table by her chair. Leaning forward, Quilley could see clearly what they were: one showed him standing with Peplow outside the Park Plaza, and the other caught the two of them talking outside the Scotiabank at Bloor and Spadina. Mrs. Peplow flipped the photos over, and Quilley saw that they had been date-stamped by the processors.

"You met with my husband at least twice to help him plan my death."

"That's ridiculous. I do remember him, now I've seen the picture. I just couldn't recollect his name. He was a fan. We talked about mystery, novels. I'm very sorry to hear that he's passed away."

"He had a heart attack, Mr. Quilley, and now I'm all alone in the world."

"I'm very sorry, but I don't see . . ."

Mrs. Peplow waved his protests aside. Quilley noticed the dark sweat stain on the tight material around her armpit. She fumbled with the catch on her purse again and brought out a pack of Export Lights and a book of matches.

"I don't allow smoking in my house," Quilley said. "It doesn't agree with me."

"Pity," she said, lighting the cigarette and dropping the spent match in the Wedgwood bowl. She blew a stream of smoke directly at Quilley, who coughed and fanned it away.

"Listen to me, Mr. Quilley," she said, "and listen good. My husband might have been stupid, but I'm not. He was not only a pathetic and boring little man, he was also an open book. Don't ask me why I married him. He wasn't even much of a man, if you know what I mean. Do you think I haven't known for some time that he was thinking of ways to get rid of me? I wouldn't give him a divorce because the one thing he did—the *only* thing he did—was provide for me, and he didn't even do that very well. I'd have got half if we divorced, but half of what he earned isn't enough to keep a bag-lady. I'd have had to go to work, and I don't like that idea. So I watched him. He got more and more desperate, more and more secretive. When he started looking smug, I knew he was up to something."

"Mrs. Peplow," Quilley interrupted, "this is all very well, but I don't see what it has to do with me. You come in here and pollute my home with smoke, then you start telling me some fairy tale about your husband, a man I met casually once or twice. I'm busy, Mrs. Peplow, and quite frankly I'd rather you left and let me get back to work."

"I'm sure you would." She flicked a column of ash into the Wedgwood bowl. "As I was saying, I knew he was up to something, so I started following him. I thought he might have another woman, unlikely as it seemed, so I took my camera along. I wasn't really surprised when he headed for the Park Plaza instead of going back to the office after lunch one day. I watched the elevator go up to the nineteenth floor, the bar, so I waited across the street in the crowd for him to come out again. As you know, I didn't have to wait very long. He came out with you. And it was just as easy the next time."

"I've already told you, Mrs. Peplow, he was a mystery buff, a fellow collector, that's all—"

"Yes, yes, I know he was. Him and his stupid catalogues and collection. Still," she mused, "it had its uses. That's how I found out who you were. I'd seen your picture on the book covers, of course. If I may say so, it does you more than justice." She looked him up and down as if he were a side of beef hanging in a butcher's window. He cringed. "As I was saying, my husband was obvious. I knew he must be chasing you for advice. He spends so much time escaping to his garden or his little world of books that it was perfectly natural he would go to a mystery novelist for advice rather than to a real criminal. I imagine you were a bit more accessible, too. A little flattery, and you were hooked. Just another puzzle for you to work on."

"Look, Mrs. Peplow—"

"Let me finish." She ground out her cigarette butt in the bowl. "Foxgloves, indeed! Do you think he could manage to brew up a dose of digitalis without leaving traces all over the place? Do you know what he did the first time? He put just enough in my Big Mac to make me a bit nauseous and make my pulse race, but he left the leaves and stems in the garbage! Can you believe that? Oh, I became very careful in my eating habits after that, Mr. Quilley. Anyway, your little plan didn't work. I'm here and he's dead."

Quilley paled. "My God, you killed him, didn't you?"

"He was the one with the bad heart, not me." She lit another cigarette.

"You can hardly blackmail me for plotting with your husband to kill you when *he's* the one who's dead," said Quilley. "And as for evidence, there's nothing. No, Mrs. Peplow, I think you'd better go, and think yourself lucky I don't call the police."

Mrs. Peplow looked surprised. "What are you talking about? I have no intention of blackmailing you for plotting to kill me."

"Then what . . . ?"

"Mr. Quilley, my husband was blackmailing you. That's why *you* killed *him*."

Quilley slumped back in his chair. "I what?"

She took a sheet of paper from her purse and passed it over to him. On it were just two words: "Trotton-Quilley." He recognized the neat handwriting. "That's a photocopy," Mrs. Peplow went on. "The original's where I found it, slipped between the pages of a book called *Signed in Blood* by X. J. Trotton. Do you know that book, Mr. Quilley?"

"Vaguely. I've heard of it."

"Oh, have you? It might also interest you to know that along with that book and the slip of paper, locked away in my husband's files, is a copy of your own first novel. I put it there."

Quilley felt the room spinning around him. "I . . . I . . ." Peplow had given him the impression that Gloria was stupid, but that was turning out to be far from the truth.

"My husband's only been dead for two days. If the doctors look, they'll *know* that he's been poisoned. For a start, they'll find high levels of potassium, and then they'll discover *eosinophilia*. Do you know what they are, Mr. Quilley! I looked them up. They're a kind of white blood cell, and you find lots of them around if there's been any allergic reaction or inflammation. If I was to go to the police and say I'd been suspicious about my husband's behavior over the past few weeks, that I had followed him and photographed him with you, and if they were to find the two books and the slip of paper in his files . . . Well, I think you know what they'd make of it, don't you? Especially if I told them he came home feeling ill after a lunch with you."

"It's not fair," Quilley said, banging his fist on the chair arm. "It's just not bloody fair."

"Life rarely is. But the police aren't to know how stupid and unimaginative my husband was. They'll just look at the note, read the books, and assume he was blackmailing you." She laughed. "Even if Frank had read the Trotton book, I'm sure he'd have only noticed an 'influence,' at the most. But you and I know what really went on, don't we? It happens more often than people think. A few years ago I read in the newspaper about similarities between a book by Colleen McCullough and *The Blue Castle* by Lucy Maud Montgomery. I'd say that was a bit obvious, wouldn't you? It was much easier in your case, much less dangerous. You were very clever, Mr. Quilley. You found an obscure novel, and you didn't only adapt the plot for your own first book, you even stole the character of your series detective. There was some risk involved, certainly, but not much. Your book is better, without a doubt. You have some writing talent, which X. J. Trotton completely lacked. But he did have the germ of an original idea, and it wasn't lost on you, was it?"

Quilley groaned. Thirteen solid police procedurals, twelve of them all his own work, but the first, yes, a deliberate adaptation of a piece of ephemeral trash. He had seen what Trotton could have done and had done it himself. Serendipity, or so it had seemed when he found the dusty volume in a second-hand bookshop in Victoria years ago. All he had had to do was change the setting from London to Toronto, alter the names, and set about improving upon the original. And now . . . ? The hell of it was that he would have been perfectly safe without the damn book. He had simply given in to the urge to get his hands on Peplow's copy and destroy it. It wouldn't have mattered, really. *Signed in Blood* would have remained unread on Peplow's shelf. If only the bloody fool hadn't written that note . . .

"Even if the police can't make a murder charge stick," Mrs. Peplow went on, "I think your reputation would suffer if this got out. Oh, the great reading public might not care. Perhaps a trial would even increase your sales—you know how ghoulish people are—but the plagiarism would at the very least lose you the respect of your peers. I don't think your agent and publisher would be very happy, either. Am I making myself clear?"

Pale and sweating, Quilley nodded. "How much?" he whispered.

"Pardon?"

"I said how much. How much do you want to keep quiet?"

"Oh, it's not your money I'm after, Mr. Quilley, or may I call you Dennis? Well, not *only* money, anyway. I'm a widow now. I'm all alone in the world."

She looked around the room, her piggy eyes glittering, then gave Quilley one of the most disgusting looks he'd ever had in his life.

"I've always fancied living near the lake," she said, reaching for another cigarette. "Live here alone, do you?"

Jim and Mary G

JAMES SALLIS

James Sallis's Introduction:

"Jim and Mary G" was written in London around 1968. At the time I'd published equal portions of poetry and science fiction, and was in the UK editing the avant-garde New Worlds, *a science fiction magazine that had contrived to pull itself up by its own bootstraps to become something else, though none of us were sure exactly what, and which published everything from Harlan Ellison's "A Boy and His Dog" to early, fine work from J. G. Ballard and D. M. Thomas. It was a magic time for me: discovering Hammett and Chandler, reading for the first time contemporary French writers like Queneau and Vian, finding my way toward Cendrars, Guillevic, Bonnefoy.*

My own work was becoming suffused with this odd parley of influences. I was just starting to try and write stories that might be read in several ways, or on several levels, simultaneously. What I wanted was a prose with a sensual surface, one as close as I could make it to actual perception itself: to that perpetual present tense in which we actually experience and expend our lives. I was also just beginning, though I'd never bring it directly up out of the shaft—and yes, I know writers are supposed to start this way, but I've always been slow to get the point—to mine the materials of my own life.

So "Jim and Mary G" became a major turning point for me. Nothing I wrote after it would be much like what I'd written before. When the story was published in Orbit, *editor Damon Knight received a number of strong letters. One woman wrote that, having come across this story, she absolutely refused to read the rest of the anthology, nor would she ever again read anything with Damon's or my name on it. And yet, first of all, it's a love story . . .*

Jim and Mary G

JAMES SALLIS

GETTING HIS LITTLE COAT down off the hook, then his arms into it, not easy because he's so excited and he always turns the wrong way anyhow. And all the time he's looking up at you with those blue eyes. We go park Papa, he says. We go see gulls. Straining for the door. The gulls are a favorite; he discovered them on the boat coming across and can't understand, he keeps looking for them in the park.

Wrap the muffler around his neck. Yellow, white. (Notice how white the skin is there, how the veins show through.) They call them scarves here don't they. Stockingcap—he pulls it down over his eyes, going Haha. He hasn't learned to laugh yet. Red mittens. Now move the zipper up and he's packed away. The coat's green corduroy, with black elastic at the neck and cuffs and a round hood that goes down over the cap. It's November. In England. Thinking, The last time I do this. Is there still snow on the ground, I didn't look this morning.

Take his hand and go on out of the flat. Letting go at the door because it takes two hands to work the latch, Mary rattling dishes in the kitchen. (Good-bye, she says very softly as you shut the door.) He goes around you and beats you to the front door, waits there with his nose on the glass. The hall is full of white light. Go on down it to him. The milk's come, two bottles, with the *Guardian* leaning between them. Move the mat so we can open the door, We go park Papa, we see gulls. Frosty foggy air coming in. Back for galoshes, all

272

the little brass-tongue buckles? No the snow's gone. Just some dirty slush. Careful. Down the steps.

Crunching down the sidewalk ahead of you, disappointed because there's no snow but looking back, Haha. We go park? The sky is flat and white as a sheet of paper. Way off, a flock of birds goes whirling across it, circling inside themselves—black dots, like iron filings with a magnet under the paper. The block opposite is lined with trees. What kind? The leaves are all rippling together. It looks like green foil. Down the walk.

Asking, Why is everything so still. Why aren't there any cars. Or a mailtruck. Or milkcart, gliding along with bottles jangling. Where is everyone. It's ten in the morning, where is everyone.

But there is a car just around the corner, stuck on ice at the side of the road where it parked last night with the wheels spinning Whrrrrr. Smile, you understand a man's problems. And walk the other way. His mitten keeps coming off in your hand. Haha.

SHE HAD BROKEN DOWN only once, at breakfast.

The same as every morning, the child had waked them. Standing in his bed in the next room and bouncing up and down till the springs were banging against the frame. Then he climbed out and came to their door, peeking around the frame, finally doing his tiptoe shyly across the floor in his white wool nightshirt. Up to their bed, where they pretended to be still asleep. Brekpust, Brekpust, he would say, poking at them and tugging the covers, at last climbing onto the bed to bounce up and down between them until they rolled over: Hello. Morninggg. He is proud of his G's. Then, Mary almost broke down, remembering what today was, what they had decided the night before.

She turned her face toward the window (they hadn't been able to afford curtains yet) and he heard her breathe deeply several times. But a moment later she was up—out of bed in her quilted robe and heading for the kitchen, with the child behind her.

He reached and got a cigarette off the trunk they were using as a night table. It had a small wood lamp, a bra, some single cigarettes, and a jarlid full of ashes and filters on it. Smoking, listening to water running, pans clatter, cupboards, and drawers. Then the sounds stopped and he heard them, together in the bathroom: the tap ran for a while, then the toilet flushed and he heard the child's pleased exclamations. They went back into the kitchen and the sounds resumed. Grease crackling, the child chattering about how good he had been. The fridge door opened and shut, opened again, Mary said something. He was trying to help.

He got out of bed and began dressing. How strange that she'd forgotten to take him to the bathroom first thing, she'd never done that before. Helpinggg, from the kitchen by way of explanation, as he walked to the bureau. It was square and ugly, with that shininess peculiar to cheap furniture, and it had been in the flat when they moved in, the only thing left behind. He opened a drawer and took out a shirt. All his shirts were white. Why, she had once asked him, years ago. He didn't know, then or now.

He went into the kitchen with the sweater over his head. "Mail?" Through the wool. Neither of them looked around, so he pulled it the rest of the way on, reaching down inside to tug the shirt collar out. Then the sleeves.

"A letter from my parents. They're worried they haven't heard from us, they hope we're all right. Daddy's feeling better, why don't we write them."

The child was dragging his highchair across the floor from the corner. Long ago they had decided he should take care of as many of his own needs as he could—a sense of responsibility, Mary had said—but this morning Jim helped him carry the chair to the table, slid the tray off, lifted him into it, and pushed the chair up to the table. When he looked up, Mary turned quickly away, back to the stove.

Eggs, herring, toast, and ham. "I thought it would be nice," Mary said. "To have a good breakfast." And that was the time she broke down.

The child had started scooping the food up in his fingers, so she got up again and went across the kitchen to get his spoon. It was heavy silver, with an ivory *K* set into the handle, and it had been her own. She turned and came back across the tile, holding the little spoon in front of her and staring at it. Moma cryinggg, the child said. Moma cryinggg. She ran out of the room. The child turned in his chair to watch her go, then turned back and went on eating with the spoon. The plastic padding squeaked as the child moved inside it. The chair was metal, the padding white with large blue asterisks all over it. They had bought it at a Woolworth's. Twelve and six. Like the bureau, it somehow fit the flat.

A few minutes later Mary came back, poured coffee for both of them and sat down across from him.

"It's best this way," she said. "He won't have to suffer. It's the only answer."

He nodded, staring into the coffee. Then he took off his glasses and cleaned them on his shirttail. The child was stirring the eggs and herring together in his bowl. Holding the spoon like a chisel in his hand and going round and round the edge of the bowl.

"Jim . . ."

He looked up. She seemed to him, then, very tired, very weak.

"We could take him to one of those places. Where they . . . take care of them . . . for you."

He shook his head, violently. "No, we've already discussed that, Mary. He wouldn't understand. It will be easier, my way. If I do it myself."

She went to the window and stood there watching it. It filled most of one wall. It was frosted over.

"How would you like to go for a walk after breakfast?" he asked the child. He immediately shoved the bowl away and said, "Bafroom first?"

"You or me?" Mary said from the window.

Finally: "You."

He sat alone in the kitchen, thinking. Taps ran, the toilet flushed, he came out full of pride. "We go park," he said. "We go see gulls."

"Maybe." It was this, the lie, which came back to him later; this was what he remembered most vividly. He got up and walked into the hall with the child following him and put his coat on. "Where's his other muffler?"

"In the bureau drawer. The top one."

He got it, then began looking for the stockingcap and mittens. Walking through the rooms, opening drawers. There aren't any seagulls in London. When she brought the cap and mittens to him there was a hole in the top of the cap and he went off looking for the other one. Walking through rooms, again and again into the child's own.

"For God's sake go on," she finally said. "Please stop. O damn, Jim, go on." And she turned and ran back into the kitchen.

Soon he heard her moving about. Clearing the table, running water, opening and shutting things. Silverware clicking.

"We go park?"

He began to dress the child. Getting his little coat down off the hook. Wrapping his neck in the muffler. There aren't any seagulls in London. Stockingcap, Haha.

Thinking, This is the last time I'll ever do this.

Now bump, bump, bump. Down the funny stairs.

WHEN HE RETURNED, MARY was lying on the bed, still in the quilted robe, watching the ceiling. It seemed very dark, very cold in the room. He sat down beside her in his coat and put his hand on her arm. Cars moved past the window. The people upstairs had their radio on.

"Why did you move the bureau?" he asked after a while.

Without moving her head she looked down toward the foot of the bed. "After you left I was lying here and I noticed a traffic light or something like that out on the street was reflected in it. It was blinking on and off, I must have watched it for an hour. We've been here for weeks and I never saw that before. But once I did, I had to move it."

"You shouldn't be doing heavy work like that."

For a long while she was still, and when she finally moved, it was just to turn her head and look silently into his face.

He nodded, once, very slowly.

"It didn't . . ."

No.

She smiled, sadly, and still in his coat, he lay down beside her in the small bed. She seemed younger now, rested, herself again. There was warmth in her hand when she took his own and put them together on her stomach.

They lay quietly through the afternoon. Ice was re-forming on the streets; outside, they could hear wheels spinning, engines racing. The hall door opened, there was a jangle of milkbottles, the door closed. Then everything was quiet. The trees across the street drooped under the weight of the ice.

There was a sound in the flat. Very low and steady, like a ticking. He listened for hours before he realized it was the drip of a faucet in the bathroom.

Outside, slowly, obscuring the trees, the night came. And with it snow. They lay together in the darkness, looking out the frosted window. Occasionally, lights moved across it.

"We'll get rid of his things tomorrow," she said after a while.

The White Death

JUSTIN SCOTT

Justin Scott's Introduction:

The deer ate the garden and Dorothy Salisbury Davis told me to submit a short story to Sara Peretsky, who was editing an anthology called Beastly Tales. *All the writers I knew were combing their bottom drawers for typescripts featuring animals, but I'd never written a short story. I was afraid of them. I knew just enough about them to know they were harder than novels. Then Jack Carey came down from Litchfield to build me an electric deer fence and while he was stringing wire he told me a story about a murderous dog.*

Jack had built a fence to keep coyotes out of a sheep farm. But the coyotes enjoyed eating sheep so much that they were willing to endure painful electric shocks to breech the fence. They would actually scream as they slithered through the wire. Once inside, the slaughter would begin. So the farmer imported a special French sheep-guarding dog from the Pyrenees Mountains. Bred to kill wolves, the Great Pyrenees cleaned the coyotes' clocks in short order. But soon after he arrived, dogs started turning up dead.

House dogs, guard dogs, stray dogs, lap dogs all mangled to death. And before they caught the murderer, the farmer's neighbors buried many a best friend. It turned out that the French guard dog had a screw loose. Unable, or unwilling, to sort coyotes from his fellow dogs, he was murdering canines in general, just to be on the safe side.

Now there was a short story, even for someone who'd never written one. And a beastly murder mystery at that. But before I could write it, I needed to choose my central character. Who was the detective? Who on a working farm could solve the mystery and confront the murderer?

I started my first short story when I realized which animal possessed all the characteristics of a classic detective. He was a loner, beholden to no one; he was quick on his feet; he had a rep for being curious; and with few responsibilities, he had time to nose around.

The White Death

JUSTIN SCOTT

THE CAT HAD LITTLE use for dogs, but he liked action.

Comings and goings around the farm beat the long nothing times in between. So when the new dogs arrived in big red, white, and blue Air France crates peppered with air holes, the cat was on hand for the opening.

The humans were excited. They'd been tearing their hair out since the coyotes got into the sheep. There weren't even supposed to be coyotes in Connecticut, but suddenly there were, big, mean, and hungry. They were averaging a lamb a night and twice they'd taken a ewe. The humans called them a vicious pack. The cat knew better. He had done a little prowling himself and had observed, carefully, that they were not a pack, but a family—three nearly grown male pups and a mother and father, who seemed quite devoted to each other. Whether they were vicious involved subtleties that did not interest the cat. But the fact was, the coyotes regarded anything they could catch and overpower as dinner, which was why the humans had sent away for three dogs specially trained in France to protect sheep.

The cat expected standard poodles, for his only experience with French dogs was his old housemate Roger, an enormous poodle who was so old that his teeth were falling out; the cat often found them in odd corners, worn smooth like pebbles in the stream.

Instead, out of the Air France crates came three monsters as unlike old Roger as hawks from a chicken. White as clouds, big as lawn tractors, and armed with teeth you had to see to believe, they glowered about suspiciously. Attaining another perspective atop the pickup truck, the cat named the newcomers White Death One, Two, and Three to keep track of them. Even the humans were awed until, apparently satisfied no coyotes were lurking, White Death One, Two, and Three wagged their extravagant tails. Then there was a bit of applause and checking names and showing them their beds in the barn and throwing sticks and Frisbees. The cat went indoors for a nap.

With the White Death roaming the farm, that night not a sheep was killed. And when the neighbor's dog was discovered dead in the morning, the humans said the coyote pack had attacked him instead. Family, thought the cat, they're not a pack, they're a family, mother, father, three big pups. A vicious pack, the humans said, the poor dog didn't have a chance.

The cat failed to understand the tragedy. The poor dog in question was a vicious brute who had taken pleasure in annihilating rabbits, chipmunks, and cats. Things had worked out rather nicely, in fact.

The following morning, the sheep were fine and another neighbor's dog had been killed. The coyotes, the humans said, were getting desperate. One of these days they would run into the wrong dog. There was even talk of lending out the White Death. The cat went for a look at the body.

Another miscreant sent to a well-deserved grave. Curiously, though, the coyotes hadn't eaten him, just torn out his throat as neatly as if the vet had done it with his knife. "What are you looking at?" yelled a human with a shovel, obviously put out at losing his dog.

Nothing, the cat mumbled to himself and walked away.

Things were quiet for the next few nights, sheep zero, dogs zero, coyotes zero. The coyotes had gone, the humans said, which was not true. They were quiet, mulling things over. The cat could smell them and had come upon one of their kills, some dumb possum they'd caught in the open. Accordingly, he maintained cautious habits, paying particular attention to the wind direction, avoiding open spaces and, when he had to cross them, first plotting escape routes which, with coyotes, meant trees. There was no point in seeking cover they could dig up. It was trees or nothing.

Meanwhile, the White Death formed a routine of sleeping most of the day in the barn, waking occasionally to frolic with the children, doze in the sun, and eat. The cat felt their eyes on him at odd moments and made a habit of staying out of their way. Nonetheless, he had a nasty scare, thanks to the human mother who was as fast as a snake sometimes. She scooped him off the warm hood of the pickup and started one of her amusing (to her) waltzes around the yard with him in her arms, right up to the White Death, singing which of them would like the next dance, dangling him like a morsel of fresh liver. When the cat went rigid, she laughed and hugged him and said, "They won't hurt you, cat, they are very well trained. Aren't you?" she asked, and all three White Death looked up with complexity in their beady black eyes.

The humans were discussing another dead dog with a neighbor who drove up in a station wagon. Throat torn out again, the cat discovered when he went to check. A big golden retriever, dog enough to feed a whole coyote family. But his body was unmarked except, the cat noticed on closer inspection, for a crushed leg. The dog had put up a fight, all right.

It started to rain and the cat headed home, thinking things over, and regretting his curiosity. He had come a long way and he was getting wet. He broke into a smooth miles-eating gait and took a shortcut across a broad hayfield. He had known that dog, hadn't cared for him one way or another, just a dog too fat to chase cats.

Protracted thinking was not his strong suit. His mind ran more toward quick decisions, quickly forgotten. He got so tangled in his thinking that he practically broke a leg falling over a startled chipmunk. Calculating the hours until dinner, he thought what the hell and started after a snack. The chipmunk had a head start and dove into a hole. Digging him out in the rain sounded muddy. He was just turning away, when he sensed a rush from behind.

Dumb, he thought, pressing flat instinctively in the wet grass, you deserve to die. The coyote, thank the moon, flew over him like a golden express train. And die he would have, had it been the father coyote instead of a clumsy pup. Leaping twelve feet, the cat hit the grass running, searching frantically for a tree, which experience told him tended to be scarce in hayfields. *Dumb, dumb, dumb*. The coyote was after him, yapping, covering ground fast, calling his relations. Ahead was a stone wall and beyond the wall another empty hayfield. He leaped onto the wall and ran along it. The coyote practically howled for joy at how slow he went, and gathered his skinny legs for a killing jump. The cat located the hole he was hoping for and dove into a little cave among the big stones. He crouched inside, catching his breath, lowering his heartbeat, while the coyote family gathered, raging with frustration.

Other than being alive, the cat was not pleased. Rainwater was dripping on his back. The moon alone knew how long it would take a family of starving coyotes to get bored, for starving they were, all skin and bones and teeth. He hated sleeping wet. Outside the coyotes paced. Inside, the cat heard a hiss and tracked the sound through the dark until he saw a snake coiled in a corner. He had had just about enough. Spreading his foreclaws and baring his teeth, he snarled, "Screw off, scurf head!"

The snake blinked and slithered away, disappearing into a crack like a tongue between teeth.

When he got home that night, the human mother scooped him up and nearly crushed the life out of him, crying, "Thank God! I thought the coyotes got you. They killed two more dogs. I thought they'd got you, too. Poor baby, you're wet! Are you hungry?"

The cat allowed he was and the human mother heaped so much chicken in his dish that old Roger the poodle moseyed out to see what he would leave. "Don't even think about it," said the cat and Roger said, "Okay," and lay down to watch him eat, which made the very good chicken taste even more delicious.

Roger lay there, his milky eyes aglow with misguided hope, his ancient stomach rumbling, his failing ears pricking feebly at the sounds of the night.

"Coyotes," the cat explained. "Four miles."

"Right," Roger lied. "I thought so."

The cat ate some more. Roger's ears flailed about.

"Great-barred owl."

"I know."

The New York-to-Boston shuttle flew over, five minutes late, and the cat said, "Pickup truck on the wooden bridge."

"Right."

The cat sighed. "Listen, Roger, do me a favor."

"What?"

"Don't go out at night."

"Why not?"

"Just don't go out at night."

"I only go for a little walk. You know that. Oh, you think the coyotes will take a shot at me? Forget it. I don't go far. Besides, we've got the Great Pyrenees protecting us."

"Yeah."

The cat did not have a great memory. Most days started off new for him and he often delighted in discoveries like blue sky, white clouds, trees, even the taste of food. He got through the serious parts of life by instinct: his body knew to duck a flying coyote, which actually worked faster than thinking about it. But he possessed certain core memories in addition to instinct—four memories to be exact. One had to do with the smell of the human mother, which sometimes made his knees go weak. The other three all involved Roger. He had slept on Roger's huge dome of a head when he was a kitten, warm, in its woolly fuzz. Roger would be there, without moving for hours in front of the fire while the cat slept. Then, one day when he was grown and rarely noticed Roger, a fast and nasty little terrier caught him in the open and it looked bad until with a bone-chilling bay Roger came galloping from the house, a Roger he had never seen before, with long teeth and murder in his eye. As far as he knew, the terrier was still running. The third memory was vintage Roger. Some wit from New York visiting the humans had remarked that if his miniature poodle could jump over a sofa, perhaps a big standard like Roger could clear the garage. To the cat's astonishment, Roger had tried, twice, which was why the cat said, "Roger, let's just stay in, tonight. Okay?"

"Okay. But just tonight. I need my exercise."

The cat sat up with him until Roger fell asleep and the humans locked the door. It took a while and he got a later start than he had hoped, but it couldn't be helped. He slipped out, using an upstairs bathroom window instead of his cat door, in case the killer was watching.

He observed the farm from the gutter, his back to the house lights, until his eyes had adjusted fully to the dark. The sheep were grazing. He could hear their chopping at the grass. The White Death had set up their usual perimeter, one between the house and the sheep, two pacing the rim of the outer field. Every fifteen minutes or so one conferred with the other two and sometimes they exchanged positions. Once, they seemed to lay a trap, two falling back to the house, the third hiding among the sheep, white and woolly as they, tempting the coyotes to try something. The coyotes weren't buying it. The cat heard them on the wind, five miles off, at least. After two hours, the White Death changed tactics, huddling for a strategy conference before sending one of their number off into the dark.

The cat, whose hearing was superb when he remembered to listen to it, overheard their strategy and started out after the Great Pyrenees. It was White Death Two, whose rangy silhouette the cat recognized flitting through the trees.

He found it tough keeping up, at first. The big dog was putting distance between himself and the farm, and the cat had to run flat out at a pace he thought he couldn't hold more than two miles. He hung in for three before the beast slowed to sniff the wind. The cat climbed gratefully onto a low tree limb to rest. A minute later, the dog was off like a shot. The cat tore after him, heart pounding, and juggling the thought that he might become the first cat in the state of Connecticut to die of overwork. He was very much considering giving the whole thing up.

Two more logging miles, and he concluded that the dumb dog he was following was genuinely after the coyotes. He could smell them and hear them. What White Death Two couldn't seem to understand was that the coyotes had no intention of letting him get within a mile of them. The cat didn't know how they did it in France, but here, if you really wanted to surprise a family of coyotes you had better approach downwind. The cat called it a night and went home.

He awakened stiff and sore late in the afternoon to angry humans shouting. The replacement dog at the neighboring farm, a highly trained German attack hound, had been killed, which pleased the cat mightily. As he knew that both the coyote family and White Death Two had been miles away, his suspects were reduced to White Death One and Three. On the other hand, he worried about what would happen if he trailed the wrong dog tonight and Roger took a walk. Fortunately, Roger was exhausted, having spent the entire day watching the cat sleep, which gave the poodle pleasures the cat could not begin to fathom.

The White Death repeated the same strategy that night and soon the cat found himself following the designated hunter, the barrel-chested White Death One, the biggest of the three. He started off slowly into the night, the cat pacing him easily. It was a little scary, knowing there was a fifty-fifty chance that this was the killer.

A mile from the farm he veered toward a wood that bordered a horse farm with a Doberman pinscher. The new Doberman pinscher, the cat recalled, the original, a truly horrible dog, having mislaid his throat. The cat got too close in his eagerness, and for an eerie second White Death One slowed and stared in his direction. The cat assumed the shape of a bent hemlock. The dog kept moving. When he came to the edge of the woods, close enough to the stables for the cat to hear the horses whispering, the white dog suddenly dropped to his belly, opened his toothsome mouth in a mighty yawn, and went to sleep.

The cat felt his jaw fall. White Death One was a slacker. He wasn't chasing coyotes, he was sleeping. The cat climbed a shaggy maple and stretched out to watch from a limb. An hour after the moon set, the Great Pyrenees got up, loped home, and reported to his colleagues that the coyotes had eluded him.

White Death Three, the one with the scariest light in his black eyes, sneered that One and Two were sorry excuses for hunters. He would make a sweep and settle the coyotes' hash once and for all. White Death One suggested that Three button his lip while he still had one. Both dogs went stiff-legged, hackles rising like wire, and for a pleasant moment the cat thought there would be bloodshed.

But White Death Two, shouldered between them with a prissy reminder that they had come a long way from a fine French school to do an important job. "This isn't about you or me, it's about the sheep." This made no sense to the cat, but One and Three mumbled abashed apologies and resumed patrol.

So Three was the killer, thought the cat. Lean, rangy Two couldn't catch a coyote in a million years and barrel-chested One was asleep at the switch. Three had a screw loose. Three was going out and killing dogs instead of coyotes. Why, the cat didn't know and didn't care, though it occurred to him that if, as the humans claimed, dogs and coyotes were so closely related they could mate—and there was a truly awful picture—maybe White Death Three just couldn't tell them apart.

The humans had come home late. The pickup truck was still warm. He climbed onto the tire under the front fender and luxuriated in the heat of the ticking engine. He had a marvelous thought. White Death Three could go on for years, killing every dog in the county, while the humans blamed the coyotes. How pleasant, how lovely. But what got him onto this subject? He felt a slight disquiet. Something had . . . Oh, moon! Roger. Poor, dumb, stupid, old Roger. One of these nights White Death Three would kill Roger. And the cat liked Roger, for some damned reason he couldn't remember at the moment. Stupid dog. Wouldn't have a chance, even if it was true that he had been in the navy. He said he was a commando with the Navy SEALS. Strongest bite in the Sixth Fleet or some stupid thing. Bit the propeller off a submarine. Now all he did was drop teeth. He hadn't a chance against White Death Three. Slowly, it all drifted back to the cat—the soft, fuzzy head, the terrier, the garage.

The pickup engine started with a roar. The cat jumped up, banged his head hard on the fender, and scrambled off the rolling tire. Moon! He had fallen asleep and hadn't heard them get in.

"Look out for the cat," the human mother said.

"Damned fool cat can look out for himself. Roger, you stay up on the porch 'fore them coyotes get ya." The truck roared down the drive, throwing gravel on the cat, and when it was quiet enough to hear again, the cat wandered onto the porch where Roger was mumbling, "I'm not staying on the porch. I'm going for a walk."

"Yeah, I'll walk with you to the barn," said the cat.

"No, I'm going for a real walk."

White Death Three was out there, and it was no night for a walk. "Let's just walk to the barn."

"You walk where you want, Cat. I'm going for a walk."

"The coyotes—"

"Did I ever tell you I was a commando?"

"Nightly, for seven years."

Roger didn't hear him. "I could take any three coyotes they can field."

"What if all five come?" asked the cat, knowing that there was no way he could explain White Death Three to dumb Roger.

"I would hear them coming in time to get back to the porch, taking you with me. All right?"

"Amtrak Metroliner, southbound," the cat lied.

"I know. I hear it."

They were at the barn and Roger showed no sign of stopping and the cat was wondering what to do with him when White Death One loomed suddenly from behind a feed crib. "Where you going, boys?"

"For a walk," said the cat. "What does it look like?"

"I wouldn't wander too far," White Death One replied. "Least until we finish off the coyotes." Fat chance, Sleeping Beauty, thought the cat.

"We'll keep an ear cocked," said Roger, breezing by the Great Pyrenees. The cat had to admire Roger's sense of self. Dumb, he certainly was, but he was a classy act, taking no guff from some foreign fieldhand. White Death One fell into pace alongside.

"Okay, I'll cover you."

"No need," said Roger.

The cat, thinking of White Death Three roaming the dark and five coyotes roaming the dark, said, "Suit yourself." To his relief, the huge white guard dog stayed with them.

After a mile of walking and sniffing, Roger asked, "Who's watching the sheep?"

"Two's plenty."

The cat's mind was drifting. With the moon down there wasn't a lot to see. He could smell the coyotes on the wind. And he could hear them, talking quietly among themselves three miles off. He was listening for White Death Three, listening for the sounds of a short scuffle and sudden death as the killer nailed another farm dog.

He felt safe as long as One was here. Three wasn't about to kill Roger in front of One.

One had gotten quiet. He and Roger had been talking at first, trading war stories, Roger going on about some escapade in the Mediterranean and One about wolf tracking. He admitted that he and his colleagues thought the coyotes were a bit of a joke, having tousled with mountain wolves.

"Then how come they're still out there?" the cat had asked and One got very quiet. They had stopped in a small clearing. The cat was picking up strange sounds and went up a beech tree to try to get a fix on them. It was the coyotes, closer now, two miles, and whispering, urgently. The cat climbed higher, until he could hear the conversation.

"It's the white dog, again. The dumb one, Crazy Eyes." Three, thought the cat. Crazy Eyes was Three. Tracking coyotes instead of killing dogs. What in moon was going on?

"If that dumb Crazy Eyes ever learns to attack from downwind, we're in trouble," growled the coyote mother.

"I have half a mind to rip his head off before he does."

"There are easier ways to earn a living, son. Let's go, everyone. Make tracks."

"Damn. Where's Big Chest?" Big Chest would be Two.

"Patrolling the farm."

"Where's Sleepy Head?"

"Sleeping, probably."

"I said make tracks. Head down that stream."

The cat looked down from his tree limb. Roger was sitting on his haunches, smiling at the dark. He had apparently interpreted the coyote talk as the UPS van on a late-night delivery. White Death One was standing behind him, slowly wagging his tail. And he didn't look one bit sleepy.

The cat dropped from the tree, landing on stinging feet. "Let's go home, Roger."

"In a minute."

"Fight much in the navy?" asked White Death One.

Roger looked at him. "No." He was moving his jaw side to side, working a loose tooth with his tongue.

The cat heard the coyotes splashing down the stream bed, a quarter mile off, which paralleled the door trail they were on. Cocking his cars, he heard White Death Three moving further away, tracking the coyotes in the wrong direction. You really had to wonder about that French dog school.

The cat nuzzled up to Roger, rubbed his leg, and whispered very softly, "Roger, this dog is a psychotic killer. He's killed every dog in the neighborhood and now he's going to kill you."

"What did you say? Why are you mumbling?"

The cat glanced at White Death One, whose tail was starting to swish in a weird rhythm. White Death looked down at him and the cat thought, You know that I know, you misery. You *did* spot me tonight. You just pretended to sleep.

He tried to whisper another warning to Roger.

White Death One snarled, "Why don't you go home, you little reptile?"

"Don't bother the cat," Roger said mildly. "He can't help himself."

"What the *hell* is that supposed to mean?" the cat demanded.

"Get out of here while you still can," said White Death One.

"Leave the cat atone," said Roger, standing up and facing the big Pyrenees.

This stupid dog, thought the cat, is going to try to gum this killer to death on my behalf. He said, "Roger, I'm running down to the stream for a drink. Come with me."

"I'll wait."

"Come with me. I can't see too well in the dark."

Roger laughed, "You've got eyes like a cat. Okay, okay, I'll come." They started through the brush, the cat leading at a brisk trot, the Great Pyrenees trailing close.

They were still downwind of the coyotes, but at an angle, and any minute they would catch the dog scent or White Death One would hear them. It was now or never.

The cat bolted to the stream and ran up the bed, leaping from rock to rock. Around a bend, he came face to face with the golden eyes of a hungry coyote.

"Your mother mates with dogs."

The cat spun on his tail and raced back downstream.

They howled after him. The mother coyote forged ahead of her husband and sons, screaming, "I'll eat your liver, cat."

The cat scrambled from mossy stone to slippery log to cold wet gravel, then up the bank, through the brush, and smack into Roger, whom the Great Pyrenees had backed against a tree.

The cat was pleased to see the old poodle's instincts were still good, covering his back, but otherwise he looked helpless and utterly bewildered that White Death One would want to hurt him.

Tail thrashing, the Great Pyrenees poised to spring, so intent on murder that he didn't hear the coyotes until they had burst into the clearing. For one long second, no one moved. Then the cat jumped on Roger's back, said, "Jump!" and sunk his teeth in.

Roger gathered his old bones and jumped. The fact was he had made a pretty good shot at the garage, attaining the gutter the second try, and the cat felt that if there had only been a garage there in the woods, he might have made it this time. He jumped so high and so far that the cat nearly fell off. He saved himself with his claws, causing old Roger to jump again and leaving White Death One alone in the clearing with five angry coyotes.

The cat longed to stay for the carnage, but he feared Roger would get lost and blunder back into it, so he stayed aboard, nipping the old dog to steer him home, and sometimes just for the fun of it.

White Death Two and Three were at the house. The cat waited for the sounds of battle to die down.

"Your partner said he needs some help, couple miles down the deer path. He said one of you go now, the other wait five minutes."

Crazy Eyes charged into the night. Three minutes later Big Chest roared after him.

"I didn't hear that," said Roger, collapsing on the porch.

"With a little luck, we'll end up with maybe one Great Pyrenees and no coyotes."

"But I didn't hear him say that."

"Maybe you missed it when the train went by."

The Tinder Box

MINETTE WALTERS

Introduction for Minette Walters:

Jane Gregory, agent for Minette Walters, furnished this note on the origin of "The Tinder Box":

In 1998, CCMB, the Organization for the Promotion of the Dutch Book, invited Minette Walters to write the promotional suspense novella for 1999. Participating booksellers ordered three hundred thousand copies, a record number, and Minette traveled to Holland in May 1999 to support the promotion. Consequently, sales of all her novels soared.

Following first publication in Dutch, all Minette's foreign publishers are printing and publishing the story in different ways. In America it first appeared in Ellery Queen. In Australia the story was incorporated in the paperback edition of The Breaker. *French, German, and Norwegian editions will be published as a slim novella.*

The Tinder Box

MINETTE WALTERS

***THE DAILY TELEGRAPH—WEDNESDAY, 24TH JUNE, 1998
Sowerbridge Man Arrested

Patrick O'Riordan, thirty-five, an unemployed Irish laborer, was charged last night with the double murder of his neighbors Lavinia Fanshaw, ninety-three, and her live-in nurse, Dorothy Jenkins, sixty-seven. The murders have angered the small community of Sowerbridge where O'Riordan and his parents have lived for fifteen years. The elderly victims were brutally battered to death after Dorothy Jenkins interrupted a robbery on Saturday night. "Whoever killed them is a monster," said a neighbor. "Lavinia was a frail old lady with Alzheimer's who never hurt a soul." Police warned residents to remain calm after a crowd gathered outside the O'Riordan home when news of the arrest became public. "Vigilante behavior will not be tolerated," said a spokesman. O'Riordan denies the charges.

11:30 P.M.—MONDAY, 8TH MARCH 1999
Even at half past eleven at night, the lead news story on local radio was still the opening day of Patrick O'Riordan's trial. Siobhan Lavenham, exhausted after a fourteen-hour stint at work, listened to it in

298

the darkness of her car while she negotiated the narrow country lanes back to Sowerbridge village.

"... O'Riordan smiled as the prosecution case unfolded ... harrowing details of how ninety-three-year-old Lavinia Fanshaw and her live-in nurse were brutally bludgeoned to death before Mrs. Fanshaw's rings were ripped from her fingers ... scratch marks and bruises on the defendant's face, probably caused by a fight with one of the women ... a crime of greed triggered by O'Riordan's known resentment of Mrs. Fanshaw's wealth ... unable to account for his whereabouts at the time of the murders ... items of jewelry recovered from the O'Riordan family home which the thirty-five-year-old Irishman still shares with his elderly parents ..."

With a sinking heart, Siobhan punched the off button and concentrated on her driving. "The Irishman ..." Was that a deliberate attempt to inflame racist division, she wondered, or just careless shorthand? God, how she loathed journalists! Confident of a guilty verdict, they had descended on Sowerbridge like a plague of locusts the previous week in order to prepare their background features in advance. They had found dirt in abundance, of course. Sowerbridge had fallen over itself to feed them with hate stories against the whole O'Riordan family.

She thought back to the day of Patrick's arrest, when Bridey had begged her not to abandon them. "You're one of us, Siobhan. Irish through and through, never mind you're married to an Englishman. You know my Patrick. He wouldn't hurt a fly. Is it likely he'd beat Mrs. Fanshaw to death when he's never raised a hand against his own father? Liam was a devil when he still had the use of his arm. Many's the time he thrashed Patrick with a stick when the drunken rages were on him, but never once did Patrick take the stick to him."

It was a frightening thing to be reminded of the bonds that tied people together, Siobhan had thought as she looked out of Bridey's window toward the silent, angry crowd that was gathering in the road. Was being Irish enough of a reason to side with a man suspected of slaughtering a frail bedridden old woman and the woman who looked after her?

"Patrick admits he stole from Lavinia," Siobhan had pointed out.

Tears rolled down Bridey's furrowed cheeks. "But not her rings," she said. "Just cheap trinkets that he was too ignorant to recognize as worthless paste."

"It was still theft."

"Mother of God, do you think I don't know that?" She held out her hands beseechingly. "A thief he may be, Siobhan, but never a murderer."

And Siobhan had believed her because she wanted to. For all his sins, she had never thought of Patrick as an aggressive or malicious man—too relaxed by half, many would say—and he could always make her and her children laugh with his stories about Ireland, particularly ones involving leprechauns and pots of gold hidden at the ends of rainbows. The thought of him taking a hammer to anyone was anathema to her.

And yet . . . ?

In the darkness of the car she recalled the interview she'd had the previous month with a detective inspector at Hampshire Constabulary Headquarters who seemed perplexed that a well-to-do young woman should have sought him out to complain about police indifference to the plight of the O'Riordans. She wondered now why she hadn't gone to him sooner.

Had she really been so unwilling to learn the truth . . . ?

WEDNESDAY, 10TH FEBRUARY, 1999

The detective shook his head. "I don't understand what you're talking about, Mrs. Lavenham."

Siobhan gave an angry sigh. "Oh, for goodness sake! The hate campaign that's being waged against them. The graffiti on their walls, the constant telephone calls threatening them with arson, the fact that Bridey's too frightened to go out for fear of being attacked. There's a war going on in Sowerbridge which is getting worse the closer we come to Patrick's trial, but as far as you're concerned, it doesn't exist. Why aren't you investigating it? Why don't you respond to Bridey's telephone calls?"

He consulted a piece of paper on his desk. "Mrs. O'Riordan's made fifty-three emergency calls in the eight months since Patrick was remanded for the murders," he said, "only thirty of which were considered serious enough to send a police car to investigate. In every case, the attending officers filed reports saying Bridey was wasting police time." He gave an apologetic shrug. "I realize it's not what you want to hear, but we'd be within our rights if we decided to prosecute her. Wasting police time is a serious offense."

Siobhan thought of the tiny, wheelchair-bound woman whose terror was so real she trembled constantly. "They're after killing us, Siobhan," she would say over and over again. "I hear them creeping about the garden in the middle of the night and I think to myself, there's nothing me or Liam can do if this is the night they decide to break in. To be sure, it's only God who's keeping us safe."

"But who *are* they, Bridey?"

"It's the bully boys whipped up to hate us by Mrs. Haversley and Mr. Jardine," wept the woman. "Who else would it be?"

Siobhan brushed her long dark hair from her forehead and frowned at the detective inspector. "Bridey's old, she's disabled, and she's completely terrified. The phone never stops ringing. Mostly it's long silences, other times it's voices threatening to kill her. Liam's only answer to it all is to get paralytically drunk every night so he doesn't have to face up to what's going on." She shook her head impatiently. "Cynthia Haversley and Jeremy Jardine, who seem to control everything that happens in Sowerbridge, have effectively given carte blanche to the local youths to make life hell for them. Every sound, every shadow has Bridey on the edge of her seat. She needs protection, and I don't understand why you're not giving it to her."

"They were offered a safe house, Mrs. Lavenham, and they refused it."

"Because Liam's afraid of what will happen to Kilkenny Cottage if he leaves it empty," she protested. "The place will be trashed in half a minute flat . . . You know that as well as I do."

He gave another shrug, this time more indifferent than apologetic. "I'm sorry," he said, "but there's nothing we can do. If any of these attacks actually happened . . . well, we'd have something concrete to investigate. They can't even name any of these so-called vigilantes . . . just claim they're yobs from neighboring villages."

"So what are you saying?" she asked bitterly. "That they have to be dead before you take the threats against them seriously?"

"Of course not," he said, "but we do need to be persuaded the threats are real. As things stand, they seem to be all in her mind."

"Are you accusing Bridey of lying?"

He smiled slightly. "She's never been averse to embroidering the truth when it suits her purpose, Mrs. Lavenham."

Siobhan shook her head. "How can you say that? Have you ever spoken to her? Do you even *know* her? To you, she's just the mother of a thief and a murderer."

"That's neither fair nor true." He looked infinitely weary, like a defendant in a trial who has answered the same accusation in the same way a hundred times before. "I've known Bridey for years. It's part and parcel of being a policeman. When you question a man as often as I've questioned Liam, you get to know his wife pretty well by default." He leaned forward, resting his elbows on his knees and clasping his hands loosely in front of him. "And sadly, the one sure thing I know about Bridey is that you can't believe a word she says. It may not be her fault, but it is a fact. She's never had the courage to speak out honestly because her drunken brute of a husband beats her within an inch of her life if she even dares to think about it."

Siobhan found his directness shocking. "You're talking about things that happened a long time ago," she said. "Liam hasn't struck anyone since he lost the use of his right arm."

"Do you know how that happened?"

"In a car crash."

"Did Bridey tell you that?"

"Yes."

"Not so," he countered bluntly. "When Patrick was twenty, he tied Liam's arm to a tabletop and used a hammer to smash his wrist to a pulp. He was so wrought up that when his mother tried to stop him, he shoved her through a window and broke her pelvis so badly she's never been able to walk again. That's why she's in a wheelchair and why Liam has a useless right arm. Patrick got off lightly by pleading provocation because of Liam's past brutality toward him, and spent less than two years in prison for it."

Siobhan shook her head. "I don't believe you."

"It's true." He rubbed a tired hand around his face. "Trust me, Mrs. Lavenham."

"I can't," she said flatly. "You've never lived in Sowerbridge, Inspector. There's not a soul in that village who doesn't have it in for the O'Riordans and a juicy tidbit like that would have been repeated a thousand times. Trust *me.*"

"No one knows about it." The man held her gaze for a moment, then dropped his eyes. "It was fifteen years ago and it happened in London. I was a raw recruit with the Met, and Liam was on our ten-most-wanted list. He was a scrap-metal merchant, and up to his neck in villainy, until Patrick scuppered him for good. He sold up when the lad went to prison and moved himself and Bridey down here to start a new life. When Patrick joined them after his release, the story of the car crash had already been accepted."

She shook her head again. "Patrick came over from Ireland after being wounded by a terrorist bomb. That's why he smiles all the time. The nerves in his cheek were severed by a piece of flying glass." She sighed. "It's another kind of disability. People take against him because they think he's laughing at them."

"No, ma'am, it was a revenge attack in prison for stealing from his cell mate. His face was slashed with a razor. As far as I know, he's never set foot in Ireland."

She didn't answer. Instead she ran her hand rhythmically over her skirt while she tried to collect her thoughts. *Oh, Bridey, Bridey, Bridey . . . have you been lying to me . . . ?*

The inspector watched her with compassion. "Nothing happens in a vacuum, Mrs. Lavenham."

"Meaning what, exactly?"

"Meaning that Patrick murdered Mrs. Fanshaw—" he paused— "and both Liam and Bridey know he did. You can argue that the

physical abuse he suffered at the hands of his father as a child pro-
voked an anger in him that he couldn't control—it's a defense that
worked after the attack on Liam—but it won't cut much ice with a
jury when the victims were two defenseless old ladies. That's why
Bridey's jumping at shadows. She knows that she effectively signed
Mrs. Fanshaw's death warrant when she chose to keep quiet about
how dangerous Patrick was, and she's terrified of it becoming
public." He paused. "Which it certainly will during the trial."

Was he right, Siobhan wondered? Were Bridey's fears rooted in
guilt? "That doesn't absolve the police of responsibility for their
safety," she pointed out.

"No," he agreed, "except we don't believe their safety's in question. Frankly, all the evidence so far points to Liam himself being the
instigator of the hate campaign. The graffiti is always done at night
in car spray paint, at least a hundred cans of which are stored in
Liam's shed. There are never any witnesses to it, and by the time
Bridey calls us the perpetrators are long gone. We've no idea if the
phone rings as constantly as they claim, but on every occasion that a
threat has been made, Bridey admits she was alone in the cottage.
We think Liam is making the calls himself."

She shook her head in bewilderment. "Why would he do that?"

"To prejudice the trial?" he suggested. "He has a different mind-
set to you and me, ma'am, and he's quite capable of trashing
Kilkenny Cottage himself if he thinks it will win Patrick some sympathy with a jury."

Did she believe him? Was Liam that clever? "You said you were
always questioning him. Why? What had he done?"

"Any scam involving cars. Theft. Forging M.O.T. certificates.
Odometer fixing. You name it, Liam was involved in it. The scrap-
metal business was just a front for a car-laundering operation."

"You're talking about when he was in London?"

"Yes.

She pondered for a moment. "Did he go to prison for it?"

"Once or twice. Most of the time he managed to avoid conviction. He had money in those days—a lot of money—and could pay
top briefs to get him off. He shipped some of the cars down here,

presumably with the intention of starting the same game again, but he was a broken man after Patrick smashed his arm. I'm told he gave up grafting for himself and took to living off disability benefit instead. There's no way anyone was going to employ him. He's too unreliable to hold down a job. Just like his son."

"I see," said Siobhan slowly.

He waited for her to go on, and when she didn't he said: "Leopards don't change their spots, Mrs. Lavenham. I wish I could say they did, but I've been a policeman too long to believe anything so naive."

She surprised him by laughing. "Leopards?" she echoed. "And there was me thinking we were talking about dogs."

"I don't follow."

"Give a dog a bad name and hang him. Did the police *ever* intend to let them wipe the slate clean and start again, Inspector?"

He smiled slightly. "We did . . . for fifteen years . . . Then Patrick murdered Mrs. Fanshaw."

"Are you sure?"

"Oh, yes," he said. "He used the same hammer on her that he used on his father."

Siobhan remembered the sense of shock that had swept through the village the previous June when the two bodies were discovered by the local milkman after his curiosity had been piqued by the fact that the front door had been standing ajar at 5:30 on a Sunday morning. Thereafter, only the police and Lavinia's grandson had seen inside the house, but the rumor machine described a scene of carnage, with Lavinia's brains splattered across the walls of her bedroom and her nurse lying in a pool of blood in the kitchen. It was inconceivable that anyone in Sowerbridge could have done such a thing, and it was assumed the Manor House had been targeted by an outside gang for whatever valuables the old woman might possess.

It was never very clear why police suspicion had centered so rapidly on Patrick O'Riordan. Gossip said his fingerprints were all over the house and his toolbox was found in the kitchen, but Siobhan had always believed the police had received a tip-off. Whatever the reason, the matter appeared to be settled when a search warrant unearthed Lavinia's jewelry under his floorboards and Patrick was formally charged with the murders.

Predictably, shock had turned to fury but, with Patrick already in custody, it was Liam and Bridey who took the full brunt of Sowerbridge's wrath. Their presence in the village had never been a particularly welcome one—indeed, it was a mystery how "rough trade like them" could have afforded to buy a cottage in rural Hampshire, or why they had wanted to—but it became deeply unwelcome after the murders. Had it been possible to banish them behind a physical pale, the village would most certainly have done so; as it was, the old couple were left to exist in a social limbo where backs were turned and no one spoke to them.

In such a climate, Siobhan wondered, could Liam really have been stupid enough to ratchet up the hatred against them by daubing anti-Irish slogans across his front wall?

"If Patrick *is* the murderer, then why didn't you find Lavinia's diamond rings in Kilkenny Cottage?" she asked the inspector. "Why did you only find pieces of fake jewelry?"

"Who told you that? Bridey?"

"Yes."

He looked at her with a kind of compassion. "Then I'm afraid she was lying, Mrs. Lavenham. The diamond rings were in Kilkenny Cottage along with everything else."

2.

11:45 P.M.—MONDAY, 8TH MARCH, 1999

Siobhan was aware of the orange glow in the night sky ahead of her for some time before her tired brain began to question what it meant. Arc lights? A party? Fire, she thought in alarm as she approached the outskirts of Sowerbridge and saw sparks shooting into the air like a giant Roman candle. She slowed her Range Rover to a crawl as she approached the bend by the church, knowing it must be the O'Riordans' house, tempted to put the car into reverse and drive away, as if denial could alter what was happening. But she could see the flames licking up the front of Kilkenny Cottage by that time and knew it was too late for anything so simplistic. A police car was blocking the narrow road ahead, and with a sense of foreboding she obeyed the torch that signaled her to draw up on the grass verge beyond the church gate.

She lowered her window as the policeman came over, and felt the warmth from the fire fan her face like a Saharan wind. "Do you live in Sowerbridge, madam?" he asked. He was dressed in shirt-sleeves, perspiration glistening on his forehead, and Siobhan was amazed that one small house two hundred yards away could generate so much heat on a cool March night.

"Yes." She gestured in the direction of the blaze. "At Fording Farm. It's another half-mile beyond the crossroads."

He shone his torch into her eyes for a moment—his curiosity whetted by her soft Dublin accent, she guessed—before lowering the beam to a map. "You'll waste a lot less time if you go back the way you came and make a detour," he advised her.

"I can't. Our driveway leads off the crossroads by Kilkenny Cottage and there's no other access to it." She touched a finger to the map. "There. Whichever way I go, I still need to come back to the crossroads."

Headlights swept across her rearview mirror as another car rounded the bend. "Wait there a moment, please." He moved away to signal toward the verge, leaving Siobhan to gaze through her windscreen at the scene of chaos ahead.

There seemed to be a lot of people milling around, but her night sight had been damaged by the brilliance of the flames; and the water glistening on the tarmac made it difficult to distinguish what was real from what was reflection. The rusted hulks of the old cars that littered the O'Riordans' property stood out in bold silhouettes against the light, and Siobhan thought that Cynthia Haversley had been right when she said they weren't just an eyesore but a fire hazard as well. Cynthia had talked dramatically about the dangers of petrol, but if there was any petrol left in the corroded tanks, it remained sluggishly inert. The real hazard was the time and effort it must have taken to maneuver the two fire engines close enough to weave the hoses through so many obstacles, and Siobhan wondered if the house had ever stood a chance of being saved.

She began to fret about her two small boys and their nanny, Rosheen, who were alone at the farmhouse, and drummed her fingers impatiently on the steering wheel. "What should I do?" she asked the policeman when he returned after persuading the other driver to make a detour. "I need to get home."

He looked at the map again. "There's a footpath running behind the church and the vicarage. If you're prepared to walk home, I suggest you park your car in the churchyard and take the footpath. I'll radio through to ask one of the constables on the other side of the crossroads to escort you into your driveway. Failing that, I'm afraid you'll have to stay here until the road's clear, and that could take several hours."

"I'll walk." She reached for the gear stick, then let her hand drop. "No one's been hurt, have they?"

"No. The occupants are away."

Siobhan nodded. Under the watchful eyes of half of Sowerbridge village, Liam and Bridey had set off that morning in their ancient Ford Estate, to the malignant sound of whistles and hisses. "The O'Riordans are staying in Winchester until the trial's over."

"So we've been told," said the policeman.

Siobhan watched him take a notebook from his breast pocket. "Then presumably you were expecting something like this? I mean, everyone knew the house would be empty."

He flicked to an empty page. "I'll need your name, madam."

"Siobhan Lavenham."

"And your registration number, please, Ms. Lavenham."

She gave it to him. "You didn't answer my question," she said unemphatically.

He raised his eyes to look at her but it was impossible to read their expression. "What question's that?"

She thought she detected a smile on his face and bridled immediately. "You don't find it at all suspicious that the house burns down the minute Liam's back is turned?"

He frowned. "You've lost me, Ms. Lavenham."

"It's *Mrs.* Lavenham," she said irritably, "and you know perfectly well what I'm talking about. Liam's been receiving arson threats ever since Patrick was arrested, but the police couldn't have been less interested." Her irritation got the better of her. "It's their son who's on trial, for God's sake, not them, though you'd never believe it for all the care the English police have shown them." She crunched the car into gear and drove the few yards to the churchyard entrance where she parked in the lee of the wall and closed the window. She was preparing to open the door when it was opened from the outside.

"What are you trying to say?" demanded the policeman as she climbed out.

"What am I trying to say?" She let her accent slip into broad brogue. "Will you listen to the man? And there was me thinking my English was as good as his."

She was as tall as the constable, with striking good looks, and color rose in his cheeks. "I didn't mean it that way, Mrs. Lavenham. I meant, are you saying it was arson?"

"Of course it was arson," she countered, securing her mane of brown hair with a band at the back of her neck and raising her coat collar against the wind which two hundred yards away was feeding the inferno. "Are you saying it wasn't?"

"Can you prove it?"

"I thought that was your job."

He opened his notebook again, looking more like an earnest student than an officer of the law. "Do you know who might have been responsible?"

She reached inside the car for her handbag. "Probably the same people who wrote 'IRISH TRASH' across their front wall," she said, slamming the door and locking it. "Or maybe it's the ones who broke into the house two weeks ago during the night and smashed Bridey's Madonna and Child before urinating all over the pieces on the carpet. Who knows?" She gave him credit for looking disturbed at what she was saying. "Look, forget it," she said wearily. "It's late and I'm tired, and I want to get home to my children. Can you make that radio call so I don't get held up at the other end?"

"I'll do it from the car." He started to turn away, then changed his mind. "I'll be reporting what you've told me, Mrs. Lavenham, including your suggestion that the police have been negligent in their duty."

She smiled slightly. "Is that a threat or a promise, Officer?"

"It's a promise."

"Then I hope you have better luck than I've had. I might have been speaking in Gaelic for all the notice your colleagues took of my warnings." She set off for the footpath.

"You're supposed to put complaints in writing," he called after her.

"Oh, but I did," she assured him over her shoulder. "I may be Irish, but I'm not illiterate."

"I didn't mean—"

But the rest of his apology was lost on her as she rounded the corner of the church and vanished from sight.

THURSDAY, 18TH FEBRUARY, 1999

It had been several days before Siobhan found the courage to confront Bridey with what the detective inspector had told her. It made her feel like a thief even to think about it. Secrets were such fragile things. Little parts of oneself that couldn't be exposed without inviting changed perceptions toward the whole. But distrust was corroding her sympathy and she needed reassurance that Bridey at least believed in Patrick's innocence.

She followed the old woman's wheelchair into the sitting room and perched on the edge of the grubby sofa that Liam always lounged upon in his oil-stained boiler suit after spending hours poking around under his unsightly wrecks. It was a mystery to Siobhan what he did under them, as none of them appeared to be driveable, and she wondered sometimes if he simply used them as a canopy under which to sleep his days away. He complained often enough that his withered right hand, which he kept tucked out of sight inside his pockets to avoid upsetting people, had deprived him of any chance of a livelihood, but the truth was, he was a lazy man who was only ever seen to rouse himself when his wife left a trailing leg as she transferred from her chair to the passenger seat of their old Ford.

"There's nothing wrong with his left hand," Cynthia Haversley would snort indignantly as she watched the regular little pantomime outside Kilkenny Cottage, "but you'd think he'd lost the use of both hands the way he carries on about his disabilities."

Privately, and with some amusement, Siobhan guessed the demonstrations were put on entirely for the benefit of the Honorable Mrs. Haversley, who made no bones about her irritation at the level of state welfare which the O'Riordans enjoyed. It was axiomatic, after all, that any woman who had enough strength in her arms to heave herself upstairs on her bottom, as Bridey did every night, could lift her own leg into a car . . .

The Kilkenny Cottage sitting room—Bridey called it her "parlour"—was full of religious artifacts: a shrine to the Madonna and Child on the mantelpiece, a foot-high wooden cross on one wall, a print of William Holman Hunt's "The Light of the World" on another, a rosary hanging from a hook. In Siobhan, for whom religion was more of a trial than a comfort, the room invariably induced a sort of spiritual claustrophobia which made her long to get out and breathe fresh air again.

In ordinary circumstances, the paths of the O'Riordans, descendants of a roaming tinker family, and Siobhan Lavenham (nee Kerry), daughter of an Irish landowner, would never have crossed. Indeed, when she and her husband, Ian, first visited Fording Farm and fell in love with it, Siobhan had pointed out the eyesore of Kilkenny Cottage with a shudder and had predicted accurately the kind of people who were living there. Irish Gypsies, she said.

"Will that make life difficult for you?" Ian had asked.

"Only if people assume we're related," she answered with a laugh, never assuming for one moment that anyone would . . .

Bridey's habitually cowed expression reminded Siobhan of an ill-treated dog, and she put the detective inspector's accusations reluctantly, asking Bridey if she had lied about the car crash and about

Patrick never striking his father. The woman wept, washing her hands in her lap as if, like Lady Macbeth, she could cleanse herself of sill.

"If I did, Siobhan, it was only to have you think well of us. You're a lovely young lady with a kind heart, but you'd not have let Patrick play with your children if you'd known what he did to his father, and you'd not have taken Rosheen into your house if you'd known her uncle Liam was a thief."

"You should have trusted me, Bridey. If I didn't ask Rosheen to leave when Patrick was arrested for murder, why would I have refused to employ her just because Liam spent time in prison?"

"Because your husband would have persuaded you against her," said Bridey truthfully. "He's never been happy about Rosheen being related to us, never mind she grew up in Ireland and hardly knew us till you said she could come here to work for you."

There was no point denying it. Ian tolerated Rosheen O'Riordan for Siobhan's sake, and because his little boys loved her, but in an ideal world he would have preferred a nanny from a more conventional background. Rosheen's relaxed attitude to child rearing, based on her own upbringing in a three-bedroomed cottage in the hills of Donegal where the children had slept four to a bed and play was adventurous, carefree, and fun, was so different from the strict supervision of his own childhood that he constantly worried about it. "They'll grow up wild," he would say. "She's not disciplining them enough." And Siobhan would look at her happy, lively, affectionate sons and wonder why the English were so fond of repression.

"He worries about his children, Bridey, more so since Patrick's arrest. We get telephone calls too, you know. Everyone knows Rosheen's his cousin."

She remembered the first such call she had taken. She had answered it in the kitchen while Rosin was making supper for the children, and she had been shocked by the torrent of anti-Irish abuse that had poured down the line. She raised stricken eyes to Rosheen's and saw by the girl's frightened expression that it wasn't the first such call that had been made. After that, she had had an answerphone installed, and forebade Rosin from lifting the receiver unless she was sure of the caller's identity.

Bridey's sad gaze lifted toward the Madonna on the mantelpiece. "I pray for you every day, Siobhan, just as I pray for my Patrick. God knows, I never wished this trouble on a sweet lady like you. And for why? Is it a sin to be Irish?"

Siobhan sighed to herself, hating Bridey's dreary insistence on calling her a "lady." She did not doubt Bridey's faith, nor that she prayed every day, but she doubted God's ability to undo Lavinia Fanshaw's murder eight months after the event.

And if Patrick was guilty of it, and Bridey knew he was guilty . . .

"The issue isn't about being Irish," she said bluntly, "it's about whether or not Patrick's a murderer. I'd much rather you were honest with me, Bridey. At the moment, I don't trust any of you, and that includes Roshen. Does she know about his past? Has she been lying to me, too?" She paused, waiting for an answer, but Bridey just shook her head. "I'm not going to blame you for your son's behavior," she said more gently, "but you can't expect me to go on pleading his cause if he's guilty."

"Indeed, and I wouldn't ask you to," said the old woman with dignity. "And you can rest your mind about Rosheen. We kept the truth to ourselves fifteen years ago. Liam wouldn't have his son blamed for something that wasn't his fault. We'll call it a car accident, he said, and may God strike me dead if I ever raise my hand in anger again." She grasped the rims of her chair wheels and slowly rotated them through half a turn. "I'll tell you honestly, though I'm a cripple and though I've been married to Liam for nearly forty years, it's only in these last fifteen that I've been able to sleep peacefully in my bed. Oh yes, Liam was a bad man, and oh yes, my Patrick lost his temper once and struck out at him, but I swear by the Mother of God that this family changed for the better the day my poor son wept for what he'd done and rang the police himself. Will you believe me, Siobhan? Will you trust an old woman when she tells you her Patrick could no more have murdered Mrs. Fanshaw than I can get out of this wheelchair and walk. To be sure, he took some jewelry from her—and to be sure, he was wrong to do it—but he was only trying to get back what had been cheated out of him."

"Except there's no proof he was cheated out of anything. The police say there's very little evidence that any odd jobs had been done in the manor. They mentioned that one or two cracks in the plaster had been filled, but not enough to indicate a contract worth three hundred pounds."

"He was up there for two weeks," said Bridey in despair. "Twelve hours a day every day."

"Then why is there nothing to show for it?"

"I don't know," said the old woman with difficulty. "All I can tell you is that he came home every night with stories about what he'd been doing. One day it was getting the heating system to work, the next relaying the floor tiles in the kitchen where they'd come loose. It was Miss Jenkins who was telling him what needed doing, and she was thrilled to have all the little irritations sorted out once and for all."

Siobhan recalled the detective inspector's words. *"There's no one left to agree or disagree,"* he had said. *"Mrs. Fanshaw's grandson denies knowing anything about it, although he admits there might have been a private arrangement between Patrick and the nurse. She's known to have been on friendly terms with him . . ."*

"The police are saying Patrick only invented the contract in order to explain why his fingerprints were all over the manor house."

"That's not true."

"Are you sure? Wasn't it the first idea that came into his head when the police produced the search warrant? They questioned him for two days, Bridey, and the only explanation he gave for his fingerprints and his toolbox being in the manor was that Lavinia's nurse had asked him to sort out the dripping taps in the kitchen and bathroom. Why didn't he mention a contract earlier? Why did he wait until they found the jewelry under his floorboards before saying he was owed money?"

Teardrops watered the washing hands. "Because he's been in prison and doesn't trust the police . . . because he didn't kill Mrs. Fanshaw . . . because he was more worried about being charged with the theft of her jewelry than he was about being charged with murder. Do you think he'd have invented a contract that didn't exist?

My boy isn't stupid, Siobhan. He doesn't tell stories that he can't back up. Not when he's had two whole days to think about them."

Siobhan shook her head. "Except he couldn't back it up. You're the only person, other than Patrick, who claims to know anything about it, and your word means nothing because you're his mother."

"But don't you see?" the woman pleaded. "That's why you can be sure Patrick's telling the truth. If he'd believed for one moment it would all be denied, he'd have given some other reason for why he took the jewelry. Do you hear what I'm saying? He's a good liar, Siobhan—for his sins, he always has been—and he'd not have invented a poor, weak story like the one he's been saddled with."

3.

TUESDAY, 23RD JUNE, 1998

It was a rambling defense that Patrick finally produced when it dawned on him that the police were serious about charging him with the murders. Siobhan heard both Bridey's and the inspector's versions of it, and she wasn't surprised that the police found it difficult to swallow. It depended almost entirely on the words and actions of the murdered nurse.

Patrick claimed Dorothy Jenkins had come to Kilkenny Cottage and asked him if he was willing to do some odd jobs at the Manor House for a cash sum of three hundred pounds. "I've finally persuaded her miserable skinflint of a grandson that I'll walk out one day and not come back if he doesn't do something about my working conditions, so he's agreed to pay up," she had said triumphantly. "Are you interested, Patrick? It's a bit of moonlighting . . . no VAT . . . no Inland Revenue . . . just a couple of weeks' work for money in hand. But for goodness sake don't go talking about it," she had warned him, "or you can be sure Cynthia Haversley will notify social services that you're working and you'll lose your unemployment benefit. You know what an interfering busybody she is."

"I needed convincing she wasn't pulling a fast one," Patrick told the police. "I've been warned off in the past by that bastard grandson of Mrs. F's and the whole thing seemed bloody unlikely to me. So she takes me along to see him, and he's nice as pie, shakes me by the hand and says it's a kosher contract. We'll let bygones be bygones, he says. I worked like a dog for two weeks and, yes, of course I went into Mrs. Fanshaw's bedroom. I popped in every morning because she and I were mates. I would say 'hi,' and she would giggle and say 'hi' back. And yes, I touched almost everything in the house—most of the time I was moving furniture around for Miss Jenkins. 'It's so boring when you get too old to change things,' she'd say to me. 'Let's see how that table looks in here.' Then she'd clap her hands and say: 'Isn't this exciting?' I thought she was almost as barmy as the old lady, but I wasn't going to argue with her. I mean, three hundred quid is three hundred quid, and if that's what was wanted I was happy to do the business."

On the second Saturday—"the day I was supposed to be paid . . . shit . . . I should have known it was a scam . . . "—Mrs. Fanshaw's grandson was in the Manor House hall waiting for him when he arrived.

"I thought the bastard had come to give me my wages, but instead he accuses me of nicking a necklace. I called him a bloody liar, so he took a swing at me and landed one on my jaw. Next thing I know, I'm out the front door, facedown on the gravel. Yeah, of course that's how I got the scratches. I've never hit a woman in my life, and I certainly didn't get into a fight with either of the old biddies at the manor."

There was a two-hour hiatus during which he claimed to have driven around in a fury wondering how "to get the bastard to pay what he owed." He toyed with the idea of going to the police—"I was pretty sure Miss Jenkins would back me up, she was that mad with him, but I didn't reckon you lot could do anything, not without social services getting to hear about it, and then I'd be worse off than I was before . . ."—but in the end he opted for more direct action and sneaked back to Sowerbridge Manor through the gate at the bottom of the garden.

"I knew Miss Jenkins would see me right if she could. And she did. 'Take this, Patrick,' she said, handing me some of Mrs. F's jewelry, 'and if there's any comeback I'll say it was my idea.' I tell you," he finished aggressively, "I'm gutted she and Mrs. F are dead. At least they treated me like a friend, which is more than can be said of the rest of Sowerbridge."

He was asked why he hadn't mentioned any of this before. "Because I'm not a fool," he said. "Word has it Mrs. F was killed for her jewelry. Do you think I'm going to admit having some of it under my floorboards when she was battered to death a few hours later?"

Thursday, 18th February, 1999

Siobhan pondered in silence for a minute or two. "Weak or not, Bridey, it's the one he has to go to trial with, and at the moment no one believes it. It would be different if he could prove any of it."

"How?"

"I don't know." She shook her head. "Did he show the jewelry to anyone *before* Lavinia was killed?"

A sly expression crept into the woman's eyes as if a new idea had suddenly occurred to her. "Only to me and Rosheen," she said, "but, as you know, Siobhan, not a word we say is believed."

"Did either of you mention it to anyone else?"

"Why would we? When all's said and done, he took the things without permission, never mind it was Miss Jenkins who gave them to him."

"Well, it's a pity Rosheen didn't tell me about it. It would make a world of difference if I could say I knew on the Saturday afternoon that Patrick already had Lavinia's necklace in his possession."

Bridey looked away toward her Madonna, crossing herself as she did so, and Siobhan knew she was lying. "She thinks the world of you, Siobhan. She'd not embarrass you by making you a party to her cousin's troubles. In any case, you'd not have been interested. Was your mind not taken up with cooking that day? Was that not the Saturday you were entertaining Mr. and Mrs. Haversley to dinner to pay off all the dinners you've had from them but never wanted?"

There were no secrets in a village, thought Siobhan, and if Bridey knew how much Ian and she detested the grinding tedium of Sowerbridge social life, which revolved around the all-too-regular "dinner party," presumably the rest of Sowerbridge did as well. "Are we really that obvious, Bridey?"

"To the Irish, maybe, but not to the English," said the old woman with a crooked smile. "The English see what they want to see. If you don't believe me, Siobhan, look at the way they've condemned my poor Patrick as a murdering thief before he's even been tried."

Siobhan had questioned Rosheen about the jewelry afterward and, like Bridey, the girl had wrung her hands in distress. But Rosheen's distress had everything to do with her aunt expecting her to perjure herself and nothing at all to do with the facts. "Oh, Siobhan," she had wailed, "does she expect me to stand up in court and tell her? Because it'll not do Patrick any good when they find me out. Surely it's better to say nothing than to keep inventing stories that no one believes?"

11:55 P.M.—MONDAY, 8TH MARCH, 1999
It was cold on the footpath because the wall of the Old Vicarage was reflecting the heat back toward Kilkenny Cottage, but the sound of the burning house was deafening. The pine rafters and ceiling joists popped and exploded like intermittent rifle fire while the flames kept up a hungry roar. As Siobhan emerged onto the road leading up from the junction, she found herself in a crowd of her neighbors, who seemed to be watching the blaze in a spirit of revelry—almost, she thought in amazement, as if it were a spectacular fireworks display put on for their enjoyment. People raised their arms and pointed whenever a new rafter caught alight, and "oohs" and "ahs" burst out of their mouths like a cheer. Any moment now, she thought cynically, and they'd bring out an effigy

of that other infamous Catholic, Guy Fawkes, who was ritually burnt every year for trying to blow up the Houses of Parliament.

She started to work her way through the crowd but was stopped by Nora Bentley, the elderly doctor's wife, who caught her arm and drew her close. The Bentleys were far and away Siobhan's favorites among her neighbors, being the only ones with enough tolerance to stand against the continuous barrage of anti-O'Riordan hatred that poured from the mouths of almost everyone else. Although as Ian often pointed out, they could afford to be tolerant. "Be fair, Siobhan. Lavinia wasn't related to them. They might feel differently if she'd been *their* granny."

"We've been worried about you, my dear," said Nora. "What with all this going on, we didn't know whether you were trapped inside the farm or outside."

Siobhan gave her a quick hug. "Outside. I stayed late at work to sort out some contracts, and I've had to abandon the car at the church."

"Well, I'm afraid your drive's completely blocked with fire engines. If it's any consolation, we're all in the same boat, although Jeremy Jardine and the Haversleys have the added worry of sparks carrying on the wind and setting light to their houses." She chuckled suddenly. "You have to laugh. Cynthia bullied the firemen into taking preventative measures by hosing down the front of Malvern House, and now she's tearing strips off poor old Peter because he left their bedroom window open. The whole room's completely saturated."

Siobhan grinned. "Good," she said unsympathetically. "It's time Cynthia had some of her own medicine."

Nora wagged an admonishing finger at her. "Don't be too hard on her, my dear. For all her sins, Cynthia can be very kind when she wants to be. It's a pity you've never seen that side of her."

"I'm not sure I'd want to," said Siobhan cynically. "At a guess, she only shows it when she's offering charity. Where are they, anyway?"

"I've no idea. I expect Peter's making up the spare-room beds and Cynthia's at the front somewhere behaving like the chief constable. You know how bossy she is."

"Yes," agreed Siobhan, who had been on the receiving end of Cynthia's hectoring tongue more often than she cared to remember. Indeed, if she had any regrets about moving to Sowerbridge, they were all centered around the overbearing personality of the Honorable Mrs. Haversley.

By one of those legal quirks of which the English are so fond, the owners of Malvern House had title to the first hundred feet of Fording Farm's driveway while the owners of the farm had right of way in perpetuity across it. This had led to a state of war existing between the two households, although it was a war that had been going on long before the Lavenhams' insignificant tenure of eighteen months. Ian maintained that Cynthia's insistence on her rights stemmed from the fact that the Haversleys were, and always had been, the poor relations of the Fanshaws at the Manor House. ("You get slowly more impoverished if you inherit through the distaff side," he said, "and Peter's family has never been able to lay claim to the manor. It's made Cynthia bitter.") Nevertheless, had he and Siobhan paid heed to their solicitor's warnings, they might have questioned why such a beautiful place had had five different owners in under ten years. Instead, they had accepted the previous owners' assurances that everything in the garden was lovely—*You'll like Cynthia Haversley. She's a charming woman*—and put the rapid turnover down to coincidence.

Something that sounded like a grenade detonating exploded in the heart of the fire and Nora Bentley jumped. She tapped her heart with a fluttery hand. "Goodness me, it's just like the war," she said in a rush. "*So* exciting." She tempered this surprising statement by adding that she felt sorry for the O'Riordans, but her sympathy came a poor second to her desire for sensation.

"Are Liam and Bridey here?" asked Siobhan, looking around.

"I don't think so, dear. To be honest, I wonder if they even know what's happening. They were very secretive about where they were staying in Winchester; unless the police know where they are, well—" she shrugged—"who could have told them?"

"Rosheen knows."

Nora gave an absent-minded smile. "Yes, but she's with your boys at the farm."

"We are on the phone, Nora."

"I know, dear, but it's all been so sudden. One minute, nothing; the next, mayhem. As a matter of fact, I did suggest we call Rosheen, but Cynthia said there was no point. Let Liam and Bridey have a good night's sleep, she said. What can they do that the fire brigade haven't already done? Why bother them unnecessarily?"

"I'll bear that in mind when Cynthia's house goes up in flames," said Siobhan dryly, glancing at her watch and telling herself to get a move on. Curiosity held her back. "When did it start?"

"No one knows," said Nora. "Sam and I smelt burning about an hour and a half ago and came to investigate, but by that time the flames were already at the downstairs windows." She waved an arm at the Old Vicarage. "We knocked up Jeremy and got him to call the fire brigade, but the whole thing was out of control long before they arrived."

Siobhan's eyes followed the waving arm. "Why didn't Jeremy call them earlier? Surely he'd have smelt burning before you did? He lives right opposite." Her glance traveled on to the Bentleys' house, Rose Cottage, which stood behind the Old Vicarage, a good hundred yards distant from Kilkenny Cottage.

Nora looked anxious, as if she, too, found Jeremy Jardine's inertia suspicious. "He says he didn't, says he was in his cellar. He was horrified when he saw what was going on."

Siobhan took that last sentence with a pinch of salt. Jeremy Jardine was a wine shipper who had used his Fanshaw family connection some years before to buy the Old Vicarage off the church commissioners for its extensive cellars. But the beautiful brick house looked out over the O'Riordans' unsightly wrecking ground, and he was one of their most strident critics. No one knew how much he'd paid for it, although rumor suggested it had been sold off at a fifth of its value. Certainly questions had been asked at the time about why a substantial Victorian rectory had never been advertised for sale on the open market, although, as usual in Sowerbridge, answers were difficult to come by when they involved the Fanshaw family. Prior to the murders, Siobhan had been irritated enough by Jeremy's unremitting criticism of the O'Riordans to ask him why he'd bought the Old Vicarage, knowing what the view was going to be. "It's not as though you didn't know about Liam's cars," she told him. "Nora Bentley says you'd been living with Lavinia at the manor for two years before the purchase." He'd muttered darkly about good investments turning sour when promises of action failed to materialize and she had interpreted this as meaning he'd paid a pittance to acquire the property from the church on the mistaken understanding that one of his district councilor buddies could force the O'Riordans to clean up their frontage.

Ian had laughed when she told him about the conversation. "Why on earth doesn't he just offer to pay for the cleanup himself? Liam's never going to pay to have those blasted wrecks removed, but he'd be pleased as punch if someone else did."

"Perhaps he can't afford it. Nora says the Fanshaws aren't half as well off as everyone believes, and Jeremy's business is no great shakes. I know he talks grandly about how he supplies all the top families with quality wine, but that case he sold us was rubbish."

"It wouldn't cost much, not if a scrap-metal merchant did it."

Siobhan had wagged a finger at him. "You know what your problem is, husband of mine? You're too sensible to live in Sowerbridge. Also, you're ignoring the fact that there's an issue of principle at stake. If Jeremy pays for the cleanup then the O'Riordans will have won. Worse still, they will be seen to have won because *their* house will also rise in value the minute the wrecks go."

He shook his head. "Just promise me you won't start taking sides, Shiv. You're no keener on the O'Riordans than anyone else, and there's no law that says the Irish have to stick together. Life's too short to get involved in their ridiculous feuds."

"I promise," she had said, and at the time she had meant it.

But that was before Patrick had been charged with murder . . .

There was no doubt in the minds of most of Sowerbridge's inhabitants that Patrick O'Riordan saw Lavinia Fanshaw as an easy target. In November, two years previously, he had relieved the confused old woman of a Chippendale chair worth five hundred pounds after claiming a European directive required all hedgerows to be clipped to a uniform standard. He had stripped her laurels to within four feet of the ground in return for the antique, and had sold the foliage on to a crony who made festive Christmas wreaths.

Nor had he shown any remorse. "It was a bit of business," he said in the pub afterward, grinning happily as he swilled his beer, "and she was pleased as punch about it. She told me she's always hated that chair." He was a small, wiry man with a shock of dark hair and penetrating blue eyes which stared unwaveringly at the person he was talking to—like a fighting dog whose intention was to intimidate. "In any case, I did this village a favor. The manor looks a damn sight better since I sorted the frontage."

The fact that most people agreed with him was neither here nor there. The combination of Lavinia's senility and extraordinary longevity meant Sowerbridge Manor was rapidly falling into disrepair, but this did not entitle anyone, least of all an O'Riordan, to take advantage of her. What about Kilkenny Cottage's frontage? people protested. Liam's cars were a great deal worse than Lavinia's overgrown hedge. There was even suspicion that her live-in nurse had connived in the fraud, because she was known to be extremely critical of the deteriorating conditions in which she was expected to work.

"I can't be watching Mrs. Fanshaw twenty-four hours a day," Dorothy Jenkins had said firmly, "and if she makes an arrangement behind my back, then there's nothing I can do about it. It's her grandson you should be talking to. He's the one with power of attorney over her affairs, but he's never going to sell this place before she's dead because he's too mean to put her in a nursing home. She could live forever the way she's going, and nursing homes cost far more than I do. He pays me peanuts because he says I'm getting free board and lodging, but there's no heating, the roof leaks, and the whole place is a death trap of rotten floorboards. He's only waiting for the poor old thing to die so that he can sell the land to a property developer and live in clover for the rest of his life."

Monday, 8th March, 1999

The crowd seemed to be growing bigger and more boisterous by the minute, but as Siobhan recognized few of the faces, she realized word of the fire must have spread to surrounding villages. She couldn't understand why the police were letting thrill-seekers through until she heard one man say that he'd parked on the Southampton Road and cut across a field to bypass the police block. There was much jostling for position; the smell of beer on the breath of one man who pushed past her was overpowering. He barged against her and she jabbed him angrily in the ribs with a sharp elbow before taking Nora's arm and shepherding her across the road.

"Someone's going to be hurt in a minute," she said. "They've obviously come straight from the pub." She maneuvered through a knot of people beside the wall of Malvern House, and ahead of her she saw Nora's husband, Dr. Sam Bentley, talking with Peter and Cynthia Haversley. "There's Sam. I'll leave you with him and then be on my way. I'm worried about Rosheen and the boys." She nodded briefly to the Haversleys, raised a hand in greeting to Sam Bentley, then prepared to push on.

"You won't get through," said Cynthia forcefully, planting her corseted body between Siobhan and the crossroads. "They've barricaded the entire junction and no one's allowed past." Her face had turned crimson from the heat, and Siobhan wondered if she had any idea how unattractive she looked. The combination of dyed blond hair atop a glistening beetroot complexion was reminiscent of sherry trifle, and Siobhan wished she had a camera to record the fact. Siobhan knew her to be in her late sixties because Nora had let slip once that she and Cynthia shared a birthday, but Cynthia herself preferred to draw a discreet veil over her age. Privately (and rather grudgingly) Siobhan admitted she had a case, because her plumpness gave her skin a smooth, firm quality which made her look considerably younger than her years, though it didn't make her any more likable.

Siobhan had asked Ian once if he thought her antipathy to Cynthia was an "Irish thing." The idea had amused him. "On what basis? Because the Honorable Mrs. Haversley symbolizes colonial authority?"

"Something like that."

"Don't be absurd, Shiv. She's a fat snob with a power complex who loves throwing her weight around. No one likes her. I certainly don't. She probably wouldn't be so bad if her wet husband had ever stood up to her, but poor old Peter's as cowed as everyone else. You should learn to ignore her. In the great scheme of things, she's about as relevant as birdshit on your windscreen."

"I *hate* birdshit on my windscreen."

"I know," he had said with a grin, "but you don't assume pigeons single your car out because you're Irish, do you?"

She made an effort now to summon a pleasant smile as she answered Cynthia. "Oh, I'm sure they'll make an exception of me. Ian's in Italy this week, which means Rosheen and the boys are on their own. I think I'll be allowed through in the circumstances."

"If you aren't," said Dr. Bentley, "Peter and I can give you a leg up over the wall and you can cut through Malvern House garden."

"Thank you." She studied his face for a moment. "Does anyone know how the fire started, Sam?"

"We think Liam must have left a cigarette burning."

Siobhan pulled a wry face. "Then it must have been the slowest burning cigarette in history," she said. "They were gone by nine o'clock this morning."

He looked as worried as his wife had done earlier. "It's only a guess."

"Oh, come on! If it was a smoldering cigarette you'd have seen flames at the windows by lunchtime." She turned her attention back to Cynthia. "I'm surprised that Sam and Nora smelt burning before you did," she said with deliberate lightness. "You and Peter are so much closer than they are."

"We probably would have done if we'd been here," said Cynthia, "but we went to supper with friends in Salisbury. We didn't get home until after Jeremy called the fire brigade." She stared Siobhan down, daring her to dispute the statement.

"Matter of fact," said Peter, "we only just scraped in before the police arrived with barricades. Otherwise they'd have made us leave the car at the church."

Siobhan wondered if the friends had invited the Haversleys or if the Haversleys had invited themselves. She guessed the latter. None of the O'Riordans' neighbors would have wanted to save Kilkenny Cottage, and unlike Jeremy, she thought sarcastically, the Haversleys had no cellar to skulk in. "I really must go," she said then. "Poor Rosheen will be worried sick." But if she expected sympathy for Liam and Bridey's niece, she didn't get it.

"If she were *that* worried, she'd have come down here," declared Cynthia. "With or without your boys. I don't know why you employ her. She's one of the laziest and most deceitful creatures I've ever met. Frankly, I wouldn't have her for love or money."

Siobhan smiled slightly. It was like listening to a cracked record, she thought. The day the Honorable Mrs. Haversley resisted an opportunity to snipe at an O'Riordan would be a red-letter day in Siobhan's book. "I suspect the feeling's mutual, Cynthia. Threat of death might persuade her to work for you, but not love or money."

Cynthia's retort, a pithy one if her annoyed expression was anything to go by, was swallowed by the sound of Kilkenny Cottage collapsing inward upon itself as the beams supporting the roof finally gave way. There was a shout of approval from the crowd behind them, and while everyone else's attention was temporarily distracted, Siobhan watched Peter Haversley give his wife a surreptitious pat on the back.

4.

SATURDAY, 30TH JANUARY, 1999

Siobhan had stubbornly kept an open mind about Patrick's guilt, although as she was honest enough to admit to Ian, it was more for Rosheen and Bridey's sake than because she seriously believed there was room for reasonable doubt. She couldn't forget the fear she had seen in Rosheen's eyes one day when she came home early to find Jeremy Jardine at the front door of the farm. "What are you doing here?" she had demanded of him angrily, appalled by the ashen color in her nanny's cheeks.

There was a telling silence before Rosheen stumbled into words.

"He says we're murdering Mrs. Fanshaw all over again by taking Patrick's side," said the girl in a shaken voice. "I said it was wrong to condemn him before the evidence is heard—you told me everyone would believe Patrick was innocent until the trial—but Mr. Jardine just keeps shouting at me."

Jeremy had laughed. "I'm doing the rounds with my new wine list," he said, jerking his thumb toward his car. "But I'm damned if I'll stay quiet while an Irish murderer's cousin quotes English law at me."

Siobhan had controlled her temper because her two sons were watching from the kitchen window. "Go inside now," she told Rosheen, "but if Mr. Jardine comes here again when Ian and I are at work, I want you to phone the police immediately." She waited while the girl retreated with relief into the depths of the house. "I mean it, Jeremy," she said coldly. "However strongly you may feel about all of this, I'll have you prosecuted if you try that trick again. It's not as though Rosheen has any evidence that can help Patrick, so you're simply wasting your time."

He shrugged. "You're a fool, Siobhan. Patrick's guilty as sin. You know it. Everyone knows it. Just don't come crying to me later when the jury proves us right and you find yourself tarred with the same brush as the O'Riordans."

"I already have been," she said curtly. "If you and the Haversleys had your way, I'd have been lynched by now, but, God knows, I'd give my right arm to see Patrick get off, if only to watch the three of you wearing sackcloth and ashes for the rest of your lives."

Ian had listened to her account of the conversation with a worried frown on his face. "It won't help Patrick if he does get off," he warned. "No one's going to believe he didn't do it. Reasonable doubt sounds all very well in court, but it won't count for anything in Sowerbridge. He'll never be able to come back."

"I know."

"Then don't get too openly involved," he advised. "We'll be living here for the foreseeable future, and I really don't want the boys growing up in an atmosphere of hostility. Support Bridey and Rosheen by all means—" he gave her a wry smile—"but do me a favor, Shiv, and hold that Irish temper of yours in check. I'm not convinced Patrick is worth going to war over, particularly not with our close neighbors."

It was good advice, but difficult to follow. There was too much overt prejudice against the Irish in general for Siobhan to stay quiet indefinitely. War finally broke out at one of Cynthia and Peter Haversley's tedious dinner parties at Malvern House, which were impossible to avoid without telling so many lies that it was easier to attend the wretched things. "She watches the driveway from her window," sighed Siobhan when Ian asked why they couldn't just say they had another engagement that night. "She keeps tabs on everything we do. She knows when we're in and when we're out. It's like living in a prison."

"I don't know why she keeps inviting us," he said.

Siobhan found his genuine ignorance of Cynthia's motives amusing. "It's her favorite sport," she said matter-of-factly. "Bearbaiting . . . with me as the bear."

Ian sighed. "Then let's tell her the truth, say we'd rather stay in and watch television."

"Good idea. There's the phone. *You* tell her."

He smiled unhappily. "It'll make her even more impossible."

"Of course it will."

"Perhaps we should just grit our teeth and go?"

"Why not? It's what we usually do."

The evening had been a particularly dire one, with Cynthia and Jeremy holding the platform as usual, Peter getting quietly drunk, and the Bentleys making only occasional remarks. A silence had developed round the table and Siobhan, who had been firmly biting her tongue since they arrived, consulted her watch under cover of her napkin and wondered if nine forty-five was too early to announce departure.

"I suppose what troubles me the most," said Jeremy suddenly, "is that if I'd pushed to have the O'Riordans evicted years ago, poor old Lavinia would still be alive." He was a similar age to the Lavenhams and handsome in a florid sort of way—*Too much sampling of his own wares*, Siobhan always thought—and loved to style himself as Hampshire's most eligible bachelor. Many was the time Siobhan had wanted to ask why, if he was so eligible, he remained unattached, but she didn't bother because she thought she knew the answer. He couldn't find a woman stupid enough to agree with his own valuation of himself.

"You can't evict people from their own homes," Sam Bentley pointed out mildly. "On that basis, we could all be evicted any time our neighbors took against us."

"Oh, you know what I mean," Jeremy answered, looking pointedly at Siobhan as if to remind her that she was tarred with the O'Riordans' brush. There must be something I could have done—had them prosecuted for environmental pollution, perhaps?"

"We should never have allowed them to come here in the first place," declared Cynthia. "It's iniquitous that the rest of us have no say over what sort of people will be living on our doorsteps. If the Parish Council was allowed to vet prospective newcomers, the problem would never have arisen."

Siobhan raised her head and smiled in amused disbelief at the other woman's arrogant assumption that the Parish Council was in her pocket. "What a good idea!" she said brightly, ignoring Ian's warning look across the table. "It would also give prospective newcomers a chance to vet the people already living here. It means house prices would drop like a stone, of course, but at least neither side could say afterward that they went into it with their eyes closed."

The pity was that Cynthia was too stupid to understand irony. "You're quite wrong, my dear," she said with a condescending smile. "The house prices would go *up*. They always do when an area becomes exclusive."

"Only when there are enough purchasers who want the kind of exclusivity you're offering them, Cynthia. It's basic economics." Siobhan propped her elbows on the table and leaned forward, stung into pricking the fat woman's self-righteous bubble once and for all, even if she did recognize that her real target was Jeremy Jardine. "And for what it's worth, there won't be any competition to live in Sowerbridge when word gets out that, *however* much money you have, there's no point in applying unless you share the Fanshaw Mafia's belief that Hitler was right."

Nora Bentley gave a small gasp and made damping gestures with her hands.

Jeremy was less restrained. "Well, my God!" he burst out aggressively. "That's bloody rich coming from an Irishwoman. Where was Ireland in the war? Sitting on the sidelines, rooting for Germany, that's where. And you have the damn nerve to sit in judgment on us! All you Irish are despicable. You flood over here like a plague of sewer rats looking for handouts, then you criticize us when we point out that we don't think you're worth the trouble you're causing us."

It was like a simmering saucepan boiling over. In the end, all that had been achieved by restraint was to allow resentment to fester. On both sides.

"I suggest you withdraw those remarks, Jeremy," said Ian coldly, rousing himself in defense of his wife. "You might be entitled to insult Siobhan like that if your business paid as much tax and employed as many people as hers does, but as that's never going to happen I think you should apologize."

"No way. Not unless she apologizes to Cynthia first."

Once roused, Ian's temper was even more volatile than his wife's. "She's got nothing to apologize for," he snapped. "Everything she said was true. Neither you nor Cynthia has any more right than anyone else to dictate what goes on in this village, yet you do it anyway. And with very little justification. At least the rest of us bought our houses fair and square on the open market, which is more than can be said of you or Peter. He inherited his, and you got yours cheap via the old-boy network. I just hope you're prepared for the consequences when something goes wrong. You can't incite hatred and then pretend you're not responsible for it."

"Now, now, now!" said Sam with fussy concern. "This sort of talk isn't healthy."

"Sam's right," said Nora. "What's said can never be unsaid."

Ian shrugged. "Then tell this village to keep its collective mouth shut about the Irish in general and the O'Riordans in particular. Or doesn't the rule apply to them? Perhaps it's only the well-to-do English like the Haversleys and Jeremy who can't be criticized?"

Peter Haversley gave an unexpected snigger. "Well-to-do?" he muttered tipsily. "Who's well-to-do? We're all in hock up to our blasted eyeballs while we wait for the manor to be sold."

"Be quiet, Peter," said his wife.

But he refused to be silenced. "That's the trouble with murder. Everything gets so damned messy. You're not allowed to sell what's rightfully yours because probate goes into limbo." His bleary eyes looked across the table at Jeremy. "It's your fault, you sanctimonious little toad. Power of bloody attorney, my arse. You're too damn greedy for your own good. Always were . . . always will be. I kept telling you to put the old bloodsucker into a home but would you listen? Don't worry, you kept saying, she'll be dead soon . . ."

00:23 A.M.—TUESDAY, 9TH MARCH, 1999

The hall lights were on in the farmhouse when Siobhan finally reached it, but there was no sign of Rosheen. This surprised her until she checked the time and saw that it was well after midnight. She went into the kitchen and squatted down to stroke Patch, the O'Riordans' amiable mongrel, who lifted his head from the hearth in front of the Aga and wagged his stumpy tail before giving an enormous yawn and returning to his slumbers. Siobhan had agreed to look after him while the O'Riordans were away and he seemed entirely at home in his new surroundings. She peered out of the kitchen window toward the fire, but there was nothing to see except the dark line of trees bordering the property, and it occurred to her then that Rosheen probably had no idea her uncle's house had gone up in flames.

She tiptoed upstairs to check on her two young sons who, like Patch, woke briefly to wrap their arms around her neck and acknowledge her kisses before closing their eyes again. She paused outside Rosheen's room for a moment, hoping to hear the sound of the girl's television, but there was only silence and she retreated downstairs again, relieved to be spared explanations tonight. Rosheen had been frightened enough by the anti-Irish slogans daubed across the front of Kilkenny Cottage; God only knew how she would react to hearing it had been destroyed.

Rosheen's employment with them had happened more by accident than design when Siobhan's previous nanny—a young woman given to melodrama—had announced after two weeks in rural Hampshire that she'd rather "die" than spend another night away from the lights of London. In desperation, Siobhan had taken up Bridey's shy suggestion to fly Rosheen over from Ireland on a month's trial—"*She's Liam's brother's daughter and she's a wonder with children. She's been looking after her brothers and her cousins since she was knee-high to a grasshopper, and they all think the world of her.*"— and Siobhan had been surprised by how quickly and naturally the girl had fitted into the household.

Ian had reservations—"*She's too young . . . she's too scatterbrained . . . I'm not sure I want to be quite so cozy with the O'Riordans.*"—but he had come to respect her in the wake of Patrick's arrest when, despite the hostility in the village, she had refused to abandon either Siobhan or Bridey. "Mind you, I wouldn't bet on family loyalty being what's keeping her here."

"What else is there?"

"Sex with Kevin Wyllie. She goes weak at the knees every time she sees him, never mind he's probably intimately acquainted with the thugs who're terrorizing Liam and Bridey."

"You can't blame him for that. He's lived here all his life. I should imagine most of Sowerbridge could name names if they wanted to. At least he's had the guts to stand by Rosheen."

"He's an illiterate oaf with an IQ of ten," growled Ian. "Rosheen's not stupid, so what the hell do they find to talk about?"

Siobhan giggled. "I don't think his conversation is what interests her."

Recognizing that she was too hyped-up to sleep, she poured herself a glass of wine and played the messages on the answerphone. There were a couple of business calls followed by one from Ian. "*Hi, it's me. Things are progressing well on the Ravenelli front. All being well, hand-printed Italian silk should be on offer through Lavenham Interiors by August. Good news, eh? I can think of at least two projects that will benefit from the designs they've been showing me. You'll love them, Shiv. Aquamarine swirls with every shade of terra cotta you can imagine.*"

Pause for a yawn. *"I'm missing you and the boys like crazy. Give me a ring if you get back before eleven, otherwise I'll speak to you tomorrow. I should be home on Friday."* He finished with a slobbery kiss which made her laugh.

The last message was from Liam O'Riordan and had obviously been intercepted by Rosheen. *"Hello? Are you there, Rosheen? It's . . ."* said Liam's voice before it was cut off by the receiver being lifted. Out of curiosity, Siobhan pressed one-four-seven-one to find out when Liam had phoned, and she listened in perplexity as the computerized voice at the other end gave the time of the last call as "twenty thirty-six hours," and the number from which it was made as "eight-two-seven-five-three-eight." She knew the sequence off by heart but flicked through the telephone index any way to make certain. *Liam & Bridey O'Riordan, Kilkenny Cottage, Sowerbridge, Tel. 827538.*

For the second time that night her first instinct was to rush toward denial. It was a mistake, she told herself . . . Liam couldn't possibly have been phoning from Kilkenny Cottage at eight-thirty . . . The O'Riordans were under police protection in Winchester for the duration of Patrick's trial . . . Kilkenny Cottage was empty when the fire started . . .

But, oh dear God! Supposing it wasn't?

"Rosheen!" she shouted, running up the stairs again and hammering on the nanny's door. "Rosheen! It's Siobhan. Wake up! Was Liam in the cottage?" She thrust open the door and switched on the light, only to look around the room in dismay because no one was there.

WEDNESDAY, 10TH FEBRUARY, 1999

Siobhan had raised the question of Lavinia Fanshaw's heirs with the detective inspector. "You can't ignore the fact that both Peter Haversley and Jeremy Jardine had a far stronger motive than Patrick could ever have had," she pointed out. "They both stood to inherit from her will, and neither of them made any bones about wanting her dead. Lavinia's husband had one sister, now dead, who produced a single child, Peter, who has *no* children. And Lavinia's only child, a daughter, also dead, produced Jeremy, who's never married."

He was amused by the extent of her research. "We didn't ignore it, Mrs. Lavenham. It was the first thing we looked at, but you know better than anyone that they couldn't have done it because you and your husband supplied their alibis."

"Only from eight o'clock on Saturday night until two o'clock on Sunday morning," protested Siobhan. "And not out of choice either. Have you any idea what it's like living in a village like Sowerbridge, Inspector? Dinner parties are considered intrinsically superior to staying in of a Friday or Saturday night and watching telly, never mind the same boring people get invited every time and the same boring conversations take place. It's a status thing." She gave a sarcastic shrug. "Personally, I'd rather watch a good Arnie or Sly movie any day than have to appear interested in someone else's mortgage or pension plan, but then—*hell*—I'm Irish and everyone knows the Irish are common as muck."

"You'll have status enough when Patrick comes to trial," said the inspector with amusement. "You'll be the one providing the alibis."

"I wouldn't be able to if we'd managed to get rid of Jeremy and the Haversleys any sooner. Believe me, it wasn't Ian and I who kept them there—we did everything we could to make them go—they just refused to take the hints. Sam and Nora Bentley went at a reasonable time, but we couldn't get the rest of them to budge. Are you *sure* Lavinia was killed between eleven and midnight? Don't you find it suspicious that it's *my* evidence that's excluded Peter and Jeremy from the case? Everyone knows I'm the only person in Sowerbridge who'd rather give Patrick O'Riordan an alibi if I possibly could."

"What difference does that make?"

"It means I'm a reluctant witness, and therefore gives my evidence in Peter and Jeremy's favor more weight."

The inspector shook his head. "I think you're making too much of your position in all of this, Mrs. Lavenham. If Mr. Haversley and Mr. Jardine had conspired to murder Mrs. Fanshaw, wouldn't they have taken themselves to—say, Ireland—for the weekend? That would have given them a much stronger alibi than spending hours in the home of a hostile witness. In any case," he went on apologetically, "we are sure about the time of the murders. These days, pathologists' timings are extremely precise, particularly when the bodies are found as quickly as these ones were."

Siobhan wasn't ready to give up so easily. "But you must see how odd it is that it happened the night Ian and I gave a dinner party. We *hate* dinner parties. Most of our entertaining is done around barbecues in the summer when friends come to stay. It's always casual and always spur-of-the-moment and I can't believe it was coincidence that Lavinia was murdered on the one night in the whole damn year for which we'd sent out invitations—" her mouth twisted—"*six weeks in advance . . .*"

He eyed her thoughtfully. "If you can tell me how they did it, I might agree with you."

"Before they came to our house or after they left it," she suggested. "The pathologist's timings are wrong."

He pulled a piece of paper from a pile on his desk and turned it toward her. "That's an itemized British Telecom list of every call made from Sowerbridge Manor during the week leading up to the murders." He touched the last number. "This one was made by Dorothy Jenkins to a friend of hers in London and was timed at ten-thirty P.M. on the night she died. The duration time was just over three minutes. We've spoken to the friend and she described Miss Jenkins as at 'the end of her tether.' Apparently Mrs. Fanshaw was a difficult patient to nurse—Alzheimer's sufferers usually are—and Miss Jenkins had phoned this woman—also a nurse—to tell her that she felt like "smothering the old bitch where she lay." It had happened several times before, but this time Miss Jenkins was in tears and rang off abruptly when her friend said she had someone with her and couldn't talk for long." He paused for a moment. "The friend was worried enough to phone back after her visitor had gone," he went on, "and she estimates the time of that call at about a quarter past midnight. The line was engaged so she couldn't get through, and she admits to being relieved because she thought it meant Miss Jenkins had found someone else to confide in."

Siobhan frowned. "Well, at least it proves she was alive after midnight, doesn't it?"

The inspector shook his head. "I'm afraid not. The phone in the kitchen had been knocked off its rest—we think Miss Jenkins may have been trying to dial nine-nine-nine when she was attacked—" he tapped his finger on the piece of paper—"which means that, with or without the pathologist's timings, she must have been killed between that last itemized call at ten-thirty and her friend's return call at fifteen minutes past midnight, when the phone was already off the hook."

5.

00:32 A.M.—TUESDAY, 9TH MARCH, 1999

Even as Siobhan lifted the receiver to call the police and report Rosheen missing, she was having second thoughts. They hadn't taken a blind bit of notice in the past, she thought bitterly, so why should it be different today? She could even predict how the conversation would go simply because she had been there so many times before.

Calm down, Mrs. Lavenham . . . It was undoubtedly a hoax . . . Let's see now . . . Didn't someone phone you not so long ago pretending to be Bridey in the throes of a heart attack . . . ? We rushed an ambulance to her only to find her alive and well and watching television . . . You and your nanny are Irish . . . Someone thought it would be entertaining to get a rise out of you by creeping into Kilkenny Cottage and making a call . . . Everyone knows the O'Riordans are notoriously careless about locking their back door . . . Sadly we can't legislate for practical jokes . . . Your nanny . . . ? She'll be watching the fire along with everyone else . . .

With a sigh of frustration, she replaced the receiver and listened to the message again. *"Hello? Are you there, Rosheen? It's . . ."*

She had been so sure it was Liam the first time she heard it, but now she was less certain. The Irish accent was the easiest accent in the world to ape, and Liam's was so broad any fool could do it. For want of someone more sensible to talk to, she telephoned Ian in his hotel bedroom in Rome. "It's me," she said, "and I've only just got back. I'm sorry to wake you but they've burnt Kilkenny Cottage and Rosheen's missing. Do you think I should phone the police?"

"Hang on," he said sleepily. "Run that one by me again. Who's they?"

"I don't know," she said in frustration. "Someone—anyone— Peter Haversley patted Cynthia on the back when the roof caved in. If I knew where the O'Riordans were I'd phone them, but Rosheen's the only one who knows the number—and she's not here. I'd go back to the fire if I had a car—the village is swarming with policemen—but I've had to leave mine at the church and yours is at Heathrow—and the children will never be able to walk all the way down the drive, not at this time of night."

He gave a long yawn. "You're going much too fast. I've only just woken up. What's this about Kilkenny Cottage burning down?"

She explained it slowly.

"So where's Rosheen?" He sounded more alert now. "And what the hell was she doing leaving the boys?"

"I don't know." She told him about the telephone call from Kilkenny Cottage. "If it was Liam, Rosheen may have gone up there to see him, and now I'm worried they were in the house when the fire started. Everyone thinks it was empty because we watched them go this morning." She described the scene for him as Liam helped Bridey into their Ford Estate then drove unsmilingly past the group of similarly unsmiling neighbors who had gathered at the crossroads to see them off. "It was awful," she said. "I went down to collect Patch, and bloody Cynthia started hissing at them so the rest joined in. I really hate them, Ian."

He didn't answer immediately. "Look," he said then, "the fire brigade don't just take people's words for this kind of thing. They'll have checked to make sure there was no one in the house as soon as they got there. And if Liam and Bridey *did* come back, their car would have been parked at the front and someone would have noticed it. Okay, I agree the village is full of bigots, but they're not murderers, Shiv, and they wouldn't keep quiet if they thought the O'Riordans were burning to death. Come on, think about it. You know I'm right."

"What about Rosheen?"

"Yes, well," he said dryly, "it wouldn't be the first time, would it? Did you check the barn? I expect she's out there getting laid by Kevin Wyllie."

"She's only done it once."

"She's used the barn once," he corrected her, "but it's anyone's guess how often she's been laid by Kevin. I'll bet you a pound to a penny they're tucked up together somewhere and she'll come wandering in with a smile on her face when you least expect it. I hope you tear strips off her for it, too. She's no damn business to leave the boys on their own."

She let it ride, unwilling to be drawn into another argument about Rosheen's morals. Ian worked on the principle that what the eye didn't see the heart didn't grieve over, and refused to recognize the hypocrisy of his position, while Siobhan's view was that Kevin was merely the bit of "rough" that was keeping Rosheen amused while she looked for something better. *God knew every woman did it . . . the road to respectability was far from straight . . .* In any case, she agreed with his final sentiment. Even if it were Liam who phoned from the cottage, Rosheen's first responsibility was to James and Oliver. "So what should I do? Just wait for her to come back?"

"I don't see you have much choice. She's over twenty-one so the police won't do anything tonight."

"Okay."

He knew her too well. "You don't sound convinced."

She wasn't, but then she was more relaxed about the way Rosheen conducted herself than he was. The fact that they'd come home early one night and caught her in the barn with her knickers down had offended Ian deeply, even though Rosheen had been monitoring the boys all the time via a two-way transmitter that she'd taken with her. Ian had wanted to sack her on the spot, but Siobhan had persuaded him out of it after extracting a promise from Rosheen that the affair would be confined to her spare time in future. Afterward, and because she was a great deal less puritanical than her English husband, Siobhan had buried her face in her pillow to stifle her laughter. Her view was that Rosheen had shown typical Irish tact by having sex outside in the barn rather than under the Lavenhams' roof. As she pointed out to Ian: *"We'd never have known Kevin was there if she'd smuggled him into her room and told him to perform quietly."*

"It's just that I'm tired," she lied, knowing she could never describe her sense of foreboding down the telephone to someone over a thousand miles away. Empty houses gave her the shivers at the best of times—a throwback to the rambling, echoing mansion of her childhood, which her overactive imagination had peopled with giants and specters . . . "Look, go back to sleep and I'll ring you tomorrow. It'll have sorted itself out by then. Just make sure you come home on Friday," she ended severely, "or I'll file for divorce immediately. I didn't marry you to be deserted for the Ravenelli brothers."

"I will," he promised.

Siobhan listened to the click as he hung up at the other end, then replaced her own receiver before opening the front door and looking toward the dark shape of the barn. She searched for a chink of light between the double doors but knew she was wasting her time even while she was doing it. Rosheen had been so terrified by Ian's threat to tell her parents in Ireland what she'd been up to that her sessions with Kevin were now confined to somewhere a great deal more private than Fording Farm's barn.

With a sigh she retreated to the kitchen and settled on a cushion in front of the Aga with Patch's head lying across her lap and the bottle of wine beside her. It was another ten minutes before she noticed that the key to Kilkenny Cottage, which should have been hanging from a hook on the dresser, was no longer there.

WEDNESDAY, 10TH FEBRUARY, 1999

"But why are you so sure it was Patrick?" Siobhan had asked the inspector then. "Why not a total stranger? I mean, anyone could have taken the hammer from his toolbox if he'd left it in the kitchen the way he says he did."

"Because there were no signs of a break-in. Whoever killed them either had a key to the front door or was let in by Dorothy Jenkins. And that means it must have been someone she knew."

"Maybe she hadn't locked up," said Siobhan, clutching at straws. "Maybe they came in through the back door."

"Have you ever tried to open the back door to the manor, Mrs. Lavenham?"

"No."

"Apart from the fact that the bolts were rusted into their sockets, it's so warped and swollen with damp you have to put a shoulder to it to force it ajar, and it screams like a banshee every time you do it. If a stranger had come in through the back door at eleven o'clock at night, he wouldn't have caught Miss Jenkins in the kitchen. She'd have taken to her heels the minute she heard the banshee-wailing and would have used one of the phones upstairs to call the police."

"You can't know that," argued Siobhan. "Sowerbridge is the sleepiest place on earth. Why would she assume it was an intruder? She probably thought it was Jeremy paying a late-night visit to his grandmother."

"We don't think so." He picked up a pen and turned it between his fingers. "As far as we can establish, that door was never used. Certainly none of the neighbors report going in that way. The milkman said Miss Jenkins kept it bolted because on the one occasion when she tried to open it, it became so wedged that she had to ask him to force it shut again."

She sighed, admitting defeat. "Patrick's always been so sweet to me and my children. I just can't believe he's a murderer."

He smiled at her naivete. "The two are not mutually exclusive, Mrs. Lavenham. I expect Jack the Ripper's neighbor said the same about him."

1:00 A.M.—TUESDAY, 9TH MARCH, 1999

People began to shiver as the smoldering remains were dowsed by the fire hoses and the pungent smell of wet ashes stung their nostrils. In the aftermath of excitement, a sense of shame crept among the inhabitants of Sowerbridge—*schadenfreude* was surely alien to their natures?—and bit by bit the crowd began to disperse. Only the Haversleys, the Bentleys, and Jeremy Jardine lingered at the crossroads, held by a mutual fascination for the scene of devastation that would greet them every time they emerged from their houses.

"We won't be able to open our windows for weeks," said Nora Bentley, wrinkling her nose. "The smell will be suffocating."

"It'll be worse when the wind gets up and deposits soot all over the place," complained Peter Haversley, brushing ash from his coat.

His wife clicked her tongue impatiently. "We'll just have to put up with it," she said. "It's hardly the end of the world."

Sam Bentley surprised her with a sudden bark of laughter. "Well spoken, Cynthia, considering you'll be bearing the brunt of it. The prevailing winds are southwesterly, which means most of the muck will collect in Malvern House. Still—" he paused to glance from her to Peter—"you sow a wind and you reap a whirlwind, eh?"

There was a short silence.

"Have you noticed how Liam's wrecks have survived intact?" asked Nora then, with assumed brightness. "Is it a judgment, do you think?"

"Don't be ridiculous," said Jeremy.

Sam gave another brief chortle. "Is it ridiculous? You complained enough when there were only the cars to worry about. Now you've got a burnt-out cottage to worry about as well. I can't believe the O'Riordans were insured, so it'll be years before anything is done. If you're lucky, a developer will buy the land and build an estate of little boxes on your doorstep. If you're unlucky, Liam will put up a corrugated-iron shack and live in that. And do you know, Jeremy, I hope he does. Personal revenge is so much sweeter than anything the law can offer."

"What's that supposed to mean?"

"You'd have been wiser to call the fire brigade earlier," said the old doctor bluntly. "Nero may have fiddled while Rome burned, but it didn't do his reputation any good."

Another silence.

"What are you implying?" demanded Cynthia aggressively. "That Jeremy could somehow have prevented the fire?"

Jeremy Jardine folded his arms. "I'll sue you for slander if you *are*, Sam."

"It won't be just me. Half the village is wondering why Nora and I smelt burning before you did, and why Cynthia and Peter took themselves off to Salisbury on a Monday evening for the first time in living memory."

"Coincidence," grunted Peter Haversley. "Pure coincidence."

"Well, I pray for all your sakes you're telling the truth," murmured Sam, wiping a weary hand across his ash-grimed face, "because the police aren't the only ones who'll be asking questions. The Lavenhams certainly won't stay quiet."

"I hope you're not suggesting that one of us set fire to that beastly little place," said Cynthia crossly. "Honestly, Sam, I wonder about you sometimes."

He shook his head sadly, wishing he could dislike her as comprehensively as Siobhan Lavenham did. "No, Cynthia, I'm suggesting you knew it was going to happen, and even incited the local youths to do it. You can argue that you wanted revenge for Lavinia and Dorothy's deaths, but aiding and abetting any crime is a prosecutable offense and—" he sighed—"you'll get no sympathy from me if you go to prison for it."

Behind them, in the hall of Malvern House, the telephone began to ring . . .

WEDNESDAY, 10TH FEBRUARY, 1999

Siobhan had put an opened envelope on the desk in front of the detective inspector. "Even if Patrick is the murderer and even if

Bridey knows he is, it doesn't excuse this kind of thing," she said. "I can't prove it came from Cynthia Haversley, but I'm a hundred percent certain it did. She's busting a gut to make life so unpleasant for Liam and Bridey that they'll leave of their own accord."

The inspector frowned as he removed a folded piece of paper and read the letters pasted onto it.

> HAnGInG IS TOo GOoD foR THE LikEs of YOU.
> BUrN in h e l l

"Who was it sent to?" he asked.

"Bridey."

"Why did she give it to you and not to the police?"

"Because she knew I was coming here today and asked me to bring it with me. It was posted through her letterbox sometime the night before last."

("They'll take more notice of you than they ever take of me," the old woman had said, pressing the envelope urgently into Siobhan's hands. "Make them understand we're in danger before it's too late.")

He turned the envelope over. "Why do you think it came from Mrs. Haversley?"

Feminine intuition, thought Siobhan wryly. "Because the letters that make up 'hell' have been cut from a *Daily Telegraph* banner imprint. It's the only broadsheet newspaper that has an 'h,' an 'e,' and two 'l's in its title, and Cynthia takes the *Telegraph* every day."

"Along with how many other people in Sowerbridge?"

She smiled slightly. "Quite a few, but no one else has Cynthia Haversley's poisonous frame of mind. She loves stirring. The more she can work people up, the happier she is. It gives her a sense of importance to have everyone dancing to her tune."

"You don't like her." It was a statement rather than a question.

"No."

"Neither do I," admitted the inspector, "but it doesn't make her guilty, Mrs. Lavenham. Liam and/or Bridey could have acquired a *Telegraph* just as easily and sent this letter to themselves."

"That's what Bridey told me you'd say."

"Because it's the truth?" he suggested mildly. "Mrs. Haversley's a fat, clumsy woman with fingers like sausages, and if she'd been wearing gloves the whole exercise would have been impossible. This—" he touched the letter—"is too neat. There's not a letter out of place."

"Peter then."

"Peter Haversley's an alcoholic. His hands shake."

"Jeremy Jardine?"

"I doubt it. Poison-pen letters are usually written by women. I'm sorry, Mrs. Lavenham, but I can guarantee the only fingerprints I will find on this—other than yours and mine, of course—are Bridey O'Riordan's. Not because the person who did it wore gloves, but because Bridey did it herself."

1:10 A.M.—TUESDAY, 9TH MARCH, 1999

Dr. Bentley clicked his tongue in concern as he glanced past Cynthia to her husband. Peter was walking unsteadily toward them after answering the telephone, his face leeched of color in the lights of the fire engines. "You should be in bed, man. We should all be in bed. We're too old for this sort of excitement."

Peter Haversley ignored him. "That was Siobhan," he said jerkily. "She wants me to tell the police that Rosheen is missing. She said Liam called the farm from Kilkenny Cottage at eight-thirty this evening, and she's worried he and Rosheen were in there when the fire started."

"They can't have been," said Jeremy.

"How do you know?"

"We watched Liam and Bridey leave for Winchester this morning."

"What if Liam came back to protect his house? What if he phoned Rosheen and asked her to join him?"

"Oh, for God's sake, Peter!" snapped Cynthia. "It's just Siobhan trying to make trouble again. You know what she's like."

"I don't think so. She sounded very distressed." He looked around for a policeman. "I'd better report it."

But his wife gripped his arm to hold him back. "No," she said viciously. "Let Siobhan do her own dirty work. If she wants to employ a slut to look after her children then it's her responsibility to keep tabs on her, not ours."

There was a moment of stillness while Peter searched her face in appalled recognition that he was looking at a stranger, then he drew back his hand and slapped her across the face. "Whatever depths you may have sunk me to," he said, "I am *not* a murderer . . ."

***LATE NEWS—THE *TELEGRAPH*—TUESDAY, 9TH MARCH, A.M.

Irish Family Burnt Out by Vigilantes

The family home of Patrick O'Riordan, currently on trial for the murder of Lavinia Fanshaw and Dorothy Jenkins, was burnt to the ground last night in what police suspect was a deliberate act of arson. Concern has been expressed over the whereabouts of O'Riordan's elderly parents, and some reports suggest bodies were recovered from the gutted kitchen. Police are refusing to confirm or deny the rumors. Suspicion has fallen on local vigilante groups who have been conducting a "hate" campaign against the O'Riordan family. In face of criticism, Hampshire police have restated their policy of zero tolerance toward anyone who decides to take the law into his own hands. "We will not hesitate to prosecute," said a spokesman. "Vigilantes should understand that arson is a very serious offense."

6.

TUESDAY, 9TH MARCH, 1999

When Siobhan heard a car pull into the driveway at 6:00 A.M. she prayed briefly, but with little hope, that someone had found Rosheen and brought her home. Hollow-eyed from lack of sleep, she opened her front door and stared at the two policemen on her doorstep. They looked like ghosts in the gray dawn light. Harbingers of doom, she thought, reading their troubled expressions. She recognized one of them as the detective inspector and the other as the young constable who had flagged her down the previous night. "You'd better come in," she said, pulling the door wide.

"Thank you."

She led the way into the kitchen and dropped onto the cushion in front of the Aga again, cradling Patch in her arms. "This is Bridey's dog," she told them, stroking his muzzle. "She adores him. *He* adores her. The trouble is he's a hopeless guard dog. He's like Bridey—" tears of exhaustion sprang into her eyes—"not overly bright—not overly brave—but as kind as kind can be."

The two policemen stood awkwardly in front of her, unsure where to sit or what to say.

"You look terrible," she said unevenly, "so I presume you've come to tell me Rosheen is dead."

"We don't know yet, Mrs. Lavenham," said the inspector, turning a chair to face her and lowering himself onto it. He gestured to the young constable to do the same. "We found a body in the kitchen area, but it'll be some time before—" He paused, unsure how to continue.

"I'm afraid it was so badly burnt it was unrecognizable. We're waiting on the pathologist's report to give us an idea of the age and—" he paused again—"sex."

"Oh, God!" she said dully. "Then it must be Rosheen."

"Why don't you think it's Bridey or Liam?"

"Because . . ." she broke off with a worried frown, "I assumed the phone call was a hoax to frighten Rosheen. Oh, my God! Aren't they in Winchester?"

He looked troubled. "They were escorted to a safe house at the end of yesterday's proceedings but it appears they left again shortly afterward. There was no one to monitor them, you see. They had a direct line through to the local police station and we sent out regular patrols during the night. We were worried about trouble coming from outside, not that they might decide to return to Kilkenny Cottage without telling us." He rubbed a hand around his jaw. "There are recent tire marks up at the manor. We think Liam may have parked his Ford there in order to push Bridey across the lawn and through the gate onto the footpath beside Kilkenny Cottage."

She shook her head in bewilderment. "Then why didn't you find three bodies?"

"Because the Estate isn't there now, Mrs. Lavenham, and whoever died in Kilkenny Cottage probably died at the hands of Liam O'Riordan."

WEDNESDAY, 10TH FEBRUARY, 1999

She had stood up at the end of her interview with the inspector. "Do you know what I hate most about the English?" she told him.

He shook his head.

"It never occurs to you, you might be wrong." She placed her palm on the poison-pen letter on his desk. "But you're wrong about this. Bridey cares about my opinion—she cares about *me*—not just as a fellow Irishwoman but as the employer of her niece. She'd never do anything to jeopardize Rosheen's position in our house, because Rosheen and I are her only lifeline in Sowerbridge. We shop for her, we do our best to protect her, and we welcome her to the farm when things get difficult. Under no circumstances *whatsoever* would Bridey use me to pass on falsified evidence, because she'd be too afraid I'd wash my hands of her and then persuade Rosheen to do the same."

"It may be true, Mrs. Lavenham, but it's not an argument you could ever use in court."

"I'm not interested in legal argument, Inspector, I'm only interested in persuading you that there is a terror campaign being waged against the O'Riordans in Sowerbridge and that their lives are in danger." She watched him shake his head. "You haven't listened to a word I've said, have you? You just think I'm taking Bridey's side because I'm Irish."

"Aren't you?"

"No." She straightened with a sigh. "Moral support is alien to Irish culture, Inspector. We only really enjoy fighting with each other. I thought every Englishman knew *that . . .*"

TUESDAY, 9TH MARCH, 1999

The news that Patrick O'Riordan's trial had been adjourned while police investigated the disappearance of his parents and his cousin was broadcast across the networks at noon, but Siobhan switched off the radio before the names could register with her two young sons.

They had sat wide-eyed all morning watching a procession of policemen traipse to and from Rosheen's bedroom in search of anything that might give them a lead to where she had gone. Most poignantly, as far as Siobhan was concerned, they had carefully removed the girl's hairbrush, some used tissues from her wastepaper basket, and a small pile of dirty washing in order to provide the pathologist with comparative DNA samples.

She had explained to the boys that Rosheen hadn't been in the house when she got back the previous night, and because she was worried about it she had asked the police to help find her.

"She went to Auntie Bridey's," said six-year-old James.

"How do you know, darling?"

"Because Uncle Liam phoned and said Auntie Bridey wasn't feeling very well."

"Did Rosheen tell you that?"

He nodded. "She said she wouldn't be long but that I had to go to sleep. So I did."

She dropped a kiss on the top of his head. "Good boy."

He and Oliver were drawing pictures at the kitchen table, and James suddenly dragged his pencil to and fro across the page to obliterate what he'd been doing. "Is it because Uncle Patrick killed that lady?" he asked her.

Siobhan searched his face for a moment. *The rules had been very clear . . . Whatever else you do, Rosheen, please do not tell the children what Patrick has been accused of . . .* I didn't know you knew about that," she said lightly.

"Everyone knows," he told her solemnly. "Uncle Patrick's a monster and ought to be strung up."

"Goodness!" she exclaimed, forcing a smile to her lips. "Who said that?"

"Kevin."

Anger tightened like knots in her chest. *Ian had laid it on the line following the incident in the barn . . . You may see Kevin in your spare time, Rosheen, but not when you're in charge of the children . . .* "Kevin Wyllie? Rosheen's friend?" She squatted down beside him, smoothing a lock of hair from his forehead. "Does he come here a lot?"

"Rosheen said we weren't to tell."

"I don't think she meant you mustn't tell me, darling."

James wrapped his thin little arms round her neck and pressed his cheek against hers. "I think she did, Mummy. She said Kevin would rip her head off if we told you and Daddy anything."

LATER—TUESDAY, 9TH MARCH, 1999

"I can't believe I let this happen," she told the inspector, pacing up and down her drawing room in a frenzy of movement. "I should have listened to Ian. He said Kevin was no good the minute he saw him."

"Calm down, Mrs. Lavenham," he said quietly. "I imagine your children can hear every word you're saying."

"But why didn't Rosheen tell me Kevin was threatening her? God knows, she should have known she could trust me. I've bent over backward to help her and her family."

"Perhaps that's the problem," he suggested. "Perhaps she was worried about laying any more burdens on your shoulders."

"But she was responsible for my *children*, for God's sake! I can't believe she'd keep quiet while some low-grade Neanderthal was terrorizing her."

The inspector watched her for a moment, wondering how much to tell her. "Kevin Wyllie is also missing," he said abruptly. "We're collecting DNA samples from his bedroom because we think the body at Kilkenny Cottage is his."

Siobhan stared at him in bewilderment. "I don't understand."

He gave a hollow laugh. "The one thing the pathologist *can* be certain about, Mrs. Lavenham, is that the body was upright when it died."

"I still don't understand."

He looked ill, she thought, as he ran his tongue across dry lips. "We're working on the theory that Liam, Bridey, and Rosheen appointed themselves judge, jury, and hangman before setting fire to Kilkenny Cottage in order to destroy the evidence."

***The *Telegraph*—Wednesday, 10th March, a.m.
Couple Arrested
Two people, believed to be the parents of Patrick O'Riordan, whose trial at Winchester Crown Court was adjourned two days ago, were arrested on suspicion of murder in Liverpool yesterday as they attempted to board a ferry to Ireland. There is still no clue to the whereabouts of their niece Rosheen, whose family lives in County Donegal. Hampshire police have admitted that the Irish guardee have been assisting them in their search for the missing family. Suspicion remains that the body found in Kilkenny Cottage was that of Sowerbridge resident Kevin Wyllie, twenty-eight, although police refuse to confirm or deny the story.

THURSDAY, 11TH MARCH, 1999—4:00 A.M.

Siobhan had lain awake for hours, listening to the clock on the bed-side table tick away the seconds. She heard Ian come in at two o'clock and tiptoe into the spare room, but she didn't call out to tell him she was awake. There would be time enough to say sorry tomorrow. Sorry for dragging him home early . . . sorry for saying Lavenham Interiors could go down the drain for all she cared . . . sorry for getting everything so wrong . . . sorry for blaming the English for the sins of the Irish . . .

Grief squeezed her heart every time she thought about Rosheen. But it was a complicated grief that carried shame and guilt in equal proportions, because she couldn't rid herself of responsibility for what the girl had done. "I thought she was keen on Kevin," she told the inspector that afternoon. "Ian never understood the attraction, but I did."

"Why?" he asked with a hint of cynicism. "Because it was a suit-able match? Because Kevin was the same class as she was?"

"It wasn't a question of class," she protested.

"Wasn't it? In some ways you're more of a snob than the Eng-lish, Mrs. Lavenham. You forced Rosheen to acknowledge her rela-tionship with Liam and Bridey because *you* acknowledged them," he told her brutally, "but it really ought to have occurred to you that a bright girl like her would have higher ambitions than to be known as the niece of Irish gypsies."

"Then why bother with Kevin at all? Wasn't he just as bad?"

The inspector shrugged. "What choice did she have? How many unattached men are there in Sowerbridge? And you had to believe she was with someone, Mrs. Lavenham, otherwise you'd have started asking awkward questions. Still—" he paused—"I doubt the poor lad had any idea just how much she loathed him."

"No one did," said Siobhan sadly. "Everyone thought she was besotted with him after the incident in the barn."

"She was playing a long game," he said slowly, "and she was very good at it. You never doubted she was fond of her aunt and uncle."

"I believed what she told me."

He smiled slightly. "And you were determined that everyone else should believe it as well."

Siobhan looked at him with stricken eyes. "Oh, God! Does that make it my fault?"

"No," he murmured. "Mine. I didn't take you seriously when you said the Irish only really enjoy fighting each other."

THURSDAY, 11TH MARCH, 1999—3:00 P.M.

Cynthia Haversley opened her front door a crack. "Oh, it's you," she said with surprising warmth. "I thought it was another of those beastly journalists."

Well, well! How quickly times change, thought Siobhan ruefully as she stepped inside. Not so long ago Cynthia had been inviting those same "beastly" journalists into Malvern House for cups of tea while she regaled them with stories about the O'Riordans' iniquities. She nodded to Peter, who was standing in the doorway to the drawing room. "How are you both?"

It was three days since she had seen them, and she was surprised by how much they had aged. Peter, in particular, looked haggard and gray, and she assumed he must have been hitting the bottle harder than usual. He made a rocking motion with his hand. "Not too good. Rather ashamed about the way we've all been behaving, if I'm honest."

Cynthia opened her mouth to say something, but clearly thought better of it. "Where are the boys?" she asked instead.

"Nora's looking after them for me."

"You should have brought them with you. I wouldn't have minded."

Siobhan shook her head. "I didn't want them to hear what I'm going to say to you, Cynthia."

The woman bridled immediately. "You can't blame—"

"Enough!" snapped Peter, cutting her short and stepping to one side. "Come into the drawing room, Siobhan. How's Ian bearing up? We saw he'd come home."

She walked across to the window from where she could see the remains of Kilkenny Cottage. "Tired," she answered. "He didn't get back till early this morning and he had to leave again at crack of dawn for the office. We've got three contracts on the go and they're all going pear-shaped because neither of us has been there."

"It can't be easy for you."

"No," she said slowly, "it's not. Ian was supposed to stay in Italy till Friday, but as things are . . ." She paused. "Neither of us can be in two places at once, unfortunately." She turned to look at them. "And I can't leave the children."

"I'm sorry," said Peter.

She gave a small laugh. "There's no need to be. I do rather like them, you know, so it's no hardship having to stay at home. I just wish it hadn't had to happen this way." She folded her arms and studied Cynthia curiously. "James told me an interesting story yesterday," she said. "I assume it's true, because he's a truthful child, but I thought I'd check it with you anyway. In view of everything that's happened, I'm hesitant to accept anyone's word on anything. Did you go down to the farm one day and find James and Oliver alone?"

"I saw Rosheen leave," she said, "but I knew no one was there to look after them because I'd been—well—watching the drive that morning." She puffed out her chest in self-defense. "I told you she was deceitful and lazy but you wouldn't listen to me."

"Because you never told me why," said Siobhan mildly.

"I assumed you knew and that it didn't bother you. Ian made no secret of how angry he was when you came home one night and found her with Kevin in the barn, but you just said he was overreacting." She considered the wisdom of straight-speaking, decided it was necessary, and took a deep breath. "If I'm honest, Siobhan, you even seemed to find it rather amusing. I never understood why. Personally, I'd have sacked her on the spot and looked for someone more respectable."

Siobhan shook her head. "I thought it was a one-off. I didn't realize she'd been making a habit of it."

"She was too interested in sex not to, my dear. I've never seen anyone so shameless. More often than not, she'd leave your boys with Bridey if it meant she could have a couple of hours with Kevin Wyllie. Many's the time I watched her sneak into Kilkenny Cottage only to sauce out again five minutes later without them. And then she'd drive off in your Range Rover, bold as brass, with that unpleasant young man beside her. I did wonder if you knew what your car was being used for."

"You should have told me."

Cynthia shook her head. "You wouldn't have listened."

"In fact, Cynthia tried several times to broach the subject," said Peter gently, "but on each occasion you shot her down in flames and all but accused her of being an anti-Irish bigot."

"I never had much choice," murmured Siobhan without hostility. "Could you not have divorced Rosheen from Liam, Bridey, and Patrick, Cynthia? Why did every conversation about my nanny have to begin with a diatribe against her relatives?"

There was a short, uncomfortable silence.

Siobhan sighed. "What I really don't understand is why you should have thought I was the kind of mother who wouldn't care if her children were being neglected?"

Cynthia looked embarrassed. "I didn't, not really. I just thought you were—well, rather more relaxed than most."

"Because I'm Irish and not English?"

Peter tut-tutted in concern. "It wasn't like that," he said. "Hang it all, Siobhan, we didn't know what Rosheen's instructions were. To be honest, we thought you were encouraging her to make use of Bridey in order to give the poor old thing a sense of purpose. We didn't applaud your strategy—as a matter of fact, it seemed like a mad idea to us—" He broke off with a guilty expression. "As Cynthia kept saying, there's no way she'd have left two boisterous children in the care of a disabled woman and a drunken man, but we thought you were trying to demonstrate solidarity with them. If I trust the O'Riordans with my children, then so should the rest of you . . . that sort of thing."

Siobhan turned back to the window and the blackened heap that had been Kilkenny Cottage. *For want of a nail the shoe was lost . . . for want of a shoe the horse was lost . . . for want of mutual understanding lives were lost* . . . "Couldn't you have told me about the time you went to the farm and found James and Oliver on their own?" she murmured, her breath misting the glass.

"I did," said Cynthia.

"When?"

"The day after I found them. I stopped you and Ian at the end of the drive as you were setting off for work and told you your children were too young to be left alone. I must say I thought your attitude was extraordinarily casual but—well—" she shrugged—"I'd rather come to expect that."

Siobhan remembered the incident well. Cynthia had stood in the drive, barring their way, and had then thrust her indignant red face through Ian's open window and lectured them on the foolishness of employing a girl with loose morals. "We both assumed you were talking about the night she took Kevin into the barn. Ian said afterward that he wished he'd never mentioned it, because you were using it as a stick to beat us."

Cynthia frowned. "Didn't James and Oliver tell you about it? I sat with them for nearly two hours, in all conscience, and gave Rosheen a piece of my mind when she finally came back."

"They were too frightened. Kevin beat them about the head because they'd opened the door to you and said if I ever asked them if Mrs. Haversley had come to the house they were to say no."

Cynthia lowered herself carefully onto a chair. "I had no idea," she said in an appalled tone of voice. "No wonder you took it so calmly."

"Mm." Siobhan glanced from the seated woman to her husband. "We seem to have got our wires crossed all along the line, and I feel very badly about it now. I keep thinking that if I hadn't been so quick to condemn you all, *no one* would have died."

Peter shook his head. "We all feel the same way. Even Sam and Nora Bentley. They're saying that if they'd backed your judgment of Liam and Bridey instead of sitting on the fence—" He broke off on a sigh. "I can't understand why we allowed it to get so out of hand. We're not unkind people. A little misguided . . . rather too easily prejudiced perhaps . . . but not *unkind*."

Siobhan thought of Jeremy Jardine. Was Peter including Lavinia's grandson in this general absolution? she wondered.

7.

9:00 A.M.—FRIDAY, 12TH MARCH, 1999

"Can I get you a cup of tea, Bridey?" asked the inspector as he came into the interview room.

The old woman's eyes twinkled mischievously. "I'd rather have a Guinness."

He laughed as he pulled out a chair. "You and Liam both. He says it's the first time he's been on the wagon since his last stretch in prison nearly twenty years ago." He studied her for a moment. "Any regrets?"

"Only the one," she said. "That we didn't kill Mr. Jardine as well."

"No regrets about killing Rosheen?"

"Why would I have?" she asked him. "I'd crush a snake as easily. She taunted us with how clever she'd been to kill two harmless old ladies and then have my poor Patrick take the blame. And all for the sake of marrying a rich man. I should have recognized her as the devil the first day I saw her."

"How did you kill her?"

"She was a foolish girl. She thought that because I'm in a wheelchair she had nothing to fear from me, when, of course, every bit of strength I have is in my arms. It was Liam she was afraid of, but she should have remembered that Liam hasn't been able to hurt a fly these fifteen years." She smiled as she released the arm of her wheelchair and held it up. The two metal prongs that located it in the chair's framework protruded from each end. "I can only shift myself to a bed or a chair when this is removed, and it's been lifted out that many times the ends are like razors. Perhaps I'd not have brought it down on her wicked head if she hadn't laughed and called us illiterate Irish bastards. Then again, perhaps I would. To be sure, I was angry enough."

"Why weren't you angry with Kevin?" he asked curiously. "He says he was only there that night because he'd been paid to set fire to your house. Why didn't you kill him, too? He's making no bones about the fact that he and his friends have been terrorizing you for months."

"Do you think we didn't know that? Why would we go back to Kilkenny Cottage in secret if it wasn't to catch him and his friends red-handed and make you coppers sit up and take notice of the fearful things they've been doing to us these many months? As Liam said, fight fire with fire. Mind, that's not to say we wanted to kill them—give them a shock, maybe."

"But only Kevin turned up?"

She nodded. "Poor greedy creature that he is. Would he share good money with his friends when a single match would do the business? He came creeping in with his petrol can and I've never seen a lad so frightened as when Liam slipped the noose about his throat and called to me to switch on the light. We'd strung it from the beams and the lad was caught like a fly on a web. Did we tell you he wet himself?"

"No."

"Well, he did. Pissed all over the floor in terror."

"He's got an inch-wide rope burn round his neck, Bridey. Liam must have pulled the noose pretty tight for that, so perhaps Kevin thought you were going to hang him?"

"Liam hasn't the strength to pull anything tight," she said matter-of-factly, slotting the chair arm back into its frame. "Not these fifteen years."

"So you keep saying," murmured the inspector.

"I expect Kevin will tell you he slipped and did it himself. He was that frightened he could hardly keep his feet, but at least it meant we knew he was telling the truth. He could have named anybody . . . Mrs. Haversley . . . Mr. Jardine . . . but instead he told us it was our niece who had promised him a hundred quid if he'd burn Kilkenny Cottage down and get us out of her hair for good."

"Did he also say she had been orchestrating the campaign against you?"

"Oh, yes," she murmured, staring past him as her mind replayed the scene in her head. "'She calls you thieving Irish trash,' he said, 'and hates you for your cheap, common ways and your poverty. She wants rid of you from Sowerbridge because people will never treat her right until you're gone.'" She smiled slightly. "So I told him I didn't blame her, that it can't have been easy having her cousin arrested for murder and her aunt and uncle treated like lepers—" she paused to stare at her hands—"and he said Patrick's arrest had nothing to do with it."

"Did he explain what he meant?"

"That she hated us from the first day she met us." She shook her head. "Though, to be sure, I don't know what we did to make her think so badly of us."

"You lied to your family, Bridey. We've spoken to her brother. According to him, her mother filled her head with stories about how rich you and Liam were and how you'd sold your business in London to retire to a beautiful cottage in a beautiful part of England. I think the reality must have been a terrible disappointment to her. According to her brother, she came over from Ireland with dreams of meeting a wealthy man and marrying him."

"She was wicked through and through, Inspector, and I'll not take any of her fault on me. I was honest with her from the beginning. We are as you see us, I said, because God saw fit to punish us for Liam and Patrick's wrongdoing, but you'll never be embarrassed by it, because no one knows. We may not be as rich as you hoped, but we're loving, and there'll always be a home for you here if the job doesn't work out with Mrs. Lavenham."

"Now Mrs. Lavenham's blaming herself, Bridey. She says if she'd spent less time at the office and more time with Rosheen and the children, no one would have died."

Distress creased Bridey's forehead. "It's always the same when people abandon their religion. Without God in their lives, they quickly lose sight of the devil. Yet for you and me, Inspector, the devil exists in the hearts of the wicked. Mrs. Lavenham needs reminding that it was Rosheen who betrayed this family . . . and only Rosheen."

"Because you gave her the means when you told her about Patrick's conviction."

The old woman's mouth thinned into a narrow line. "And she used it against him. Can you believe that I never once questioned why those poor old ladies were killed with Patrick's hammer? Would you not think—knowing my boy was innocent—that I'd have put two and two together and said, there's no such thing as coincidence?"

"She was clever," said the inspector. "She made everyone believe she was only interested in Kevin Wyllie, and Kevin Wyllie had no reason on earth to murder Mrs. Fanshaw."

"I have it in my heart to feel sorry for the poor lad now," said Bridey with a small laugh, "never mind he terrorized us for months. Rosheen showed her colors soon enough when she came down after Liam's phone call to find Kevin trussed up like a chicken on the floor. That's when I saw the cunning in her eyes and realized for the first time what a schemer she was. She tried to pretend Kevin was lying, but when she saw we didn't believe her, she snatched the petrol can from the table. 'I'll make you burn in hell, you stupid, incompetent bastard,' she told him. 'You've served your purpose, made everyone think I was interested in you when you're so far beneath me I wouldn't have wasted a second glance on you if I hadn't had to.' Then she came toward me, unscrewing the lid of the petrol can as she did so and slopping it over my skirt. Bold as brass she was with her lighter in her hand, telling Liam she'd set fire to me if he tried to stop her phoning her fancy man to come and help her." Her eyes hardened at the memory. "She couldn't keep quiet, of course. Perhaps people can't when they believe in their own cleverness. She told us how gullible we were . . . what excitement she'd had battering two old ladies to death . . . how besotted Mr. Jardine was with her . . . how easy it had been to cast suspicion on a moron like Patrick . . . And when Mr. Jardine never answered because he was hiding in his cellar, she turned on me in a fury and thrust the lighter against my skirt, saying she'd burn us all anyway. Kevin will get the blame, she said, even though he'll be dead. Half the village knows he's been sent down here to do the business."

"And that's when you hit her?"

Bridey nodded. "I certainly wasn't going to wait for the flame to ignite."

"And Kevin witnessed all this?"

"He did indeed, and will say so at my trial if you decide to prosecute me."

The inspector smiled slightly. "So who set the house on fire, Bridey?"

"To be sure, it was Rosheen who did it. The petrol spilled all over the floor as she fell and the flint struck as her hand hit the quarry tiles." A flicker of amusement crossed her old face as she looked at him. "Ask young Kevin if you don't believe me."

"I already have. He agrees with you. The only trouble is, he breaks out in a muck sweat every time the question's put to him."

"And why wouldn't he? It was a terrible experience for all of us."

"So why didn't you go up in flames, Bridey? You said your skirt was saturated with petrol."

"Ah, well, do you not think that was God's doing?" She crossed herself. "Of course, it may have had something to do with the fact that Kevin had managed to free himself and was able to push me to the door while Liam smothered the flames with his coat, but for myself I count it a miracle."

"You're lying through your teeth, Bridey. We think Liam started the fire on purpose in order to hide something."

The old woman gave a cackle of laughter. "Now why would you think that, Inspector? What could two poor cripples have done that they didn't want the police to know about?" Her eyes narrowed. "Never mind a witch had tried to rob them of their only son?"

2:00 P.M.—FRIDAY, 12TH MARCH, 1999

"Did you find out?" Siobhan asked the inspector.

He shrugged. "We think Kevin had to watch a ritual burning and is too terrified to admit to it because he's the one who took the petrol there in the first place." He watched a look of disbelief cross Siobhan's face. "Bridey called her a witch," he reminded her.

Siobhan shook her head. "And you think that's the evidence Liam wanted to destroy?"

"Yes."

She gave an unexpected laugh. "You must think the Irish are very backward, Inspector. Didn't ritual burnings go out with the Middle Ages?" She paused, unable to control her amusement. "Are you going to charge them with it? The press will love it if you do. I can just imagine the headlines when the case comes to trial."

"No," he said, watching her. "Kevin's sticking to the story Liam and Bridey taught him, and the pathologist's suggestion that Rosheen was upright when she died looks too damn flaky to take into court. At the moment, we're accepting a plea of self-defense and accidental arson." He paused. "Unless you know differently, Mrs. Lavenham."

Her expression was unreadable. "All I know," she told him, "is that Bridey could no more have burnt her niece as a witch than she could get up out of her wheelchair and walk. But don't go by what I say, Inspector. I've been wrong about everything else."

"Mm. Well, you're right. Their defense against murder rests entirely on their disabilities."

Siobhan seemed to lose interest and fell into a thoughtful silence which the inspector was loath to break. "Was it Rosheen who told you Patrick had stolen Lavinia's jewelry?" she demanded abruptly.

"Why do you ask?"

"Because I've never understood why you suddenly concentrated all your efforts on him."

"We found his fingerprints at the manor."

"Along with mine and most of Sowerbridge's."

"But yours aren't on file, Mrs. Lavenham, and you don't have a criminal record."

"Neither should Patrick, Inspector, not if it's fifteen years since he committed a crime. The English have a strong sense of justice, and that means his slate would have been wiped clean after seven years. Someone—" she studied him curiously—"must have pointed the finger at him. I've never been able to work out who it was, but perhaps it was you? Did you base your whole case against him on privileged knowledge that you acquired fifteen years ago in London? If so, you're a shit."

He was irritated enough to defend himself. "He boasted to Rosheen about how he'd got the better of a senile old woman and showed her Mrs. Fanshaw's jewelry to prove it. She said he was full of himself, talked about how both old women were so gaga they'd given him the run of the house in return for doing some small maintenance jobs. She didn't say Patrick had murdered them—she was too clever for that—but when we questioned Patrick and he denied ever being in the manor house or knowing anything about any stolen jewelry, we decided to search Kilkenny Cottage and came up trumps."

"Which is what Rosheen wanted."

"We know that now, Mrs. Lavenham, and if Patrick had been straight with us from the beginning, it might have been different then. But unfortunately, he wasn't. His difficulty was he had the old lady's rings in his possession as well as the costume jewelry that Miss Jenkins gave him. He knew perfectly well he'd been palmed off with worthless glass, so he hopped upstairs when Miss Jenkins's back was turned and helped himself to something more valuable. He claims Mrs. Fanshaw was asleep so he just slipped the rings off her fingers and tiptoed out again."

"Did Bridey and Rosheen know he'd taken the rings?"

"Yes, but he told them they were glass replicas which had been in the box with the rest of the bits and pieces. Rosheen knew differently, of course—she and Jardine understood Patrick's psychology well enough to know he'd steal something valuable the minute his earnings were denied—but Bridey believed him."

She nodded. "Has Jeremy admitted his part in it?"

"Not yet," murmured the inspector dryly, "but he will. He's a man without scruples. He recognized a fellow traveler in Rosheen, seduced her with promises of marriage, then persuaded her to kill his grandmother and her nurse so that he could inherit. Rosheen didn't need an alibi—she was never even questioned about where she was that night because you all assumed she was with Kevin."

"On the principle that shagging Kevin was the only thing that interested her," agreed Siobhan. "She *was* clever, you know. No one suspected for a minute that she was having an affair with Jeremy. Cynthia Haversley thought she was a common little tart. Ian thought Kevin was taking advantage of her. *I* thought she was having a good time."

"She was. She had her future mapped out as Lady of the Manor once Patrick was convicted and Jardine inherited the damn place. Apparently, her one ambition in life was to lord it over Liam and Bridey. If you're interested, Mrs. Haversley is surprisingly sympathetic toward her." He lifted a cynical eyebrow. "She says she recognizes how easy it must have been for a degenerate like Jardine to manipulate an unsophisticated country girl when he had no trouble persuading *sophisticated*—" he drew quote marks in the air—"types like her and Mr. Haversley to believe whatever he told them."

Siobhan smiled. "I'm growing quite fond of her in a funny sort of way. It's like fighting your way through a blackened baked potato. The outside's revolting but the inside's delicious and rather soft." Her eyes strayed toward the window, searching for some distant horizon. "The odd thing is, Nora Bentley told me on Monday that it was a pity I'd never seen the kind side of Cynthia . . . and I had the bloody nerve to say I didn't want to. God, how I wish—" She broke off abruptly, unwilling to reveal too much of the anguish that still churned inside her. "Why did Liam and Bridey take Kevin with them?" she asked next.

"According to him, they all panicked. *He* was scared he'd get the blame for burning the house down with Rosheen in it if he stayed behind, and *they* were scared the police would think they'd done it on purpose to prejudice Patrick's trial. He claims he left them when they got to Liverpool because he has a friend up there he hadn't seen for ages."

"And according to you?"

"We don't think he had any choice. We think Liam dragged him by the noose round his neck and only released him when they were sure he'd stick by the story they'd concocted."

"Why were Liam and Bridey going to Ireland?"

"According to them, or according to us?"

"According to them."

"Because they were frightened . . . because they knew it would take time for the truth to come out . . . because they had nowhere else to go . . . because everything they owned had been destroyed . . . because Ireland was home . . ."

"And according to you?"

"They guessed Kevin would start to talk as soon as he got over his fright, so they decided to run."

She gave a low laugh. "You can't have it both ways, Inspector. If they released him because they were sure he'd stick by the story, then they didn't need to run. And if they knew they could never be sure of him—as they most certainly should have done if they'd performed a ritual murder—he would have died with Rosheen."

"Then what are they trying to hide?"

She was amazed he couldn't see it. "Probably nothing," she hedged. "You're just in the habit of never believing anything they say."

He gave a stubborn shake of his head. "No, there *is* something. I've known them too long not to know when they're lying."

He would go on until he found out, she thought. He was that kind of man. And when he did, his suspicion about Rosheen's death would immediately raise its ugly head again. Unless . . . "The trouble with the O'Riordans," she said, "is that they can never see the wood for the trees. Patrick's just spent nine months on remand because he was more afraid of being charged with what he *had* done . . . theft . . . than what he *hadn't* done . . . murder. I suspect Liam and Bridey are doing the same—desperately trying to hide the crime they have committed, without realizing they're digging an even bigger hole for themselves on the one they haven't."

"Go on."

Siobhan's eyes twinkled as mischievously as Bridey's had done. "Off the record?" she asked him. "I won't say another word otherwise."

"Can they be charged with it?"

"Oh, yes, but I doubt it'll trouble your conscience much if you don't report it."

He was too curious not to give her the go-ahead. "Off the record," he agreed.

"All right, I think it goes something like this. Liam and Bridey have been living off the English taxpayer for fifteen years. They get disability benefit for his paralyzed arm, disability benefit for her broken pelvis, and Patrick gets a care allowance for looking after both of them. They get mobility allowances, heating allowances, and rate rebates." She tipped her forefinger at him. "But Kevin's built like a gorilla and prides himself on his physique, and Rosheen was as tall as I am. So how did a couple of elderly cripples manage to overpower both of them?"

"You tell me."

"At a guess, Liam wielded his useless arm to hold them in a bear hug while Bridey leapt up out of her chair to tie them up. Bridey would call it a miracle cure. Social Services would call it deliberate fraud. It depends how easily you think English doctors can be fooled by professional malingerers."

He was visibly shocked. "Are you saying Patrick never disabled either of them?"

Her rich laughter peeled round the room. "He must have done at the time. You can't fake a shattered wrist and a broken pelvis, but I'm guessing Liam and Bridey probably prolonged their own agony in order to milk sympathy and money out of the system." She canted her head to one side. "Don't you find it interesting that they decided to move away from the doctors who'd been treating them in London to hide themselves in the wilds of Hampshire where the only person competent to sign their benefit forms is—er—medically speaking—well, past his sell-by date? You've met Sam Bentley. Do you seriously think it would ever occur to him to question whether two people who'd been registered disabled by a leading London hospital were ripping off the English taxpayer?"

"Jesus!" He shook his head. "But why did they need to burn the house down? What would we have found that was so incriminating? Apart from Rosheen's body, of course."

"Sets of fingerprints from Liam's right hand all over the door knobs?" Siobhan suggested. "The marks of Bridey's shoes on the kitchen floor? However Rosheen died—whether in self-defense or not—they couldn't afford to report it because you'd have sealed off Kilkenny Cottage immediately while you tried to work out what happened."

The inspector looked interested. "And it wouldn't have taken us long to realize that neither of them is as disabled as they claim to be."

"No."

"And we'd have arrested them immediately on suspicion of murder."

She nodded. "Just as you did Patrick."

He acknowledged the point with a grudging smile. "Do you know all this for a fact, Mrs. Lavenham?"

"No," she replied. "Just guessing. And I'm certainly not going to repeat it in court. It's irrelevant anyway. The evidence went up in flames."

"Not if I get a doctor to certify they're as agile as I am."

"That doesn't prove they were agile before the fire," she pointed out. "Bridey will find a specialist to quote psychosomatic paralysis at you, and Sam Bentley's never going to admit to being fooled by a couple of malingerers." She chuckled. "Neither will Cynthia Haversley, if it comes to that. She's been watching them out of her window for years, and she's never suspected a thing. In any case, Bridey's a great believer in miracles, and she's already told you it was God who rescued them from the inferno."

"She must think I'm an absolute idiot."

"Not you personally. Just your . . . er . . . kind."

He frowned ominously. "What's that supposed to mean?"

Siobhan studied him with amusement. "The Irish have been getting the better of the English for centuries, Inspector." She watched his eyes narrow in instinctive denial. "And if the English weren't so blinded by their own self-importance," she finished mischievously, "they might have noticed."

Arrest

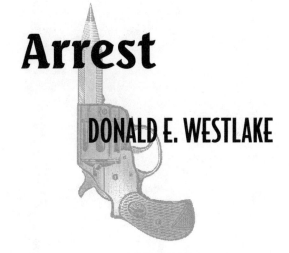

DONALD E. WESTLAKE

Donald E. Westlake's Introduction:

Memory lane. I was at the time a wannabe, with a job with a New York literary agent named Scott Meredith, whose clients ranged from P. G. Wodehouse and Norman Mailer to every hardworking hack you've never heard of. A lot of beginning writers worked briefly at that agency, including our now-illustrious anthologist, Mr. Block, and me, oh, Lord, I was one. A whole lot of manuscripts moved through that office, on their way to publication, so I started tossing my own into the same stream. They kept being tossed back, but every failure produced a lesson, so I was improving without being aware of it.

Manhunt was a magazine from the final generation of pulps. The first pulps added their flavor to the new world of paperback originals, and now the world of paperbacks juiced up the closing days of the pulps. Manhunt was the best of that world, and Scott Meredith was, I believe, their primary supplier. When I finally did a story the agency felt worthy of putting their sticker on, Manhunt took it, and I thought I was now a new and better person. The lesson I eventually learned from that first success was that I was still the same person, who had taken his first tottering step.

And the further lesson I'm just learning now is, we never know where we're going, we can barely see where we are, and it's astonishing to look back at where we've been.

Arrest

DONALD E. WESTLAKE

WILLIAM WINTHROP TURNED THE key in its lock, pushed open the apartment door, and stepped inside. Kicking the door shut behind him, he stopped in the foyer and looked at the key in the palm of his hand. He grinned to himself and slowly turned the hand palm downward. The key made no sound at all as it hit the carpet.

Winthrop moved from the foyer to the living room, leaving hat and tie on a sofa as he went by. He walked into the bedroom, tossing his coat and shirt at a chair in the corner of the room as he removed them. Then he sat down on the edge of the bed and put his head in his hands.

He could feel his hands trembling against his cheeks, and was surprised. He felt his chest for his cigarettes, realized he didn't have his shirt on, and walked over to where the shirt lay, on the floor beside his chair. He picked it up, took the cigarettes from the pocket, and dropped it on the floor again. Removing one cigarette, he dropped the pack on the floor beside the shirt, then lit the cigarette with his pocket lighter. He looked at the lighter for a long moment, then dropped that, too.

He stuck the cigarette into the corner of his mouth, walked over to the dresser on the other side of the room, and opened the top drawer. He felt under a pile of shirts, came up with a .45 automatic. The gun dangling from his hand, he went back and sat down on the bed again. He dropped the cigarette on the floor and stepped on it.

He took the clip from the handle of the gun, looked at the eight bullets, then put the clip back. He pressed the barrel of the gun against the side of his head, just above the ear, and sat there, his finger trembling on the trigger. Perspiration broke out on his forehead. He stared at the floor.

Finally, he looked up from the floor and saw his own reflection in the mirror on the closet door. He saw a young man of twenty-four, long brown hair awry, face contorted, dressed in brown pants, brown shoes, and a sweaty undershirt, a gun held to his head.

He hurled the gun at the mirror. The crash startled him and he jumped. Then he lay facedown on the bed, his head in the crook of his left arm, his right fist pounding the bed. "Damn it," he cried, over and over, in time to the pounding of his fist. "Damn it, damn it, damn it."

At last, he stopped swearing and beating the bed, and a sob shook his body. He cried, wrackingly, for almost five minutes, then rolled over and stared at the ceiling, breathing hard.

When he had calmed down, he rolled out of the bed to his feet and walked across the room to where his cigarettes lay. This time, after he'd lit the cigarette, he stuffed cigarettes and lighter in his pants pocket, then recrossed the room, past the bed and the dresser and the shattered mirror and the gun on the floor, and on into the bathroom.

With water filling the sink, he took a comb and ran it through his hair, to get it out of the way while he washed. Then he turned the tap off, dipped a washcloth in the water, and scrubbed his face until it hurt. Grabbing a towel, he dried face and hands, and looked at himself in the mirror. Again he took the comb, this time combing more carefully, patting his hair here and there until it looked right to him.

The cigarette had gone out in the ashtray, so he lit another. Then he went back to the bedroom.

Kicking the gun and the larger pieces of glass out of the way, he opened the closet door and looked over the clothing inside. He selected a dark blue suit, shut the closet door, and tossed the suit on the bed.

Back at the dresser, he took out a clean shirt, underwear, and socks. From the tie rack on the back of the bedroom door he took a conservative gray number and brought all back to the bed.

He changed rapidly, transferring everything from the pockets of the pants he'd been wearing to the suit. Then he went back to the living room and made himself a drink at the bar in the corner. He gulped the drink, lit another cigarette, and went to the front door, to make sure it was unlocked. On the way back, he picked up his key and put it in his pocket.

He sat down, crossed and recrossed his legs, buttoned and unbuttoned his suit coat, played with the empty glass. After a minute he crushed the cigarette in an ashtray, got up, and made another drink. He swallowed half, lit another cigarette, threw away the empty pack, and went to his room for another. When he came back, he reached for the half-full glass on the bar, but his hand shook and the glass went over, shattering on the floor behind the bar. He jumped again.

Leaning back against the wall, eyes squeezed shut, he whispered to himself, "Take it easy. Take it easy. Take it easy."

After a while, he moved away from the wall. He'd dropped the cigarette when the glass broke, and it was still smoldering on the rug. He stepped on it and took out another. He got another glass and made a drink, then went back to the sofa and sat down again.

He was just finishing the drink when the knock came. He was facing the door. "Come in," he called.

The door opened, and the two of them came in through the foyer to the living room. "William Winthrop?" asked one.

Winthrop nodded.

The man took out his wallet, flipped it open to show a badge. "Police," he said.

"I know," said Winthrop. He got to his feet. "Anything I say can be used against me. I demand my right to make one phone call."

"To your lawyer," said the detective. It wasn't a question.

"Of course," said Winthrop. He crossed to the phone. "Care for a drink? The makings are over there, in the corner."

"No thanks," said the detective. He motioned and the other one walked into the bedroom.

"Don't mind the mess in there," called Winthrop. "I tried to commit suicide."

The detective raised his eyebrows and walked over to the bedroom door to take a look. He whistled. "What happened to the mirror?"

"I threw the gun at it."

"Oh." The detective came back. "At least you're sane. A lot of guys try to cash in. Only the nuts do."

"That's a relief," said Winthrop. He dialed.

The detective grunted and sat down. The other one came back from his inspection, shook his head, and sat down near the door.

Winthrop heard the click as a receiver was lifted, and a man's voice said, "Arthur Moresby, attorney."

"Hello, Art? This is Bill."

There was a pause, then, "Who?"

"Bill. Bill Winthrop."

"I'm afraid I don't recognize the name. Are you sure you have the right number?"

"Oh," said Winthrop. "Like that. It's in the papers already, eh?"

"On the radio."

"You don't know me, is that right?"

"That's right," said Arthur Moresby, attorney. "Good-bye."

Winthrop heard the click, but continued to hold the phone against his ear.

"What's the matter?" asked the detective.

Winthrop shook his head and returned the phone to its cradle. He grinned crookedly at the detective. "Wrong number," he said.

"How a wrong number?"

"I'm a sinking ship."

"And your lawyer?"

"He's a rat. He doesn't know me. He never heard the name."

"Oh," said the detective. He stood up. "I guess we can go then, huh?"

Winthrop shrugged. "I guess so."

He followed them out of the apartment. They walked to the elevator, Winthrop pushed the button, and they waited without speaking. When the elevator came. they stepped in and the detective pushed the button marked "1."

On the way down, the detective said, "Mind if I ask you a question?"

"For the insurance," said Winthrop. "I was in debt. Either I paid or *chhhk*. He ran a finger across his neck.

"That isn't the question. I want to know why you waited for us to come before you called the lawyer. You had a lot of time before we got there. Why did you wait?"

Winthrop stared at the door. Why had he waited? He thought a minute, then said, "I don't know. Bravado or something."

"Okay," said the detective. The door slid open and they walked across the vestibule to the street. A few passersby watched curiously as Winthrop got into the back seat of the police car.

"I'm twenty-four," said Winthrop, as they drove through the streets to police headquarters.

"So?" said the detective.

"Seems like a hell of an age to stop at."

"How old was your mother?" asked the cop.

Winthrop closed his eyes. "Do you hate me?"

"No," said the cop.

Winthrop turned and looked at the cop. "I do," he said. "I hate my guts."

You Can't Lose

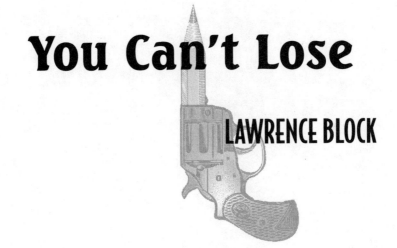

LAWRENCE BLOCK

Lawrence Block's Introduction:

In the summer of 1956, I was living on Barrow Street in Greenwich Village and working in the mail room at Pines Publications. I was an Antioch student, and this was a co-op job, designed to add some vocational experience to one's education. One Saturday afternoon, toward the end of my three-month stint, I set up my typewriter at the kitchen table and wrote a short story.

Months later, back on campus, I hauled it out and looked at it. It occurred to me that it was a crime story—I hadn't thought in categorical terms when I wrote it—and I knew there was a magazine, Manhunt, that published tough-minded crime stories. I had never actually seen a copy of Manhunt, but I'd read The Jungle Kids, a collection of stories by Evan Hunter, and had noted that most of the contents had originally appeared in that magazine.

That was good enough for me. I looked up the magazine's address, sent off the story, and waited for another ejection slip to add to my collection.

Instead I got a letter from the editor. He liked the story, but it just sort of trailed off. If I could come up with a snappy ending, he'd like to see it again.

Wow!

I went and bought Manhunt, read it cover to cover, and thought of an ending for my story. It owed a lot to "The Man at the Top," by O. Henry, and consisted of the narrator confidently investing all his ill-gotten gains in what we know is some worthless stock. Off it went to Manhunt, and back it came; the editor said it was trite and predictable, and he was right.

Then some more months passed, and the following spring I had a bout of creative insomnia and saw how to revise the story. I drove to Cape Cod, where I rented a room in an attic over a barber shop for eight bucks a week and started writing stories. First thing I did was take another run at "You Can't Lose." I shipped it off to Manhunt, natch, and got a note back from an assistant editor. Francis X. Lewis, the editor in chief, was on vacation, but the assistant was sure he'd like the new version, so could he hold it until Mr. Lewis returned? You bet he could.

Six weeks later I was in New York, where I answered a blind ad and wound up working as an editor at Scott Meredith Literary Agency, reading bad manuscripts and telling the authors to keep writing, and to keep sending in their stories with their reading fees. What I didn't know—what nobody knew—was that Scott Meredith edited Manhunt. There was no Francis X. Lewis. That was Scott. And it was also Scott pretending to be Mr. Lewis's assistant, because Manhunt had cash flow problems and, if they could hold the story for awhile, they wouldn't have to pay for it right away.

Here's what happened—someone in the office, to bait the new kid, made a disparaging remark about Manhunt. "Hey, don't knock Manhunt," I said. "They're buying a story of mine. At least I think they are, when Mr. Lewis gets back."

Somebody ducked into the other office and checked the files, and there was my story, sitting in inventory. Scott actually was on vacation that week, but his brother Sid came to talk to me. Since I had a story that Manhunt wanted to buy, he explained, they'd have me sign an agency contract, and then I'd be a Scott Meredith client, and I'd get more money. Ordinarily the magazine paid two cents a word, so I'd get fifty or sixty bucks, but Scott Meredith clients got a minimum of $100 for Manhunt stories. "So you can see the advantage," he said. "Sign here."

I signed. "That's great," I said. "So that means the story's sold? And I'll get a hundred dollars?"

He shook his head.

"It's not sold? I thought—"

"Oh, it's sold," he said, "but you don't get a hundred. You get ninety. We get ten."

You Can't Lose

LAWRENCE BLOCK

ANYONE WHO STARVES IN this country deserves it. Really. Almost any-body who is dumb enough to want to work can get a job without any back-breaking effort. Blindies and crips haul in twenty-five bucks an hour bumming the Times Square district. And if you're like me—able-bodied and all, but you just don't like to work, all you got to do is use your head a little. It's simple.

Of course, before you all throw up your jobs, let me explain that this routine has its limitations. I don't eat caviar, and East Third Street is a long way from Sutton Place. But I never cared much for caviar, and the pad I have is a comfortable one. It's a tiny room a couple blocks off the Bowery, furnished with a mattress, a refrigerator, a stove, a chair, and a table. The cockroaches get me out of bed, dress me, and walk me down to the bathroom down the hall. Maybe you couldn't live in a place like that, but I sort of like it. There's no problem keeping it up, 'cause it couldn't get any worse.

My meals, like I said, are not caviar. For instance, in the refrigerator right now I have a sack of coffee, a dozen eggs, and part of a fifth of bourbon. Every morning I have two fried eggs and a cup of coffee. Every evening I have three fried eggs and two cups of coffee. I figure, you find something you like, you should stick with it.

And the whole thing is cheap. I pay twenty a month for the room, which is cheap anywhere and amazing in New York. And in this neighborhood food prices are pretty low, too.

379

All in all, I can live on ten bucks a week with no trouble. At the moment I have fifty bucks in my pocket, so I'm set for a month, maybe a little more. I haven't worked in four months, haven't had any income in three.

I live, more or less, by my wits. I hate to work. What the hell, what good are brains if you have to work for a living? A cat lives fifty, sixty, maybe seventy years, and that's not a long time. He might as well spend his time doing what he likes. Me, I like to walk around, see people, listen to music, read, drink, smoke, and get a dame. So that's what I do. Since nobody's paying people to walk around or read or anything, I pick up some gold when I can. There's always a way.

By this I don't mean that I'm a mugger or a burglar or anything like that. It might be tough for you to get what I'm saying, so let me explain.

I mentioned that I worked four months ago, but I didn't say that I only held the job for a day. It was at a drugstore on West Ninety-sixth Street. I got a job there as a stock and delivery boy on a Monday morning. It was easy enough getting the job. I reported for work with a couple of sandwiches in a beat-up gym bag. At four that afternoon I took out a delivery and forgot to come back. I had twenty shiny new Zippo lighters in the gym bag, and they brought anywhere from a buck to a buck-seventy-five at the Third Avenue hockshops. That was enough money for three weeks, and took me all of one day to earn it. No chance of him catching me, either. He's got a fake name and a fake address, and he probably didn't notice the lighters were missing for a while.

Dishonest? Obviously, but so what? The guy deserved it. He told me straight off the Puerto Ricans in the neighborhood were not the cleverest mathematicians in the world, and when I made a sale I should shortchange them and we'd split fifty-fifty. Why should I play things straight with a bum like that? He can afford the loss. Besides, I worked one day free for him, didn't I?

It's all a question of using your head. If you think things out carefully, decide just what you want, and find a smart way to get it, you come out ahead, time after time. Like the way I got out of going into the army.

The army, as far as I'm concerned, is strictly for the sparrows. I couldn't see it a year ago, and I still can't. When I got my notice I had to think fast. I didn't want to try faking the eye chart or anything like that, and I didn't think I would get away with a conscientious objector pitch. Anyway, those guys usually wind up in stir or working twice as hard as everybody else. When the idea came to me it seemed far too simple, but it worked. I got myself deferred for homosexuality.

It was a panic. After the physical I went in for the psychiatric, and I played the beginning fairly straight, only I acted generally hesitant.

Then the Doc asks, "Do you like girls?"

"Well," I blurt out, "only as friends."

"Have you ever gone with girls?"

"Oh, no!" I managed to sound somewhat appalled at the idea.

I hesitated for a minute or two, then admitted that I was homosexual. I was deferred, of course.

You'd think that everybody who really wanted to avoid the army would try this, but they won't. It's psychological. Men are afraid of being homosexual, or of having people think they're homosexual. They're even afraid of some skull doctor who never saw them before and never will see them again. So many people are so stupid, if you just act a little smart you can't miss. After the examination was over I spent some time with the whore who lives across the hall from me. No sense talking myself into anything. A cat doesn't watch out, he can be too smart, you know.

To get back to my story—the money from the Zippos lasted two weeks, and I was practically broke again. This didn't bother me, though. I just sat around the pad for a while, reading and smoking, and sure enough, I got another idea that I figured would be worth a few bucks. I showered and shaved, and made a half-hearted attempt at shining my shoes. I had some shoe polish from the drugstore. I had some room in the gym bag after the Zippos, so I stocked up on toothpaste, shoe polish, aspirins, and that kind of junk. Then I put on the suit that I keep clean for emergencies. I usually wear dungarees, but once a month I need a suit for something, so I always have it clean and ready. Then, with a tie on and my hair combed for a change, I looked almost human. I left the room, splurged fifteen cents for a bus ride, and got off at Third Avenue and Sixtieth Street. At the corner of Third and Fifty-ninth is a small semi-hockshop that I cased a few days before. They do more buying and selling than actual pawning, and there aren't too many competitors right in the neighborhood. Their stock is average—the more common and lower-priced musical instruments, radios, cameras, record players, and the cheap stuff—clocks, lighters, rings, watches, and so on. I got myself looking as stupid as possible and walked in.

There must be thousands of hockshops in New York, but there are only two types of clerks. The first is usually short, bald, and over forty. He wears suspenders, talks straight to the lower-class customers and kowtows to the others. Most of the guys farther downtown fit into this category. The other type is like the guy I drew: tall, thick black hair, light-colored suit, and a wide smile. He talks gentleman-to-gentleman with his upper-class customers and patronizingly to the bums. Of the two, he's usually more dangerous.

My man came on with the Johnny-on-the-spot pitch, ready and willing to serve. I hated him immediately.

"I'm looking for a guitar," I said, "preferably a good one. Do you have anything in stock at the moment?" I saw six or seven on the wall, but when you play it dumb, you play it dumb.

"Yes," he said. "Do you play guitar?" I didn't, and told him so. No point in lying all the time. But, I added, I was going to learn.

He picked one off the wall and started plucking the strings. "This is an excellent one, and I can let you have it for only thirty-five dollars. Would you like to pay cash or take it on the installment plan?"

I must have been a good actor, because he was certainly playing me for a mark. The guitar was a Pelton, and it was in good shape, but it never cost more than forty bucks new, and he had a nerve asking more than twenty-five. Any minute now he might tell me that the last owner was an old lady who only played hymns on it. I held back the laugh and plunked the guitar like a nice little customer.

"I like the sound. And the price sounds about right to me."

"You'll never find a better bargain." Now this was laying it on with a trowel.

"Yes, I'll take it." He deserved it now. "I was just passing by, and I don't have much money with me. Could I make a down payment and pay the rest weekly?"

He probably would have skipped the down payment. "Surely," he said. For some reason I've always disliked guys who say "surely." No reason, really. "How much would you like to pay now?"

I told him I was really short at the moment, but could pay ten dollars a week. Could I just put a dollar down? He said I could, but in that case the price would have to be forty dollars, which is called putting the gouge on.

I hesitated a moment for luck, then agreed. When he asked for identification I pulled out my pride and joy.

In a wallet that I also copped from that drugstore I have the best identification in the world, all phony and all legal. Everything in it swears up and down that my name is Leonard Blake and I live on Riverside Drive. I have a baptismal certificate that I purchased from a sharp little entrepreneur at our high school back in the days when I needed proof of age to buy a drink. I have a Social Security card that can't be used for identification purposes but always is, and an unapproved application for a driver's license. To get one of these you just go to the Bureau of Motor Vehicles and fill it out. It isn't stamped, but no pawnbroker ever noticed that. Then there are membership cards in everything from the Captain Marvel Club to the NAACP. Of course he took my buck and I signed some papers.

I made it next to Louie's shop at Thirty-fifth and Third. Louie and I know each other, so there's no haggling. He gave me fifteen for the guitar, and I let him know it wouldn't be hot for at least ten days. That's the way I like to do business.

Fifteen bucks was a week and a half, and you see how easy it was. And it's fun to shaft a guy who deserves it, like that sharp clerk did. But when I got back to the pad and read some old magazines, I got another idea before I even had a chance to start spending the fifteen.

I was reading one of those magazines that are filled with really exciting information, like how to build a model of the Great Wall of China around your house, and I was wondering what kind of damn fool would want to build a wall around his house, much less a Great

Wall of China type wall, when the idea hit me. Wouldn't a hell of a lot of the same type of people like a Sheffield steel dagger, twenty-five inches long, an authentic copy of a twelfth-century relic recently discovered in a Bergdorf castle? And all this for only two bucks post-paid, no CODs? I figured they might.

This was a big idea, and I had to plan it just right. A classified in that type of magazine cost two dollars, a post office box cost about five for three months. I was in a hurry, so I forgot about lunch, and rushed across town to the Chelsea Station on Christopher Street, and Lennie Blake got himself a post office box. Then I fixed up the ad a little, changing "twenty-five inches" to "over two feet." And customers would please allow three weeks for delivery. I sent ads and money to three magazines, and took a deep breath. I was now president of Cornet Enterprises. Or Lennie Blake was. Who the hell cared?

For the next month and a half I stalled on the rent and ate as little as possible. The magazines hit the stands after two weeks, and I gave people time to send in. Then I went west again and picked up my mail.

A hell of a lot of people wanted swords. There were about two hundred envelopes, and after I finished throwing out the checks and requests for information, I wound up with $196 and sixty-seven three-cent stamps. Anybody want to buy a stamp?

See what I mean? The whole bit couldn't have been simpler. There's no way in the world they can trace me, and nobody in the post office could possibly remember me. That's the beauty of New York—so many people. And how much time do you think the cops will waste looking for a two-bit swindler? I could even have made another pick-up at the post office, but greedy guys just don't last long in this game. And a federal rap I need like a broken ankle.

Right now I'm 100 percent in the clear. I haven't heard a rumble on the play yet, and already Lennie Blake is dead—burned to ashes and flushed down the toilet. Right now I'm busy establishing Warren Shaw. I sign the name, over and over, so that I'll never make a mistake and sign the wrong name sometime. One mistake is above par for the course.

Maybe you're like me. I don't mean with the same fingerprints and all, but the same general attitudes. Do you fit the following general description: smart, coldly logical, content with coffee and eggs in a cold-water walk-up, and ready to work like hell for an easy couple of bucks? If that's you, you're hired. Come right in and get to work. You can even have my room. I'm moving out tomorrow.

It's been kicks, but too much of the same general pattern and the law of averages gets you. I've been going a long time, and one pinch would end everything. Besides, I figure it's time I took a step or two up the social ladder.

I had a caller yesterday, a guy named Al. He's an older guy, and hangs with a mob uptown on the West Side. He always has a cigar jammed into the corner of his mouth and he looks like a holdover from the twenties, but Al is a very sharp guy. We gassed around for awhile, and then he looked me in the eyes and chewed on his cigar.

"You know," he said, "we might be able to use you."

"I always work alone, Al."

"You'd be working alone. Two hundred a night."

I whistled. This was sounding good. "What's the pitch?"

He gave me the look again and chewed his cigar some more. "Kid," he said, "did you ever kill a man?"

Two hundred bucks for one night's work! What a perfect racket! Wish me luck, will you? I start tonight.

Authors' Biographies

David Black is an award-winning journalist, novelist, screenwriter, and producer. His most recent film, *The Confession*, won the Writer's Guild of America Award for Best Television Movie of the Year. He has also won the Writer's Foundation of America Gold Medal for Excellence in Writing, a National Endowment of the Arts grant for fiction, and the *Atlantic Monthly*'s "first" award for fiction. His novel *Like Father* and his autobiography of August Belmont were both *New York Times* Notable Books of the Year. He was nominated for a Pulitzer Prize for his novel *The Plague Years*, and he won a National Magazine Reporting award and the National Science Writers Award.

Charm is something few of us in these pages possess, in reality or as writers. Charm is what **Simon Brett**'s most famous creation, middle-aged British actor Charles Paris, has aplenty—a charm that is a mixture of melancholy, alcohol and the stubborn heart of a romantic. The first Paris novel, *Cast in Order of Disappearance*, appeared in 1975. They're still appearing regularly, even though Brett has turned an increasing amount of his attention to the Christie-like widow Mrs. Pargeter.

When **Max Allan Collins**'s *True Detective* appeared in 1983, the subgenre of historical detective fiction was changed forever. Rather than being a history-heavy treatise, the novel was filled with historical figures portrayed with a vitality and dash never before seen in the genre. In the center of it all was Nathan Heller, Collins's gumshoe, who has now told us in wry and intimate detail about his adventures with everybody from Bugsy Siegel to Amelia Earhart. Collins has written several other series, including a number of books about a hitman (Quarry) and a professional criminal (Nolan). Probably his best novel outside the Hellers is *Butcher's Dozen*, a series book about Eliot Ness's attempt to track down Cleveland's infamous Mad Butcher of Kingsbury Run.

Hard to believe that **Dorothy Salisbury Davis** published her first novel, *The Judas Cat*, in 1949. Her run as a major figure in the world of mystery fiction was confirmed when Mystery Writers of America made her a Grand Master in 1984. Davis's work brilliantly explores the moral conundrums of modern-day life. Her current novels and stories are as fresh and piquant as the work that won her the Grand Master award. It is easy to be cynical, much more difficult to find the redemptive values that Davis celebrates in life and literature alike.

Loren D. Estleman has distinguished himself in a number of literary fields including mainstream, western, private eye, and thriller. He has been nominated for the Pulitzer Prize and won a couple of shelves of literary awards. Everybody from John D. MacDonald to the reviewers at *People* magazine have showered him with the kind of adjectives writers like to keep in their wall safes at home. Because he started so young, his list of novels and story collections is not only long but luminous with style, innovation, and a particular love of all things American. Well, most things American. He has never been known to hide his opinions, especially in his fiction.

It's not often that an important poet sits down to crank out series western novels. But that's just what **John Harvey** did before giving us Charlie Resnick and the police procedurals that brought us a London that few had ever seen before—including many Londoners. The Resnicks are cutting-edge contemporary mystery fiction—sly, sad, sexy, harsh, and quite frequently powerful and poetic. They are also Maughamesque in a revisionist sort of way—but this time the empire that is crumbling is the police department and many of its bobbies.

Joan Hess, on or off the page, is funny. Off the page that's great. On the page, that's not always so good. At least not when reviewers, trained to look for Deep Meanings, look over her books. Nothing this enjoyable, they seem to think, can possibly have real merit. Not true, as she continues to demonstrate in novel after novel. Hess's spirited takes on her home state of Arkansas combines the cozy form with her own version of black comedy—domestic comedy that is set down with the same neurotic glee one finds in the stories of Anne Beatty. Whether she's writing about Clare Malloy, her young widow who runs a bookstore, or Arly Hanks, who is police chief of Magody, Arkansas, Hess's two series are engaging, but also quite serious, takes on relationships, middle age, parental duties, and life in small-town America.

Few pleasures match that of coming upon a new **Susan Isaacs** novel. Whether she chooses to be funny or bittersweet (or both), writing about World War II or today, showing us suburbia or the city, her books are truly unputdownable—and not because of any goofy high concept or sleazy docudramatics—but just because her people are so engaging and her writing style so nimble and quick. While she gets better each time out, it's still fun to go back and read her first formal mystery, *Compromising Positions*. The reputations of horny, deceitful dentists were never the same after that book began climbing the best-seller lists.

A pro's pro is somebody who can work in a variety of styles and forms with equal skill. One such man is **Peter Lovesey**. Whether he's writing about Victorian times (his Cribb and Thackery novels), early Hollywood (*Keystone*), or World War II (*On the Edge*), Lovesey is always in artful command of his material. His humor is genuinely funny and his dramatics genuinely moving, especially in the elegiac *Rough Cider*. Many of his novels and stories have been adapted to film and television.

Margaret Maron's passionate and poetic novels such as *Bootlegger's Daughter* (1992), which won the Agatha, Anthony, Edgar, and Macavity awards, and her latest, *Storm Track* (2000), offer readers the depth and resonance of a good literary novel. Maron took the conventional mystery and made it uniquely her own to examine both the old and new South. Possibly the most amazing thing about Maron's career is that she continues to get even better as she goes along. She has created her own niche in contemporary fiction.

Cassandra Swann (what a nice name) is a British bridge professional while Penny Wanawake (another nice name) is a black English diplomat's photographer daughter whose lover steals jewelry and donates the proceeds to famine relief programs. Both are the creations of a savvy, wily writer named Susan Moody, a talented woman who lived in Tennessee for a decade before returning to her native England. She writes very well, has a good deal to say about our shared lives on this planet, and is unflaggingly entertaining and original.

"Rambo" became a part of world language with the release of the Sylvester Stallone movie *First Blood*. **David Morrell**, the English professor who wrote the novel upon which the film was based, has become a successful author the world over with more than ten international best-sellers. Morrell is an accomplished writer in several fields as his recent collection of horror and dark suspense stories in

Black Evening demonstrates. He also wrote a moving book, *Fireflies*, about the death of his teenage son.

Sara Paretsky put the female private eye on the bestseller list. She and her private investigator, V. I. Warshawski, are very much of their generation—social causes, including feminism, playing key parts in the attitudes and story lines of the novels. Paretsky is also an excellent short-story writer, a chance she got to demonstrate with her accomplished 1995 collection *Windy City Blues*. She continues to grow and has surprises in store for everybody.

The Canadian crime writers give out the Arthur Ellis award for excellence in suspense fiction. **Peter Robinson** has won the Ellis for short story ("Innocence") and novel (*The Hanging Valley* and *Past Reason*). Most of his novels deal with the subtle changes in the life of one Chief Inspector Alan Banks, who presently works out of Yorkshire England's Swainsdale area. Robinson has often spoken of his fondness for Simenon and this influence is especially marked in the clarity of his prose and the melancholy truths discovered during the investigations. Robinson is also a first-rate short-story writer, and the piece chosen for inclusion in the volume hints at the long and successful career ahead of him.

Talented **James Sallis** has a devoted audience that greets the publication of his novels as important moments. He has remarked that his best-received novel *The Long-Legged Fly* is "what might have happened if Raymond Chandler and Samuel Beckett had collaborated on a detective novel." He persists in writing the detective novel on his own terms, and that is admirable in so commercial an age.

The Shipkiller and *Rampage* are exemplary best-sellers—unique in concept, filled with interesting characters, and structured to keep those pages turning at an ever-accelerating rate. But **Justin Scott** added one thing that many best-selling authors leave out, a true love of language. There's an eloquence, even elegance in the books that keep them from dating. They are as fresh today as when they were first published in the previous two decades. Lately, Scott has turned his skilled hands to the mystery novel, with equally excellent results.

It seems that every year a major star is born in the mystery field. Some of them fall quickly aside. Too much too soon; not worthy of all the quick airy praise. Britisher **Minette Walters** rocked the mystery world with her first novel *The Ice House* and she's continued to rock it with each subsequent novel. While her books faintly resemble those of Agatha Christie, she's definitely put a New Millennium spin on her material. She's always a pleasure to read because you can never quite guess where she's taking you. Already a major force in mystery, she sets her sights higher with every novel, and then, seemingly effortlessly, achieves it.

Few would disagree with the contention that, page for page, **Donald E. Westlake** is the best crime fiction writer of his generation. He has written at least three bona fide masterpieces—*Adios, Scheherazade*, *The Ax*, and *The Hunter*—the latter written under his Richard Stark pen name, and the novel which single-handedly dragged the caper novel out of its W. R. Burnett rut (where it had been since 1928) and brought it into the last half of the century. *The Ax* may well be the most notable utterance yet made about downsizing in the world of corporate America. And *Adios, Scheherazade*—hilarious and heartbreaking—is one of the two or three funniest and truest books ever written about a writer. In 1990 Westlake wrote the screenplay for the film *The Grifters*, based on the Jim Thompson novel of the same name. His script earned him an Academy Award nomination.

Lawrence Block has done it all and done it well. From ribald sex farce (*Ronald Rabbit Is a Dirty Old Man*) to the caper comedy (his Bernie Rhoenbarr novels) to the private eye novel as social realism (his Matt Scudder books), Block has brought style, wit, and enormous skill to every book he's undertaken. His prose is the cleanest in mystery fiction and his ability to create characters of every social stripe is amazing. As someone once remarked, even a walk-on waiter comes to two-line life in a Block story. He's that good. In 1994, the Mystery Writers of America made him a Grand Master.

Copyrights and Permissions